Cadillac
Road

Essential Prose Series 132

Canada Council   Conseil des Arts
for the Arts   du Canada

ONTARIO ARTS COUNCIL
CONSEIL DES ARTS DE L'ONTARIO
an Ontario government agency
un organisme du gouvernement de l'Ontario

Canadä

Guernica Editions Inc. acknowledges the support of the Canada Council
for the Arts and the Ontario Arts Council. The Ontario Arts Council
is an agency of the Government of Ontario.

We acknowledge the financial support of the Government of Canada.

Cadillac Road

Kristin Andrychuk

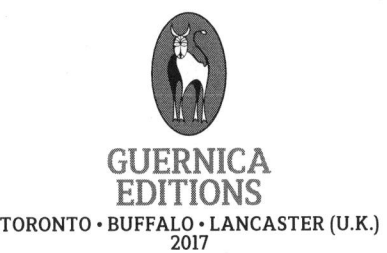

GUERNICA
EDITIONS
TORONTO · BUFFALO · LANCASTER (U.K.)
2017

Michael Mirolla, general editor
Lindsay Brown, editor
David Moratto, interior and cover design
Guernica Editions Inc.
1569 Heritage Way, Oakville, (ON), Canada L6M 2Z7
2250 Military Road, Tonawanda, N.Y. 14150-6000 U.S.A.
www.guernicaeditions.com

Distributors:
University of Toronto Press Distribution,
5201 Dufferin Street, Toronto (ON), Canada M3H 5T8
Gazelle Book Services, White Cross Mills,
High Town, Lancaster LA1 4XS U.K.

First edition.
Printed in Canada.

Legal Deposit—First Quarter
Library of Congress Catalog Card Number: 2016952732
Library and Archives Canada Cataloguing in Publication
Andrychuk, Kristin, author
Cadillac road / Kristin Andrychuk. -- First edition.
(Essential prose series ; 132)
Issued in print and electronic formats.
ISBN 978-1-77183-150-5 (paperback).--ISBN 978-1-77183-151-2 (epub).
-- ISBN 978-1-77183-152-9 (mobi)
I. Title. II. Series: Essential prose series ; 132
PS8551.N395C33 2017   C813'.54   C2016-905965-0   C2016-905966-9

For my husband Don and my children:
Paul, Patricia, Sylvia, and Charles

*A*N OLD GREY house and in the distance dark bush-covered hills in Cadillac, Quebec, where I was born. I remember the board sidewalks high above the muddy streets and Mom's warning to keep away from the edge. There's no snow. Must be a summer memory.

Cadillac, Quebec—unpainted or tarpaper-covered houses, dirt yards, mud everywhere. Me and Suzette Belanger in rubber boots and overalls, dig in the dirt back of my house. We find a battered lunch bucket, a rusty spoon and a piece of a blue-flowered cup.

Our houses have faces. Mine has a sad face — the pointed porch roof makes the nose and its sagging floor, the mouth. The lighted windows above are the eyes. Shades half down like it's squinting or ducking a blow.

Belangers' next door its twin, but so different. Is it the porch with the baby carriage, the half-built go-cart, and at least three bikes? The upstairs in both is one big room, more a large attic with slanting walls. Me and my little sister Gloria share the iron-pipe bedstead. We also share the hiding place below.

Mommy takes out her hairpins and lets down her wavy red hair. I brush it for her. Though I'm only four or five—must be under six, because we leave when I'm six, I know my mother is beautiful, blue-green eyes, and long red hair. I love how her hair lifts itself to the brush. And how, when I climb on her lap, it makes a shawl around us. Sometimes we have tea, milky tea for me. Gloria, a year younger, is already asleep in the big bed upstairs. My hair is red and curly like Mommy's. Gloria's is dark.

Not all good—we hear the end-of-shift whistle at the mine. I run upstairs and burrow under the covers next to my sister. Then comes the heart-thumping wait. Sometimes, laughter rises from below, his loud, hers tinkling. Nights that he curses, glass shatters, Mommy screams, and I pull Gloria from the bed to our hiding place. She whimpers, too scared to cry out. We have a blanket under the bed and sometimes, fall asleep there.

My mother's long red hair, the unpainted house, the iron-pipe bed, my whimpering little sister.

That's not all. Those trips to our cousins' place. The car heater doesn't work. Mommy makes us nests in the back seat, pillows, blankets, and hot water bottles. Gravel flies, bush crowds the road. Every so often a branch scrapes the car, and Papa swears.

When we set out the road is gravel, but I remember the bump, bump over corduroy roads. Such a funny name. My overalls are made of corduroy. The roads are logs laid down in a row.

Me and Gloria giggle as the car bounces along. Papa sings *O claire de la lune*, something like that, and another one *Sur le pont*.

Our old car rumbles up the lane, and Aunt Lisette, Uncle Yves, and all the cousins spill out of the house. Papa and his brother hug, smack each other on the back. My aunt and uncle hug and kiss me and Gloria. Mommy hangs back, like she's shy.

The farm: a cow, pigs—never more than a couple—and chickens all over the place. The wonderful animals are uncle's horses. Clydesdales—reddish coats, black manes and tails, and a white hairy ruffle around each hoof. Once my uncle lifts me up, and I sit on the wide warm back, more thrilled than scared.

Their log house and barn are so old the wood's mossy. Great piles of fresh cut trees fill the yard. Uncle Yves sells wood.

Falling asleep, I occasionally see that log house and barn sinking into the green hillside. The neat stacks of cordwood. The wall of bush. The trees grow so close together I can't walk between them. The farm has its own corduroy roads. Me and my cousins—Gloria's too little to come—follow these roads to the clearings where Uncle Yves' been cutting. Cowboys and Indians. Run, run, run. *Vite, vite*. My feet stay warm in a cousin's rubber boots, wool socks. The sharp spruce smell in the cold air.

My cousins: Louisette, Jacques, Pierre, Marie. There were a lot more than those four. I can't remember the others' names. Was Pierre the redhead or was that Jacques?

They didn't speak any English. I spoke French as I did with the

Cadillac children. Papa spoke French, but English to Mommy unless he was mad at her. She didn't speak French. She met Papa when he was working on the railway in Buffalo, before he went back to Quebec to work in the gold mines.

I can't speak French now—I've forgotten it all. A strange feeling because the lost words are in my head, sometimes they almost come to me. When I start high school in September and take French, will I remember then?

I do have good memories of when we lived in Cadillac. I occasionally dream of my cousins' log house, but more often of hiding under the iron-pipe bed and listening to my parents fight.

Papa is mean. Mommy yells: "Leave my baby alone!" He's holding Gloria by one skinny arm and smacking her bum. She's just wearing an undershirt. I'm under the table and tuck my nightie tightly around me. Gloria's shrieking and trying to twist out of his reach. There's a loud thud. A piece of firewood lands by the table leg. Mommy must've hit him because he curses and lets Gloria go. She crawls under the table and I hold her tight.

Mommy yells: "Sharon, take her to Belangers'."

I grab Gloria's hand and run, but not before I see blood pouring from my mother's mouth.

At Belangers' we have brown sugar spread on white bread. The big girl fixes it for us. What is her name? I don't remember. Upstairs a curtain divides the girls' side from the boys'. We sleep in a wide bed along with the big girl's little sisters.

Gloria won't tell what bad thing she did. Most likely pooped behind the door. Mommy told her when she turned five she had to stop using the potty and use the big toilet. She's scared she'll go down the drain. She's a silly.

I don't remember how long we stay at Belangers', only that, when our mother comes for us, she looks ugly—her mouth puffy and bruised, and her front teeth are gone.

I remember my mother telling somebody, maybe Aunt Jean in Buffalo: "I hit the bastard with a piece of cordwood—too bad it was his arm and not his head. I should've killed him."

That memory's from later. My last Cadillac memory is the train.

The seats are dark red plush. Gloria keeps petting them. She does things like that. She'll sit real quiet and stroke and stroke the ratty old fur collar on Mommy's coat.

We have two big seats facing each other. I have one all to myself for a bed. Gloria sleeps on the other one, her head on Mommy's lap. We play paper dolls—the cuttings are all over the floor, and Mommy makes us clean up. We eat bread and cheese and big sugar cookies Mrs. Belanger made. We get water in little paper cups from the tap by the bathroom. A nice lady gives us an orange to share. We're on the train all day and all night and all the next day.

Miles and miles of snow, trees, rocks, and lakes.

WAKE UP IN Toronto, Mommy telling me to hurry. "Get your coat on. Hold your sister's hand."

Gloria leaves her favourite paper doll behind and bawls.

Trains are everywhere, huffing and shunting. Some go right into the building. I'm a little bit scared, but don't let on. Gloria's still wailing. Is she scared of the trains or mourning her lost paper doll?

I carry the small suitcase and Mommy the big one. We climb stairs that go up and up into an enormous building with an arched ceiling more grand than the church in Rouyn-Noranda where me and Papa went one time.

Another train and finally, Buffalo. In the taxi, cars honk all around us. With my face pressed against the window, I see tall buildings and red lights that make a picture of a bottle—flashing off and on. The taxi driver honks at the blue and white bus blocking our path. A woman in a turquoise coat, holding a tiny plaid-coated dog under her arm, crowds between our taxi and the bus. We have left the grey North far behind.

Grandma looks just like the grandma in *Grandma and Stony River Farm*. She's white-haired, short and plump and wears glasses. Her apartment's warm and everything is so pretty. The floors are shiny wood. The living room rug has designs of tiny flowers, blue, green, red, with a blue border and white fringe Gloria likes to make all straight and nice.

Grandma's dishes are pink and white and all match. We have orange juice and waffles for breakfast, much nicer than oatmeal. Mommy, me, and Gloria all sleep in one big soft bed.

There's a playground next to the apartment building. Lots of kids. They all speak English. Gloria's too shy to speak and scared to get on the big swings. I push her on the baby swings, then take her to the monkey bars and tell her to watch. At first, I just climb and swing a bit. Much easier climbing than on the trees back of our old house. A girl in a red jacket goes hand over hand from one side to the other. I try it. The first time I fall, the second, make it across. Not as hard as it looks.

"Where you from?" Red Jacket asks.

"Cadillac. We came on the train."

"She lived in a car," a girl says.

"No, we had a big house with good climbing trees."

"Dummy, a Cadillac's a car," a boy says.

"It's the name of a town," I tell them.

"Funny name," Red Jacket says, and the other kids all laugh.

"Not as funny as Buffalo. A buffalo is a big smelly animal." I swing myself up on the bars, and go hand over hand from one end to the other without falling.

Red Jacket and the boy follow, and we take turns until Red Jacket says: "Let's go on the swings. My name's Ruth. What's yours?"

"Sharon Desjardins, and that's my little sister Gloria."

We soar high on the big swings. I feel I could fly right over the fence. Gloria hides behind the post. When I take her hand to go home, her teeth are chattering, and she's peed her pants.

"I want Mommy," she whispers.

"Come back tomorrow," Ruth yells.

"Yeah, see ya," I call back.

In Buffalo, Cadillac is the name of a car.

***

I get out of bed. Need a drink of water. Mommy and Grandma are in the kitchen. Mommy says something about Papa and high-grading.

"Mommy, what's high-grading?"

"You're supposed to be in bed."

"What's high-grading?"

"Taking gold home from the mine."

"Stealing?"

"Yeah."

"Did Papa?"

"I sure never saw any gold. Now you get back to bed."

* * *

The day before Christmas, we pile into Grandma's car. It's called a station wagon and has wood sides and leather seats that smell new, though Grandma says it's eight years old. But there are no dents or scratches and no rope to tie the trunk shut. Mommy drives.

We pass other apartment buildings like Grandma's—red brick, three stories high. Streets and streets of brick houses and tall wood ones, but not like Cadillac—these are painted pale blue or white. One is yellow. Some have shutters. The yards have big trees. Mommy says they're maples and oaks and will be beautiful in the spring when they get their leaves. They're beautiful now with every branch iced in snow. Cement sidewalks, no wooden ones. We go down Main Street, past Grants where Mommy worked as a girl, and J&M's Department Store where last week she bought herself a Christmas dress. There's the bus terminal where the legless man was selling pencils. I don't see him today.

Bethlehem Steel is the biggest factory I've ever seen, makes Wood-Cadillac mine look like a bunch of shacks. Towers belch flames and smoke. All the buildings are grey. The houses around the factory are grey, too. Grey like in the North, but street after street and no trees or wood piles.

And the people are dark, too. Negroes, Mommy calls them. I haven't seen negroes before.

We drive past more factories. One really stinks. "P.U., what's that?"

"They make beer," Grandma says.

Papa drank beer. Mommy, too. Grandma drinks tea or hot water. Makes cocoa for me and Gloria.

The houses look better again and have big yards, lots of trees, some with yellow leaves still hanging. We pass open fields. "Look, Gloria, horses." I give her a poke. This farm's not at all like our cousins' place. The house is huge, white with green shutters. There's a green barn with a shiny metal roof. People in funny suits and hats are riding the horses, jumping over gates.

"The Buffalo Country Club," Mommy says and sighs. "Remember Charlie Baird, Mother? I danced with him at Crystal Beach. Should've married him."

"He didn't ask you, did he?"

"Na, those swanks were just playing around. Well, here we are—Blossom City. Ritzville."

Wide streets lined with small trees. The houses are newer, shorter, more spread out. That one is white with blue trim and a little porch with black iron railings. We stop in front of a red brick house. The windows have many little panes outlined in black. A curving, cement drive and a brick garage and a sidewalk right up to the front porch, and the door is shiny wood with a coloured-glass window—flowers in the glass. Only place I've seen this is the church in Rouyn-Noranda.

Aunt Jean's at the door. She's wearing a creamy dress. She hugs Mommy.

"Oh, Muriel, you poor thing. We've got to get you to a dentist."

Mommy puts her hand over her mouth. It doesn't look that bad now. Not swollen and she's wearing her new lipstick—really bright red. Just no front teeth. I don't have front teeth either. Different though. Mine fell out on their own, and the tooth fairy came and brought nickels.

Aunt Jean hugs me and Gloria, both at once. Her dress is soft wool, and she smells nice.

"John's still at the bank," she says to Grandma.

Last night Mommy told me Uncle John is a bank manager.

Our cousin Barbara is seven and very beautiful. She has long blond hair, white butterfly barrettes, a red plaid skirt, white stockings and shiny black shoes with straps. She just stands there though, with a stuck-up look.

Aunt Jean says: "Why don't you show the girls your room?"

Barbara, with a little shrug, leads us down the hall and up the stairs.

Her room has all white furniture, a pink-flowered quilt, and curtains and the same pink flowers on the wallpaper. There's a long shelf with dolls all in row, like in a store. They look brand new. Gloria touches one, and Barbara says: "Don't, you'll mess up her dress."

I have a feeling I'm not going to like this cousin. I take Gloria's hand, and we go back down to the living room where the grownups are having tea.

Supper's amazing—a gigantic ham, a Jell-O salad in the shape of a Christmas tree, and more fancy desserts than we can possibly eat. Uncle John says grace, and that's all he says. He's not a bit like Uncle Yves, who has a very loud laugh and pretends to be a bear and chases us kids all through the house.

After, we sit by the Christmas tree. It looks like the ones in J&M's windows. The ornaments are made of glass. I hold Gloria's hand, though she's stopped trying to touch everything.

We had a tree last year. Papa cut it in the bush. Me and Mommy made popcorn strings and red crepe paper bows. It was pretty, and after Christmas, we ate the popcorn. It was really hard to chew.

We're in a big bed in a room by ourselves. The bed's soft and the room warm. Gloria's scared. She's such a crybaby. I have to tell her stories. I tell her about Santa Claus coming down the chimney. She cries harder. So I make up a story.

"Once there were two little girls, and they went to visit their grandma. They had to go a long way through the bush." I'm about to mention the big bad wolf, but think better of it. "They took the train. Miles and miles of snow, rocks, and bush. It was a long, long way, but they didn't have to be afraid of wolves and bears because they were on the train. The whistle went *ooouu ooouu*, and all the wild animals ran away. Grandma lived in a big city in a beautiful house and all the windows had coloured glass flowers in them."

"Grandma lives in the apartment."

"This is a story, silly."

"Okay."

"It was Christmas Eve, and the children went right to sleep because they knew there would be presents the next morning."

"What did they get?" whispers Gloria.

"The smaller girl got a beautiful doll with blond curly hair and eyes that open and shut, and the doll was wearing a red silk dress and black shiny shoes."

"Really, she got a doll?"

"Really, now go to sleep. Soon it'll be morning."

***

Christmas morning is far better than my story. We both get red velvet dresses, long white stockings and shiny black shoes with straps. Mommy says the shoes are called Mary Janes.

Aunt Jean says: "We maybe should've got Sharon green. Red-heads shouldn't wear red."

"Sharon's so pretty she looks good in any colour," Mommy says.

"You'll make her vain," Grandma says.

I'm not sure I like being dressed exactly like my little sister. We both get oranges, candy canes, and best of all dolls with blond curls and open-and-shut eyes, and the dolls have red velvet dresses, too.

Barbara gets a plaid taffeta dress and whispers: "Velvet's for babies."

"You're an idiot. Your mother's dress is velvet," I whisper back.

All day Gloria holds her doll. She strokes and strokes its velvet dress. She strokes her own velvet dress too. She won't play Snakes and Ladders. She won't colour in our new books. I colour with Barbara who doesn't like it when I draw pictures in the margins. "You're supposed to colour within the lines," she says.

"It's my book. I'll colour wherever I please."

*J*ANUARY IS A very good month. I start school and learn to read in two weeks. Miss Cherry says I'm very smart. What she doesn't know is that I was already reading with Mommy. In Cadillac we had a whole box of books that she had when she was little.

Mommy gets new teeth and is beautiful again. She also gets a job at Grants department store. On the last Friday of the month, the day she gets paid, she takes me and Gloria on the blue and white bus to Grants. We have supper at the snack bar: hamburgers, French fries, and grape phosphates. We watch the waitress squirt the syrup in the glass and then shoot the fizzy water from the machine. And *voila*, grape pop. There are twelve different flavours. Grape was Mommy's favourite when she worked here as a teenager. Gloria and I stick our purple tongues out at each other. Mommy smokes and chats with our waitress, Holly, who tells us she and our mommy are old friends. Grandma doesn't like it when Mommy smokes. Says it isn't ladylike.

We go to the girls' department, and Mommy buys us new underwear in different colours with the days of the week stamped on them. In Cadillac at Ducharme's store, they sold only white underwear, and Mommy says it was more expensive. Everything's prettier and cheaper at Grants. We get red plaid skirts and white blouses, and flannelette nighties with kittens printed on them. In the toy department there's a counter covered with doll clothes. Dresses are 25 cents, and we each pick one out and socks for 5 cents and shoes for 10. Mommy says next week she'll buy us new dolls. Gloria wants the soft-bodied baby doll, while I would like the grownup lady doll with the ruffled taffeta skirt.

"Are we rich now?" I ask Mommy.

"Not quite," she says and laughs.

February is good, too. Gloria gets her baby doll and me a lady doll. Each Friday we eat at the snack bar. We've had cherry, orange, lime, as well as the grape phosphates. Every week we get new clothes, and almost every night she brings us a colouring or paper-doll book, or some candy. It's like every day is Christmas.

Gloria has stopped wetting the bed and pooping in corners. Grandma bought a child-sized toilet seat and covered it in pink furry fabric. Gloria stopped being afraid of toilets.

It's cozy being in the big bed with Mommy and Gloria, but I can't always go to sleep right away.

I'm still awake when Mommy comes to bed and snuggles down beside me.

"What was your papa like?" I ask her.

"A good man. Critical, though."

"What's critical?"

"Oh, just how he thought about people. My best friend was Mary Talbot, our next-door neighbour. Her folks had a store downtown, Talbot's Gifts and Confectionary. Their store sold beautiful china dolls, and Mary got one each Christmas. I knew my folks could get me one through the store at half price. I heard our mothers talking. I never got one though."

"Did you get ordinary dolls instead?"

"Once, but after that she would say, 'You have a doll. What do you need another one for?'"

"Was Mary nice?"

"Oh, yes. She always shared everything. Lent me clothes and even her dolls. My dad didn't like that. Anyway, when we were nine, her parents had to sell their store and move away. Dad said, 'That's what happens to big-time spenders. Serves them right.' Our families were supposed to be friends. We even had Thanksgiving dinner together, every year."

"But why did they have to sell their store?"

"It was the Depression. A lot of people lost their jobs. Nobody could buy anything. Most people were poor. The Talbots came back a year later and rented the apartment over their old store. For a while her dad was a janitor. Then he was unemployed again. Dad said, 'What does he expect, gadding around the countryside?' My mother replied, 'A rolling stone gathers no moss.'"

"What's that mean?"

"If you travel, you won't have things like a house and money. Mother loves those old sayings." Mommy sounds cross.

"Your mother's nice. I love Grandma."

"Yes, she is nice, and has been very good to us. We better get to sleep—school for you and work for me in the morning."

* * *

March starts off good. First of all, the snow melts, and we don't have to wear our itchy-wool snow-pants. If we went bare-legged in Cadillac in March, we'd freeze our behinds, as Mommy says. I learn to skip double Dutch.

Then things get very, very sad. Grandma dies. I didn't know she was sick. She did sleep a lot, but she looked after Gloria all day while Mommy was at Grants.

Grandma said: "Sweet little Gloria's no bother. I hardly know she's in the house."

Gloria had a nap every afternoon with Grandma. I can't remember ever having afternoon naps. But Gloria, with her Christmas doll, her baby doll, and the brand new Raggedy Ann doll, slept all afternoon in Grandma's bed.

Mommy and Aunt Jean have a big fight. Aunt Jean says: "Mother was too old to look after your kids, and that's why she had a heart attack."

Maybe she means me, because Grandma said Gloria was no bother. I know I'm not quiet. And sometimes, Ruth came after school, and we made a fort out of the kitchen chairs and a blanket. But Grandma said she didn't mind. She liked to see children having fun, and she gave us cocoa and graham crackers spread with peanut butter to take into our fort.

Mommy buys us pink taffeta dresses for Grandma's funeral. In the funeral home I have to tell Gloria to stop stroking hers. People will think she's a crazy.

Gloria does act crazy. First, she wants to stand by Grandma's coffin. Everybody says what a sweet little girl she is. Gloria tells everybody: "My grandma's sleeping. Doesn't she look pretty?" I try to lead her away, but she won't budge.

The man in the black suit tells everyone but the family to go in the chapel. "I'll give you a moment to say goodbye," he says to Mommy and Aunt Jean. They both kiss Grandma and step back. Don't seem to notice Gloria hasn't moved.

Black Suit closes the lid and Uncle John and some other men I don't know pick up the coffin.

Mommy picks up Gloria, and we all follow the coffin into the chapel. Mommy said a chapel is a little church. No pretty windows, but somebody is playing an organ.

At first, Gloria whimpers, then she cries louder and louder. I can't hear what the minister's saying and give her a poke to make her shut up, but she screams and screams right to the end.

Gloria has nightmares — she's in a coffin, and a man in a black suit closes the lid, and she can't breathe.

What's worse, she wets the bed. And Mommy has enough to do getting off to work without having all that extra laundry.

And then, Mommy going to work is the problem. Who's going to look after Gloria? Grandma's friend, Mrs. Jackson, does for a while, but some days she has appointments, or a headache, and her bridge club meets on Thursdays.

Everything just gets worse, and I have to stay home from school some days to look after Gloria. If I get to go to school, I have to come right home after, and Ruth's not allowed to come. Those days, Mommy leaves as soon as I get home. Me and Gloria eat the sandwiches, milk, and cookies she left for us. We colour and play with our dolls. We get too tired to wait up for her and go to bed. We're asleep before she returns. She says to keep the door locked, don't ever turn on the stove, and don't tell anybody at school we're alone.

Aunt Jean and Mommy have another big fight. Aunt Jean wants to sell Grandma's car, but she can't because Grandma gave it to Mommy. Mommy has the ownership paper and waves it in Aunt Jean's face. Aunt Jean leaves, taking the living room rug with her. She rolls it up and drags it behind her, bump, bump, bump down the stairs and out to her car. Me and Mommy watch from the front window. At first, Aunt Jean can't get it in. She pushes, folds, stuffs, heaves, kicks and finally gets the trunk shut.

When we turn around, Gloria is howling on the bare living-room floor. No more fringe for her to straighten.

***

I wake up and Mommy's not in bed with us. From the living room doorway, I see her sitting on the couch. She's smoking. She's not supposed to smoke in Grandma's house. I stand right in front of her, but she doesn't see me. She's staring at the window with a gone away look.

"Mommy, what are you looking at?"

"Just thinking, honey, just thinking." And she reaches out and pulls me onto her lap.

"About what?"

"How much I loved my mother, and never told her."

"I love you, Mommy."

"I love you too, Sharon. Never forget that. Don't ever think I don't, no matter how stupid I act."

"You don't act stupid."

"I never did anything she approved of."

"You had me and Gloria, and she loved us."

"Yes, she did." She holds me so tight I can't breathe.

"Come back to bed," I tell her.

She gets up and carries me to bed, just like a baby. She tucks me in beside Gloria and kisses me. "I'll be right back. Go to sleep now."

But I can't go to sleep, and she doesn't come back. I can smell her cigarette. Grandma didn't like Mommy smoking.

***

Mommy's late for work because Gloria clings to her leg and won't let her go. Mommy pulls her off and I hold on to her while Mommy gets out the door.

One time, Mommy sits down on the floor with Gloria on her lap and they both cry. That's scary, and I don't know what to do.

Gloria gets strep throat, and Mommy has to stay home. Gloria has pills that cost a lot of money and a high fever. Her being sick isn't all bad because every day I get to go to school.

Gloria's sick for two weeks and Mommy loses her job. "Those S.O.B.'s," she says, but won't tell me what that means. She says not to worry, we'll have the money from Grandma's estate.

Aunt Jean returns and takes the pink and white dishes, the silver platter and all the pretty things in the china cabinet. Then the movers come and take the china cabinet. The apartment doesn't look like Grandma's place anymore.

Mommy says: "It's okay. When I get my money, we'll buy new things."

In May, me and Gloria move into Grandma's room. Two men come and bring white beds with gold trim and take Grandma's old bed away. Mommy buys us pink flowered quilts and pink curtains and a pink rug for between the beds. Our room is just as pretty as our cousin Barbara's.

The only problem is Gloria's scared to sleep alone and crawls with me. I tell her I'll kill her if she wets the bed. I wake up with cold pee against my leg. She's sound asleep in her soggy mess. I give her a good poke. She bawls and Mommy comes.

***

June 12th is my birthday. I'm seven today. Gloria's still five because her birthday's not till October. We have pink and white balloons and streamers, but best of all, I get to invite Ruth and also Judy and Karen, but Ruth's my best friend.

We have a treasure hunt. Have to follow the clues. Mommy hands me a pink note: *Look in the third dresser drawer in the girls' room.*

I read the notes because I'm the best reader in our class. The next one says: *Look in the silverware drawer.*

We run to the kitchen. Ruth yanks out the drawer so hard it falls on the floor and the stuff flies all over with a great bang clatter.

"Sorry, Mrs. Desjardins," says Ruth.

"It's okay." Mommy laughs and pats her on the head. "Find the clue, quick."

I spot the piece of pink paper, and we're off to the living room. *Under the middle cushion,* the note says.

By the time we find the prize in Mommy's closet, the apartment is a big mess, but everybody's laughing, Mommy most of all.

We tear the paper off the box and there are shiny bead necklaces and bracelets for all of us.

We have hot dogs, cake and ice cream, and the cake is from the bakery, and it's white with pink candy roses and has happy birthday and my name all in pink icing.

In Cadillac, Mommy made our cakes, and they just had candles and white icing.

When Mommy's tucking me into bed, I ask her: "Did you have fun birthday parties when you were little?"

"No. My mother didn't think children needed birthday parties."

$\mathcal{T}$HE VERY NEXT week we have to put all our stuff in boxes and Mommy carries the boxes into her room and keeps the door shut.

One night I wake up and hear Mommy talking to somebody in the living room. I get up to investigate.

She tells me her friends have come to help us move. The clock says half past one—I can tell time now. "Why don't we move in the daytime?"

Nobody answers me. Mommy picks me up and says: "We're having an adventure."

They take all the boxes out, and the beds and the chesterfield and load them into Mommy's friend's truck. Gloria wakes up and cries, of course. Mommy puts down the back seat in the station wagon, and the men put a mattress in. Mommy makes us up a bed with Grandma's quilts, and gives us the big box filled with our dolls. "Go back to sleep," she says.

Pitch dark and Gloria's bawling.

* * *

Our new place is in the basement of an apartment building. The building is bigger than Grandma's, and no playground nearby. But the parking lot is cement and good for skipping, and there are lots of kids around. It's too far to go to my old school. I'll start at a new school in September. I never see Ruth again.

There's only one bedroom. It's for me and Gloria. Mommy fixes it up with all our new furniture and stuff. This apartment smells funny.

* * *

Mommy has a new job working for the *Buffalo Courier News*. She tells us it's a better job and we can help. I want to help, but don't see how Gloria can.

We get up so early it's still dark. We climb onto the mattress in the back of the station wagon. Gloria curls up with her blanket and her doll. Big help she'll be.

We go to the newspaper office and park in a lane. Mommy tells us to stay in the car. Even with my face pressed against the glass I can't see much. A big door opens and a man is talking to Mommy. Now they're coming back with bundles of papers.

Load after load of papers. I offer to help, but she waves me back. By the time they're finished, there's just room for me and Gloria to sit.

We drive for a while. Stop at the end of a very dark street. Mommy cuts open a bundle and hands us each a paper and points out the porches where the papers go. She keeps the headlights on so we can see. It's kinda fun. We don't usually get to run around outside in the dark. We've only delivered a few papers when Gloria falls and skins her knee and bawls. Now it's just me delivering. Then Mommy helps, too. She's really fast. We make it a game, but my legs and arms ache by the time we finish.

We deliver papers six days a week, even if it's raining. Mommy buys us yellow raincoats with hoods. Gloria doesn't deserve one. She doesn't deliver many papers, sits in the car, hugging one of her dolls.

Even though I get pretty tired, I like being part of the crew, as Mommy says. By the time we're done, the sun's up and we go to Hank's Diner for breakfast. We order whatever we like. One day I have pancakes and the next, bacon and eggs. Chocolate milk one day and cocoa the next. Gloria is usually asleep on Mommy's lap. Then, we go back to the apartment and sleep as long as we like. I always wake up first. Living in Buffalo is sure more exciting than dull old Cadillac.

Summer is very, very hot. Mommy says: "A good thing about our basement apartment is it's a lot cooler than Grandma's place would've been."

Everything smells like the cellar in Cadillac. The walls are getting black spots.

Sundays, when there aren't any papers, we go on adventures. We go to the zoo. The hyenas make this crazy noise, almost like they're laughing. Now I know why Mommy says her boss laughs like a hyena. He laughs really loud. He jokes around with her when they're loading the papers.

Sometimes, we go to the movies and have popcorn. A lot of movies are love stories, and Gloria falls asleep. I like *Two Years Before the Mast*. Alan Ladd's the hero. *Bambi* is really good, but Gloria cries because Bambi's mother dies. She screams so much during *The Wizard of Oz*, Mommy has to take her out and sit with her in the lobby.

My favourite Sundays are when we cross the border and go to Crystal Beach. We both have new bathing suits—mine is blue polka dot and Gloria's pink. We pack a picnic lunch and swim and play on the beach all day. I learn to swim by watching other kids. I hold my breath, go under, kick hard, reach out my arms, wriggle like a fish, surface, gulp in air. Yippee, I did it! Gloria's scared to try.

Before we go home Mommy takes us to the amusement park next to the beach. We buy sugar-puff waffles, all crispy and coated with powdered sugar. They don't taste anything like those from Grandma's waffle iron. Those were good too, but more like pancakes. We all go for a ride on the merry-go-round. My horse goes up and down. Gloria cried when Mommy put her on an up-and-down horse, so they sit in the sleigh behind my horse. Then we have ice cream and walk through the park. There's music coming from the dancehall.

"I used to go there when I was a teenager," Mommy says. "The Crystal Ballroom where all sorts of famous bands played—Tommy Dorsey, Duke Ellington." She looks sad.

"Was that when you worked at Grants and bought pretty dresses?"

"Sure was. Now, let's go get all-day suckers."

My favourite's cinnamon, Gloria likes butterscotch, and Mommy gets lemon or peanut.

One Sunday, we cross the border and go to Niagara Falls. Gloria doesn't like the roaring water, but I do. We see an old wooden barge stuck in the river.

Mommy says: "It got stuck a long time ago. The men on it thought at any moment they'd be swept over the falls. They were so scared their hair turned white. The next morning they were rescued. The barge never did go over."

"There's a tree growing on it, like a little island."

"Amazing, eh?"

"Did other boats go over?"

"Lots of them."

"I wanna go home," Gloria says.

We go see the whirlpool—a great funnel of water going down, down, down. If the railing broke, I'd be sucked miles down to the centre of the earth. I'm glad when we leave. I wasn't afraid at the falls. Looked like it might be fun to go over, like swishing down a giant slide, but I have nightmares about the whirlpool. I don't usually have nightmares. After a while they stop.

***

Me and Gloria are in bed. She goes to sleep right away—always does. I can't get to sleep. I'm going to ask Mommy to make me cocoa. She does when I can't sleep.

She's sitting at the table by the window, this dinky little window. All you can see, even in the daytime, is feet going by. Mommy's staring up at the window with that gone away look. "Are you sad?" I ask her.

"Just thinking, honey. Can't you sleep?"

"Can I have cocoa?"

She makes us both some, and we sit on the couch, with her quilt over our knees. This apartment's chilly at night, even though it's July.

"Mommy, when you were a little girl, was your family poor?"

"Whatever gave you that idea?"

"Your friend Mary lent you clothes and you didn't have birthday parties."

"We weren't poor. My dad was a high-school principal. He always had a job. But I didn't have nice clothes like Mary's. My parents were frugal. One of Mother's favourite sayings was *a penny saved is a penny earned.*"

"Huh?"

"Just means you should save your money."

"Is that bad?"

"No, but can be overdone. Like, I never went to high-school dances because I didn't have anything suitable to wear. Funny thing is, Sharon, they weren't always so saving. The year I started high school, my sister got married. Jean is seven years older. She was in her second year of university. My parents made a big deal out of us getting a good education. Were always telling me to work harder. Getting good marks was all that mattered. Yet they didn't mind her getting married partway through. In fact they were delighted."

"Did she have a pretty dress?" She ignores me and goes right on talking.

"Because what was really important wasn't education but money. John was already working in the bank, and what's more, he came from a wealthy family. Jean got married at the Buffalo Country Club. Do you remember seeing it on the way to Aunt Jean's last Christmas?"

"Where we saw the horses?"

"That's right. John's parents were members, mine weren't. We went to J&M's department store, and Jean got a long white satin gown decorated with tiny pearls, and a silk suit for going away. I was to be junior bridesmaid. The bridesmaid dresses were green taffeta with sweetheart necklines and flared skirts. Pretty, and just right for a party dress. I was thrilled and already planning on going to the Christmas dance at my high school, but no, Mother had something else in mind. She thought the bridesmaid dresses too grown up for me and picked out this ruffly thing with puff sleeves. Mother never did have good taste."

"Did you go to the Christmas dance?"

"No, and I never wore that dress again. I quit school at sixteen and worked at Grants so I'd have some decent clothes."

"And you went to the Crystal Ballroom?"

"That's right, honey. And come hell or high water, I won't live as they did."

***

The week before school starts we go shopping at Grants. Mommy says there's no point holding grudges—anyway, she has friends there. I like these friends—Roseanne, I don't know her last name, and Holly Holmes, whose name sounds like a movie star. Roseanne's working in the snack bar. She's old and plump, but really nice. She serves our hamburgs, fries, and lemon phosphates. Just when we're finishing she brings us ice cream with chocolate sauce and a cherry, and whispers to Mommy: "On the house—those bastards owe ya." Mommy giggles. I love being back here.

We get to choose our dresses. I pick a quite grown-up looking, pale-blue cotton with a white eyelet collar, and Gloria, a babyish kitten print, with a big bow at the waist. We get hair ribbons, barrettes, and socks to match.

I skipped kindergarten, but Mommy thinks Gloria better go. She's going to be in afternoon kindergarten. The first day everything's fine until Mommy leaves her in the kindergarten line-up. Gloria shrieks so much, Mommy has to go with her into the school. In the grade-two line-up, I look away and pretend not to know them. The second day Mommy stays home, and after lunch, I have to take Gloria, whose sniffles turn into wails when we reach the schoolyard. "You'll make friends and have lots of fun."

"I want Mommy."

I wipe her nose with my hanky and make her stand by the monkey bars until it's time to line up. I swing upside down with my new friend Jill.

The kindergarten teacher takes Gloria's hand and tells me not to worry—lots of little ones cry the whole first week. Nobody else is bawling. The teacher's wrong because Gloria cries every day for as long as we go to that school. At least she only goes afternoons.

***

Winter comes. Delivering the *Buffalo Courier News* is no fun at all. Mommy buys me a new snowsuit with heavy wool snow-pants and boots with fur lining. I wear two pair of mitts. My fingers and toes are numb before we finish. And bundled up in those heavy clothes, I can barely walk, let alone run to each porch, so the job takes longer. My legs get red and sore from those snow-pants, though I wear my long brown stockings underneath. Mommy rubs Vaseline on me. It helps a little bit.

Even though Gloria stays curled up in the back with her quilt and her dolls, she gets an ear infection, and then tonsillitis, and has a high fever, and needs expensive medicine. I have to stay with her at the apartment while Mommy delivers all the papers by herself, and that takes a lot longer.

Still, as Mommy says, everything has a plus side — I don't have to take Gloria to school. Mommy doesn't say this is the plus. She said that when we got new stuff after Aunt Jean took Grandma's things, and when she got the newspaper job because she earns more money than at Grants.

By Christmas Gloria's all better. I told her teacher how sick she was, and the teacher gave me work sheets and green and red construction paper. I helped her with the work sheets. We play school a lot. Gloria says she likes playing school better than real school.

This Christmas is different, but fun. We don't go to Aunt Jean's. We go to Lobby's Old Spain, this really fancy restaurant. It has a fountain and white arches with little bumps, called stucco, all over them. There are white tablecloths, and a red flower in the centre of each table. We wear our red velvet dresses even though they're getting too small. We have new white stockings and black patent leather shoes.

Mommy says she didn't cook dinner because she didn't want to be alone. A funny thing to say because she's not alone, she has us. Maybe she's missing Grandma, or Papa. I do miss Grandma even though we only knew her for a little while. Papa? He knocked out Mommy's teeth. She has false ones now. I won't ever forgive him for that. He never hit me, but I'll never forget what he did to Mommy. On the trips to Uncle Yves he sang *Sur la pont*. I liked that, but I'm still mad at him. I miss the Belanger kids and my cousins.

After dinner, even though the stores are closed, we look at all the fancy Christmas displays in the department store windows. Me and Gloria catch the big soft snowflakes on our tongues. There are hardly any cars or people. As the snow covers Main Street, and more still falls, I close my eyes and see Rue Maisonneuve, our old grey house, and dark, bush-covered hills.

Then we go home and play with all our new toys.

*S*OMETIMES, MOMMY HAS to go out in the evening. She says: "A girl has to have a little fun."

She wears one of her new dresses. My favourite is black silk with a creamy velvet rose at the neck. She wears her high-heeled black shoes or her silver ones. She has a silver clip, like a big barrette, for her hair.

I'm in charge, and Gloria's already asleep.

"If anybody knocks, don't go to the door."

"Of course not. I know better than that."

"That's my big girl. I'll bring you guys a surprise."

The nights Mommy leaves, I try to stay awake and guard. Sometimes, I hear footsteps. I don't want to fall asleep, but always do.

If Gloria wakes up, she cries. I read her stories and give her peanut butter crackers, but she whines: "I want Mommy."

Why doesn't she shut up? Does she think she's the only one who wants Mommy home right now?

At some point we both fall asleep, and when we wake up there's always a surprise—an Eatmore on my pillow, and a Mars Bar on Gloria's. Once, it's little bags of ribbon candy.

Sometimes Mommy's friend, Holly Holmes, the one with the movie star name, comes to our place, and they take the station wagon and go out.

We don't usually get to meet their other friends, but one Sunday Mommy gets us all dressed up, and we drive downtown to Lobby's Old Spain. A man in a grey suit comes to our table. He looks like Alan Ladd in *Two Years Before the Mast*. Last summer we saw that movie. Mommy tells us he's her friend, Mr. Stevens. He calls us cuties. He touches my hair, and says: "My, my, a pretty, little redhead just like your Momma," and sits down at our table. He says to have whatever we want. After dinner he orders sundaes for us, though we're too full, and didn't even ask for ice cream. He's kinda bossy. Mommy seems to like him, though. She laughs a lot and touches his hand or arm when she speaks.

After, when we're in bed, Gloria says: "When I was under the table, I saw that man touch Mommy's leg."

One morning Mommy sleeps in, and it's beginning to get light when we head out to do the papers. "I'm going to be late for school."

"Don't worry so much."

"I don't like being late."

"Please, Sharon, I've got a shitty headache."

The man, where we pick up the papers, doesn't like us being late either. He yells at Mommy.

***

"C'mon, crybaby." My hands are freezing. I should've worn my mitts on the climbing bars, but they make my hands slip. Why's Gloria so slow? She's always whining to go home, yet when we're on our way, she still complains.

"Wait up," she wails.

"Hurry, Mommy'll make us grilled-cheese sandwiches, your favourite."

"I am hurrying."

We clatter down the cement stairs. Mommy opens the door before we can.

"I've got a big surprise for my girls."

"What?" we both ask.

And right behind Mommy is a small black dog with a red ribbon around his neck, tied in a big bow. He's wagging his tail so hard his whole body wriggles. Gloria hugs the dog so much, I hardly get to pet it.

"What shall we call him?" Mommy says.

"Pal," Gloria says.

"So Pal it is."

"Inky's a good name," I tell them.

"How about we let Gloria name him? He's a guard dog. He'd bark if anybody ever came around while I was out."

I think guard dogs are supposed to be bigger. "How old is he?"

"Four, twenty-eight in people years. Old enough to look after you girls."

Gloria hogs the dog. She sits beside him all evening and whispers in his ear.

When we go to bed, Pal sleeps between us, but Gloria still hogs him because she keeps her arm around him all night.

* * *

Pal may be small, but I have to admit he is a good guard dog. On Saturday we take him with us to the playground at the school. Nobody's there and I'm having such a good time I don't even feel how cold the bars are. For once Gloria's not whining. She's throwing sticks for Pal.

The next time I look over there's a man standing beside Gloria. I drop off the bars. Mommy has warned us not to talk to strangers.

"What's your dog's name?" the man asks.

"Pal," Gloria says.

I give her a kick.

"Why don't I take you girls for ice cream?" He reaches out to hold Gloria's hand.

Before I can do anything, Pal growls, the fur rises on the back of his neck, and he snaps at the man's leg. The man takes a step back. I grab Gloria's hand. "C'mon. Mommy's waiting." We run all the way home.

Besides being a guard dog Pal can do tricks. He'll sit up on his hind legs when we tell him to beg, and we feed him dog biscuits. He'll play fetch for ages. Best of all, he's taught Gloria not to wet the bed. How did he do that?

* * *

It's not fair I have to stay in and write lines — I will not be late again. A hundred times. It's not fair. I can hear the other girls out skipping. "Cinderella dressed in yella went upstairs to kiss her fella. How many kisses did she get?" and the slap of the rope as it hits the cement. "1, 2, 3, 4 ..." They're doing peppers.

One good thing—Gloria's not waiting for me. She's home sick.

Miss Wilson walks down the aisle. I write faster.

"You can finish that at home. You're to go to the principal's office now."

I pack up my books. Put everything in my Rudolph bag. I move very carefully, don't look at Miss Wilson. I won't cry. I walk slowly down the hall. I'm going to get the strap. I know it. Mommy's fault I'm late all the time. I won't cry. Won't cry.

I stand in the open doorway. The leather strap is on the desk, not far from Mr. Principal's thick, pudgy hands. "Come in," he says.

I want to run away, but stumble forward.

"You have already been late six times this month."

"I'm sorry."

"Punctuality is important. Why are you late?"

"My mother delivers newspapers real early every morning. It's her job. She has to take us with her. Sometimes it takes longer, and we're late getting home."

"Where's your father?"

"Away."

"I want you to take this note home to your mother. We can't have pupils wandering in just any old time. You may go."

I run down the hall, remember *no running in the halls*, and slow to a fast walk, my arms pressed to my sides. I push open the heavy door, don't even look towards the playground. Run all the way home.

***

We've been learning to weave with construction paper. Tomorrow, Miss Wilson says we can make Easter baskets. I'm going to choose purple and yellow. I'm giving my basket to Mommy for Easter. At Grants I'm going to buy a chocolate marshmallow egg to put in it. I skip down the sidewalk, leaping over each crack. Gloria didn't go to school. She has another cold.

In the night I wake up all hot and thirsty.

Mommy says I have a high fever. "Oh, Sharon, I just can't take it if you get sick, too."

"Don't worry, I promise I'll be better in the morning."

But I'm not. I have an itchy red rash all over my chest and I'm dizzy when I stand up. Mommy makes me stay in bed, and I cry because today I was going to make my basket.

She says I have the measles and tells me I have to stay in a dark room, because measles can affect the eyes. Gloria has to stay out of our room.

I try to read my new fairy-tale book, but the room's too dim. I get up and turn on the light. I'm so dizzy I almost fall getting back in bed. So dizzy and hot I can't read anyway.

Mommy yells: "What did I tell you? Do you want to go blind?"

Won't cry. Won't cry.

Then she's back and wants me to drink some cold water. At first, it tastes good. Then my stomach hurts, and I throw up all over the bed. "I'm sorry, Mommy!" I wail just like crybaby Gloria.

Mommy holds me, rocks me in her arms, says: "Everything'll be okay."

She cleans up the mess, and puts wet washcloths on my forehead and wrists.

When I wake up, Gloria's in bed with me and she's whimpering.

"You might as well be in together, she's got them, too."

I'm hot and push Gloria away. "There's no room."

Gloria wails. Mommy picks her up, and pushes her bed, that's never used, right next to mine to make one big bed.

Pal's whining at the door because Mommy won't let him in our room.

She brings orange juice. Yummy, we only have juice when we're sick, but it tastes funny. She says, she ground up aspirin in it, and if I drink it, my fever will go down, and I'll feel a lot better. I drink it and don't throw up. I'm so sleepy.

When I wake up, the sun's shining through the hole in the blind, and I do feel better. Gloria's asleep and looks all red. I go to find Mommy. She's asleep on the couch. "We better deliver the papers," I tell her.

She makes a big fuss about me being out of bed and in bare feet, too. "These damn cement floors are so cold," she says.

She hustles me back to bed. Then gets all upset over Gloria. Mommy wrings out washcloths for her forehead and wrists. Gloria's so hot, I can feel the heat rising off her. Mommy tells me to stay in bed—she's going put Gloria in a cold bath. She carries her into the bathroom. I hear water running, and after a while Gloria crying.

She brings her back to bed and tries to make her drink the orange juice with aspirin, but she cries.

"You keep the wet cloths on her forehead, and I'll be right back."

It's a long time before she comes back. I keep washing Gloria's face like Mommy said. Gloria whimpers and thrashes around on the bed. I try to make her drink the orange juice, but she cries. I keep the light off. Don't want us to go blind.

Mommy rushes into our room. She's got a drugstore bag. Maybe she bought treats. I'm hungry.

She picks up whimpering Gloria.

"At least she's not screaming," I tell Mommy. "I washed her like you said."

"That's good, honey, but be better if she was screaming."

Sometimes Mommy doesn't make much sense.

She fixes something in the kitchen and comes back in.

"She's not a baby."

Mommy ignores me and picks up Gloria again, cuddles her and sticks a baby bottle in her mouth. Baby Gloria sucks.

"What's in the bottle?"

"Sugar water and aspirin."

"I'm hungry."

"Thank God. You must be better. I've got some Jell-O ready for you."

"I want pancakes and sausages."

"Ah, Sharon, you're funny. Just liquids until your fever's all gone."

"But I'm really hungry."

"I'll get the Jell-O."

When Mommy puts Gloria down on the bed, she stops sucking and wails. Mommy holds her until she's finished the whole bottle and has fallen asleep.

For all of the next week Gloria drinks out of the baby bottle. I feel fine and want to go back to school, but Mommy says I have to wait until my rash is all gone and have to stay in the dark room. She puts all our dolls in bed with us. She puts a tray on my lap so that I can cut and colour. Mommy and me make new paper dolls by tracing the old ones and colouring them in. Gloria doesn't play much. Just hugs Pal. She likes me to tell her stories.

"What about your job?" I ask Mommy.

"I told them I had pneumonia and would be back in a week."

"Why didn't you say we had the measles?"

"I lost my last job when I told them Gloria had strep throat. I figure if they think it's me who's sick, they can't object. Next week you should be able to stay with Gloria."

"I want to go to school."

"You can go like you always do when I get back."

"But I can't be late."

"I do the best I can."

***

The next Monday Mommy wakes me up when it's still dark and says she's going to work. "Keep the light off in the bedroom. You can turn the light on in the living room as long as Gloria stays in here."

"Don't worry. I'll look after her."

"You're my big girl, and here's breakfast."

Breakfast is in the picnic basket. After she leaves, I check Gloria's still sleeping. She is, with her arm around Pal. He looks at me and thumps his tail, but doesn't move. I bet he'd like to join me for breakfast. He always stays on the bed till Gloria wakes up.

I carry the picnic basket into the living room. Two bottles for Gloria—one with red sugar water and one with milk. For me there are pancakes layered with peanut butter and red jam, and a thermos of cocoa. Yummy!

I climb on the couch, wrap myself up in Mommy's blankets, and eat breakfast. I check to make sure Gloria's still sleeping. Then I read *Snipp, Snapp, Snurr and The Buttered Bread*.

It's still dark when Mommy returns.

She's crying, striding around the room, and saying over and over: "Those god damn bastards."

I figure she's lost her job. I offer her the last of the cocoa. She sits down on the couch and hugs me.

"What'll I do?" she sobs.

"We'll use Grandma's money."

"Oh, Sharon, there wasn't much. She sold her house after my dad died for a few thousand. It was the war years and prices were still at Depression lows. I'm so stupid. Why didn't I save what money I got? I'm so bloody stupid."

"Mommy, you're not stupid. You'll get another job." I pat her back.

She stops crying. "My big girl, what would I do without you?"

*E*VERYTHING ALWAYS HAS a good side. Mommy says that a lot. I agree. Even losing her job has one because I'm never late for school. Mind you, she didn't say anything about losing her job having a good side. She goes job hunting afternoons while we're both at school.

Then things get very, very bad, and there's no good side at all. One night we pack all our toys and clothes and Pal into the station wagon and drive a long way to another apartment building. We're going to stay with Mommy's friend Holly Holmes.

"What about our beds?"

"I'm sorry," says Mommy. "Holly will have beds for us to sleep in."

Holly doesn't. We're sleeping on the living room rug. Pal's between us, and we both hug him. I can't go to sleep—the floor's too hard.

Mommy and Holly are arguing in the bedroom, but the next morning Holly gives us big bowls of cornflakes and milk, pats our heads, and calls us cuties. Mommy hustles us and Pal into the car, and I get to school an hour early. She says to wait by the gate at noon for her and Gloria.

I meet them and we have lunch in the car. She'll pick us up at three-thirty, right when the bell rings. She drives away with Pal.

Gloria whines: "Why can't Pal stay with us?"

"Somebody might steal him while we're in school."

This shuts her up, but she still looks sad.

***

Mommy's always there when we get out of school. And everything would've continued just fine, if it wasn't for that baby, Gloria.

Miss Wilson has just handed back our spelling tests and I'm feeling good—got 100. If I get one more perfect test, I'll get a Thomas Jefferson card. I've already got my George Washington one. There's a knock on the door. Miss Wilson tells me to gather up my things and go to the office. I haven't been late once this week, but I'm still scared. I pack up my Rudolph bag.

I knock gently on the closed door. If nobody comes, maybe I can tell Miss Wilson there was nobody there.

The kindergarten teacher opens the door, and I see Gloria, head hanging and sobbing. The principal is beside her. What have they done to her? I hate fat-faced Mr. Principal with his squinty pig eyes. If I was big and had a knife, I'd chop off his pudgy fingers one by one.

"Your sister's had an accident," he says. "You must take her home."

Sure enough, Gloria's brown stockings are wet. I don't say anything, just take Gloria's hand and lead her down the hall. Once outside, we run until we're out of sight of the school.

"Where are we going?" Gloria wails.

"We'll go to that big park where Mommy sometimes takes us."

"How'll she find us?"

"We'll come back."

The big park has a turnabout. I put Gloria on it and spin her around. It's a sunny day, but she complains she's cold, and her wet pants feel awful.

To make matters worse, an old man comes over and says: "Shouldn't you little girls be in school?"

I grab Gloria's hand, and we run down the street until we're panting, and have to stop.

"We're going to get lost," Gloria wails.

"No, we're not. This is Lincoln Street. See that sign. The library where Mommy took us isn't very far. It'll be warm, and we can see what time it is. I can tell time, you know."

It's further than I thought, but we find it, and the door isn't locked. "Stop crying, Gloria, or the library lady won't let us stay."

She chokes back her sobs, and I use her skirt to clean the snot and tears off her face. "Your pants must be dry by now."

"They're not."

"It'll be warm inside, and they'll dry quick."

Together we pull open the heavy door. I hold Gloria's hand and hurry her upstairs to the children's department. I find the door

marked—girls. We hide in a stall and both pee. I tell her to leave her brown stockings off. I stuff them in her Mickey Mouse lunch box. She has half of a baloney sandwich left, and we share it. I fold toilet paper into the crotch of her panties. "We should've come here first," I tell her, and lead her out to the books.

I pick out two, and we sit down at a table. "This looks like a good one, *Three Smart Squirrels and Squee.*" I start to read: "Chatterbox and Chubby-Chunk and Timothy were three little squirrels. They had a brother whose name was Squee."

"When will Mommy be here?"

"See that clock? When the big hand gets to twelve and the little hand is at three, we'll start walking back. 'Little Squee, why don't you use your tail for a blanket to keep you warm?' said Mother Squirrel. 'I forgot,' said Squee.'"

"Little girls, where is your mother?" A plump grey-haired woman leans over us.

Gloria clutches my arm.

"Oh, she's waiting for us outside," I say and give the woman my best smile.

"Then go and get her. Small children aren't supposed to be alone in the library."

I hand Gloria her lunch box, pick up my Rudolph bag, and lead her back down the stairs and out the heavy doors.

"Mommy won't find us," Gloria whimpers.

"Don't be a crybaby. We'll walk back slow, and she'll be there."

She isn't, and now it's raining. We hide behind the big tree on the corner for a long time.

When we spot the station wagon turning the corner, we rush right up to it. She screeches to a stop and leaps out. "You girls crazy? I almost hit you. What's the matter?"

Sobbing Gloria leaps into Mommy's arms.

"I looked after her. There was a man in the park, and the library lady wouldn't let us stay, and it's cold."

She opens the car door and sets Gloria down next to Pal, who licks her face. I climb in the front.

"Now, tell me what happened."

"Gloria wet her pants, and I was supposed to take her home and ..."

"Those fuckin' bastards, those fuckin' bastards!" And she bangs her fist again and again against the steering wheel.

"Mommy, don't."

She hugs me and starts up the car. We drive all the way to Hank's diner.

She roots through our boxes, and we change into dry clothes. We go in and have cocoa. She says she's sorry she doesn't have enough for French fries. She's not drinking anything.

Hank comes over to our table, sets a coffee down in front of Mommy, and puts his arm around her. He gives her a cigarette and lights it for her. She tells him all about the school and the stupid library lady. She calls her a dumb bitch. Then we all have hamburgs and fries. When we leave, Hank gives her his pack of cigarettes and a bag of donuts for us.

"They're day-olds," he says. "But still good."

At Holly's place Mommy gives Gloria a bath and puts her in her kitten nightie.

"Mommy, my throat hurts," Gloria says.

"Oh, honey, please don't get sick." Mommy looks like she's going to cry. "Do you want cocoa?"

"I'm tired."

She fixes Gloria in her quilts on the floor. Pal stretches out right next to her.

Mommy smokes, and I have more cocoa. We listen to the Jack Benny show until Holly gets home, and then I have to go to bed.

I can't get to sleep because Mommy and Holly are arguing in the kitchen.

"He says it's too many people, and there's a no-pet rule," Holly says.

"What can I do?" Mommy says.

Then they're whispering, and I think Mommy's crying. I'm never going to fall asleep.

But I must've, 'cause it's morning, and Mommy's packing up our stuff. Her face is all puffy. She's been crying. Holly's nowhere in sight.

"I hate Holly," I tell her.

"It's not her fault. Her landlord's kicking us out."

"I hate him."

"Hate all landlords, baby."

We drive around for a while, and then we go to a new park. Mommy sits on a bench and smokes. "I need time to think," she says.

"Why don't you call Mr. Stevens? He bought us sundaes when we were too full to eat them."

"Oh, honey, believe me, men like him don't want to hear from you when you need money."

"I didn't like him anyway."

"Take Gloria on the swings, would you?"

"Sure, c'mon Gloria."

Mommy makes a phone call from the booth on the corner. There weren't phone booths in Cadillac. I wish we were back home in Cadillac. I could play with the Belangers, and their big sister would give us bread and brown sugar.

Mommy comes back and says she's got a cleaning job for the day. We get back in the car and drive to a big fancy house with a tree house in the back. "Can we play in the yard?"

We can't. She parks a block away. "Stay in the car, play with your dolls, and if you have to pee, use the potty." She puts the potty in the dip down place behind our mattress.

"Potties are for babies," I tell her.

"Don't fuss. And here's the bag of donuts, and there's milk in the thermos."

"Don't go, Mommy," Gloria wails.

"You'll be fine. Sharon will look after you, and you have Pal."

"Why don't we go to school?" I ask her.

"Too risky. Keep the doors locked. I'll be back at lunchtime."

I'm never going to get my Thomas Jefferson card. Gloria won't even play stories with our dolls. She's under the blanket with her thumb in her mouth and her arm around Pal.

"You're a baby," I tell her.

She closes her eyes. I read for a while in my fairy-tale book. I've read all the stories before. We never got to finish the squirrel book. There's nothing to do. Just wait and wait and wait.

Ages later, Mommy comes back and moves the car next to a park.

"You can play on the swings, and if you get cold, come back to the car." She puts the key on a string and hangs it around my neck. "Keep the car locked."

Then she has me take the key off my neck and show her I know how to lock and unlock the door.

"Keep Pal with you and don't talk to anybody."

I do my stunts on the monkey bars. I'm wearing my playsuit with the ruffles over the shoulders—so much better for climbing than a dress. I try to teach Gloria to swing across, but she's scared and won't even try. I push her on the swings for a while, and that's when I see the big sandbox. We get our dolls, and I carefully lock the car door. We play our dolls are at the beach.

There are big houses all around this park and no old men on the benches. This isn't too bad a place. Gloria gets bored and throws sticks for Pal.

Then she has to pee, and I take her back to the car. I dump the pee under the car so it won't stink things up. We eat another donut and drink some milk, and I read her stories for a while.

Mommy comes back and hugs and kisses us. "Three bloody dollars," she says and starts up the car.

We go to a gas station, and she pays the man a dollar. "I won't get far running on empty," she tells him. We use the bathroom—toilet paper and cigarette butts all over the floor, and boy, does this place stink.

We stop at a store and buy bread, peanut butter, chocolate milk, and cigarettes. Mommy parks on a side street, next to a different playground.

We eat supper and then go play on the swings. Mommy sits on the bench and smokes. It's getting dark.

"I'm tired," Gloria tells Mommy. "I wanna go home."

"It's okay, honey. We're camping tonight."

Camping means we're going to sleep in the back of the station wagon. We can't find the flashlight. Gloria's crying. I feel like crying, but won't. Mommy has enough to worry about without us both acting like babies.

"Never mind," Mommy says. "We'll all cuddle up under the quilts. I'll tell you stories."

Gloria's scared of the dark. Silly. The streetlight shines a little bit into the car. Mommy tells the story about us and our friends the elephants. We're sleeping in the circus tent.

Pal curls up at our feet. He watches her talk, thumps his tail. When the bad men come to steal the elephants Pal barks and wakes us up. I bet Pal likes being in the story.

I guess we all fall asleep because the next thing I know is it's very dark in the car. I hear a man's voice. Mommy puts her hand over my mouth.

"Shh," she says. She's holding the paring knife.

Someone rattles the door.

Gloria wakes up, but before she can cry, Mommy holds her tight and whispers, "Shh."

Pal goes wild, growling and barking.

"Wha' the fuck?" the man mumbles.

We wait and wait.

Mommy puts down the paring knife and hugs all of us, even Pal. Then she climbs in the front seat, starts up the car. We drive around for a while and then park again.

"Go back to sleep, girls. It'll be okay now."

I stay awake a long time after Gloria falls asleep. What are we going to do? We don't have anywhere to live. That boy at the playground said: "She lived in a car." Now we really do live in a car. My heart goes thump, thump, thump.

Mommy sits in the front seat, blowing her smoke out the window.

I must've gone to sleep because when I wake up, it's morning. Mommy's still sitting in the front seat, having a cigarette. I climb up front with her.

"I've had a brain wave," she says. "We're going to Crystal Beach. Remember all the fun we had there?"

"Where'll we live?"

"The park's opening soon. There'll be lots of jobs, and we'll rent a tourist cabin."

"Can I go to school?"

"We'll see. First thing is to get across the border."

CRYSTAL BEACH DOESN'T look anything like before. I remember the streets of cottages, but there aren't any people and the cottage windows are all boarded up.

"Where's everybody gone?"

"They haven't opened up their cottages yet. In a couple of weeks it'll be booming."

"Is Papa meeting us here?"

"No."

"You told the border man he was."

"He saw all our stuff and knew we weren't just coming for the day."

"So?"

"If he knew I was on my own with you kids, he might not have let us across."

"Why not?"

"Sharon, too many questions. Let's get something to eat."

She stops at Smith's Groceries. It's open, but there are boarded up restaurants on either side. She buys a big bag of Puffs cereal and a bottle of chocolate milk.

At the beach we change in the car. Nobody's around. It feels good to get off our too-tight pink dresses. She made us get all dressed up to cross the border. We have pots and spoons to dig with, and Mommy says she'll be back in an hour. Gloria, for once, isn't bawling. She's throwing sticks for Pal.

I'm digging a moat for my castle. It's warm enough to go swimming, but we're not to go in the water. I take off my socks and stick my toes in. Brrr! But if I had my bathing suit, I'd run right in.

Funny thing is, before she left, Mommy changed into her black slacks and a red blouse that's too small, and her silver sandals with the really high heels. And she took out her hairpins. She's pretty. My hair is red and curly just like hers.

It's a long time before she comes back, but she's got a big grin on her face. She hugs us both.

"Hey, kids, I've got a job painting the roller coaster."

"You get to ride on it?"

"Not ride, climb up with a paint pail. Phil Whitmore, he's the boss, said it was no job for a lady. You should've seen their faces when I climbed right to the top and laughed at them. I took off my shoes and tossed them down to Phil. I know him from before. He has a reputation."

"What's reputation?"

"He likes the ladies, honey, but your mommy can handle him."

She changes into her old slacks, t-shirt, and sneakers, and ties her hair into a high ponytail with a yellow scarf. "I start work right away so I won't be back till suppertime. I'm counting on you to look after Gloria."

She leaves the car by the beach. Puts the key string around my neck. I'm to take Gloria to the car when she's tired and read her stories. I'm going to ask Mommy to get us a new book. We can eat all the Puffs we want and finish off the chocolate milk.

We play for a long time before going back to the car. We eat and I read stories. Pal falls asleep first, then Gloria. Mommy's gone a long, long time. I make sure all the car doors are locked. I'm the guard. Mommy said, if anybody comes around, Pal will bark and chase them away. "Whatever you do, don't unlock the car."

I know Pal will wake up if anybody comes so I lie down beside him.

I never take naps, but today I do and don't wake up until I hear voices. I peek out the window. Mommy's here talking to a man. He's tall and has wavy brown hair. He and Mommy look like movie stars. He's got his hand on her shoulder.

I roll down the window. "Hi, Mommy."

"Here's my big girl. Sharon, this is Mr. Whitmore." She steps away from him.

"Hi," I say.

"Whadda you know? A miniature version of your pretty Momma."

I like him saying that.

"Seeya tomorrow, Phil. I'd better be getting my girls some supper." She unlocks her door, and we drive away. She tosses a five-dollar bill in my lap. "That'll buy us a nice dinner."

We drive out of Crystal Beach to Ridgeway. It's the little town nearby. We drive down Main Street. Nothing like Main Street in Buffalo. No high buildings, no bus terminal, and no legless man selling pencils. "Where are all the people?"

"In their houses. Small towns close up tight at six o'clock."

Big maple trees line the street. She's been teaching me the different tree names. In the North it was spruce, pine, and birch. In the South it's maples, oaks, and elms.

The restaurant is more like Hank's Diner than Lobby's Old Spain, but there's hardly any people. Just two old ladies in dark dresses and little hats — they make me think of Grandma. A man in a brown suit is at another table. We get the big table in the corner. We order fish and chips. I want cocoa, but Mommy says it better be white milk, because we already drank a whole quart of chocolate. Gloria doesn't eat her fish and falls asleep with her head on Mommy's lap. Me and Mommy finish off her plate too, though we save one piece of fish for Pal. He's only had Puffs today. Also a dead fish he found on the beach. He threw that up. Tomorrow we're buying dog food and biscuits.

Back in the car she tells me her plan. Tonight we'll find a quiet place and sleep in the car. Tomorrow, when she gets to know Mr. Whitmore a little better, she'll get an advance on her wages, and we'll rent a tourist cabin.

"Is Mr. Whitmore a good roller-coaster painter?"

She laughs. "You wouldn't catch Phil Whitmore with a paint brush in his hand — too much like work. He's the park manager. The big boss."

We go a long way to a place Mommy says is called Lowbanks. We drive down a dirt road through ploughed fields to a big empty beach. "How did you know it was here?"

"I came here with a friend eons ago." She smiles.

"What's eons?"

"A long time ago. Another lifetime."

"Mommy, we each have one life."

"I know, honey, but believe me, sixteen was a different lifetime."

We fix our bed up in the back of the station wagon. Once Gloria's asleep, we take Pal for a run. Me and Mommy are both barefoot. In the dark, the wet sand and seaweed smell mixes with the sound the waves make hitting the beach. So dark, and the stars so bright, it's hard to tell where sand and water end and sky begins. We run and run, and I remember the farm, running with my cousins in the clearing in the bush. I smell spruce trees.

We're walking back to the car now. "Mommy, when we were running, did you smell spruce trees?"

"Spruce trees? No trees here, just beach and fields."

Even curled up against Mommy's warm back, it takes me a long time to get to sleep. I think about Uncle Yves' farm, corduroy roads and Papa singing *Sur le pont*. The car window's open a bit. I smell wet seaweed and dead fish.

***

The next morning we have a big problem. Mommy has to be at work for eight o'clock, and Smith's Groceries doesn't open till nine. We drive to Ridgeway. The two towns are really close together. The restaurant's closed and so are the stores. There's a store I want to go in—Dell's Five to a Dollar. There are books, a Mickey Mouse sand pail, and all sorts of good stuff in the window.

We drive back to Crystal Beach. Smith's Groceries and the beach where we played yesterday are both on Erie Road, but a long way apart. She parks the car halfway between and gives me the $1.45 left over from supper. She puts her watch on the dashboard.

"Can you tell when it's nine o'clock?"

"Sure, I learned to tell time eons ago."

She laughs at my little joke. "Okay, at nine, go to Smith's, buy a loaf of bread, peanut butter, and milk. You can buy treats with the change. Come back and eat in the car."

"What about dog biscuits?"

"If you have enough, get some, or Pal can have some bread."

"Then can we go to the beach?"

"Well, keep the key around your neck. It might be too far for Gloria to walk."

"Don't go, Mommy," Gloria wails. "I'm hungry."

"Your sister will look after you. Read her stories, will you, Sharon?"

"I need a new book."

"We'll get one as soon as we can."

She leaves, and Gloria keeps whining she's hungry. I smack her and tell her to shut up. She bawls so loud I'm scared somebody'll hear us. I have to promise her both a red licorice and a Mars Bar to make her be quiet.

We wait and wait, and nine o'clock just won't come. I decide we'll wait at the store.

It's a long walk.

"I'm cold," Gloria whines.

We sit on the stone steps with our arms around Pal to keep warm.

A lady opens the door. "You little girls must be freezing out here. C'mon in."

"We're okay. Our mother sent us for some groceries. She'll have the pancakes ready when we get back."

She helps find the things, and there's enough for dog biscuits, and change for licorice and chocolate bars for us both. "We'd like Mars Bars."

"Sorry, we don't have those. They're American. Neilson's Malted Milk is pretty much the same. Are you girls from Buffalo?"

"We live here now."

There's still six cents, but I hurry us out. This lady asks too many questions.

We've just started back with our bags when Gloria says: "I'm going to have three giant pancakes with syrup."

I get the car unlocked and make Gloria a big peanut butter sandwich. Thought we'd have to eat the peanut butter with our fingers, but I found a knife.

She eats one mouthful and says: "I want pancakes."

"Stupid, there aren't any pancakes."

She bawls and crawls under her blanket.

Pal eats her sandwich, but the peanut butter sticks in his throat,

and he brings up—a big stinky pile right on our mattress. I use Gloria's yesterday underpants to wrap it up and throw the whole mess under the car. They're her pink Thursday panties. Too bad for her. She just lies there under her blanket, with her thumb in her mouth.

I finish my sandwich, stash the milk on the floor of the front seat, put our candy in my Rudolph bag, and tell Gloria: "C'mon, time to go to the beach."

She closes her eyes and pulls her blanket right over her head. When I poke her, she starts crying. I lie down beside her and say: "Once there were four little squirrels: Chatterbox, Chubby-Chunk, Timothy and Squee."

Gloria sits up. "I want Mommy to make pancakes."

"She'll make them for supper."

"We don't have a stove."

"We're going to rent a cabin when she gets back. It'll have a big stove like Grandma's, and we'll have lots of pancakes."

"Okay," she says and lies back down.

"Now, let's go to the beach."

"No, I'm waiting here for Mommy."

I throw myself down on the mattress. I hate my sister.

***

This is our third night at Lowbanks. I hate having to use the potty, but most of the time I like camping. We gather lots of sticks and drift-wood for the campfire. Pal helps. He has a big branch in his mouth and is trying to haul it down the beach. Looks like he's trying to move a tree. Me and Gloria help him. Pal's a good wood gatherer. The only trouble is, once we get the wood piled up, he wants to haul it away again.

We give him a hot dog, and Mommy lights the fire. It's our first time to roast marshmallows. Mommy and her friend had marshmal-lows when they camped here. My marshmallow gets on fire, and we have to blow it out. I like the taste, but you have to be careful not to burn your mouth. Of course, Gloria burns hers, and won't stop crying until Mommy lets her have milk in the baby bottle. My sister's really stupid.

The next morning we wake up cold, even with Grandma's three quilts over us. It's raining so hard I can't see out the car windows. I have to poop and don't want to use the potty and stink things up. Mommy says to go and she'll dump it out real quick.

"I don't want to use the potty."

"Well, hold it then till we get to a restaurant."

"Can't."

"Then use the potty."

I wrap up in my quilt and feel rotten in my guts.

"Sharon, I don't have to go to work this morning. I have a plan."

We drive down Erie Road to the park. Mommy runs through the pouring rain to the phone booth. I really need to go to the bathroom.

"I wanna go with Mommy," Gloria whines.

"Shut up." I smack her and she howls.

Mommy's back and opening the door. "Gloria, hush. Sharon, we're going to my friend's place. Norma's husband's part of the painting crew. You'll have fun. They have a kid."

"How old?"

"A boy around your age."

The front steps are broken and the porch is covered with junk, but who cares, they have a bathroom, and I'm the first one in.

Teddy's eight. I'm almost eight. His mother cuts open grocery bags for paper to draw on, and we share the crayons. He draws battles. At first I draw movie stars, but I change them into soldiers and draw battles, too. Then we go in the bedroom and play with his army truck and tin soldiers. We build forts for them with his blocks. "Ask if you can come to the beach with us. The sand's great for building forts."

"I'll go ask Mom," he says.

In the kitchen our mothers are at the table giggling and smoking. Mommy has changed her clothes—she's wearing her too-small red blouse and a tight black skirt. Her hair is wet. She must've just had a bath. I haven't had a bath in days. We just wash in the lake when it's not too cold. Her pretty hair hangs almost to her waist.

"Mom, can we go to the beach?" Teddy asks.

"Not now," she says. "It's raining."

"Sharon," Mommy says, "you and Gloria are going to stay here while I go see Mr. Whitmore."

"You stay, too," Gloria wails.

"Your sister will look after you. Sharon, include her in whatever you're playing."

"Okay." As if she could play Battles. "When are you coming back?"

"Soon. You be good and do what Norma says."

She puts on her raincoat and spike-heeled silver sandals and leaves.

"Where do you live?" Teddy asks.

"Buffalo." But we don't. We don't live anywhere, but I won't tell him that. "Let's play Battles."

We line up all his soldiers and run them down with the cars. Gloria sits on the couch with her doll. I don't think she wants to play. Anyway, she wouldn't know how to play Battles.

Teddy's Mom makes big yummy pancakes with syrup. He calls her Mom, not Mommy. She's not pretty like mine. She's fat and has short plain brown hair. Nice, though.

Gloria's stupid. She doesn't eat anything, in spite of all the fuss she made before over not having pancakes.

***

Mommy comes back and barely gets her raincoat off before Gloria's bawling and clinging to her. She sits down with Gloria on her lap. I can't see Mommy's face. It's buried in Gloria's hair.

"How'd it go," asks Teddy's mom.

"I need a smoke." Her voice sounds funny, and she rocks back and forth, back and forth with Gloria. "It's okay, baby. It's okay." She still doesn't look up.

I'm scared, and if I wasn't nearly eight, I'd climb on her lap, too.

Teddy's mom lights two cigarettes and hands one to Mommy. "Well?"

"Slimy bastard," she mumbles.

I still can't see her face.

"But I'm going to ... manage the popcorn stand—I've got enough to rent a place." She holds the cigarette, but keeps her face to the wall.

"Good, but he's still an ass," Teddy's mom says.

Mommy mashes her cigarette into the ashtray. "I need a shower." She pushes Gloria toward me. "Play with her, Sharon."

I put my arm around Gloria. "Stop crying, and I'll teach you to play Battles."

* * *

We're back in the station wagon and going to find our cabin. Mommy's real cross and doesn't even answer when I ask if there'll be a playground.

The first place we stop is Top of the Hill.

"You girls stay in the car with Pal, while I have a look."

"Can't we look, too? I want to pick our cabin."

"No, stay with your sister!"

Why's she mad at me? I didn't do anything. She should be happy. We're going to sleep in a cabin tonight. I'm going to have a bath and wash my hair. The cabins are pretty, white with green roofs, and they have little porches.

She's going into number three with the lady. Bet that one's going to be ours.

It's not. She gets back in the car and we drive off.

"Didn't you like the cabins?"

"Too expensive," she snaps.

We drive around for a while and stop at a place called Maple Grove. I know better than to ask to go to the office with her. She's still cross. Oh, I hope, hope, hope, this is the place. There are a lot of cabins all painted blue with white trim. The big trees look good for climbing.

First, Mommy and the lady go in a blue cabin, then into a green one off by itself next to a big field. The field would be great for playing. Pal would like it, too.

She's coming back. She still looks mad. She gets in and starts up the car. "I'm so sick of begging. They don't want kids. They don't want dogs. Who in the hell do they want?"

I guess we're not staying here either, but then she drives over to the green one. Up close I see it's not that nice — the paint's peeling, and no porch like the others. "Is it ours?"

"All ours. Let's go and explore." She's not cross. Everything's all right again.

Inside there's a bed, a cot, and a dresser. I don't like the bed—an iron pipe one like we had in Cadillac. "Where's the bathroom?"

"We share with the other campers. Let's go see everything."

The bathrooms have three showers and three toilets. No bathtub. One building for women and one for men. There's a big room with two stoves and tables and chairs, two couches, and a shelf with books and magazines and a Please Return sign. "Can we read the books?"

"Sure can."

Most are grownup books, but I find one, *Bedtime Stories,* that looks good.

***

Everything's okay now. We went shopping and unpacked all our stuff from the station wagon into the cabin. Mommy showed us how to take showers. It's like playing in warm rain. I washed my own hair. Got soap in my eyes, but didn't cry. Just washed it out. Gloria got scared, and Mommy had to wash her in the sink.

We're the only campers. Mommy says there'll be lots once the park opens. She makes hot dogs, and we have applesauce and jelly-roll cake for dessert. I show Gloria how to unroll hers and lick off the jam. We get jam on our noses.

"You're Rudolph." Gloria giggles.

"We're both Rudolphs." And I laugh too.

Still raining so we wear our raincoats everywhere. In the cabin there are hooks for our coats. Mommy rubs Pal dry with a towel.

All three of us put on our flannelette pyjamas and get in the big bed. The cabin only came with one thin blanket, but that doesn't matter. We have lots of quilts, ones Grandma made. Pal has to lie on the end of the bed. He doesn't mind. Mommy says he'll keep everybody's feet warm. She tells us circus adventures. We're friends with all the animals. She tells the one where the lion rescues us kids from the evil sword-swallower.

Gloria says: "Tell the one where we find the kittens."

And Mommy does.

When I wake up I can hear birds chirping, and it's just getting light. Mommy's sitting on the side of the cot, smoking. She has that gone-away look I don't like. I sit down beside her, and she puts her arm around me and nuzzles my hair like Pal does. This makes me giggle.

"It's going to be better now. While I'm working you can play in the picnic grove. Do you remember last summer how you loved the big slide?"

"We can come to the park with you?"

"That's right."

"Yippee!"

"Shh, don't wake your sister. On my breaks I can come see you. You'll still be looking after Gloria all day, though."

"That's okay."

"Once the park opens and I have the popcorn stand, you'll be able to spend some time there with me. A whole summer in an amusement park, a real adventure, eh?"

E HAVE A quick breakfast in our cabin—corn flakes and milk. Mommy has to be at work for eight. We load our dolls, books, and digging stuff into the car. Gloria and Pal get in the back, and I sit up front with Mommy. She drives around to the back of the park and through the gate to the staff parking lot, right next to the picnic grove. I see the roller coaster. It's bright yellow where it's painted. She says it's half done.

***

I push Gloria on the baby swings for a while. Mommy said it's important that we behave ourselves or Mr. Whitmore won't let us come to the park. We have to stay in the picnic grove or play in the car. I have the key around my neck. We can see the roller coaster, but it's too far away to see Mommy.

I go down the big slide ten times. The first time's a little scary. I feel like I'm gonna fly right off. From the top I can see the roller coaster and other rides, and even a bit of the lake. Be nice if there were some kids to play with. Scaredy-cat Gloria never wants to do anything.

She's throwing sticks for Pal. She'd rather play with him than me.

She falls and starts crying. I whoosh down the slide and run over. Her knee's only a little bit scraped. "C'mon we'll go to the car, and I'll fix it for you."

"I want Mommy."

"She's working."

"On the roller coaster. Gonna go see her." She runs away, Pal right behind her.

I catch up, tackle her, and bring her down. She's really bawling now. "Listen to me, Gloria. If you bother Mommy, Mr. Whitmore will smack you."

"Mommy ... won't ... let ... him."

"Just like school. He's the boss and can strap kids, like he's the principal."

She clings to me and wailing so, she's getting snot and tears all over my blouse. "C'mon, we'll go to the car." I help her up, and she holds my hand all the way there. I pat her back like Mommy would.

* * *

When Mommy comes back, we're building forts in the big sand pile. We're using sticks to be our soldiers. Gloria keeps forgetting they're supposed to be soldiers, wants hers to be babies.

"I hurt my knee." Gloria shows Mommy my bandage.

"I cut the adhesive tape and gauze like you showed me."

"My good girls." She hugs both of us and kisses Gloria's knee.

She gives us each a donut. "One of the guys brought a big box for the crew," she says.

Then she goes away again. She'll be back at lunch.

* * *

We drive to the Erie Hotel for lunch. It's the only restaurant open. Mommy says there'll be oodles once the park opens. We have hamburgs and French fries. Gloria hardly eats anything so we save hers for Pal. We get to use their bathroom and then go back to the park.

We stay in the car and colour in our books we got last night. I read the new Raggedy Ann book to Gloria. She falls asleep. I'd like to go back to the playground in the picnic grove, but I mustn't leave her alone. If I wake her up, she'll start bawling.

I read the whole Raggedy Ann book. Then I draw pictures. It's a long time till Mommy comes back.

She says it'll be better next week when the park opens and we can stay with her at the popcorn stand.

* * *

I love the Green Cabin. I don't care it's not as fixed up as the others. I peeked in a blue cabin's window. It has a wooden bed and a white knobby bedspread, and a sink in the corner, but the people who stay in the blue cabins use the same bathrooms and kitchen as we do. Mom —I'm calling her mom now like Teddy does his—says the Green Cabin's better because we have privacy. The field is ours.

Sunday night we have a little party to celebrate the park opening tomorrow. Teddy and his family come to our place for a picnic supper. Teddy's mom is going work at the sucker stand. She tells me and Gloria she can get us broken suckers for free. Mommy, I mean Mom, made fried chicken and Teddy's mom brought potato salad. We have a big bag of chocolate cookies for dessert. The grownups have beer, and we have grape Kool-Aid. I made the Kool-Aid—one package of powder, a cup of sugar, and two quarts water.

Me and Teddy make a fort in the field. We find all sorts of good stuff, boards, a car tire that's our table now, some old pots and broken china we use for dishes.

* * *

We have a schedule now, as Mom says. Mornings we're at home or doing errands. The park doesn't open till noon, so we don't leave until eleven.

Me and Gloria go to work with Mom. The popcorn stand is like a little house. It has a storeroom at the back, a kitchen part where Mom works, that opens onto a counter where the tourists come to get their popcorn. When it's closed, the counter folds up so that nobody can get in and steal the popcorn. There's a machine that pops the corn. We sell buttered popcorn, caramel corn, and popcorn balls. They're really just caramel corn with extra caramel so it'll make balls. We also sell little brown paper bags of peanuts in the shell.

Me and Gloria have to stay in the storeroom. We work though —fill the bags with peanuts from a burlap sack, and pass stuff out to Mom like when she needs more bags for popcorn. We colour in our new books and play with our dolls. When we get bored we go to the playground or the bathing beach.

I know my way around and Gloria stays with me. We can use the park bathrooms and go to the beach next to the midway. People have to pay ten cents to get onto this beach, but Steve, he's the guy who takes the money, knows us, so we get in free. This beach is nicer than the other far away beach. There's no dead fish or seaweed. Mom says they clean it every night. We can go in swimming as long as we don't go past our waists. The water is shallow way, way out, so it's no problem. I can't get Gloria to go in even up to her waist. She stays at the very edge, sits there, playing with the wet sand.

I swim. I love swimming. I can swim under the water like a fish or with my head out like Pal. The only bad thing is now that the park's open, Pal can't come with us. No dogs allowed. Just like school. Gloria bawled the first day we had to leave him behind. He has to stay in the cabin till we get home at suppertime. Some mornings we take him for a swim at the far beach. Dogs are allowed there. Mom says Pal doesn't mind being left behind. Dogs are happy to sleep all after-noon.

Mom has an hour off for supper. A teenager, Diane, takes over the stand. We go home, have supper, and then me and Gloria stay home with Pal. The park doesn't close till midnight. We can play in the field as long as we don't call attention to ourselves. Mrs. Clarkson, who owns the tourist camp, mustn't see us. She can't find out we're on our own.

"When you're outside the cabin pretend you're Indian scouts," Mom says.

She takes us into the field and shows us how to duck down in the long grass and sneak around. Mrs. Clarkson and the tourists are the cowboys who are trying to catch us and put us in jail. They mustn't hear or see us.

Mom looks funny crouched down in the long grass. The Queen Anne's lace barely comes to her shoulders. She looks stern, like this isn't a game. I spot her red hair wherever she goes. She'd make a poor Indian scout.

"When it starts to get dark come in the cabin and lock the door. If anybody comes around hide under the bed. Don't go to the central toilets. Use the potty. At nine o'clock make sure you're in bed." She

leaves her Baby Ben alarm clock on the dresser. "You can read stories until you both fall asleep."

After Mom leaves, Gloria won't play in the field.

"I don't want to go to jail," she whines.

"Silly, she was just telling us to be quiet."

"I want Mommy."

"Don't cry. I'll read you a story, and you can choose."

"I want *Sleeping Beauty*."

I'm just getting to the part where thorn bushes grow over the castle, when Gloria starts crying. "What's the matter now?"

"The castle looks like a jail."

"How about I read the Bobbsey Twins book?"

"The seashore book?"

"Yeah, the seashore is a lot like Crystal Beach."

"Okay."

"Get in your nightie first and use the potty. Then it won't matter if you fall asleep."

I don't want to go to bed this early, but I sure don't want Gloria to start really bawling. Somebody might hear her and come over.

I get in my nightgown, too. Empty the potty out the door. Then I lock the door and we get in bed, and I read the Bobbsey Twins book until Gloria, hugging Pal, closes her eyes. I read two more pages just to be sure.

I tuck the covers around Gloria and Pal and get out of bed. I look out the back window. The evening sun makes the field glow yellow. I left my sand pail in my fort. I should get it. No, better not leave Gloria.

I look out the front window for a while. Mom's Baby Ben clock is at ten past eight. The park doesn't close till midnight. Billy stays with his grandma while his mother's at work. I wish we still had a grandma.

Everything's dusky out the front window. Mrs. Clarkson's white house looms like a big ghost rising out of the trees.

I want Mommy, right now.

I wait and wait, then crawl into bed and hug Pal and Gloria. My heart goes thump, thump, thump. Pal licks my face. I close my eyes.

***

Mom and us are on our way to the library. I told her I'm running out of books, and she found out there's a library in Ridgeway. The library's in an ordinary house. Good thing there's a sign or nobody would know this is a library. The library lady is old and wears glasses.

"I'm Miss Stewart. Is there a particular book you're looking for?" She smiles at us from behind her desk.

I remember the squirrel book we never got to finish. "Do you have *Three Smart Squirrels and Squee?*"

"Why, yes we do. That's one of our newest books. Just let me check if it's in." She files through a wooden box full of cards. "Yes, it's on the shelf. Come with me."

She leads us through the big room of grownup books into a smaller one. The shelves are full of children's books, and there's a kindergarten table and chairs for kids to sit, just like the Buffalo library, but a little room with one table.

"Here you are." Miss Stewart knew right where it was. "*Grandfather Frog* is another in the same series. Would you like to read it as well?"

"Yes, please." I like this library lady. She's nothing like the mean one in Buffalo.

Mom finds *Adventures of a Brownie* and tells us it was her favourite book when she was little. She's going to read it to us.

We fill out library cards. They're ten cents each, and Mom gives our address as Maple Grove, just like we really live here.

I want to stop at the playground by the school. We went there on Saturday, but we can't today because it's Monday and the kids are in school.

"Anyway, we have to get to work," Mom says.

I made a friend at the schoolyard, Carol Beam. She lives next door to the school in a big brick house.

***

We have a new tradition, as Mom says. Each morning, after breakfast, we sit at our picnic table and she reads us a chapter from *Adventures of a Brownie*. It's about these children in England that have a brownie

living in their cellar. A brownie is something like a fairy, but isn't pretty, doesn't have wings, and likes to play tricks on the grownups.

"Winter was a grand time with the six little children, especially when they had frost and snow."

She's reading *Adventures of a Brownie,* when Mr. Whitmore drives up in his shiny black Cadillac. A Cadillac is a big expensive car, but makes me think of back home. Mr. Whitmore's car looks nothing like Papa's.

Mom gets up and goes to meet him.

"Hi, babe." He hugs her. "Let me take you guys for breakfast. There's a new place opened up on the highway."

"Sorry Phil, we're busy." She sounds cross. I don't like being interrupted while I'm reading either.

"Okay, let's go sailing Sunday evening. I bet you've never been in a sail boat, eh Sharon?"

"Nope."

"Would you like to try sailing?"

"Sure."

"Phil, we're not going sailing with you. I work twelve-hour days. I need some private time with my girls."

"Okay, babe. Just trying to help out."

"C'mon, Phil, you're a busy man." Mom laughs, takes him by the arm and leads him back to his car. They're giggling over something. He puts his hand on her bum. She steps aside, heads back to us. "Bye Phil, see you later."

He drives away.

She picks up *Adventures of a Brownie* and puts it down. "You kids go play for a while. I've got to get ready for work."

"Don't you like Mr. Whitmore?"

"He's my boss, Sharon. I don't like bosses."

Mr. Whitmore's nice. Sometimes when we're opening up the popcorn stand, he visits and gives me and Gloria dimes and, once, quarters. Mom says he's in the way and should mind his own business. She doesn't tell him that. Acts real friendly when he's around.

***

June 12th, my birthday, is a Saturday so we'll celebrate it Sunday as the park closes early. We're inviting Teddy and his family. I want to invite Carol who lives next to the school, but Mom says we don't know her well enough.

"Can I go to Ridgeway school in September?"

"If we're still here, Sharon."

"Why wouldn't we be? I love our cabin."

"My job ends when the park closes and anyway, we can't live in a tourist cabin in the winter."

"You could work in a store in Ridgeway and we could rent a house."

"That sounds like a good plan. Now, what would you like for your birthday?"

"More drawing paper, new crayons, and an all metal sand shovel. The wood-handled ones always break. Is that too many things?"

"Not at all, honey." She gives me a big hug.

My birthday's lots of fun. Teddy brings me a set of little cars and we build roads for them in the dirt pile back of the cabin. Teddy has lots of cars and says you get them at Dells — 10 cents each. Mr. Whitmore gave me 50 cents. I'm going to buy five more. Mom was cross because I told him I was having a birthday.

Teddy's already eight. We're both going to be in grade three. He moved here from Hamilton. He'll go to the Ridgeway school. There's no school in Crystal Beach.

We have hot dogs and potato salad, and a fancy bakery cake, with a tiny princess doll in the centre and eight pink candles.

After supper Teddy's daddy lights sparklers, and all of us, even the grownups, run around in the field with them. Everybody's laughing. Even Gloria who runs with Pal. Teddy's mom loses her shoe. At first, we look for it, but his mom says: "Muriel, the kids'll find it in the morning."

We all go back to the picnic table. We have more lemonade and the grownups more beer. Everybody's really thirsty.

* * *

Whenever we want, because it's summer holidays, we stop at the school playground after we get our groceries or go to the library. Carol is some-

times already there, or if she sees me arrive, she runs over from her house. She's my best friend. We have a swell time on the swings. We make Gloria hold one end for skipping. She's always tripping us up. The good thing is, she never wants a turn.

Me and Carol will both be in grade three. Carol says Miss Blake will be our teacher. She says Miss Blake is the nicest teacher in the school. She has never strapped anybody. I tell Carol that Teddy will be in our class, too. She wants to meet him. I also tell her my mom's getting a job in a store, maybe Dells, and we're going to rent a house. Carol says she hopes it's near her place. I do, too.

* * *

Because it's raining, we're going to eat in the camp kitchen. Mom's frying hamburgs. The tourist camp isn't full — only full on weekends. We have the kitchen to ourselves. Gloria colours while I look through the newspaper. The Buffalo paper had coloured funnies, but this little one doesn't. "Gloria, listen to this, 'Free kittens to good homes'."

"Mommy, can we get a kitten?" Gloria asks.

"Once we're more settled, honey."

Now I see something really interesting. Houses for rent. "Mom, look what I found — Ridgeway, small house, $60 per month. Available September first. Can we get it?"

"It's just the first week of August. We'll have to wait and see what happens in September. This is a good place for now, isn't it?"

"I love our cabin, but you said when the cold weather comes ..."

"Let's wait and see. Supper's ready."

* * *

Hard to believe we used to live in grey old Cadillac. Every morning I wake up and feel so lucky. I love the Green Cabin and everything about Crystal Beach and Ridgeway. At the midway there's a pink castle funhouse with a magic carpet ride. The guy who runs it knows Mom and lets us in for free. I whoosh down the big slide on my ruby-red carpet. I'm going to live here forever and ever.

"WE'RE HAVING A special guest for supper tonight. I want you girls on your best behaviour."

"Who is it?"

"Mr. Dutton, my new friend."

Sunday so the park doesn't open until one, but we can't go to the playground. Mom makes us clean the cabin, and put all our stuff in bags and boxes. She tells Gloria to line up all our dolls on the bed.

While we're cleaning, Mom's in the camp kitchen, cooking. She returns with fried chicken, boiled potatoes, and eggs, and puts everything in our new ice chest at the foot of our bed. We can't have any. It's all for tonight. We eat peanut butter sandwiches.

We didn't go to the school playground yesterday morning either, because we had to do the wash. Ordinarily, we do a wash when we run out of clothes.

There's a washing machine in a little room off the kitchen. We had to get our wash in before breakfast so nobody else would be using it. There are lots of tourists now. We often have to wait our turn to use the stoves. I helped Mom put the clothes through the wringer, and even Gloria helped hang them up on the line at the back of our cabin.

"Can Teddy and his family come, too?"

"Not this time. Just Mr. Dutton. He wants to meet you girls. He's a nice man. You'll like him."

***

When we get back from the park, it closes at six on Sundays, Mommy makes me and Gloria take showers.

"We're not dirty. We were in the lake all afternoon."

"It's not the same. And Gloria, there's to be no bawling."

"Mom must really like Mr. Dutton," I tell Gloria on the way to the showers.

"Don't want him to come," she says. "I want Mommy to read the Brownie book."

"He must look like a movie star, 'cause Mr. Whitmore's pretty good looking, and Mom doesn't invite him for supper. I bet Mr. Dutton looks like Alan Ladd."

"Maybe he's rich and Mommy won't have to go to work anymore," Gloria says.

"And we'll live in a big house and go to Ridgeway School."

* * *

From the moment Mr. Dutton pulls up in front of our cabin in an old mud-splattered car, I know this isn't going to be good.

He opens his car door with a big: "Hi, everybody!"

He's the funniest-looking man I've ever seen. He has short legs, a fattish body, sorta like a bug. His ears stick out and he has a bald spot. His hair's spiky and mostly grey.

Mom runs right to him, gives him a big hug, and with a goofy smile says: "Jimmy, these are my girls. Don't be shy, girls." She hauls us from the doorway. Gloria's hiding behind me.

"This is Sharon, my big helper, and this is my little one, Gloria."

We cleaned the cabin, washed our hair, and put on clean clothes for him?

* * *

Mom never finishes *Adventures of a Brownie,* because nearly every morning Mr. Dutton shows up, has breakfast with us, or we all go for a drive. Gloria and me have to crowd into the back seat of his awful old car. Move newspapers, his lunch box, and other garbage aside, even to sit down.

Doesn't do any good to complain. Mom just smiles.

"A drive will be fun," she says. "An adventure."

Some adventure. Boring! She doesn't even talk to us. She sits up front with Jimmy, and giggles a lot.

"Cedar's goodest for roofs! New-fangled asphalt, my foot!"

"You'd know, Jimmy. You've had lots of experience." And she gives him a big smile.

He'd know? It's best, not goodest. I know that and I'm just going into grade three.

I tell Mom: "He doesn't talk right, and he looks like a bug. Why do you like him?"

"Sharon, listen to me. Jimmy's a good man. Yes, he doesn't have much education, just went to grade seven. His dad died in the flu epidemic of 1919, and Jimmy had to quit school and get a job to help his mother support the family."

"Why didn't his mother get a job?"

"She had to look after the younger ones."

***

About a week after Mr. Dutton starts hanging around the Green Cabin, we're opening up the popcorn stand when Mr. Whitmore visits. He brings us princess tiaras. "For the pretty princesses," he says.

I give him my best smile. Mom frowns. "Go in the storeroom, girls."

What's she mad about?

I hear them arguing. He calls her an ungrateful bitch. She tells him to go to hell, something about 12 hours a day and 7 days a week is no prize, and neither is he.

When I peek out, he's striding away. Looks really mad.

"C'mon out, girls." She's smiling. "Well, that's the end of him, thank God."

"I like him. He gives us stuff."

"Honey, he's not a nice man."

"He's a lot better looking than Mr. Dutton."

"Jimmy Dutton is a good man. Now, why don't you girls go play on the swings for a while?"

***

Whenever Mom starts talking about how great Mr. Dutton is, I leave the cabin and go to my fort in the field. Gloria likes him. She tells me he's a carpenter and has his own house and a cat and chickens, and when the old cat has kittens he'll give her one.

"If he has a house, why haven't we seen it?"

"I dunno," she says.

***

We're having breakfast, for once Mr. Dutton's not here. Mom says he's finishing up his job in Fort Erie. He was dry-walling an apartment building. I don't ask what dry-walling means because I don't care what he does.

"Jimmy and I are getting married, and after Labour Day we'll move into his house. I'll be home every night when you come from school—no more having to leave you all alone."

"Yippee!" Gloria shouts.

I jump up from the picnic table and run through the field to my fort. "Stupid! Stupid! Dumb Dutton, why does he have to ruin everything?"

I throw myself down on the grass and bawl. Then I sit up and start thinking. Not all bad. I can go to Ridgeway School with Teddy and Carol. Mom always says there's a bright side to everything. Still mad at her, though. How could she?

***

Turns out there isn't any bright side. Mr. Dutton's house isn't here, but in a town called Grenville, a hundred miles away.

"You were going to get a job in a store in Ridgeway and we were going to rent a house."

"I never said that, Sharon."

"You did!"

"I think, honey, you wanted that, and I said maybe it would work out."

"So let's do it."

"Sharon, I'm marrying Jimmy."

"But why?"

"He loves me and I'll be able to stay home and look after you kids."

"If you have to marry somebody, why don't you marry Mr. Whitmore? He's a lot better looking."

"Sharon, I don't like Phil Whitmore and what's more, he's already married."

"You're married to Papa."

Her face turns red. "We're not married anymore."

"Do you love Mr. Dutton?"

"When you're young, you fall madly and foolishly in love, like I did with your papa. With Jimmy it's a more sensible love."

"He's too old."

"There's an old saying, *Better to be an old man's darling than a young man's fool.*" She smiles. "Jimmy's only forty. That's the right age."

* * *

Mom's taking a day off for us to go to Buffalo to shop. Diane, the girl who fills in for Mom's supper hour, is going to work all day.

"Phil will be furious, but what can he do?" Mom says and laughs. "Labour Day's a week away."

We leave Pal in the cabin and head for Fort Erie and the Peace Bridge to Buffalo. Just me, Gloria, and Mom, and I sit up front with Mom. Gloria doesn't mind I get to sit up front. She has all her dolls lined up beside her.

"Mandy and Billy, don't fidget," she says. "We'll soon be there and you guys can all get new colouring books." Gloria talks to her dolls like they're real people. Boy, she's dumb.

Mom told the border man we're just over for the day to do a little shopping and visit a friend.

"Who are we visiting?"

"Holly. We're meeting her at Grants."

"Aren't you mad at her for kicking us out?"

"She didn't kick us out—it was her landlord. She lent me her last three dollars and I already owed her money."

***

Great to be back at Grants, our favourite store in all the world. We choose our new shoes, lots of school clothes, and some fabric for Mom to make curtains for the new house. Gloria gets a new doll. I have enough dolls, and pick out a furry monkey, Veronica Lake paper-dolls, and a new skipping rope.

We meet Holly at the soda fountain. She's on her break and can sit and eat with us. Our old favourites—hamburgs, French fries, and grape phosphates make me remember the first time Mom brought us here. That was a long time ago.

Mom and Holly giggle and whisper all through lunch. When we're leaving, Mom gives her ten dollars.

"Bet you thought you'd never see that money again." Mom laughs.

Holly gives us a bag of colouring books and crayons. "For your trip," she says.

Everybody hugs. I don't believe this—Mom and Holly are crying.

"Sometimes things really do work out," Mom says.

We're crossing the street to J&M's department store. "Why were you and Holly crying?"

"Because we're happy, but sad, too. We won't see each other for a long time."

The sad part makes sense, but I don't think marrying Dumb Dutton is something to be happy about.

At J&M's Mom tries on a beautiful yellow dress with a swirly skirt and white shoes with high heels and lots of straps. She's so pretty.

"My going away outfit," she says, giggling.

***

We're leaving today. I don't know when Mom and Dumb Dutton got married, but she's got a new gold ring on her finger. It looks just like her old one, but shinier.

All our things are packed in the station wagon, his stuff, too. Dumb Dutton sold his old car. We're supposed to call him Daddy. That'll be the day. Gloria calls him Daddy all the time. Gloria is supposed to be shy, but talks to him.

"Daddy, when'll the old cat have her kittens?"

"It's August. Betcha, she's had 'em already." He picks her up and hugs her. She doesn't seem to mind.

"Can I have a striped one?"

"Honey, you can have any one ya like."

***

There's so much stuff that Mom and Jimmy put some boxes, tied up in canvas, on the roof.

Gloria and me wedge ourselves and Pal into the back. There's barely room to sit down. Jimmy climbs into the driver's seat. Mom sits up front where I used to sit.

She's wearing her yellow dress and new white shoes. Her hair, fastened with a silver clip, hangs down her back. She looks like a movie star.

Jimmy wears his same old plaid shirt and brown trousers—like a hobo.

He turns on the engine. I look back at the Green Cabin and the field. Will some other kid find my fort? I made a sign and nailed it to the clothesline tree next to the field. *Death to all who enter.* That'll keep them away for while.

I watch everything disappear. Never again just me, Mom and Gloria.

E LEFT MAPLE Grove hours ago, and it's too hot, and Pal stinks. There's no room on the mattress to curl up and sleep. I'm wedged between Pal and stacked boxes. I can't even see out the window. Gloria's on Pal's other side, next to pillows and bedding, and she has a space to look out the window. She doesn't need to see outside. She's leaning on the blankets and looks half asleep.

Pal crowds me and farts.

"Trade places," I hiss at Gloria.

"No, I'm taking a nap." She sticks her thumb in her mouth.

I reach around Pal and give her a good smack on the head.

"Mommy, Sharon hit me," she wails.

"Sharon, act your age and leave your sister alone."

"I can't see out the window."

"Stop complaining. You've done nothing but whine all day. You didn't even help load the car." She looks mean.

"Youse kids, settle down back there. Us'll be home in a couple of hours." Jimmy takes Mom's hand.

Shut up, Dumb Dutton.

Mom smiles at him.

I press my face into the boxes.

"You're crying," Gloria says.

"Am not." I bite cardboard and close my eyes.

＊

"We're here girls. C'mon, jump out," Mom chirps. Her mean face is gone.

I sit up. Gloria crawls over the tailgate with Pal right behind her. I climb over the load and jump down. We're parked beside the house. Mom should've listened to me. I tried to tell her, if Mr. Dutton owned a house, which I doubted, it would be as funny looking as he is, and it sure is.

The front part is tall and narrow with a witch-hat roof. The whole side wall has one window, a little bit crooked, and up high, off to the side. Like somebody in kindergarten drew it. The house is yellow, but I can see it used to be blue.

Funniest of all is a bunch of sheds. Maybe they were afraid the wind would blow them down, so they attached themselves to the witch's house.

Three of them, one behind the other. The yellow paint never made it this far. The first shed, wider than the house, is faded blue with a flat roof. The next has a slant roof and, many years ago, was painted white. The last is tar-papered and leans to the left.

"Sharon, here you are! The door's around front. C'mon, don't you want to see your new room?" Mom asks in that chirpy voice I hate. Not really, I think, don't say. I follow her. Doesn't she see how out of place she looks in her pretty yellow dress and high heels?

There's a porch on the front. No paint at all here. A squawking chicken flaps down the steps. Those fresh eggs Mom talked about. Delivered right to the door. I avoid stepping on what else the hen left.

The front door opens and a man, even funnier looking than Jimmy, bursts out.

"Welcome home, bro!" He hugs Jimmy, almost lifting him off the ground.

"Joey, here's my better half! Aint she a beaut?"

Joey hugs Mom and advances towards me. I back down the stairs.

"Not like Sharon to be shy," Mom says giggling. "C'mon, Sharon, say hello to Uncle Joey."

He's not my uncle.

He picks up Gloria, who's got her kitten. She's holding it up to her face and looks completely unaware of where we've landed.

Joey is as tall as Jimmy is short. Tall and very skinny. Looks like he's still growing because his shirtsleeves barely reach his wrists, and his trousers show off knobby anklebones, and huge bare feet with thick yellow nails. But anybody would know they're brothers — the same sticking-out ears and spiky hair. Joey's hair is less grey.

The house smells funny. Old wood, maybe mixed with rotten food? Mine and Gloria's room is on the second floor. I stand in the doorway and stare at the iron pipe bed just like the one in Cadillac.

"We'll get you new beds," Mom says. "And I'll make curtains."

Perhaps she does see the torn window blind.

Gloria opens a little door off the hall.

"Youse don't want to go up there," Joey says. "Hotter'n hell."

I peer up the stairs. I can just make out the bare boards of the inside of the witch's hat. I close the door.

***

I scuff my new shoes through the stones. Cherry Street, like all the others, is gravel with muddy ruts. The streets have fruity names. We live on Plum. I hate Plum Street. I hate that Mom told the principal my name was Sharon Dutton. Jimmy's not my papa.

I hate my teacher—Miss Baer. She's a cross old bear. I could've had Miss Blake who never straps kids. The Bear strapped Clinton today right in front of the class. She could've done it in the cloakroom. Four whacks on each hand. Clinton cried. I wouldn't have. Now all the kids'll make fun of him. They already call him dummy because he should be in grade four. He was supposed to write out his spelling words a hundred times. He hadn't done it. Didn't even have his book with him. What did he expect? Still, she could've done it in the cloakroom.

Gloria's way up ahead. She doesn't wait for me anymore. Our house is only four blocks from Orchard Park Public School. She knows the way home to Mom and her darling kittens as she calls them. The striped kitten, Tiger, is her very own. She tries to get it to sleep on our bed. Pal will be waiting for her at the end of the driveway. Pal and the six dumb cats are all she cares about. She doesn't have any friends.

I remember the pink castle funhouse and wish with all my heart there really was a ruby-red magic carpet. I'd fly right out of here.

When I open the front door, Mom is painting the living room light green.

"What good will paint do? This place is a mess."

"Of course it is. Jimmy and Joey have been batching it for years."

"What's batching?"

"No woman to look after them. Their mother died five years ago. This was her house. Would you like to help paint?"

I ignore her. "Joey laughs stupid."

"Uncle Joey to you." She frowns. "He'll be getting his own place soon. Their mother left the house to Jimmy. Then it'll be just our little family."

I stare at her. Never be just our little family again, me, Mom, and Gloria. "I'm going to Shirley's house to play."

"Where's your sister?"

"On the porch with the kittens."

"She does love those kittens." Mom smiles. "Be back at six for supper. I made sugar cookies if you want some."

"No thanks." I turn away. She can't make me like this place with sugar cookies.

***

"Eight o'clock, girls. Your bedtime." Mom uses her chirpy voice.

"We never used to have to go to bed so early."

"Don't sass your ma," Jimmy says.

I run upstairs to the bathroom and hook the door. Jimmy's pride and joy. He and Joey put in the bathroom two years ago. Funny, 'cause nothing looks new. I asked Mom: "How come it looks so old?"

"We'll paint it, dear. The tub and sink Jimmy got from a house he was working on."

Gloria pounds the door. "Let me in. I have to go."

I open the door, walk past her without speaking. I'm in bed with the blanket over my head before she comes back.

When Mom comes in to kiss us goodnight, I pretend to be already asleep.

"C'mon, Sharon, I know you're not asleep."

I pull the blanket off my face. "Before, we went to bed real late."

"Oh, Sharon, I'm a proper mother now. Children are supposed to

get twelve hours sleep every night. You'll see. Gloria won't get sick so much."

"I didn't get sick much."

"No, you're my tough little girl."

"I can't go to sleep this early."

"Read Gloria stories until you both fall asleep. I'll leave the lamp on by your bed." She kisses us both and walks out of the room. Closes the door behind her.

"What are you going to read me?"

"Shut up or I'll smack you."

I switch off the lamp. She snuffles for a while, finally shuts up. Music's coming through a grate in the floor. Somebody must've turned the radio on. Me and Mom used to listen to *Jack Benny*. Sometimes *The Thin Man*—that's a scary show.

I get out of bed and peek through the grate. Mom's on the couch—Jimmy's arm around her shoulders. Can only see part of the couch so can't see the rest of him. Hear his low voice though. Mom's fluty laugh. Joey's in the chair by the woodstove.

Back in bed I put the pillow over my head. Still hear them. Joey gives his hyena laugh.

I listen to the branches scrape the window. Never again just me, Mom, and Gloria.

***

Saturday morning—a perfect day for exploring, sunny, not too hot. Wait till Shirley sees my packsack. I found it in the back shed. Musty, but washed up good. Mom said it was Uncle Joey's when he was in the army. I've got cheese, apples, cold-pancake-sandwiches and a jar of water.

Shirley drew me a map to her house—Plum to Cherry to Courtland. Follow Courtland to where it bends around the big tree, then count houses. Hers is the third. It's green.

The tree's a giant chestnut. The ground's covered. Some shells are splitting, and I pry out the shiny nuts. Boy, they stain your hands.

At school I'll trade them to Clinton for marbles. He wins everybody's marbles.

Shirley's house is worse than ours. No front steps—just a wooden box turned on its side. Good thing the porch is near the ground. Newspapers, jars, a car tire. I knock.

Shirley opens the door.

"Ready to go," I say.

"Can't." She's holding a baby wearing only a diaper, and another kid is holding onto her skirt.

"You said you could go."

"Ma's sick. I gotta mind the kids. C'mon in. You can help."

I go in for a little while, but the baby stinks, and the other one never stops whining for a cookie. Clothes are piled on the couch and boxes are stacked half way to the ceiling. Stuff's spilling out of the boxes. The kitchen stinks like a toilet. No wonder—there's a half-full kid's potty under the table, poop floating in it.

"Christ, can't youse make those damn kids shut up?" a snarly voice from the room off the kitchen.

"Pa's sick, too."

"I better go."

***

I gulp in the sunny air and head to the lake. At least Jimmy's not like Shirley's dad. Jimmy never yells or swears at us.

Shirley said Courtland ends at the lake. Poor Shirley—looking after Gloria was bad enough. I find the beach. It's great—big rocks. By the park the beach is all sand like Crystal Beach. Orchard Park is a lot like Crystal Beach. There's even a few rides—a merry-go-round and a roller coaster, not big though, like the one Mom painted. Clinton said in the summer there are bumper cars and a pony track.

I sit on a rock and eat my pancakes. Orchard Park is part of Grenville, but downtown Grenville is like Ridgeway. Nice houses, lots of flower gardens, a big two-storey school that has a paved playground with swings and teeter totters. Our school is just five rooms and the kindergarten room is an add-on. Shirley said they didn't have kinder-

garten when she started. The schoolyard is gravel, not as good as pavement for skipping.

Maybe we'll move downtown. I'd hate to be Shirley, her dad yelling and those stinky kids.

* * *

I'm on my way to feed the chickens and gather the eggs—that's my job. Mom made Jimmy mend the chicken-yard fence so they don't get on the porch anymore. She wants him to paint the house, too, but he hasn't had time.

"He doesn't fix much," I told her.

"Sharon, Jimmy works hard. He's tired at the end of the day. In the spring I'll paint the house. After all, I painted a roller coaster." She laughed. "Don't you worry—we'll get everything fixed up."

"I can help."

"Sure, the way you climb trees, a high ladder won't bother you."

"Mom, when you were a little girl, did you like climbing trees?"

"Yes, but it wasn't allowed."

"Your mom was mean."

"She was protecting me. I was clumsy. You could climb the big pines back of the Cadillac house when you were five. When I was ten, I fell out of a tree and broke my arm."

"You're not clumsy."

"If we went hiking, I was always the one who fell in the creek and came home covered in mud. No wonder Mother was angry."

"You don't get mad when we get muddy."

"True, but it meant she knew I was in the ravine."

"So?"

"In a big city like Buffalo, derelicts and bad men hang out in ravines. Grenville's much safer for kids."

Me and Mom will paint the house. The inside already looks so much better. She painted the living room, the kitchen, mine and Gloria's room. She went to an auction sale and bought beds for us. Wood, but dingy brown. We painted them sky blue. I helped.

I don't mind feeding the chickens. I wear my new rubber boots that are just for chores and play, so it doesn't much matter where I step. I leave them in the tarpapered shed. It already smells so a little more stink doesn't matter.

The rooster used to chase me, but I bopped him on the head with the water pail so now he leaves me alone. There's a little shed that's part of the henhouse. I go in there to get the feed out of the grain bin. Sometimes there's a mouse in the bin. I'm not scared of mice, but don't like putting my hand in and touching one. Old Cat hangs out in the little shed. She eats mice. Crunches them right down, though once I found a head she left behind.

I climb up in the nests to find the eggs. It's kinda fun. The hens never mess in their nests. I find six eggs this morning. Mom will scramble them for breakfast. She does them this really good way with cheese and onion.

***

"Sharon, open the door. I'm going to be sick." Mom pounds on the door.

I flush quick, pull up my pants and open the door. She brushes past me, kneels down and vomits.

"Mom, you better lie down. I'll wring out a wash cloth for your forehead."

"It's okay, Sharon." She gets to her feet, splashes water on her face and smiles. "I'm not really sick. You better be off to school now."

Sometimes, she doesn't make a lot of sense.

***

We're having roast beef and mashed potatoes that Mom only makes on special occasions.

"Your ma has a big somethin' to tell youse." Jimmy giggles.

"I'm going to have a baby." She's smiling.

"When?" Gloria says.

"In the spring."

"Can I help look after it?" Gloria asks.

I jump up from the table.

"Where are you going?" Mom asks.

I ignore her. Go upstairs and throw myself down on the bed. I don't want a brother or another sister. I pull the blanket up over my head. I'm gonna end up like Shirley.

Mom pulls the blanket down. She's sitting on the edge of my bed. "What's the matter, honey?"

"Aren't me and Gloria enough for you?"

"Sharon, parents love all their children. Didn't I still love you after Gloria arrived?"

"But why have another baby?"

"Jimmy and I love children. You'll see it's going to be all right."

Never again just me, Mom, and Gloria.

***

At first, it's all right. In fact, one good thing happens. Uncle Joey gets his own place. Uncle Joey's worse than Jimmy. At least Jimmy doesn't say much. Joey is loud, has a laugh like a hyena, and a bad smell. Also, he picks kids up, swings them around, and tosses them up in the air. He does this with Gloria. She giggles like crazy. He tried it once with me and I bit him. He didn't even get mad. Just laughed his idiot laugh and called me little red spitfire. I'm always getting teased about my red hair. I don't care 'cause I like my red hair, just like Mom's. Gloria's is plain brown. Uncle Joey calls me little red spitfire all the time now, but doesn't try to pick me up.

Jimmy said spitfire is the name of a warplane. It's also the name of a chocolate bar I like—brown sugar inside and chocolate outside.

Me and Mom haul all the junk from Joey's room to the back shed. He took his furniture with him, but left piles of newspapers, magazines, old rags, clothes, beer bottles. I look in one of the magazines —pictures of ladies in bathing suits. One lady's in a too-short nightgown.

"I'll take that." Mom puts his magazines in the wood box and piles wood on top. "Those aren't for children."

The next day all the magazines are gone. Mom paints the old

wallpaper in Uncle Joey's room pale blue. Jimmy brings home an iron crib, most of the paint chipped off. Mom paints it white. She puts its mattress in the garage and the next day Jimmy comes home with a brand new one.

***

Mom's belly gets bigger, but she's happy. All the while she gets supper and does the dishes, she sings that song about you are my sunshine. "I'm so lucky," she says. "I have you two girls, a good man, and a new baby coming."

A good man, huh! Skinflint Jimmy won't even give me money for a chocolate bar. Mom never has any money for treats now. He gives her just enough for groceries. Not really enough because sometimes when she's paying she has to put stuff back.

STICK MY NOSE out from under the quilt. Brrr, it's cold! I smell wood smoke so Mom and Jimmy must have the fires going. The grate in our floor lets warm air come up. Two weeks till Christmas! Last year just me, Mom, and Gloria, and we got lots of stuff. But that was before Mom married Jimmy. Here, I don't know what I'll get. I want skates—white ones. There's a pond off Courtland Road. Used to be a gravel pit, not very deep, so it's already frozen over. Me and Gloria went sliding there. All Gloria wants is another baby doll.

Somebody is snoring. I get out of bed, dragging my quilt with me, and peek through the grate. I can see one end of the couch. Somebody's feet are hanging over the edge. Phooey! Uncle Joey is back. The kids at school call him Crazy Joey. He calls hallo to everybody and tries to give kids candy. And now he's worn boots to bed.

I stomp down to the kitchen. I smell coffee perking. Mom and Jimmy are sitting at the kitchen table. "Why's Uncle Joey back?"

She gives me a real cross look. "That's not Joey. Uncle Raymond is visiting."

"Who's he?"

"Daddy's youngest brother. He's been out west."

"Is he a cowboy?"

Jimmy chuckles.

"No," says Mom. "He was a soldier in the war like Uncle Joey. Now, go wake Gloria up, and both of you get dressed for school. Uncle Raymond got in real late so you'll meet him tonight."

***

Uncle Raymond's not here when we get home from school. "Out for a walk," Mom says and sends me out to feed the chickens.

He comes in just as we're sitting down at the table. Jimmy introduces us and Uncle Raymond just nods. Doesn't even smile. Uncle Joey's come for supper, too. Now there are three Dumb Duttons at the table. Mom has roasted two chickens. Uncle Raymond is even skinnier than Joey. I can tell he's a Dutton. He has the ears.

"So's the prairies flat like they say?" Jimmy asks. Raymond just nods.

"Ya kept the pants." Joey gives his crazy laugh. Raymond stares at him.

"You're wearing army issue," Jimmy says.

"They owe me more'n a pair of pants."

That's the only thing he says during supper. To most questions he just nods or doesn't even do that. Mom tells us to hurry up and eat our supper. Then she tells us to go play in our room.

***

Most nights Raymond doesn't have supper with us, but every night he sleeps in our living room, and he never, ever, takes off his boots — leather lace-ups, all scuffed and dirty. I bet he wore them in the war. He always keeps his battered-up, cardboard suitcase next to the couch.

Sometimes I wake up in the night and hear him snoring. Tonight he's yelling. Oh, no, another crazy uncle. Words all jumbled together like Uncle Joey's nightmares.

***

Jimmy brings home a big Christmas tree and puts it up in the living room. There's a china angel in a white satin dress for the top of the tree and glass balls and stars. Only one string of lights works. Jimmy says the decorations were their mother's. I pick up a little angel, made of folded crepe paper with a puffy dress.

Jimmy takes her from me, and says: "Remember, Ray? This was Annie's."

Uncle Raymond glares at him and leaves the room. The front door slams. Raymond doesn't really look much like Uncle Joey because Joey always smiles and Raymond never does.

"Here," Jimmy says to me. "You hang 'er in a nice spot."

"Who's Annie?"

"Our sister."

"Where is she?"

"In heaven," he says and leans in to give me a hug, but I back away. I hang the angel up real quick. I don't like dead girls' stuff.

Uncle Joey holds up a little snowman made from knitting yarn. "Maw fixed 'im for Annie." He gives his big laugh, and hangs the snowman next to my angel.

***

Christmas morning I wake up when it's still dark. Snow pings against the window. I peer out—too dark to see anything. I smell wood smoke and peek through the grate. The Christmas lights are on. Can see Uncle Raymond's blanket, but can't see his boots. Hope he's gone out.

I shake Gloria awake. "It's Christmas!"

"Has Santa been here yet?" she whispers.

"Must've. C'mon, Mom's up."

I hold her hand and we go barefoot downstairs. Pal, who always sleeps with Gloria, follows us down.

"Merry Christmas, darlings," Mom says. She and Jimmy are standing together in the kitchen doorway. He has his arm around her. I don't see Raymond.

"Merry Christmas," I say and head for my bulging stocking. Last night we hung our long brown stockings over kitchen chairs Jimmy hauled in by the tree.

I pull a rolled-up colouring book out first—Sleeping Beauty. Gloria's holding up a Cinderella one. Next, crayons—love the smell of new crayons. Next, there's a metal paint box—eight colours. Gloria gets one, too.

I also get butterfly barrettes, very pretty, two pair of underwear, plain white, new brown stockings, and pink garters. Good, my old ones are falling apart.

Then comes the yummy stuff. A Jersey Milk chocolate bar and a brown paper bag with a Santa Claus sticker. I open it, and it's filled with hard candy. I find a cinnamon one. I mean to suck on it, but forget and crunch it. Next, I try a lemon one.

Mom and Jimmy sit on the couch and watch us empty our stockings.

In the very toe is the orange that always smells like Christmas.

I want to open the wrapped parcels under the tree, but Mom says we'll wait for Uncle Joey and Uncle Raymond. "C'mon to the kitchen. We're having pancakes and sausages."

The old oilcloth's gone from the table. The new one has red flowers.

"Where's the teapot cloth? I liked it." says Gloria.

"It was worn through," Mom says, "but you can make doll tablecloths from the good bits."

"The new one's snazzy," I tell Gloria. Snazzy is Joanne Newman's favourite word. Her father owns The Red and White grocery store. She has white figure skates and takes lessons. Her mother said Uncle Joey should be put away. I push the stupid cat off the table. I bet cats don't jump on the table at Joanne's house.

We're eating our pancakes when Uncle Joey comes in covered with snow. He shakes himself just like Pal does and we all get showered. He laughs and I laugh too because it's Christmas. He has some pancakes and then we all go back to the tree.

Jimmy says: "Better us don't wait for Raymond. He just might walk all day."

I get my skates—white figure skates! Can't wait to go skating. Gloria gets her baby doll. Mom and Jimmy also give us a *365 Bedtime Stories* and Monopoly to share. Uncle Joey gives us both pink fuzzy sweaters. Mine has a Spitfire bar tucked into it, and Gloria gets Crackerjack. I give Uncle Joey a hug because it's Christmas. We give Jimmy and Joey grey woolly socks. Mom bought a pair for Raymond, too, but he doesn't come back till dinnertime. He doesn't give anybody presents and doesn't open his. I want to go skating.

"Wait till tomorrow," Mom says. "The ice won't be cleared."

She teaches us to play Monopoly. I catch on quicker than Uncle Joey. Uncle Raymond's out walking again.

Mom's wearing the blue chenille housecoat Jimmy gave her, and

he's wearing the red plaid shirt she gave him. Mom sits my china lady and Gloria's china cat on the sideboard next to the little blue bottle of Evening in Paris perfume Jimmy gave her. We bought her gifts at Stedmans. Jimmy gave us each a dollar. He turns the cat over and reads out—*Made in Occupied Japan*. "Good thing the Yanks are keeping 'em in line," he says. Jimmy doesn't make much sense.

Old Cat didn't come to the house for her supper. Jimmy tells Gloria not to worry. She'll maybe be in the henhouse having her kittens.

"Funny place to have kittens," I tell him.

"Her likes the shed where us keeps the feed."

"Can we go look?" Gloria asks.

"Wait 'til morning," Mom says.

We play Monopoly way past our bedtime. Mom makes hot chocolate with marshmallows. We haven't had marshmallows since we came here.

Uncle Raymond still isn't back when we go to bed. Mom says I can go to the pond right after breakfast.

The wind and snow rattle-bang at our window, but I'm not cold. I have Grandma's big quilt pulled right up to my nose. I can see my skates hanging on the end of my bed. I liked it when we lived in the tourist cabin, but now I have skates just like Joanne Newman.

***

Mom's going to make scrambled eggs for breakfast and sends me out to feed the chickens first thing because she needs the eggs.

"Wait for me," Gloria says. "I wanna see if Old Cat's had her kittens."

"Hurry up and get your snow pants on."

I make her help carry the water bucket. We wade through the fresh snow. There's going to be lots to clear off the rink. When I unhook the chicken house door, there's somebody in there on the floor. I see his blue plaid shirt and army boots. There's a different bad smell, and blood, and the chickens are pecking him. Gloria's screaming.

We drop the bucket and run back to the house. Gloria screams and screams. Mom carries her up to our room and tells me to stay with her.

I don't remember much after that. I hold my skates, but my head hurts. I do remember Jimmy yelling and wailing louder than Gloria. I'm scared to look through the grate.

I don't go downstairs, though I can hear people talking, and Jimmy still wailing. I'm sure once I hear Uncle Joey's hyena laugh. He is crazy.

Dr. Stewart comes upstairs with Mom. Gloria's face down on her bed, sobbing. Pal's licking her ear. The doctor gives Gloria a needle, right in her behind.

I back away from him. "I feel fine," I tell him.

"She's a tough one," Mom says. Her eyes are red. She's been crying too. "Stay in your room. You can read your new book."

"You said I could go skating."

She gives me a funny look. "Not now."

I curl up on my bed with my skates. Guess I fell asleep, because Mom's here with peanut butter sandwiches and milk. "You must be hungry, didn't have any breakfast. Good—Gloria's still sleeping."

"We went to the chicken house ..."

"That's right, dear. Uncle Raymond is dead. Poor Jimmy. His baby brother."

She doesn't make sense. Uncle Raymond wasn't a baby. He was the man on the floor.

All day we have to stay in our room. People come and go downstairs. This is a very long day. I have supper in our room, too. Finally, Gloria wakes up and we play with the new doll she calls Lucy. I pretend I'm skating round and round.

"What happened to Old Cat?" Gloria asks.

"Nothing."

"Did she have her kittens?"

"I don't know."

There's a tap on our door. I open it and here's Uncle Joey with a big grin on his face. He hands me a bag and goes away. In the bag are two Spitfire chocolate bars, two boxes of Crackerjack, and two bottles of Coke. We eat the bars and the Crackerjack. My prize is a tin brooch, really great. Gloria gets a tiny celluloid doll. Not nearly as nice as my flower brooch, but she likes it. We can't get the bottles open. I try with my teeth, but we need an opener.

"I'm going down to get one," I tell Gloria.

"Don't. We're supposed to stay in our room."

"I don't care. I'm thirsty."

"Don't go."

"You hug Pal till I get back."

I open our door very carefully. Sneak downstairs and along the hall. I peek in the living room. The Christmas tree lights aren't on. Mom's sitting with her arm around Jimmy. Other people I don't know are silent or talk in low voices.

Uncle Joey's in the rocker. He winks at me.

I hurry to the kitchen. Get the opener out of the drawer and scurry back upstairs.

I open both Cokes and hand Gloria one. My, this tastes yummy even though it's warm. Mom doesn't buy us Coke. Uncle Joey's nice even if he is crazy.

"Where did you get that?"

Oh, oh, Mom's here. She looms over us.

"Uncle Joey," I say.

"He brought us Cracker Jack too," Gloria says.

"We wondered where he went. Out buying treats for you kids —that's Joey all right. Bet he marched through Italy giving his rations to the children."

***

I wake while it's still dark, but know Mom's downstairs because warm air's coming up.

I peek through the grate. There's a light on, but not the Christmas tree lights. I can see the end of the couch, but not Uncle Raymond feet, or even his blanket. I'm a little bit scared to go downstairs.

I give Gloria a shake, but she won't wake up. She's snuffling like she does when she has a cold. She better not be sick, 'cause I want her to go skating.

All tremble-y I go downstairs. Mom comes to meet me and does a really odd thing. She picks me up, like she doesn't know I'm eight, and carries me into the kitchen. She sits down in the rocker and cuddles me. She's warm and smells pretty.

"How are you feeling this morning?" she asks.

"Fine. Can I go skating?"

"Better wait till after the funeral."

"When's that?"

"Tomorrow."

"Can I go?"

She looks at me kinda funny. "No. You and Gloria'll stay here."

"We went to Grandma's funeral."

"And Gloria had nightmares for months."

"I don't have nightmares."

"I know. You're my tough little girl. How about some pancakes?"

"Yeah, I'm hungry."

Jimmy's not up yet, just me and Mom. At the table, we sit side by side to eat our pancakes. I wish we were back at Grandma's. Grandma has white hair and smells like lavender. Sometimes I forget she's dead. "Why did Uncle Raymond die?"

"He was very sad."

"Why?"

"Because of the war. He was shell-shocked."

"What's that mean?"

"Some of the men couldn't take the noise of the guns and the shells going off. It made them nervous and sick."

"Can I have more pancakes?" He wasn't sick. Sick is when you throw up.

"Certainly, hungry girl. Then we better wake Gloria. I'm counting on you to look after her for the next couple of days. Can you do that?"

"Sure. What if we went skating just for an hour?"

"Not today. You'll have to play quietly in your room. Daddy's very upset and there'll be a lot of people visiting."

***

Boring, boring, boring! I want to go skating. We've coloured most of the pictures in our new books by the time Mom brings newspapers up and spreads them on the floor. She cuts open brown grocery bags for us to paint on. We have jars of water and our new paints.

Hard to get the colours dark enough, and they run together. I paint me and Joanne skating, but it goes all smeary. Gloria cries 'cause she's trying to draw Mom, and her picture's a mess.

"We'll make paint soup," I tell her, and we mix up all the colours in our water jars. It's pretty before the water turns brown.

We paint the newspapers, but Gloria spills her water and it drips through the grate. Mom comes up. She doesn't get mad, just gathers the newspapers and mops the floor with a raggedy towel. "Read Gloria some stories." She hands me our *Three Hundred and Sixty-Five Bedtime Stories*. "This should keep you busy for a while."

People come and go all day. Me and Gloria watch through the grate. Most of the people are strangers, but I recognize our next-door neighbours, the Reubels. They have their son Billy with them. He's in grade eight. I've seen him at school.

Everybody talks in low voices so I can't hear what they're saying. Sometimes, I hear Jimmy crying again or Uncle Joey's crazy laugh. You're not supposed to laugh when your brother just died.

This is a very boring day until Mom comes up carrying a big box. Old Cat is following right behind her.

In the box are four brand new kittens, two black, one yellow, and one tiger and white like Old Cat.

Mom takes our shoes and stuff off the closet floor and puts the box in. Old Cat jumps right in and starts washing her kittens.

"You can pet Old Cat, but don't pick up the kittens—it'll hurt them."

Mom goes back downstairs. Me and Gloria sit by the box. The kittens aren't much bigger than mice, and they can't open their eyes. Gloria wants to hold one, but I don't let her. "You want it to die?"

She starts bawling. "Be quiet, you're scaring Old Cat," I tell her.

That shuts her up. We pet with our fingers very gently. Old Cat purrs and purrs.

In the night, Gloria wakes up screaming. Mom comes in and holds her for a long time. Then she puts Gloria in bed with me. I don't mind 'cause I'm a little bit scared, too.

***

Mrs. Reubel's staying with us while everybody's at the funeral. She brought us paper-doll books. They're paper-doll twins. The boy twins are brown-haired and the girl twins blond. I cut mine out and Mrs. Ruebel helps Gloria. These are really good paper dolls with two of everything—even twin dogs and twin cats.

We play at the kitchen table until Mom, Jimmy, and Uncle Joey come back from the funeral, and then we have to go upstairs.

Mom brings us good stuff to eat, all arranged on a special plate. Homemade donuts, really yummy, and little sandwiches with the crusts cut off. It all tastes good, but I'll be glad when this day is over. Mom's promised I can go skating tomorrow.

***

I have to wait till after breakfast to go skating. We have scrambled eggs. Mom went out to get the eggs. Supposed to be my job. Mom's not scared of anything. I bet the chickens are scared. I'm glad Old Cat's safe in our room with her kittens.

After breakfast me and Gloria get all bundled up and head to the pond. Gloria doesn't have skates, but she can slide on the ice.

Jimmy's still not up by the time we leave.

"Hurry up," I tell Gloria.

There are a lot of kids here already. I push my feet into my skates and lace 'em up good. The big boys have shovels and have cleared the snow off. There's Billy Reubel. I don't know the other boys.

I land on my behind a few times, but I'm getting the hang of it. By the time Joanne sees me skate, I'll be as good as her.

Billy Reubel comes over and talks to me, which is funny because grade eight boys don't talk to grade three girls.

"How are you girls doing?" he asks just like his mother would.

"Fine."

"Did you see the gun?"

"What gun?"

"The Nazi Luger, your uncle did it with."

"There wasn't any gun."

"You found the body, didn't ya?"

"So what?" I skate over to Gloria. "C'mon, Mom needs us." I go to take Gloria's hand, but slip on the ice. Jump back up, really mad, and skate all the way around the pond. So mad, I don't even think about falling. *Crazy Dumb Duttons.* Go round and round and round. *Crazy Dumb Duttons.*

Gloria catches up. "Let's go home." She grabs my arm and I sit down hard.

"Stupid!"

"Sharon, I'm cold," she whines.

Billy's watching. Doesn't he know it's bad manners to stare?

"Okay, okay."

I have trouble getting my skates off. Have to take my mitts off and now both my fingers and toes are freezing. I put on my cold shoes and overshoes, and we run to warm up.

Gloria lags behind, and I let her catch up. We walk side by side kicking hunks of icy snow. I keep my hunk going the longest.

"I saw the gun," Gloria says.

"There wasn't any gun."

"It was right where all the blood was, where his face ..."

"Shut up about it or I'll smack you."

Gloria's bawling and won't move.

I dig my Christmas candy out of my pocket, and give her a green one. I have a red one. I wipe her face with my hanky. She stops crying.

I see the white's all rubbed off the toes of my skates. They're all scuffed up. They weren't new. Just white shoe polish making them look good. What a dirty trick! Everything's a dirty trick.

When we get home, the tree's been taken down and all the decorations put away.

***

Crossing the schoolyard I hear kids whispering behind me. I know they're talking about me. Joanne Newman comes right up to me and says: "Your family's crazy."

"Are not."

"Your uncle killed himself."

"Did not."

"My dad went to the funeral."

"He died from shell-shock."

"He shot himself in the head," Bobby says.

"Blew his brains all over your hen house," Dougie Baker says.

"You're a bunch of liars." I run all the way to Plum Street. He wasn't my uncle anyway. Jimmy's not my papa.

***

Gloria's back having nightmares and her screaming wakes me up. I'm tired all the time, and if her keeping me awake isn't bad enough, on the way to school she wants to tell me her dreams.

"The chickens were pecking Uncle Raymond. I saw the blood and ran away, but my feet wouldn't move and ..."

"If you'd shut up about it, you'd stop having bad dreams. I don't have nightmares." That's not exactly true. Sometimes, I wake up really scared, but can't remember what I was dreaming.

***

The kids at school won't leave me alone. "I saw your other crazy uncle last night," Joanne says. "He tries to give kids candy. My mother said he should be put away."

Dougie Baker says: "Did you keep the gun? I'd give ya five dollars for it."

Clinton McClary says: "Shut the fuck up, Dougie, or I'll pound ya."

Clinton's the only one who doesn't say mean things. I like him even if he is the class dummy. Last night, he walked part way home with me and gave me a cat's eye marble. It's blue-y green. I added it to my collection.

*M*OM KEEPS GETTING bigger and bigger. She said the baby's due right after Easter.

"How do you know?"

"A baby takes nine months to grow big enough to be born. Kittens only take sixty days. Lucky mother cat."

Mom has to sit with her feet up. I make her cups of tea. I'm feeding the chickens again, too. Mom or Jimmy did it for a while or Mom went with me.

Gloria asks: "Aren't you scared to go in there?"

"Why should I be? There's nothing there but a bunch of squawky hens."

* * *

I'm to be in charge while Mom's in the hospital. There's a whole shelf of food for while she's away — tins of soup and beans, Spam, and even a tinned ham. I can make soup and sandwiches for lunch and supper. We can have boiled eggs and toast for breakfast, and Puffs, corn flakes, and shredded wheat. Gloria's to set the table and help wash dishes.

Thursday, when I come home from school, Mom's gone. Jimmy says he took her to the hospital and she's having the baby.

"Can we go see her?"

"No kids allowed," he says.

I make hotdogs and chicken noodle soup for supper. I wash dishes and Gloria dries. Jimmy leaves for the hospital.

"When's Mommy coming home?" Gloria asks me.

"She said she'll be away a week."

"Wanna go see her and the baby." She looks like she's about to bawl.

"Jimmy said no kids allowed. I'm going to do my homework." She follows me upstairs.

Mom's fixed a small table and chair next to my bed. I write out my spelling words for the end of the month test. I usually get perfect. At this school, we don't get picture cards of the presidents for perfect spelling tests.

When I look up, Gloria, already in her pyjamas, is sitting on her bed with Pal and Tiger. Since it got warm Jimmy put Old Cat and her new kittens out in the garage.

"Read me a story."

"Can't you read your own stories now?"

"Don't read good enough."

"Okay, just let me finish this."

When I come back from the bathroom, she and Pal are in my bed. She's got the big fairy-tale book. "Read me Cinderella, please Sharon."

"Okay, shove over."

I'm sick of *Cinderella* and read *Rumplestiltskin* and *The Twelve Dancing Princesses*. Pal lies across the foot of the bed. "Okay, now get in your own bed."

She lies down tight against the wall. "Please, I won't take up much space. Don't wanna sleep in my bed. I'm scared."

I let her stay 'cause I'm just a little bit scared, too.

* * *

The baby's a girl, Debra Jane, but we're calling her Debbie.

Gloria wants to hold her all the time. "She's like a doll. Look at her tiny hands and feet."

A scary doll and Mom shouldn't let Gloria hold her 'cause she might drop her. I don't like holding the baby. She looks like she could break very easily. I remember holding Gloria, and she was cuddly like a teddy bear. This one's skinny with thrashing around blue-red arms and legs. I think she got born too soon, but Mom says all new babies look like this.

My new sister cries all the time. I wake up at night and listen to her wail. I think that's what a wolf sounds like caught in a trap. I remember at my cousins' farm we heard the wolves. Why does my baby

sister cry like that? I want to wail along with her. Never again just me, Mom, and Gloria.

＊＊＊

Mom's so busy with the baby that I'm surprised when she says I can have a party. June 12th is my birthday, and I invite six girls and Clinton. I don't think Clinton will come, but he does. We have a treasure hunt like we did for my birthday in Grandma's apartment. Even more fun than the last time because Mom hides clues all over the yard, in the garage, in the back shed, even in the attic. Joanne fusses that her party dress is all dusty. Why did she wear it? We wrote on the invitations—wear your play clothes. Everybody else wore shorts. One clue's up in the maple tree. Clinton climbs up before I can. That's okay. You're supposed to let your friends go first at a party.

When we find the prize hidden in an old butter box in the garage, I'm a little surprised it's just chocolate bars. I remember the jewellery last time. Of course, Clinton wouldn't want jewellery.

I get lots of gifts. Colouring books, crayons, a paint set, and paper dolls. Joanne gives me blue socks and pink socks with matching barrettes and hair ribbons. Gloria thinks this is the best gift ever and keeps lining up the socks with their matching barrettes and ribbons. My favourite gift is the cap gun Clinton gives me. I don't think it's new. It must've been his.

Well, I guess my really favourite gift is my bike from Mom and Jimmy. I was disappointed that it's an old one, but it's freshly painted. Mom says we have to economize because we've had a lot of expenses with the baby, and the property taxes are due.

When I told her my shoes were too tight and I wanted the t-strap ones in the catalogue, Jimmy said: "Youse get new ones in September. Youse don't need no shoes in the summer."

When Mom's tucking me in, I say: "I hate being poor."

"We're not poor."

"I got lots of new shoes when we lived in Buffalo."

"I never was any good with money. Jimmy's careful with money."

"A penny saved is a penny earned!" And I laugh meanly. Mom hated Grandma's old sayings. "I don't even have shoes that fit."

"Sharon, it's not the same at all. My parents had money, but wouldn't buy me things I needed. Jimmy has to be saving. That's how he's kept this house."

"You told me his mother gave it to him."

"Yes, but there are expenses, like taxes, and he's saving for a new roof."

"I need shoes."

"Oh, honey, it'll be fine. All the children around here go barefoot in the summer." She kisses me goodnight.

I lie awake a long time. I wish we were back in Buffalo, delivering papers, having breakfast at Hank's Diner. We've never gone to a restaurant in Grenville.

After breakfast Mom cuts the toes out of my sneakers so they'll fit. "They're like sandals now," she says.

When we lived in Buffalo I had real sandals. Who cares if Jimmy and his brothers went barefoot all summer? They're Dumb Duttons.

Me and Gloria wear our holey sneakers to the beach. Mom cut the toes out of Gloria's too. Joanne's there in her new red sandals and a new red gingham bathing suit. Mom said all the kids go barefoot around here. What does she know? We bury our old sneakers in the sand.

Jimmy won't give Mom money for us to get new shoes, but when they sent me and Gloria up to bed tonight, Mom and Jimmy were sitting on the porch, drinking beer. Almost every Friday night Jimmy brings home three bottles of beer, one each for him and Joey and Mom.

Beer costs money. If he'd stop buying beer, I could have new shoes. I wouldn't mind going without the t-strap sandals, if I could just have new sneakers. They only cost two dollars.

* * *

Jimmy's scared to chop a chicken's head off. He says blood makes him faint. His brother, Joey, comes on Saturday to kill the chicken for Sunday dinner. The trouble is he kills two chickens and takes one

home with him. Not right then—comes back the next day when Mom has the chickens ready for the oven. Usually, he stays for dinner and eats half of our chicken, too. Maybe not half, but enough that me and Gloria only get the wings.

Joey asked Mom: "Where does a city girl like you learn to clean chickens?"

"When I lived in Quebec."

"Frog country, eh?" And gives his crazy laugh.

I do sorta remember Mom and Mrs. Belanger cleaning chickens. "Did Belangers have a farm?"

"No, her sister would send in a crate. Mr. Belanger would kill them. I'd go over and help her clean them, and she'd give us one for our dinner."

"Like we give Joey?"

Mom laughs. "Chopping a chicken's head off takes two seconds. Cleaning them is work."

"I could help. I'm nine now."

"What would I do without my big girl?"

I do help. Stay up long after Gloria's in bed. Once we get Debbie asleep, we clean chickens. Debbie still cries a lot, but she's not so skinny now, and I rock her to sleep while Mom starts on the chickens. Jimmy's usually not around—either out at Joey's or in bed early. Mom says his back is acting up. He hurt it years ago, falling off a roof. "Is that why he's scared to paint the house?"

"Oh, Sharon," Mom says, laughing.

Cleaning chickens is a big job. First, hang upside down to bleed. Then dip them in boiling water to get the feathers off. Singe them, holding a match to the pinfeathers. Cut the chicken open. There's this one little part you mustn't cut into or the meat will be ruined. Haul out the innards and give them to Pal and the cats. Save heart, liver and gizzard. Jimmy and Joey like those. I'm not surprised they like the uggy bits. Now the chicken's ready to stuff and put in the oven.

Every time we get chickens ready for the oven, Joey shows up for his and helps us eat ours.

One day Mom says: "Bet you and I could kill a chicken."

"Sure."

We go out to the hen yard, and Mom grabs a young cockerel—he's a boy bird. Hens don't get eaten until they're too old to lay eggs. Mom has him by the legs, but he twists his neck around and pecks her hand. "Shit," she makes a face, but doesn't let go. She's got one hand around his neck and the other holding his legs.

"You bring the axe."

We go to the stump, and Mom presses his head down between the two nails.

"Hold his legs really tight, cause he'll get you with his spurs if he can."

I hold on tight.

Mom picks up the axe, and wham, his head flies off.

I'm so surprised I let go, and the headless, spurting-blood chicken runs in circles. I stare opened-mouthed. Suddenly, Gloria's here. She screams and runs away.

"Oh cripes, I should've kept her in the house," Mom says.

The chicken drops and I pick it up by its legs. "How come it could run?"

"Just nerves. You okay?"

"Sure," I say, giggling. "We don't need Uncle Joey no more."

Mom laughs. "That's my girl."

E'RE GOING ON a trip. Holly Holmes invited us to her wedding in Buffalo.

"Can we go to Grants and get school clothes?"

"I'm planning on it. Everything's cheaper there than in Grenville," Mom says.

None of my dresses fit me—all too short. Gloria's are too short, too, but she can wear my outgrown ones.

***

We get up while it's still dark and load the station wagon. Last night, Mom made Jimmy clean all his junk out—tools, newspapers, paint tins, bits of lumber, rags. He and Joey both collect newspapers and rags.

Jimmy said: "Lotsa room for the kids."

"I'm not going to Buffalo in a car full of garbage," Mom said.

"Jeez, it's not garbage."

"Jimmy, clean it out!" Mom yelled.

His ears turned red and he mumbled: "Cripes." But went out and did it. When Mom gets mad, Jimmy does what he's told.

Looks a little more like Grandma's car again. Still smells of Jimmy's stuff and there's a big cut in the front seat upholstery with stuffing puffing out.

Mom's packed the picnic basket full. It's in the back with me and Gloria and our suitcase. Mom made Jimmy put our mattress in. It was stored in the garage and smells musty, but she spread a clean sheet over it. Baby Debbie is up front with Mom. Debbie has a little bit of red hair now.

Pal has to stay home. Joey's coming over to feed him, the cats, and the chickens.

We drive for a long time. We stop at a park in Dunville and have

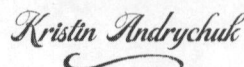

our picnic. There's a store nearby, and Jimmy buys us ice cream. Then we're on our way again.

"Stop!" I yell. "There's the sign for Crystal Beach!"

"Oh, Sharon, we don't have time to stop," Mom says.

"We could visit Teddy's family."

"Would be nice, but we're going to Holly's wedding, remember?"

"Couldn't we do both?"

"There isn't time. I want to get to Grants to buy you a dress and both of you need school shoes."

"I'd like a blue dress."

"That shouldn't be too hard to find."

"I'd like doll clothes," Gloria says. "Remember all the doll clothes, Sharon, even roller skates? I'm getting roller skates for Lucy."

***

I've found my blue dress. It's taffeta with a lace collar. Just right for a wedding.

"Sorry, honey. That one's too expensive, and we need to get one you could wear to school, too." She leads me to a rack marked "Clearance."

They're all summer dresses, most of them sundresses. "I can't wear a sundress to school."

"Here's one with sleeves. Yellow goes nicely with your red hair. Us redheads look good in yellow."

I try it on. Not bad—white eyelet collar and pockets and a full skirt, but not as nice as the blue taffeta. "Can I get white shoes with straps?"

"Sorry, we better get Oxfords for school."

We both get ugly brown Oxfords. I spot some really cute white baby shoes that are only $1.49, but Mom won't buy them. Gloria gets her doll roller skates, but doesn't seem to notice she didn't get a new dress. Mom buys us each three pairs of white panties. They're cheaper than the days of the week kind.

***

We park on a side street and change in the car. Gloria's wearing my blue dress I got in Ridgeway for my eighth birthday. Doesn't matter 'cause it's too short on me. The brown shoes look dumb. Mom brushes our hair and fixes it with barrettes. She dresses Debbie in the pink ruffly dress our neighbours, the Ruebels, gave her when she was born —way too small now. She's barefoot. Mom should've bought those baby shoes. She changes into her black silk dress with the creamy rose at the neck. I remember that dress from when we lived in Buffalo.

As we're following Mom into the church, I notice her shoes are scuffed and her black dress looks too big on her. She got real skinny since Debbie was born. She's still beautiful. Her red curls hang down her back. She's wearing her silver clip I really like. Somebody gave it to her when we lived in Buffalo. Jimmy's wearing the black suit he wore to Uncle Raymond's funeral. The back of his jacket is wrinkled and shiny.

Gloria and me sit down between Mom and Jimmy. How did I get stuck next to him? Even though he did slick back his hair with water, it's already spiking up. And nothing can be done about his ears. His jacket isn't buttoned up. His belly's too big. At least he's not wearing his awful brown pants with the patched knee. All the other men have their suit jackets buttoned up.

Mom looks over and smiles at me. Nobody is as pretty as her. Debbie, wrapped up in a pink blanket, smiles too and waves her arms. You can't see she's barefoot.

Holly's wearing a white satin dress with a train. The groom is tall and dark, and wearing a fancy suit. Mom whispers it's called a tuxedo. They look like a picture in a magazine.

***

We're in this really fancy dining room with white tablecloths. Dinner took a long time, and there were a lot of speeches. Now the tables are pushed against the walls—for the dancing, Mom says. The band starts playing. This is maybe like the ballroom at Crystal Beach where Mom used to go dancing.

First, Holly and her husband danced and now, everybody is. Mom tells me and Gloria we can dance. At first, I don't want to, but I see some other kids dancing so I haul Gloria out on the floor. It's fun. You just listen to the music and jump around.

Mom's not dancing. Jimmy says he never learned. That doesn't surprise me.

"Mom, dance with me."

She gets up. "This one's a waltz." She holds me and says: "Count one, two, three, one big step, two little steps, turn."

Holly comes to our table with Steve, that's the groom. He asks Mom to dance, and Holly asks Jimmy. Jimmy won't, of course. Holly sits down, holds the baby and talks to us while Mom dances with Steve. I watch them. They look good—like a movie star couple. Holly, even in her beautiful, white dress, isn't pretty like Mom. She has a big nose and even with all the makeup she's wearing, I can see her pimples. I feel like crying, and I hate Jimmy. If Mom hadn't had me and Gloria to look after, she could've married somebody like Steve. Holly and Steve are going to live in California. I could swim year 'round there. Because of us, Mom's stuck with Jimmy.

We leave before the end 'cause we have to drive back to Grenville. "Why can't we stay in a tourist cabin at Crystal Beach?"

Jimmy laughs, turns his pockets inside out. "No money, honey." And he giggles as a balled up handkerchief, cigarette butts, and other garbage fall to the ground.

At least we're in the parking lot and not the hotel. I want to hit him.

Mom says: "C'mon girls. Curl up in the back, and you'll be asleep in no time."

I can't fall asleep. I listen to Gloria's snuffling breath. How come she can go to sleep? Baby Debbie cries and cries.

Mom says: "Baby, please go to sleep. I'm so tired."

If she didn't have me and Gloria, she'd be on her way to California, instead of stupid old Grenville.

$\mathcal{S}$ATURDAY AFTERNOON, I look down at my bare knees going up down, up down, strong as a machine. The bike swerves, I giggle and watch where I'm going. Stand up on the pedals and go even faster. Bet I could pedal all the way to Crystal Beach. I don't hang around the house much since I got my bike. Learned to ride in one day—fell ten times. Skinned both elbows and knees. I didn't care.

Mom says I'm lucky to be able to go off bike-riding. As a kid she had to darn stockings and clean her room every Saturday morning. And every Saturday afternoon go with her mother to do errands. Her job was to carry the bags.

I'm glad to leave the Plum behind. That's what I call our house, though it's more of a pit.

My favourite way is through Orchard Park, past Courtland Street to where the farms start and then follow Grey's Road. Finally, I'm away from those stupid fruity streets—Cherry, Peach, Plum. Grey's Road turns away from the lake so there are farms on both sides. One more turn and I'll be at the beach, great for bike-riding, though watch out for rocks. I know to ride on the wet sand—dry jams the wheels. There's never anybody around.

Warm for the end of September, and my hair sticks to my bare back—should've put it up in a ponytail. I'm wearing my raggedy sneakers. My Oxfords are stiff and uncomfortable, but I'm glad I have them for school 'cause Joanne and Betty wear Oxfords, too. The poor kids wear sneakers to school. So warm I put on the bibbed sundress I got when we lived in Buffalo. Mom moved the buttons to the very end of the straps so it still fits. Uncle Joey's packsack from the army is in my bike carrier. Mom let me make baloney sandwiches.

Clinton pedals up behind me. What's he doing here? He's wearing this funny old jacket about three sizes too big for him.

"Where ya headed?" he asks.

"To the lake."

"Me, too." He rides up beside me. "I'm building a fort back in the woods. You wanna see it?"

"Sure."

We pedal along the beach to the swampy part where cattails grow. Too muddy to go further.

Clinton shows me a path through the field above the beach. We ride our bikes all the way to the woods. The trees are big and the leaves thick on the ground. We have to wheel our bikes 'cause the trees are close together. His fort's in a little clearing.

"Musta been a house here once," he says.

"How do you know?"

"Lilacs and apple trees—somebody planted 'em."

We cover up our bikes with loose brush.

"Don't want some dummy snitching 'em," he says.

He pulls some hanging vines aside so I can crawl in. Once through there's room to stand up.

"Two old apple trees," he says. "Grape vines took 'em over."

"It's great!" He's made a ceiling by weaving pine branches through the vines. There are cut logs for stools. I sit on one. "Where'd you find these?"

"The farmer was cuttin' wood. Helped myself."

"Want some food?" I open my packsack.

"Thanks, if ya got enough."

I share my baloney sandwiches, apples, and jar of cherry Kool-Aid.

There's a piece of a plaid blanket spread out in a corner. "You could camp here overnight."

"Yeah, when Pa's on the warpath."

"What do you mean?"

"Pa's a bugger when he's drunk."

"I had a papa like that."

"Huh?"

"In Cadillac where we used to live. In Quebec."

"Did he beat youse up?"

"Not me, but my mom, and he hit my sister once. We left."

"Wish Pa would leave."

"Why don't you and your mom leave?"

"No money. Anyway, she's scared of 'im and I've got three little brothers. When I'm big I'll beat 'im up. Surprise the bugger."

Dusk by the time we're on our way home. Clinton's pedal falls off. "Fix er up in a jiffy," he says.

He pulls a wrench and a screwdriver out of his jacket's big pockets and fastens the pedal back on.

"Thread's worn—gotta get me a new one."

"You're good at fixing stuff."

"Gonna be a mechanic. Uncle Mike's got himself a garage."

Me and Clinton go to his fort every chance we get—our secret place. He's never told anybody but me. We tell each other things that we would never tell anybody else.

I tell him I hate Jimmy because he makes Mom have babies. Debbie's only five months old, and Mom's having another one in January. We're supposed to be pleased.

Clinton says he feels the same. His mom's having another one, too.

I found a sleeping bag in the back shed. Mom washed it for me and I stuffed it in my bike carrier and took it to the fort. It's better than his blanket. Now when his pa's drunk, Clinton won't freeze to death.

***

I was in grade four. Now I'm in grade five. It's a grade five-six class so I'm in with the big kids. The work's tough, but I don't mind. The principal put me ahead because I'm smart. Those snots Joanne Newman and her friend Betty Moyer got put ahead, too. I can't escape them.

I don't care too much that Clinton and me aren't in the same grade anymore. He never has his homework done and is always getting in trouble. He's two years older. Should be in grade six, but he had to repeat grade one and grade two. Even Gloria passed grade one and she's pretty stupid.

Outside of school though, he's real smart and my best friend. He's really good at building things, and he fixed my bike chain.

***

Mom's sick a lot, and I have to stay home after school, get supper, and look after Debbie. Debbie's real cute, but I want to go bike-riding. Gloria has to help, too. She's no good at getting supper. She burns herself just making tea. Mom's taught me to boil potatoes and vegetables, and even roast a chicken.

I can peel potatoes pretty well, but I hate doing carrots. Our carrots are in boxes of sand in the basement. They're bendy and hard to scrape. Most nights when Mom's sick and I have to get supper, we have hot dogs, and tinned soup or beans. Jimmy complains if I don't cook vegetables.

"Don't youse kids wanna be healthy?"

***

"Why doesn't he cook something?" I ask Clinton.

"Maybe he don't know how."

"Sometimes he doesn't even go to work. Either has a cold or says his back is acting up again, and he has to rest and wants me to make tea."

"At least he don't hit nobody," Clinton says.

***

We didn't get much for Christmas. I wanted a sled with steel runners. I got new pyjamas, underwear, and socks. Not too exciting. Though I did get coloured pencils and a book. Gloria got a doll, but I know it came from the church rummage sale. I saw Mom buy it. Gloria still believes in Santa Claus. Mom said: "Let her believe a little longer."

She also said she was sorry about the sled. Mom says sorry a lot.

Jimmy giggles. "Cardboard works good."

ECEMBER 28TH, MOM has Emily Louise. Another girl —know they wanted a boy because Jimmy says: "When ya gonna pop me out a son?"

Emily came a month early and cries all the time. When she was born, she only weighed five pounds. Now we have two babies to look after.

***

A good thing happens in January. Jimmy gets a job dry-walling in Toronto. He takes Uncle Joey with him. They'll be gone six weeks. Mom says when they get back we're getting a new roof, and there'll be money for school clothes. That's good because I've had to wear some stuff she bought at the church rummage sale. "What if I run into the girl who owned it?"

Mom says: "Don't worry so much. Anyway, those girls go to Grenville Public, not Orchard Park."

She's probably right. Because I've caught on that Orchard Park is where the poor kids live. The rich ones live in downtown Grenville. In the rummage sale stuff I found a pair of red dungarees that fit really well. Wish I could wear them to school, but we have to wear dresses. I wear them under my skirts and take them off when I get there. I don't have snow pants anymore. That's okay—snow pants are itchy. Too cold to go barelegged, and we don't have long brown stockings now either. Lotsa kids at Orchard Park go barelegged all winter. There's one girl in my class who wears rubber boots with no socks. One day last fall I was downtown with Mom when the Grenville Public kids were just getting out. Most of the girls had brown stockings, a few had navy knees socks, and a couple were even wearing white stockings like we had to go with our red velvet dresses.

* * *

The doctor said the alarm would go when it's time. I reach under my pillow and stare at Mom's clock. Too dark to make out the numbers. But I don't want it to wake Gloria. She'll bawl. She's eight and still acts like a baby.

Gloria coughs.

Don't wake up, scaredy cat. Mom's not going to die. The medicine'll make her better—Dr. Stewart said so.

He came to the house after Mrs. Ruebel called him. It was scary —Mom on the floor and couldn't get up. She whispered: "Get Mrs. Ruebel."

Gloria wailed: "Mommy's gonna die."

Mom didn't need to hear that. I smacked my sister and told her to shut up.

"Mrs. Ruebel," I yelled all the way next door. She came over and got Mom up on the couch. Mom was mumbling: "The ceiling's falling. Get the children ..."

Mrs. Ruebel said: "Don't pay any attention. She's delirious from fever." She ran back to her place and called the doctor. Dr. Stewart says Mom has pneumonia.

She mustn't die. I'll have to look after Gloria and the babies forever.

Maybe turn on the light? No. Both Gloria and Baby Emily'll wake up, but the alarm will wake them. Gloria coughs, sniffles—always has a cold.

Cradling the steel clock, I climb out of bed. Shiver as my bare feet touch the linoleum. I peek in the basket. Emily's asleep. She still has that bluish, new-baby look. Mom says we have to keep a close eye on her. That's why she's not in the baby room with Debbie. Until Mom got sick she nursed Emily and kept the baby basket right next to her bed.

I go to the window. In the moonlight I can see it's twenty to two. I guess Dr. Stewart doesn't know I'm nine. He patted my head. *When the big hand's at twelve and the little hand's at two, but never mind the alarm will ring. Wake your mother up. Give her a glass of water and two pills, just*

two now. That's important. Mrs. Ruebel will have the water and pills by the bed. You're a big girl, and you can help out. I know I'm a big girl and can read and tell time. I could read when I was six and tell time when I was seven. Gloria's eight and still reads baby books.

I pull the quilt off my bed and wrap up in it on the mat by the window. The window's down near the floor, like there was barely room to make a window, 'cause the ceiling slants above it, right up to the witch-hat roof. The moonlight glints off the icy-stiff diapers on the line and the doorless icebox in the yard. Wrapped in the quilt and still shivering, I study the clock and wait. I pick up my sweater off the floor and put it on. Sit back down and wait. The wind rattles the window. Gloria would be scared, thinking a burglar was trying to get in.

At two minutes to two, I push down the knob on top of the clock, throw off the quilt, and go to Mom, and turn on the light.

She's asleep — her red hair spread out around her head is the exact same shade as mine. She looks old. Her cheeks sunk in. Her teeth are in the cup. She breathes noisily. I touch her forehead. It's hot. I stroke her like I pet the cats. She stirs.

"Mom, time for your pills."

"Wha, who is it?"

"Me, Mom. Time for your pills."

She struggles to sit up.

"I'll help, here's your pillow. It was on the floor." I hold out the glass of water in one hand, the pills in the other.

"Thanks, Sharon. I'm so hot."

"Do you want a wet washcloth for your forehead? I could fix one."

"That would be nice."

I run down to the kitchen. Push the yellow cat out of the laundry basket and root around for a washcloth. Can't find one, so I use a tea towel.

I sit on Mom's bed and hold the wet cloth on her forehead. She's already back asleep. I lie down beside her and the heat from her fever warms me. Want to sleep here, but mustn't. Baby Emily will be waking up for her bottle.

***

The baby's crying and rubbing her tiny fists all over her face. She woke me up. Still dark, but must be morning because I hear Mrs. Ruebel fixing the fires. She comes over every morning since Mom got sick. Me and Gloria aren't allowed to touch the woodstoves. Last night Mrs. Ruebel brought Billy with her. He goes to high school now. He brought the wood up from the cellar.

I hear Debbie rattling the bars of her crib. Better get her before she wakes Mom up.

I bring her into our room, and lay her on a blanket on the floor. When I undo her soggy diaper I see she's had a poopie—P-U! "Gloria, get up and help me."

"I'm too cold, and my throat hurts."

"I can't carry them both downstairs at once."

She pulls her quilt over her head.

I take Debbie down to the kitchen and stick her in the playpen, then go back up and get Emily. As I pass Gloria's bed, I yank her covers off and throw them on the floor. I carry Emily down and put her in the buggy.

Mrs. Ruebel sterilized the baby bottles and made up formula. She brought milk with her, but we have the corn syrup that goes in Emily's bottle. Debbie gets plain milk.

I sit in Mom's rocker and feed Emily. Debbie can hold her own bottle now.

"Go see if your mother's awake and would like some tea," Mrs. Reubel says.

Mom's awake. She still looks awful. There's dried spittle at the corner of her mouth, and her hair's all matted. Gloria's in bed with her.

"Gloria's supposed to be helping," I tell Mom.

"She's just having a little cuddle first. Is Mrs. Ruebel here?"

"Yep, she wants to know if you want tea. I can make it."

Mom nods. "Are the babies fed?"

"I gave them their bottles. Mrs. Ruebel fixed them."

"Come here a minute."

She reaches out, and I climb in bed on the other side from Gloria.

"Now girls, I'm depending on you. Gloria, you too can help. You're my big girls."

"Is Daddy coming home?" Gloria says.

"Not till February."

"We need him to help," my whiny sister says.

We don't need him at all—managed fine before on our own, I think, don't say.

"Your daddy is helping by earning money. When he comes home, we'll have the money for a new roof. No more pails sitting around in the attic to catch the drips."

Mrs. Ruebel thumps up the stairs and pokes her head in the door. "Oh, here you all are. Muriel, how are you feeling? I sent Sharon up to see if you wanted tea."

"Much better, and tea would be lovely. Are you able to stay so the girls can go to school?"

"Yes, they should be getting ready. Hurry up now, girls. Don't bother your mother." She shoos us out of the bed. "Your oatmeal's waiting."

***

Mrs. Ruebel comes every day for a week, and every night I get up to give Mom her pills and Baby Emily her bottle. Mrs. Ruebel said: "If you can't wake your mother up, come next door and get me. But the worst is over."

Dr. Stewart comes and tells us Mom's a lot better, but has to stay in bed at least another week. "Isn't there a relative that could come in and nurse her?" he says to Mrs. Reubel.

"Doesn't appear so."

Mom sets the alarm for herself, and I don't need to get up at night anymore, except when baby Emily wakes up. She still sleeps in her basket next to my bed so I'll hear her. I bring a bottle up with me when I go to bed. Don't have to worry about the milk souring. Our room's as cold as the icebox. Gloria draws pictures in the frost on our window. Some nights I wake up and go in and check on Mom. If she's awake, I get her a drink of water.

***

This week Mom can come downstairs and sit in the rocking chair by the kitchen woodstove. She keeps a blanket over her shoulders. I stay home to look after the babies. Gloria wants to stay, too, but Mom says she's missed too much and is behind. Mrs. Ruebel still comes morning and night to fix the fires. Mom shows me how to add wood and make sure the stove door is tight closed, and how to fix the damper. I must never touch the fires when Mom's not around.

I like this time, just me and Mom. I wish Jimmy would never come back. We don't need him.

"Mom, did your papa go away and not come back?"

"Whatever gave you that idea? My father died just before I turned fifteen. A heart attack, hadn't even been sick."

"Then it was just you and Grandma because Aunt Jean was already married?"

"For two years, until I married Maurice."

I know it's Jimmy's fault Mom keeps having babies. We can look after these two, but no more. Jimmy's made Mom old—her hair's different, sorta limp and her cheeks are sunk in. She walks different, too—hunched over. All Jimmy's fault. I told her no more babies.

She laughed and said: "Oh, Sharon, Jimmy and I want a big family. My family's gone and so is his—just him and Joey left. We love children. I want Jimmy to have a son. For us to have a little Jimmy."

That's all the world needs—another Jimmy. Maybe Jimmy will have a heart attack like Mom's papa.

Someone's knocking. When I open the door, I'm surprised to see Clinton. I haven't seen him much this winter. Don't often go bike-riding and there's too much snow to ride on the beach. We never played together at school. Boys get teased if they play with girls. And we're in different grades.

"Hi, Gloria told me your mom's sick. Here." He hands me a brown paper bag.

Inside is a tin of soup—chicken noodle.

"Ma says ... soup's good for sick people." His face turns bright red.

"Thanks. C'mon in."

With Clinton I don't care the house's a mess. I've only seen the

outside of his, but it's an old summer cottage with a crate instead of front steps. At least we have steps.

I lead him out to the kitchen. Mom's in her rocker with Baby Emily.

"Mom, Clinton brought soup." I sit the tin on the work table.

"Hi, Clinton. Thank you. That's very kind. Sharon, why don't you make some cocoa?"

I make cocoa while Mom finishes feeding Emily.

"I'm going up for a little lie-down. Bring Debbie down when she wakes up, willya?"

"Sure."

"There's cookies in the tin Mrs. Ruebel brought over. Clinton, thanks for the soup."

Clinton blushes again.

I give him his cocoa and we sit down at the table. "You skipping?"

"Yeah, had stuff to do. I've got a paper route now. When Pa's not working, I buy the groceries."

"Maybe I'll get a paper route."

"Girls don't do papers."

"You're stupid. When we lived in Buffalo Mom and I delivered hundreds. She worked for the *Buffalo Courier News*. That's a big thick newspaper with coloured funnies, not a bit like the dumb little *Grenville Times*."

"Didn't know that," he mumbles.

"How'd you get hired?"

"Ad in the window at the *Grenville Times* downtown."

"I'm going to get a job, too."

***

After school on Thursday I ride my bike downtown. We're having a mild spell so the road's bare. That's one good thing about Grenville. When we lived in Cadillac there was never bare ground in January. The *Grenville Times* office is on Main Street right next to the bank.

There's an old man sitting at a desk behind the counter. He's wearing a tweed jacket and smoking a pipe. Looks friendly.

"What can I do for you, little girl?"

"I'd like a job delivering papers."

"You want to be a paper boy?"

"Yes."

"Honey, that's not a job for a sweet little girl like you." And he chuckles.

"In Buffalo me and my mom delivered lots of papers."

"Well, there's no accounting for the Yanks. Believe me, sweetie, lugging papers around is heavy work. Let the boys do it."

"Bugger," I say and walk out.

E HAVE A new roof. Jimmy and Uncle Joey did it. There's been pounding for days. The wood under the shingles was all rotten.

"Big job," Jimmy said.

We have a gas space heater for the living room. Jimmy's not completely useless. Mom ordered our new clothes out of Eaton's Catalogue. She let me pick out a spring jacket. Both me and Gloria got new underwear and socks.

***

Clinton's supposed to be here. He said he'd call for me around nine. Last night we rode home from school together and planned on going to the fort today. Most of the snow's melted so we can ride down the beach.

Mom says: "Just finish hanging out the wash and you can go."

Hate hanging out wash when it's cold. Can't wear mitts, 'cause they get soggy, and make it hard to work the clothespins.

Gloria's sick with bronchitis—always has some excuse.

I put hardboiled eggs, bread, and apples in my packsack. The apples are from the barrel in the cellar, and their skins are all wrinkly. Still taste good though. Jimmy got them last fall from a man whose porch he fixed. I fill a Mason jar with water. "If Clinton comes by, tell him I've gone to the beach."

"Okay," Mom says, smiling.

"What's so funny?"

"He's sweet on you."

"Is not. We just like bike-riding. I'm sick of Shirley and Norma. They just want to play dolls."

"Okay. Have fun, my little tomboy."

I pedal as hard as I can. The ditches are flowing, and the sun warms my back. A red-winged blackbird, first one I've seen this year, darts from a fence post. Yippee—winter's over.

I'm mad at Clinton. He didn't show up, and it's not fair he's got a job. Why are there only paper boys? Me and Mom were paper girls.

The beach is clear, and I ride all the way to the field. I wheel my bike to the brush pile and see Clinton's bike thrown carelessly on top. He came without me, the bugger! Didn't even hide his bike properly. Serve him right if somebody stole it.

I follow his tracks. There's still snow in the bush. Funny, some people say woods and some bush. Mom says it's a North-South thing. Northerners say bush and Southerners say woods. I'm half and half. Would Papa say bush? How do you say bush in French? Bet I used to know.

I push the vines aside and crawl in. At first, I don't think he's here, then see his curly brown hair sticking out of the sleeping bag. "Clinton!" What's he sleeping for?

He sits up and I want to run away. He looks awful. His one eye is swollen shut and there's a big purple bruise on his jaw. "What happened?"

"Nuttin', just Pa, as usual."

"Did you come here in the night?"

"Yep. Bring any food?"

"Eggs and stuff." I hand him my packsack. He's really hungry. He gobbles down an egg and most of the bread. "Are your little brothers okay?"

"Yeah, Pa don't bother them none. Sorry, I'm eatin your food. Wanna an egg?"

"Nah, I'm not hungry. Eat it all, if you want."

"Really thirsty." He gulps down most of the water.

"You better go to the doctor."

"Be okay."

"How come your dad only hits you?"

"Not his kid."

"Your mom was married before like mine?"

"Sorta. Youse lucky, Jimmy Dutton's a nice guy."

"At least he doesn't hit anybody."

"Pa beats on Ma, too. Someday, I'll bash his head in."

* * *

Sunday morning and I was supposed to meet Clinton at the fort, but here I am climbing into the Cowans' brand new '51 Ford. They're taking me and Gloria to Sunday school at Saint James Anglican—the big stone church right across from the bank. Jimmy thought it a good idea. As if he ever has good ideas. His mother used to go to this church, and he and his brothers went to Sunday school. The minister came to call last week and arranged everything.

In the Sunday-school room, I sit down on the chair next to Suzie Cowan in her crisp pink and white striped cotton dress. Mom insisted we get dressed up. I'm wearing a limp red-plaid taffeta dress that no doubt was some kid's Christmas dress years ago. Suzie moves her skirt aside as I sit down, and turns away from me. Is she afraid I'll get her skirt dirty? I tuck my feet in their scuffed up Oxfords under my chair. She's wearing shiny Mary Janes and spotless white half-socks.

I hate Sunday school—Suzie and her friend, Nancy, sit together and whisper. I bet they're talking about us.

* * *

Sunday mornings are ruined. I can't go to the fort because every week we have to go to Sunday school. Perfect bike-riding weather and I'm stuck in church. Gloria loves church and Sunday school. She's too dumb to know they don't really like us. She even joined the junior choir. Mrs. Cowan's the leader and drives Gloria to the practices Thursday nights.

One good thing for Gloria is on Sundays she gets to cover up her shabby dress with a choir gown.

* * *

I don't have a birthday party this year, though Mom does make me a cake. Who cares about birthdays anyway? I do get new sneakers, drawing paper and crayons. Mom's been sick a lot. I know she's going to have another baby. I hate Jimmy.

*** *

It's just getting light when I carry Baby Emily down to get a bottle. She's ten months, but still wakes up at five for a bottle. Debbie didn't and she was walking by nine months. Good though this one's slower —not walking, not into everything. Debbie fell out of the pear tree and broke her arm. She's still got the cast on. Jimmy said: "Why wasn't ya watching her?" How was I supposed to know she'd climb the tree? Even I wasn't climbing trees when I was two. She's a lot like me. Mom calls us her little tomboys and we both have Mom's curly red hair.

I freeze. There's a snorting, growling sound coming from the living room. What the hell! I tiptoe over to the doorway.

Uncle Joey is sprawled on our couch, one knobby bare foot touching the floor. Just wearing trousers. I see the scars on his chest—ridges of red skin with the odd black hair. The first time I saw them, he was washing himself at the pump. I thought I'd puke. He laughed his crazy laugh. "Good thing they didn't get my face, eh?"

I know he got hurt in the war. He snuffles, snorts, and mumbles in his sleep. At least he's not yelling. When he lived with us, sometimes he'd yell in the middle of the night. Could never make out what he was saying, but it was scary.

Mom says he's got a metal plate in his head. What's he doing on our couch? He can't move in with us 'cause all the rooms are full.

*** *

Uncle Joey has moved in. All his bags and boxes are piled around the living room. "Just temporary," Mom says.

I was already mad at her 'cause she's having another baby. "Where'll everybody sleep?"

"We'll make room."

I go bike-riding whenever I get a chance. At home I'm looking after Debbie and Emily or I'm hanging out wash or getting supper because

Mom has to lie down. Gloria should help more, but she never wakes up when the babies cry and, if she tries cooking anything, she either burns herself and the food, or spills something.

All we need is Uncle Joey moving back in. Just temporary, they all say. Temporary, my eye. Jimmy and him are building another shed on the house, off the living room. At first, I think Joey's going to have a separate little house because they build the whole thing and close it in before they cut a doorway into the living room. The new shed's covered with ugly tarpaper. Mom says it'll have boards by fall. This I doubt as the ass-end shed is still tarpaper and was when we arrived here. Now the house looks like it's got a couple of black boils both side and ass-end.

Ass is my new favourite word. "Kiss my ass," I said when that snot Betty Moyer said I shouldn't play on the climbing bars. The school just got climbing bars this spring.

"Somebody'll see something they shouldn't," she said, giggling.

Stupid girl. I always tuck my skirt between my legs before hanging up side down. They should let us wear slacks to school. A girl in grade three got sent home for wearing dungarees.

Mom gets mad if I say ass around home.

At least with Uncle Joey sleeping downstairs in his new shed, I don't hear him yelling in the night. Mom says I should feel sorry for him because he fought in the war. He was wounded in Italy.

"Was Jimmy a soldier, too?"

"No, he didn't go because he was supporting his mother and handicapped sister."

"What was wrong with her?"

"She had cerebral palsy. She died during the war years."

"His mother's dead, too."

"She died of cancer while Joey was in Italy. Poor Joey, when he finally got out of the hospital and got home, both his mother and sister were gone."

Everything about the Duttons is sad and awful. If only we'd stayed at Crystal Beach and I had gone to Ridgeway School.

***

I've had a terrible toothache for three days. My cheek's all swollen and hurts like hell. Have to walk all the way downtown to the dentist's office—more than a mile. The sun beating down on my head makes the pain worse. The only time I've been to the dentist was when we lived in Grandma's apartment. He gave us free toothbrushes. I need a new toothbrush.

I hand the little grey-haired lady drinking tea the envelope with the money in it, like Mom told me to. Mom said this lady is Dr. White's wife.

"Thank you, dear. You can sit down right over there. It won't be long." She points to the chairs.

I sit down and immediately hear a terrible noise from behind the closed door—a screeching whine followed by a rat-a-tat-tat and a moaning. Every tooth hurts now and I want to run away.

I clench my hands between my knees and wait.

The door opens and a boy about my age, holding his jaw, stumbles out followed by a huge grey-haired man. "You can come in now."

He tells me to sit in the big chair.

Dr. White cranks the chair back. "Open wide."

He's poking around in my mouth with a pointy metal thing. It hurts. I lie still and look out the window. All I can see is a brick wall.

"You have a big cavity in your molar. That's no way to treat your teeth."

"I brush my teeth every night before bed."

"Do you eat candy?"

"Yeah." Is he going to give me a treat after he fixes my tooth?

"That's why you have a cavity."

He's cranking the chair back further so that I'm almost lying down.

"This is going to hurt," he says. "Remember that the next time you want to eat candy."

He's using some kind of drill. The drill screams like I want to. I won't let him make me cry.

I stare out the window at that brick wall. I've been captured by the Nazis. I'm a spy—so is Clinton. If I talk, Clinton will be beaten and killed. I don't make a sound. The Nazi drills into my skull, stops, pushes poison into the hole, drills again. I tell him nothing.

"There, all done for now." He cranks the chair back up. "Eat lots of oatmeal, vegetables, and no candy, and there won't be a next time."

I get out of there as fast as I can. Two S.S. men are chasing me, but I race down the stairs, out the door and around the corner. Clinton blasts them with his Pa's .22 and hands me a grenade. I toss it through the second-storey window. Watch as the building explodes and Dr. White in flames flies out the window along with his little wife still holding her teacup. Too bad for her, but why did she stay with him? Me and Clinton run like hell.

I don't stop running until I reach Cherry Street. I'm panting and spit out blood. I walk the rest of the way home.

ON AUGUST, MY brother is born, and they name him Joey after our uncle. Uncle Joey works with Jimmy now. That was a mistake. I heard Jimmy telling Mom that Uncle Joey left wet cement in the mixer overnight, and it took them half a day to chip it out.

"Is Uncle Joey stupid because of the metal plate in his head?"

"Don't call him stupid. Your uncle's an okay guy."

"Kids make fun of him. He's always mumbling to himself, and he calls out hallo to everybody who comes by."

"They should respect him. He was a soldier."

"He looks funny, dresses funny, and acts funny."

"Sharon, that's no way to talk."

Mom doesn't understand. Joanne Newman, and her sidekick Betty Moyer—her dad owns Moyers' Plumbing—are such snots. It's hard enough without having an uncle like Joey.

***

I'm in grade six now and school could be good if Joanne and Betty would leave me alone. "Where'd you get that dress? At a rummage sale?" Joanne says, and Betty giggles.

I slap Joanne and push her down. Betty runs screaming for a teacher.

I'm sent to the office and given a lecture on proper behaviour for young ladies.

They leave me alone for a while after that. Then me and Gloria get lice. A lot of kids do. The nurse checks everybody for lice once a month.

We have to stay home from school and wash our hair with this awful smelling soap.

"It'd be a shame to cut off those beautiful red curls," Mom says.

"I like my long hair—it's like yours."

"Yes, you look just like I did as a child." She combs the nits out of my hair. I do Gloria's.

I'm sure glad I'm not Marlene Stinson—this kid in grade four who comes to school all winter in rubber boots with no socks. When she gets lice, her dad runs the clippers over her head.

When we get back to school, a lot of kids won't play with us. I don't care. Shirley and Norma play with me. Shirley's had lice three times. But I can't join the big group skipping. Shirley and Norma can, if they don't play with me.

I get so sick of this that one recess I walk over to the skipping group and grab the end of the rope. The kid turning, she's only in grade four, backs away. I turn the rope and Betty keeps right on skipping till she's out.

Betty tries to take the end from me. "You're not allowed to play," she says.

"Do you think we all want cooties?" Joanne says.

"I don't have cooties!" I shake my long red hair at them.

They all run away screaming, "Cooties, cooties. Cooties like carrot hair."

I catch Joanne. She never was much of a runner. I push her down and rub her face in the gravel. Boy, can she bawl.

Then Miss Haun has me by the arm and is escorting me to the principal's office. Mr. Blackwood tells me I'm a juvenile delinquent and I'll end up in reform school. He picks up the strap—thick and ugly, must be a foot long. He tells me to hold out my hand.

No way.

Miss Haun still has me by the arm, and she holds it out for me.

I won't cry. I imagine the brick wall, the Nazis, the hand grenade.

Five whacks on each hand. All afternoon my hands throb.

After school, I follow Joanne and Betty from the schoolyard. They walk quickly. I keep my distance until we're out of sight of the school. I grab Betty first and kick her in the shins.

"I'm going to tell," Joanne screams.

I grab Joanne by her braids, yank hard and push her to the ground. I sit on her and give her ratty looking braids a few more good yanks. She's bawling her head off.

"You tell anybody, you'll get this every night." I give her a final shake, get up and walk away.

After that, they leave me alone. I join the skipping group along with Shirley and Norma whenever we want to. Nobody stops me.

Clinton says: "You should ignore stuff dumb stuck-ups say."

"Nobody's going to push me around," I tell him.

Gloria just bawls when anybody teases her. I tell her she has to fight back, but she won't. Doesn't usually tell me when kids are bothering her. If I see anything going on, I walk over, and they scatter in a hurry.

* * *

Whenever I need anything, there's no money. I had to wear my too small coat all winter. My September Oxfords were too tight by January, and Mom didn't even buy me new sneakers. I have to wear some she got at a rummage sale.

"How come, when we lived in Buffalo and you worked for the *Buffalo Courier News* we had lots of money?"

"We didn't, Sharon. I couldn't even pay the rent."

"We ate at Hank's Diner. We never go to restaurants now. Me and Gloria had nice clothes."

"I was a stupid woman. Whatever money I earned, I spent. You have to save your money."

"You're just like your mother."

"What?"

"Wouldn't buy you stuff and made you do mending."

"Oh, Sharon, I'm not like her. They had money and I never made you mend socks."

Too bad you don't do some mending now. You could start with those holey underpants Gloria wore to school. It'll be a long time before she lives that down. I don't say any of that. I know Mom's tired out by the evening. Three little kids to look after all day, and she's pregnant again. I hate Jimmy. Why doesn't he leave her alone?

Long ago, Mom had a job painting the rollercoaster. In her red blouse and sparkly shoes she climbed to the top and threw down her silver spike heels on the crew below. My mom was wonderful tough.

*T*HE DAY AFTER my 11th birthday I start snitching things. Little Joey'll be a year old in August. Mom had another miscarriage, but now she's pregnant again. I used to think if I really needed something, she'd get it for me. I never expected anything from Dumb Dutton Jimmy, but Mom I could count on. Can't anymore. Not her fault —sick a lot and too many kids all needing things. When I was nine, the year after we moved to Grenville, and my favourite blue dress was too short, and there wasn't the money to buy a new one, Mom took apart a white embroidered sundress of hers and added a ruffle to my dress. She always saw to it that me and Gloria had no holes in our underwear or socks. After moving here she made a regular underwear and socks order from Eaton's catalogue. After a while she didn't seem to notice or care. I showed her the worn out elastic on my panties. "I can't wear these to school."

"Here's a safety pin."

"Mom, I need new ones."

"Sharon, don't nag. A pin will do for now."

I wish we could wear slacks to school. There'd be a lot less teasing. "I see England. I see France. I see Sharon's underpants."

"They're clean and well paid for," I yell right back.

They were clean, but greyed cotton doesn't look clean. I made sure mine didn't have any holes or rips. I'd wear the same pair the next day, if there weren't any non-holey ones dry. I never had more than three good pairs. I'd wash them out before I went to bed, but often they weren't dry by morning. Damp underwear feels horrible in the wintertime. Gloria never seems to notice what she's got on. Girls were always teasing her until I pushed a few onto the gravel. It's funny that girls, not boys sing that rhyme. Oh, boys will yell: "See your underpants." But that's different.

The first thing I snitch is a pair of pink nylon panties from Stedmans. I open my purse on the counter, make like I'm looking for something and slip the underwear into my coat pocket.

They're way too big, so I still have to use a safety pin.

Mom will notice them in the wash.

She never does. I tell Gloria I got them at the rummage sale.

***

I don't snitch stuff from Stedmans anymore. I got caught with a silk neckerchief. They've got these neckerchiefs in all sorts of colours, chartreuse, fuchsia, lime green. Everybody's wearing them. It was the new clerk. She's a fat old thing. Most of the clerks are teenagers or a bit older, and they're always chatting and giggling. But not the new one. She called Mr. Swenson—the manager. I bawled and carried on until they let me go. I said the neckerchief was a birthday present for my mother. I'm banned from Stedmans.

The only thing I snitch from home is smokes, from Mom's purse or Jimmy's jacket. I can't get them from the drugstore. Old Mrs. Poole keeps them behind the counter. I feel bad about taking anything from Mom's purse. I would never take money. Shirley can get cigarettes real easy. Her dad comes home drunk and passes out, and she cleans out his pockets. He complains somebody at the hotel stole his smokes. Her mom never tells because they share the cigarettes, and she gets any money he might've had on him.

THE SUMMER I turn 12 I get a job. Not much of a job—just leading ponies around, giving tourist kids rides. Cy, the old man who runs the pony track, hires kids to lead the ponies. If you lead ponies, you can come in the morning before the park opens and ride for free. Pony riding is fun, but I need to earn money. I told Cy this and he said if I come every afternoon, he'll pay me a dollar a day.

For a nickel I can buy a big sticky donut or a chocolate bar. For a quarter I can get a hotdog. On real hot days I buy ice cream or popsicles for the kids at home.

Every week I save some money and, just before school starts, I buy five pair of underwear, a blue skirt, and a white peasant blouse with blue embroidery. The total bill was $9.87—only have a little over three dollars left. I was scared to go into Stedmans, but Mom was with me, and it was another new clerk.

Little Joey is two now. He walked at ten months. I taught him to go upstairs on his tummy and come down sitting on his bum. He's a smart baby even if he has Jimmy's big ears.

I hoped Mom would stop having babies now that Jimmy has a son. They made such a big deal out of the baby being a boy—had a party for him. The house was full of their friends drinking beer. Us kids had cherry Kool-Aid. There was a huge cake with "Welcome Joey" written in blue icing.

But Mom kept right on getting pregnant, had another miscarriage before she got pregnant with Judy. Baby Judy was born just a week before my birthday. Another preemie—hairless, red, and scrawny.

* * *

A branch scrapes my window, such an ugly sound. Cold tonight. Fall's like that. So hot last week I went swimming, but I bet there's gonna be frost tonight. Baby Judy cries, a continuous miserable wail. She's been fed, burped, and changed. Still she cries. Mom and Jimmy are at the Legion. They needed a night out.

"Sharon's old enough to mind the young'uns," Jimmy said.

"Of course—she'll soon be a teenager. She's always been my helper."

Well, Mom, I'm sick of it. Sick, sick, sick.

What if they don't come back? The baby wails. Is she scared? Maybe she thinks the branches scraping the house are bad men trying to get in to kill her.

They'll come back. I know, but don't feel it. When we lived in Buffalo and Mom went out on dates, I knew she'd come home and bring us a treat. I'd eat my chocolate bar early in the morning while we delivered the papers. At Hank's Diner we'd have bacon and eggs. There was always something to look forward to. We never have bacon and often, not enough eggs to go around. She scrambles them, adding water, not milk. Serves Jimmy first. Barely a spoonful each for us kids. She tells us to fill up on bread.

I'm smartening up. It's my job to look after the chickens. I hide some eggs. "Too bad the hens aren't laying better," I tell Jimmy. On Saturdays, when Mom goes up to lie down, if Jimmy's at work, I find the eggs and scramble a big panful for the kids' lunch.

"Baby Judy, stop bawling! Stop, just stop it." She makes me feel like wailing right along with her. I get out of bed, pull on a sweater and go in the babies' room. How can Little Joey sleep with her wailing?

I stick the soother in her mouth, and she stops for a moment, but the soother falls out, and she starts again.

I carry baby and soother into my room. For the moment she's quiet. Good. She better not wake up the girls. Gloria, Debbie, and Emily are sound asleep. They don't hear the babies cry. How come? Gloria's only a year younger than me, but she's pretty useless and sleeps like a log.

Uncle Joey's yelling in his sleep again. He sleeps in the back shed now 'cause Mom and Jimmy have his new built-on room. But I can still hear Joey. He sounds scared. In the war he saw people get blown apart. Is that what he's seeing?

I get back in bed with Baby Judy on my chest. She scrabbles around

looking for something to suck on. She won't get any from mine. I hold the soother in her mouth and touch my breasts, first one then the other. Wish they would grow. Shirley's are bigger—mine more pointy though. When I stick out my chest, the guys notice.

Mom's breasts hang, wrinkled skin bags, purple-y-brown nipples. She tried to nurse Judy, but her milk dried up.

My breasts are smooth and white, the nipples pink. I'll never nurse a baby. I swear it.

Tomorrow's Sunday. The Cowans will be by to pick us up for Sunday school. I'm not going. They can't make me. I'll take off on my bike. Go to Clinton's fort. Maybe he'll be there.

I saw him looking at my breasts. We'd gone swimming in our clothes. The end of September, but 80 degrees. The water was freezing.

"What you gawping at?" I said.

He blushed and I laughed. He can look all he wants, but I'm not going end up married to him and living in some dump with a bunch of kids.

When we were younger, we used to swim in our underwear. I wouldn't do that now.

***

Grade eight my last year of public school, and I want out of here so bad some days I think I'll run away. But 12 is too young to get a job. Everybody says I look at least 14—still too young.

How much better my life would be if we'd stayed in Crystal Beach and I'd gone to Ridgeway school. We could've run the popcorn stand summers, and Mom could've worked in a store the rest of the time. Or maybe we could've got our own hotdog stand along Erie Road. There were lots of them. Mom, me, and Gloria could've run it. There would've been lots of things we might've done, if it had stayed just the three of us.

Everything would've been so much better if Mom hadn't married Jimmy.

All the adventures we had. Camping at Lowbanks, after Gloria was asleep, me and Mom ran on the beach. Delivering papers when it was still dark. Big breakfasts at Hank's Diner. I always thought the nice man, who gave us donuts and Mom cigarettes, was Hank. Once, when I reminded Mom of our adventures, she said that wasn't Hank, just a guy she knew who worked there.

She looked at me funny and said: "Adventures — those were scary times, Sharon."

Even the scary times were exciting, like when we were sleeping in the station wagon and that man came. I woke up and Mom was holding a paring knife. She could handle anybody in those days. And little Pal, our guard dog, barked, and the man ran away. I bet the burglar thought he was a pit bull or a police dog.

Sometimes I pretend Papa shows up and takes me to live on Uncle Yves' farm. Then I remember the last time I saw Papa. The one I'd really like to visit is Grandma, but she's dead, and I'm stuck here.

I got a pair of Lee jeans at the United Church rummage sale. They're boys', with a front zipper, not like girls' pants. They fit really well in the bum. They're big in the waist, because boys don't go in at the waist like girls do.

Shirley said I wouldn't dare wear them to school, so I do.

Joanne Newman says: "You trying to look like a boy?"

I laugh in her face and wiggle my bum. Christ, she's stupid!

If she wants a boyfriend, she better smarten up. I heard her telling Betty she likes Frank Taylor. All the girls like Frank. He's the tallest boy in our class and is really good at baseball. He just moved here this fall. Lives in a new bungalow across from the park and his dad drives a white Cadillac convertible. They're rich.

I get sent home for wearing the jeans to school. I have to change my clothes and serve a detention after school. What do I care? I change into my tight red blouse and a skirt — a dumb full skirt. Wish I had one of those pencil skirts the high-school kids wear.

We have indoor recess because of the rain. Frank's busy doing the math homework when I lean over his desk. "Can you help me with problem 5? I just can't get it."

"Sure," he says, and grins up at me. "It's just percentage — multiply by a hundred."

I put my book on top of his. "Show me," I say, letting my long red hair brush against his shoulder.

That night he walks me home from school, even though I had a detention, and his house is the other way. At the corner of Cherry and Plum, he touches my hair, runs his fingers through it. "You got gorgeous hair. Is it true what they say about redheads?" He laughs.

I giggle and twirl around, make my red curls a peacock tail. He grabs my shoulders and kisses me. I taste cigarettes and something else. I think how jealous Joanne will be and kiss him back. Then I laugh and run home.

***

Gloria, Debbie, and Emily fell asleep long ago. I'm wide awake thinking about kissing. Guys smell different. Girls go with their boyfriends to the pine grove back of the school. I'll make sure Joanne sees us. I won't do anything stupid. Don't want to end up like Mom.

***

In January, Baby Judy gets really sick. Dr. Stewart says she has bronchitis. He gave her medicine, but it's not working.

Me and Mom make a tent in the kitchen by draping sheets over the cupboard and two stepladders from the garage. We have Mom's chair in the tent. We're up all night taking turns holding and rocking the poor sick baby.

She's bright red from fever and her wispy blond hair is slick with sweat. I'm holding her up against my shoulder and rubbing her back. She wheezes, snuffles, gasps. She's sweating so, my shirt's all wet, and I just changed her nightie a little while ago. Scary when she stiffens and makes no sound at all—just for a moment. A relief when she snuffles and coughs. No matter how much my arms ache, I mustn't lie her down flat or she might stop breathing.

Mom pushes fresh steaming pots of water into the tent, and puts the cooled pots back on the woodstove.

Jimmy might as well go to bed. All he does is wander from the living room into the kitchen, wailing: "Oh Jesus help us. Oh Jesus!"

He's gone again, but I can hear the radio on in the living room. My arms ache, and I have to pee, but I won't put Judy down.

***

Finally it must be morning because the kids have come down. Little Joey keeps trying to crawl under the sheets into the tent.

I hear Gloria praying. "Dear Jesus, please make Baby Judy get better. You love little children, please help us. Tell God not to turn her into an angel."

I can't see Gloria, but know she's sitting at the kitchen table, her hands together, eyes closed, and head bowed. Be more the point if she helped Mom with the water.

Baby Judy coughs and I can't get her to breathe. "Mom, Mom, help!"

"Give her here," Mom says. She thumps her real hard on the back.

Baby Judy coughs and wails.

Bringing the steaming pots from the stove, I nearly trip over Little Joey still trying to crawl into the tent. I smack his bottom and he yowls. All we need is a scalded two-year-old, along with the sick baby. I shove the box of corn flakes into Gloria's still-praying hands. "Take those kids back upstairs, right now!"

***

This has to be the longest day ever and before night comes I'm praying, too. God, make her well, and I'll stop complaining about Sunday school.

For supper I make hotdogs, and they all eat in the living room. I've just shooed them out of the kitchen with their hotdogs when Mom comes out of the tent carrying Judy. The baby's flat in her arms, not up against her shoulder. I'm so scared, I can't breathe.

Mom smiles. "We're through the worse of it. She's asleep and breathing normally. We'll keep her in the tent tonight though, just to be on the safe side."

* * *

After school, Frank Taylor invites me to the Quick Stop downtown where the high school kids hang out. I can tell Clinton's pretty mad. He was there when Frank asked me. Me and Clinton still go bike-riding and to his fort, but he can't be my boyfriend. Even though he's older, he's only in grade seven. Joanne and Betty would laugh. When me and Frank are getting on our bikes, Clinton rides by spraying gravel. Clinton needn't think he owns me.

Me and Frank ride by Joanne and Betty in their plaid skirts. I grin and wave.

We get caught kissing in the pine grove. Kissing is fun and harmless. Frank tried to touch my breasts. I giggled and wriggled away. I'll not let him try anything else. I'm not stupid. Ruby McTag, who was repeating grade eight, quit school. Her sister said she's helping her sick aunt in London, but Joanne told me her Mom said Ruby's at the Salvation Army home for unwed mothers.

Me and Frank get detentions for a week. I get another lecture about proper deportment for young ladies, and a letter to take home to my mother.

Mom and me have a talk.

"You're only twelve."

"Almost thirteen and all we did was kiss."

"Kissing can lead to other things."

"All we did was kiss."

"I don't want you to get into trouble."

"Don't worry, Mom, I'm too smart for that."

"Maybe. Or too smart for your own good."

I feel like saying, when are you going to smarten up? She's having another one.

One time when I was mad, I said: "I hate being poor."

She was giving Baby Judy her bottle and said: "All the beautiful babies—we're rich in children." And kissed the baby's head.

That's about the stupidest thing I ever heard.

POUND UP THE stairs before anybody else can beat me to the bathroom. Thank God, for once it's empty. I hook the door and run a quick bath. No warm water—never is any after we've done the wash. I strip off my sweat-soaked shirt and shorts, undo the safety pin and step out of my panties. The elastic's already gone and I only bought them last summer.

I reach under the claw-footed tub and retrieve my Breck shampoo. Had enough trouble getting it, I'm not sharing with Gloria.

I kneel in the tub and stick my head under the tap. It's a hell of a thing to get the tangles out of my curly hair. I'll never cut it though. I giggle. Boys like it. Not just boys—I've seen men turn, take a second look at my red hair as I walk by. In the snapshot of Mom at 16, she had the hair. Now, her hair is lank and dead-looking. I won't make her mistakes.

Oh, shit, somebody's already at the door. "Hold your horses."

"Hafta pee."

"Emily, go outside and pee."

"Hafta poop, too."

"Okay, okay, give me a moment, would ya?" I soap armpits and crotch, and rinse off.

"Hafta go." Emily bangs the door and wails.

I stash my shampoo back in its hiding place, grab a towel, and wrapping up, open the door.

Emily rushes to the toilet.

I gather up my clothes. "Remember to flush."

I scowl upon entering our room. Gloria's underpants are on the floor and her scrunched-up blanket exposes her old mattress. Our mattresses came with our beds from an auction sale. The blankets may be crooked on Debbie and Emily's cots, but they've made an effort. Skinflint Jimmy should buy them proper beds. Those old army

cots from the attic, made of wood and canvas, tip over real easy. At least me and Gloria have beds.

And to think Mom wondered why I didn't want to have a sleepover for my birthday.

"You're going to be thirteen. A special time, becoming a teenager."

"Nah, be too crowded."

"You wouldn't have to sleep upstairs—you could use the living room."

"I don't want a party." I don't say, yeah, use the living room. What, sleep on the floor or even worse haul our old mattresses down? What's more we'd listen to Uncle Joey's moans and roars all night. Or, even worse, he'd wander through in his long johns on his way to the toilet.

I pull the cardboard box from under my bed and root around for clean underwear, my faded maroon shorts, my daisy blouse and the Evening in Paris perfume Mom gave me for my birthday. I dab on a little and get dressed. Remove three dolls and a stuffed dog from the dresser so I can look in the mirror. I need a bra.

If only I could get a proper job. Next year, for sure. This summer I'll have to be content with Cy's dollar a day again. I could buy a bra at Stedmans—they only cost two dollars—but Mom's always short for groceries. If it wasn't for that eagle-eyed clerk I'd have one by now. Stedmans isn't a bit like Poole's Drugs. Old Mrs. Poole wouldn't notice if I walked off with the cash register. She didn't miss my Breck shampoo. I undo the last three buttons on my blouse, twist it into two tails and tie it tightly under my breasts. That's better. These last-year shorts aren't bad—tight in the bum—good.

I brush my hair and fasten it into a high ponytail. Stash my brush in the corrugated box and push it back under my bed.

I peek in the babies' room. The new baby, Charlie, named for Jimmy's pa, is fast asleep—won't need a bottle till three. Jimmy has two sons now. That better be enough.

Mom's asleep on the couch. Poor Mom. At least the kids helped with the wash, though Debbie, who's only four is more help than Gloria, who's always off in la la land. Debbie has to stand on a chair to reach the clothesline.

The sink is piled high with dishes. The black and white cat and her last year's kitten are licking them. I'll clean things up tonight.

Debbie and Emily have Judy in their doll carriage and are pushing her up and down the rutted drive. Year-old-Judy waves her arms and giggles.

"Youse guys look after her, eh?"

"Yeah," Debbie says. "When ya coming back?"

"At three to feed the baby. Where's Little Joey?"

"In his fort," Debbie says.

I see him peeking out of the doorless icebox.

"Bring us something," Emily says.

"Be good. C'mon, Gloria, get off the swing."

"What's the rush," Gloria says, sauntering over.

"The park opened an hour ago." I start down Plum at a fast walk. Gloria trails behind.

Knowing without looking that she's chewing her hair, I stop and offer an elastic. "Here, let me fasten it up in a ponytail. You won't be so hot."

***

I hold Prince's bridle and, ignoring the tourist brat on his back, trudge around the dusty track. This spoiled brat in new clothes sticky with ice cream got a smear on my blouse when I lifted her up on the pony. Ahead of me Gretchen's leading Misty and chatting to the kid riding him.

Gretchen went to Grenville Public so I don't know much about her. Why, when she owns her own pony, does she hang around here? A purebred Welsh Cob, no less. Gretchen told everybody that. The Thortons must have lots of money. So why work, all day, every day but Sundays? Cy's paying her 14 dollars a week, twice what I'm making. Of course, she's here more than I am. Maybe he's counting the pony as a worker, too. Still, she doesn't need the money.

Donna's leading Prince. She better keep a good grip on his bridle, or he'll nip her leg. She waves and I wave back. She moved to Grenville

from Hamilton in June. They're rich, too. Her dad built all the new houses on Oak Road. She's not a bit stuck-up, not like Gretchen.

When we're just standing around waiting for more customers, Donna invites me to her house for supper.

"Sure, okay," I say.

"My turn to cook. Can't get out of it 'cause Brenda's going on a sleepover. Let's leave at five. Mom and Dad get home at six."

I tell Gloria to tell Mom where I've gone, and we ride double on her bike, a brand new C.C.M.

Her house is grand: big, two storey, stone on the first storey and painted blue above. The front porch is a semi-circle of cement with black iron railings, empty except for gigantic pots of red geraniums. This is the kind of porch I'll have one day.

We head right in the front door. There's a tiled entryway where we kick off our shoes and then a great expanse of blue carpeting. I've never been in a living room this big. There are two huge picture windows with white sheer curtains and patterned drapes with all different shapes in blues, greens, and black on a white background.

"About time you're home," a chubby girl in the red polka-dot shorts says. "I'm supposed to be at Roseanne's by now."

"Don't get your tail in a knot. I'm here now, and this is my friend Sharon."

"Hi, Sharon. I'm only grumpy 'cause she's always late. The kids are in the backyard. Tell Mom I'll be home right after breakfast. I'm off. Nice to meet you, Sharon."

"That was Brenda," Donna says, laughing. "She's a year younger than me."

"Just like me and Gloria."

"C'mon out in the kitchen. We'll rustle up some grub."

The kitchen, as big as the living room, has a black and white checkerboard tiled floor and spotless white cupboards with red Arborite counters—enough for ten kitchens. Everything smells so clean and new. I think of our rusty sink and drain board, the rickety work table beside it, and the smell—old food and diapers.

We're just setting the table when her dad gets home.

"How's the cook?" He gives Donna a hug. He's really handsome with curly brown hair just so and his ears don't stick out. He's wearing a dark blue suit. "And who's this pretty girl?"

Donna introduces me, and he shakes my hand. He smells of aftershave like our minister.

Her mom arrives wearing a white pencil skirt with a silk looking lilac blouse and a white jacket with shoulder pads. I can tell because those jackets make shoulders look square-ish. Her mother works, too — sells real estate.

They're laughing as they go upstairs together.

"Supper's ready," Donna yells up the stairs.

When her parents come down, they've both changed into Bermuda shorts.

We eat supper in what Donna calls the breakfast nook. It's a glassed-in part of the kitchen, with a white table and chairs, the seats upholstered in red. Off the living room is a dining room with a dark wood table and eight matching chairs.

Funny thing is, supper's nothing special. Donna boiled up some hotdogs and opened four tins of canned spaghetti. But the rolls are nice and fresh, not like the day-old ones we buy. And there's lots of salad stuff and bottles of different kinds of dressings. At home we just have plain lettuce and tomatoes, whatever the garden produces. Dessert is wonderful — three kinds of ice cream, and her mother brought chocolate éclairs from the bakery. I've never had one before. Delicious!

Her father's funny. "What's the best way to get rid of unwanted insects?"

"I know! I know!" Stevie, one of the little brothers, yells.

"You tell them to bug off," Tommy says.

"Not fair. I knew," Stevie whines.

"Okay, let your little brother get this one," their dad says. "What did one bug say to the other?"

"I know," Stevie shouts. "What rock did you crawl out from under?"

Both little brothers came to the table wearing nothing but grubby shorts. I like all of Donna's family. Too bad I didn't get to meet her big brother Ted.

*L*AUNDRY, LAUNDRY, LAUNDRY, I haul the basket of diapers to the line. Sun's hot already—boy, I wish I was at the beach. No such luck.

That god damn Aunt Jean! For years I've been wishing for out of town visitors. I blame it on those stupid compositions that come as faithfully every fall as Gloria's bronchitis—*What did you do on you summer holidays?*

Other kids wrote about grandparents, aunts, and cousins. I always got a B and comments like *your composition should be longer—try for more interesting details.* Yeah, sure. What? Hanging up the wash?

The first day of school in grade eight I came home with that B and wrote in my diary. Not a real diary, just a scribbler without a cover I keep hidden under my mattress:

> *Me and my sister Gloria took the train to Buffalo, that's in the United States, to visit our grandmother. Grandma sent the tickets as an end of school present. She took us shopping to Grants, this really great department store, and let us pick out whatever we wanted. I got Levis blue jeans, and my sister got a doll. Grandma took us across the Peace Bridge to Crystal Beach, and we went on all the rides. The roller coaster is my favourite. When I was little and we lived here, my mom worked on the roller coaster, part of the painting crew.*
>
> *After a week at Grandma's we got back on the train and stayed on overnight and all the next day. We had to change trains a couple of times before arriving in Rouyn-Noranda. That's in Quebec.*
>
> *Maurice, my papa, met us there and took us to our uncle's farm way out in the bush. We brought presents from Grants*

for all our cousins. We swam in the river and rode their horses.
Our uncle didn't mind even though the horses were supposed
to be hauling logs out of the bush.

My summer sure was a lot of fun.

Other kids wrote compositions like that—visits to grandparents, aunts and uncles.

I wished for more relatives, and damn it, this summer I'm getting my wish. Aunt Jean and her snotty daughter, Barbara.

I grind my teeth and hang another diaper on the line. Every last diaper was in the wash. Mom tore up an old sheet to have something to put on the babies this morning. The relatives are coming, and I sure as hell won't write a composition about it. If I did, I'd have to call it "The Most Embarrassing Summer of My Life."

Mom got a letter from Aunt Jean, and I asked her: "How do they know where we live?"

"From Grandma's sister in Florida."

"Why are they coming now?"

"Here, read it for yourself," she said.

Dear Sis,

You must've been desperate. I'm sorry I didn't help you.

John wouldn't allow me to have you stay with us. I had to beg to have you that Christmas.

John, who I now just refer to as the Bastard, said you were an embarrassment.

All the time I was trying to be Mrs. Perfection, the Bastard was carrying on with his secretary—what a cliché!

Now that I've suffered the same fate as you, I know what you were going through. To make a long story short, two years ago we got a divorce.

I'm lonely, little sister. It's not right for us to be on bad terms. I haven't seen you in nearly seven years.

*I'd like to visit, let Barbara get to know Sharon and Gloria
again. Would the first week in August be convenient?*

*Your sad and sorry sister,
Jean*

She knows what we went through? Has she ever lived in a car? She
said we killed Grandma. And that snotty Barbara. Why should I want
to see her?

Mom comes out of the cellar with another basket of wet clothes.
"Sharon, I've been thinking, we should paint the kitchen floor."

"You just had a baby. You've got to tell them, they can't come.
There's nowhere for them to sleep."

"We'll make do."

"You want them to come?"

"She's my big sister."

"She took Grandma's rug."

"She had as much right to it as I did."

"She didn't need it."

"You don't understand. When your mother dies, you want something to remember her by."

"Gloria loved that rug. Remember how she used to lie on it and
make the fringe all nice and straight, and how she cried when Aunt
Jean stole it?"

"She didn't steal it, and anyway, it would've got lost in one of our
moves. I bet Jean still has it."

"Yeah, bet she has."

Baby Charlie is two weeks old, and Mom looks like shit—thinner
than ever but with a sagging belly. Her thick red hair, that long ago I
loved to brush is fading, not grey, just dull and limp. Does Aunt Jean
even know Mom married Jimmy, and they have five more kids? Mom
falls asleep drinking her tea. I have to grab the cup before it falls.

***

Mom paints the worn linoleum blue. Says she'll stipple it in black. Like she thinks that'll make it look better?

By noon the paint's still wet so she puts Judy and Baby Charlie down for their naps, but makes us take the others with us to the pony track. She knows me and Gloria are supposed to be working. I tell Debbie: "You watch Emily and Little Joey."

There's a company picnic, and the pony track's really busy. Me and Gloria lead ponies all afternoon. Next summer I'll be 14 and can get a real job. My boss, Cy, is a nice guy though—doesn't complain the little kids are in the way, lets them have pony rides and gives them dimes for ice-creams.

The floor's still sticky at suppertime so Mom sends Gloria to the store for bread and peanut butter, and we have supper on the front porch. Along with their peanut butter sandwiches, Jimmy and Uncle Jocy share a bottle of beer from the back shed.

Mom made Jimmy fix all the leaky taps and replace the cracked toilet seat. There was a perfectly good one in the garage. He brings stuff home from his remodelling jobs. We've used that old cracked one ever since I moved here when I was eight. Why do they only fix things up when Aunt Jean's coming?

The last thing us kids do is clean all the junk off the front porch. All toys go in the backyard, newspapers and magazines to the cellar, and chairs with rungs missing to Jimmy's garage. I cover an orange crate with this blue flowered tablecloth Mom never uses.

She comes out to see how we're doing with the porch and discovers a hen on one of the chairs. She yells at Jimmy, and he and Uncle Joey spend the evening mending the chicken-yard fence.

* * *

Today's the day.

Mom said: "You know, Jean said she was in a bad way. She may think our place looks pretty good after all she's been through."

I have to admit it looks okay. Emily picked some daisies for my orange-crate table.

The grape Kool-Aid is ready. Debbie helped. "One pack powder, cup of sugar, and Mom's big jar of water," she proudly told me. I ran next door to Mrs. Reubel and borrowed ice cubes as our fridge can't make any. They're wrapped in thick newspapers in the fridge. We made mock chicken and baloney sandwiches. Jimmy got paid and gave Mom some money, fifteen dollars. "You need more than that," I told her and she got mad.

"Most of the money has to go for the taxes. We got behind when he couldn't work. Your daddy's a responsible man."

"He's not my daddy."

"He is now. And I don't know why you're so grouchy. You should have some pity for Aunt Jean and Barbara. A marriage breakup is tough."

We've scrubbed the kids, washed everybody's hair, and put them all in clean clothes. Judy's in a pink dress with ruffly panties that hide her diaper. The outfit's faded, but she looks cute. Baby Charlie's asleep in the buggy. Gloria and the little kids are sitting in a row on the front steps when Aunt Jean pulls up in a white Chevy convertible with sky-blue seats and New York license plates.

I thought she'd be poor now. She looks exactly as I remember her—sleek and blonde. Barbara's a younger version of her mother. They slip off silk scarves to reveal perfect pageboys. Both wear white bum-hugging pants. Aunt Jean's halter-top is mauve, Barbara's pink polka-dot.

Aunt Jean and Mom hug, and I want to cry or hit somebody. Aunt Jean is seven years older, and Mom in her Eaton's catalogue house-dress looks old enough to be her mother.

***

Me and Mom are getting ready for bed. The little kids already asleep. Jimmy's sleeping in the babies' room. I helped clean up the kitchen —bet there're no dirty dishes in Aunt Jean's kitchen. Mom wants to sleep on the old feather tick on our floor, but I tell her: "You're not sleeping on the floor while Aunt Jean sleeps in your bed."

"Sharon, I don't mind."

"I mind. You sleep in my bed." I lie down on the lumpy feather tick Jimmy hauled down from the attic and pull the sheet over me. "My mom's not sleeping on the floor."

* * *

When I come down the next morning, carrying Baby Charlie, Old Cat's in the sink, even though me and Mom cleaned everything up last night. Bloody hopeless! My back's sore—that feather tick must be a hundred years old. Jimmy's mother made it from dead chickens' feathers.

* * *

Mom and Aunt Jean talk and talk, but hush up when I enter the room. Sometimes Aunt Jean's crying and Mom is holding her hand or hugging her. I'd like to smack Aunt Jean. What the hell has she got to cry about?

* * *

The easiest thing to do with Barbara would be to ignore her. Mom won't allow that. "She's your cousin and only a year older. She'll like the same things as you do."

We're on our way to the pony track.

"Your Uncle Joey tried to give me a lint-covered toffee from his pocket, and when I said no, he laughed that crazy laugh. What's the matter with him, anyway?"

"He got injured in the war."

"My mother said he should be in an institution."

I grind my teeth. Hope you sit in horse shit.

At the pony track she stands around in her spotless white shorts with her nose in the air and tells everybody about the Saddle and Bridle Club where she rides in Buffalo. I feel stupid when Cy pays me and Gloria a dollar each.

On the way home she says: "He's a terrible cheapskate."

A dollar's nothing to her. I could knock her down and rub dirt into her perfect blond hair and white shorts. I don't though.

* * *

The next day we go to the beach.

I spread out our old quilt in a good spot near the water. The little kids run right in. Barbara's slipping off her beach-cover-up as she calls it—a shortie housecoat made out of the same cutesy pink gingham as her two-piece bathing suit. Looks dumb, if you ask me.

Gloria sits in the shallow water and sifts sand through her fingers.

I line up the little kids. "Now, nobody goes past their bum, got it?" They all nod.

"Bring us sumthin," Debbie says.

"Maybe. Be good. Gloria, you watch them real close, eh?"

"Okay," she says.

Sometimes I'm ashamed how easy she is to boss around. They're good kids and she'll watch them.

"C'mon," I say to Barbara. "We'll swim out to the raft. You can swim that far, can't you?" I point to where the guys are.

"Of course. We have a pool."

Bully for you, I think, don't say. She covers her hair with this ugly rubber cap.

I pull off my shorts and run in the lake before she can comment on my suit so old it always looks dirty. I swim like mad.

* * *

We're on the raft, fooling around, pushing each other off. Barbara just stands there with that snotty look. Nobody pushes her. Doesn't she know how dumb she looks in that pink rubber cap?

I've pushed every boy off except for Clinton. He's trying to get me off, but I'm holding my ground by tickling little jabs to his belly. He's laughing his head off. He grabs my shoulders. I surprise him and leap on him, and wrap my legs tight around his waist. I whip my long red ponytail across his face. His breath changes and I feel his thing stiffen. Before he knows what's happening, I leap away and give him a good push. Down he goes with a splash. I push Barbara off just for the hell of it.

I do my victory dance and feel so good, like I could push the whole damn world off.

They're all climbing back on, but before they can get me, I jump off and swim. Guess what? They all follow. Clinton's the best swimmer, though his cut-off jeans must slow him down.

On shore I undo my ponytail and shake out my red curls.

Clinton's beside me. "I just got paid," he says. "Why don't us go to the Snack Hut? I'll treat you guys."

Me and Clinton lead the way down the hot sand beach. He buys us all Cokes, and I sit on the picnic table to drink mine. Clinton leans against the table. I smile at him. "Thanks for the Coke."

He blushes. "Anytime."

"What, you suddenly a rich guy?"

"Nah, but I'm working at my uncle's garage this summer."

Barbara, still wearing that stupid cap, is just standing there sipping her Coke and, believe it or not, looking awkward.

Clinton touches my thigh. "Hey, want a hamburger?"

"Nah, but you could get Fudgsicles for the little kids. I left my sister down the beach, babysitting."

"Sure, how many?"

"Four."

"Be right back."

When he returns and hands me the bag, I jump down, give him a quick peck on the cheek and saunter off. "Thanks, gotta go," I call back over my shoulder. I feel his eyes following me. Who cares about a faded bathing suit? I smile.

"Hey, wait up." Barbara's running after me, more sorta lumbering, like she doesn't know how to run.

***

Aunt Jean's been shopping, got us southern-fried chicken from the restaurant out on the highway. She fixes drinks for the grownups. "Gin and tonics as a little treat," she says. She cuts a slice of lemon for each glass. Hoity-toity bitch! She bought the glasses, too, and a big bag

of ice cubes. I bet she and Barbara had a good laugh over our grape Kool-Aid with borrowed ice cubes. I could smack the pair of them.

We have corn and new potatoes from our garden. Swimming makes me so hungry I forget about being mad. Thinking about Clinton, I grin and chew on a drumstick.

"Barbara, didn't you wear your swim cap?" asks Aunt Jean.

"Yes, Mother, I did."

"Your hair's a mess — the cap must've leaked. Your set's ruined."

Barbara's face turns red.

"Blond hair has to be taken care of," Aunt Jean tells Mom. "When she was little, her hair was a perfect blonde. Now the hairdresser has to touch it up every couple of weeks. And it's so fine ..."

"Mother!"

"What's the matter, dear? I'm just talking to your aunt."

Barbara looks down at her plate. She hasn't even touched her chicken. For a moment I feel sorry for her. Only for a moment though — can't feel too sorry for someone who arrives in a white convertible with sky-blue seats.

***

At first, after Aunt Jean and Barbara leave, everybody tries to keep things fixed up. Mom says she really enjoyed Jean's visit and she's so happy they're friends again. I'm glad about that.

As the days go by, the doll carriage and dolls reappear on the porch. The day I find the broody hen nested down with seven eggs in the orange crate, I know life has returned to normal. I would rather have a broody hen on the porch than Aunt Jean and Barbara. I'd like to have their money, but I wouldn't want to be Barbara. The tablecloth's still on the crate, giving the hen some privacy. Seven eggs — she's been here a while.

After dark so the hen won't make a fuss, I carry the crate to the chicken house, and replace the tablecloth with a burlap sack. Two weeks later the hen hatches out seven perfect chicks. Amazing. Usually a couple of eggs are duds.

THE FIRST DAY of high school I walk by myself. Shirley and Norma are in grade eight. They didn't get put ahead when me, Joanne, and Betty did. I hoped Donna would invite me to walk with her. I bet she's with stuck-up Gretchen Thorton. I don't care. Mom gave me her yellow dress she bought in Buffalo years ago. She had it packed away in tissue paper. We shortened it on Jimmy's mother's treadle machine. I used my own money to buy a bra and white sandals—no more ugly Oxfords. Next summer I'll get a real job and all new clothes. I like the yellow dress. As Mom says, us red heads look good in yellow. She used to be so pretty. She's about the same age as Doris Day. Doris Day was really great in *Calamity Jane*. I saw it at the drive-in with Donna's family. I found out from a movie magazine that she's actually two years older than Mom.

***

I love home economics. I've already made a blouse. I went fabric shopping to London with Donna and her mom. Jimmy actually gave me three dollars for sewing supplies 'cause it was for school. My blouse is pale blue cotton.

I was the first one in our Home Ec class to start on a skirt. I thought I'd have to wait, but Mrs. Laurence gave me a piece of blue plaid somebody from last year left behind. And I didn't have to buy a pattern 'cause she has a supply to choose from, if we don't have one.

We also do cooking. It's boring. I've been cooking for years. A lot of the girls don't even know how to make scrambled eggs.

***

I'm dating Billy Sider. He's in grade 11 and has lots of spending money —bought me the saddle shoes I admired in Baiden's window. His par-

ents own the Shady Glen restaurant down by the lake. Billy says they're really busy in the summer while the tourists are in town. They stay open year round, but just serve sandwiches and hamburgs in the winter. He says he'll get me a waitressing job next summer. They hire a couple of schoolgirls for the tourist season.

I haven't seen Clinton much. High school girls don't hang out with boys still in public school. Frank Taylor's in my class, but I like older boys. They kiss better.

I lucked out. Donna and I are in the same home room and Gretchen isn't. But Donna still spends most of her time at the Thortons' house. I've not been invited to their place. In the summer I invited Gretchen over to see Baby Charlie, but she never invited me back. I bet she thought our place was dirty because the next day at the pony track she apologized for not washing her hands before feeding the baby. Asked me if he'd got sick. She was always worrying about germs. Thinks you can get lockjaw from not washing your hands. I had fun teasing her — "Lockjaw germs are sneaking up on ya." She shouldn't act so high and mighty even if the Thortons are rich. Her brother's a cripple. He's blind and walks jiggsie-jagged. I saw him on the street once.

***

I finished my skirt and complained to Mom I needed more fabric. She said: "Why don't you take apart that Black Watch tartan one I got at the rummage sale? It's way too big. I'll never wear it."

"I can't take old stuff to school."

"Cut it out at home."

I ripped it apart, washed it by hand in cold water because wool shrinks if you don't, and Mom showed me how to use a wet cloth and the iron to steam the creases out.

Now I have a pencil slim skirt that looks as good as the ones they sell at the Wool Shop.

I've started going to rummage sales with Mom. Pretend I'm picking things out for her. I got a royal blue velvet housecoat that would fit somebody two hundred pounds. I made a sheath dress to wear to the Christmas dance.

Me and Billy go out Friday and Saturday nights. I told him I wasn't allowed out weeknights. Mom hasn't actually made any rules, but two nights a week is plenty of Billy.

Mom says: "I want you to be free. Not chained by a hundred rules like I was. I trust you to be sensible. Don't be stupid and quit school like I did."

Billy's okay, but I'm not in love with him or anything.

Mrs. Laurence, in the family-living part of our class, says it's the girl's job to make the boy behave. They have impulses they can't help. We all giggled.

I can control Billy. We neck, fool around a bit, then I make him stop. Keep his hands outside my clothes. Sorta a fun game. After, when I get home if I can't sleep, just rub myself till the sparks fly.

I danced with Jimmy Waddell at the Christmas dance. Jimmy's in grade eleven and plays football. His brother, Rick, who's graduated now, was a great football player. His picture hangs in the front foyer.

Billy didn't like me dancing with Jimmy, but what could he do? I thought Jimmy might ask me out, but he didn't. Donna said he found out I was in grade nine. Billy doesn't care I'm in grade nine.

***

I should've known good things don't last. I lie in bed and stare at the peeling wallpaper—vines and baskets expose fancy ladies and faded roses. Years ago, me and Mom painted the wallpaper, but the paint peeled in places and made the paper fall off. Walls creak and shift against the slanting floors, branches scrape the window, adhesive tape peeling off the cracks. I would've fixed it, but the tape's all gone. Little Joey's fault. Kids, they're into everything. "Space gun," he said. Had a stick all taped up to the empty metal spool.

The wind and the rain pound the glass. If it breaks, we could freeze to death. February—how I hate winter, trying to find enough mitts and boots to go around.

Mom's never gone to the hospital before except to have the babies. We couldn't wake her up and there was blood dripping down her legs and on her nightie. Can't just be another miscarriage. Why couldn't we wake her up? Jimmy bawling and crying: "Oh Jesus, help us." Had the fool forgotten that's what telephones are for? I called the ambulance. Jimmy, still begging Jesus, went with Mom.

Don't die, Mom, don't die.

The old shit should leave her alone. Aren't seven kids enough? Last summer—"Why don't you guys use rubbers?" Mom slapped my face and I ran out of the house. Went to the pony track and led ponies all afternoon. When Cy paid me my dollar, I didn't take it to Mom—bought two hot dogs and an ice cream and threw up on the way home.

I was making supper for the kids—macaroni and ketchup, what a supper, and I could've bought wieners and rolls at the Red and White instead of gobbling down overpriced hot dogs at the park.

Mom looked up from giving Charlie his bottle and said: "I'm sorry I slapped you."

"No big deal."

"Jimmy and I want a big family. I want the kind of life he knew as a little boy. Didn't matter they were hard up—Jimmy worked with his dad in the blacksmith shop, and the boys all helped their mother in the house and with poor little Annie. That's it. Sharon, she wasn't poor little Annie. The boys doted on her, and took her with them on hikes and trips to the beach. All my dad cared about was us doing well in school. If you got 96 he'd want to know where you'd lost the four marks. Mind you, it was Jean getting the 90s. I, as he said, was lazy. We never had any fun." She bent down and kissed the baby's head. When she looked up, there were tears in her eyes.

"Sharon, you're too young to know about condoms. You're just a kid. Don't be in such a hurry to grow up."

"I've had enough of being a kid."

"Oh, Sharon, I don't want you to end up like me, pregnant at sixteen."

"I'm too smart for that."

"When I was your age, I thought I was pretty smart, too."

***

Oh, Mom, don't die. I'd have to quit school and look after the kids. And Jimmy—if the stupid bugger would just find a steady job. For a while he's working, then his back acts up, and he lies on the couch all day, begging for tea. And the people he's doing the job for keep phoning. Sometimes I wish we'd never got the phone in. We tell them he's sick. Often, they hire somebody else. When he isn't losing a job, Uncle Joey's making sure there isn't much profit. He pushed the scaffolding through the picture window of a house they were stuccoing. They had to pay for the window. They're both pathetic. But they don't hit people. And they're not assholes like Shirley's dad—climbing into her bed. I've told her to come here when he's after her, but if she does, he claims she's with some boy and beats her up. Jimmy's not so bad, just bloody useless.

If Mom dies …

If I stay in school till I'm 16, I can get a job in an office. Can already type 40 words a minute. I'll buy nice clothes and marry a rich guy, get the hell out of Grenville. Billy showed me the rubber he keeps in his wallet. I told him to go to hell. Then said: "Sorry, but I'm not taking chances." We lay down on the back seat and I let him rub up against me till he was done. I'm saving myself for the rich guy. Mom says: "You don't buy the cow if the milk's free."

Mom, don't die. I'm so selfish. I don't care. Oh no, the baby's crying. I better get him before he wakes everybody. Had to water the milk and there's no bottle for Judy. She's nearly two—she's gotta stop crying for bottles. And she wants milk, can't fool her with sugar water.

I get out of bed and pull on my sweater. I'm already dressed—jeans and Jimmy's torn flannel shirt, and work socks with holes in both heels and toes. My pyjamas are in the rag bag. The icy linoleum makes my feet hurt with every step I take. Someday, I'll have wall-to-wall like in Donna's house. I lift the squalling baby from the rusty buggy and carry him down the stairs, avoiding a pile of laundry, a kid's rubber boot, and Judy's one-eared rabbit. Heat the bottle in a saucepan on the stove. Maybe warm, even watery milk'll be soothing. Turn on the oven and pull over Mom's rocker, push off the sleeping cat, and sit with my feet up on the oven door. Wiggle my toes—ah, that feels good. Jimmy would whine I'm wasting electricity.

Baby Charlie waves his skinny arms and legs and cries so hard he can't latch onto the nipple. Ten months old—shouldn't be so skinny. I pull the ragged quilt off the back of Mom's chair and wrap us both up. I again offer the bottle. He latches on. Must've been too cold to suck.

"Not so fast. Too soon gone." I cuddle him tight. "You're a warm bundle, I'll say that for ya."

***

Mom's taking a long time to get better. She had a miscarriage, but she also had pneumonia. The pneumonia would clear up and then come back. Finally it's gone. She still has to rest a lot. I stayed home from school most of February and all of March. I tried to keep my schoolwork up, but I was busy with meals, laundry, and the kids. When I had them all in bed, I'd spread my books out. All too often fall sleep with my head on my desk. My marks are pretty bad. Still, there are two months before our final exams.

I feel sorry for Mom. Please God, don't let there be any more babies. Not God's fault.

Maybe Jimmy'll fall off a roof.

THINGS ARE LOOKING up in our family. Mom's all better, and I got a B average on the finals. At least I didn't fail anything.

Billy comes through on his promise and gets me a summer job at the Shady Glen. My 14th birthday is next week, but Billy's dad said I could pass for 18 real easily. He said I better watch out and laughed. I didn't like that laugh. I thought about what Mrs. Laurence said and figure he won't be a problem. He makes a pass, I'll tell Billy and Mrs. Sider. Actually, I won't tell, I'll just make a joke about it. He'll get the hint. Joking with guys is the way to handle them.

I love my uniform—dark green nylon with a flared skirt and a little half-apron trimmed in white. I do look older, like a real waitress on a TV show. Not a bit like Mrs. Taylor at the Quick Stop in her regular dowdy clothes.

***

I'm rich. Mr. Sider pays me 15 dollars a week. And after a couple of weeks, I'm more than doubling that with my tips. I learn quickly. At first, I mixed up orders, but not anymore. The other waitress, Ellen, has been here three summers. She doesn't like me. She's a slow-moving, chubby girl and thinks it'd be more fair if we shared our tips. She's caught on I'm earning more than she is. If she'd smile once in a while.

I give Mom 10 dollars each week, and I still have lots for myself. With my first pay I bought a mauve nylon bra and panty set, red pedal pushers, a white eyelet midriff blouse and white sandals with straps that wrap around my ankles. The next week I bought Gloria, Debbie and Emily new sneakers. Debbie got pink and Gloria and Emily the red ones. No more worn out sneakers with the toes cut out.

I have my own bank account. I love opening my pay envelope

and counting out the bills. Then I add up all my tips for the week. I make a deposit each week towards my school clothes.

I'm learning to drive. I got my beginner's permit and Billy's teaching me. Just once Mom let me drive. She was going to get groceries. She usually walks. Jimmy had been on the couch for two days.

When we got back, I handed out the Fudgsicles I bought everybody. I was telling Gloria about driving up to Blackstone Point when Jimmy says: "What you let her do that for? That clutch goes. A lotta money for a new one."

He thinks it's his car. Grandma gave it to Mom. I loved driving up to the point and buying Mom a big cone. When we were sitting on stools at the red Arborite counter, I remembered Buffalo and Hank's diner.

Even with my tenner Mom's often short for groceries and stuff. That's the same amount as skin-flint Jimmy gives her. I don't know how he expects her to feed seven kids on 10 dollars a week. If she says anything, he'll say: "Youse kids get weedin the garden, and your ma won't be short."

He spades up the garden each spring, and we all plant, but then he figures weeding is our job. His mother always looked after the garden.

Mom said. "But she didn't have seven children."

"Youse kids help ya ma more."

The garden starts off good, but by July nobody's remembering to water, and the weeds take over.

If Mom starts yelling, Jimmy'll give her more money, if he has it. But half the time he's not working 'cause of his back. He also gets just about as many colds as Gloria.

Jimmy likes to think he's in charge. Like last year before school started he took us to Baiden's Shoes and bought new shoes for all of us. Even the babies. Gloria and I needed shoes a lot more than the little ones. Mom could've used some of that money for her Eaton's catalogue underwear and socks order.

When I complained, she said: "You've got to humour a man."

I figure that's something like what Mrs. Laurence was talking about. Mom took the two pairs of baby shoes back and got a credit. We've got lots of old baby shoes.

***

Just two weeks before school starts, Clinton comes into the restaurant. I haven't seen him in ages. Ellen, the other waitress, says: "There's a hunk."

"That's just Clinton McClary." I say that, but he does look different. Is it he's taller, more muscular? He always slouched. One thing definitely has changed—he's wearing a clean white t-shirt.

I bring him a Coke.

"Hi, Sharon. Long time no see. How ya doin?"

"Good."

"Got myself a car. When ya get off, you wanna go for a drive?"

"I don't finish till nine."

"I'll be out front."

"Okay. I better get back to work."

"Yep, see ya at nine."

He leaves without finishing his Coke.

How'd he get a car? I don't want to go out with Clinton McClary. It's not that I care what Billy thinks. I can handle him. He gets a little possessive at times and I let him know he doesn't own me. I went out with a boy from London, just here for a holiday with his folks. He took me to the dance hall at Blackstone Point. He's 18, going into grade 13. When he found out my real age, he didn't ask me out again. Guys think I'm a lot older.

When I leave the restaurant, Clinton's waiting for me. The car is a stubby '49 Ford—pale blue with one maroon door and one black one. "She's had a lot of body work," he tells me. "Was in a bad accident." His uncle paid 35 dollars for it and let Clinton repair it in his spare time. When he has the money, he'll get it painted.

"Didn't know you were old enough to get your license."

"Turned 16, a month ago."

And just finished grade eight, I think, don't say.

"Runs good, eh? A '49 Ford's a good car—V8 engine," he says.

What I notice is how clean it is. Looks like he polished the dashboard.

"How about us go for ice cream up at Blackstone Point?" he says.

"Sure, it's a hot night."

We get our ice cream and drive on up the lake road. I don't know why, but I feel sorta awkward with him, like he was this kid I used to know, and now he's a man.

It's mainly farms along here, and the road turns away from the shore. Clinton takes a dirt side road that leads down to the beach. It's the back of somebody's farm.

"I didn't know there was a beach along here."

"Yep, found 'er years back," he says.

"It's a long way from Grenville."

"Twenty-one miles."

"Must've taken a while."

"Yep, sometimes rode me old bike all day."

"I loved bike-riding, too. You should've taken me with you."

He grins. "Am now." And parks the car. He takes a red-plaid blanket from the back seat and spreads it on the sand.

We sit down. Feels good—my legs always ache after working a ten-hour shift. I kick off my sandals. It's a sweltering night, and I'm still in my nylon waitress uniform. "So how are things?" I ask him.

"Good, real good. In the spring, Pa left. Never got to beat the shit out of 'im—too bad. How's life treating ya?"

"Fine. I like working at the restaurant. It's fun and finally have money for nice clothes. It's so damn hot. Wish I had my bathing suit."

"Would've been a good idea."

"Remember, Clinton, when we were kids, we used to swim in our underwear, down by your fort."

"I remember." Clinton smiles. "Guess us too old for that now."

"What the hell? I'm boiling in this dress. I'm going in." I strip off my uniform, and race into the water. I'm not really indecent as I'm wearing a white cotton bra and panties. Cotton's cooler all day to work in than nylon. For a moment I wish I was in the mauve nylon bra and panty set I bought in London. That is a stupid thought and I drop into the water and start swimming. Lake Erie's shallow way, way out.

I look back to shore and Clinton still in his jeans, though he's taken off his shirt, wades into the lake.

Now he's swimming. I swim hard. He never could catch me.

In a few minutes he's swimming beside me. When did he get to be so good?

I swim into shallower water, stand up and splash him. We're having a great water fight, just like when we were kids, until Clinton grabs me, and now we're kissing. The curly hair on his chest is surprisingly silky. That's the last thing I notice because I'm tingling all over, and want him to never stop.

He does stop, takes my hand and leads me back to the beach. We're kissing again, and I touch him down there and he's hard, pushing against me, and I don't care what happens.

"Better wait," he mumbles. Picks up the blanket and wraps it around me. We sit down on the sand, and he holds my hand.

He talks and talks and talks, and holds my hand. Gently strokes each finger. Tells me how good things are since his Pa left. He's got the job at his uncle's garage, and his uncle's paying him like a man now — 35 dollars a week. He's learning a lot, can take an engine apart and put it back together. Now he's going on about his mother, how much better she is — looking after the kids, cleaning up the house, and with his wages they're managing.

I'm recovering my senses. "What about school?"

"Through with that."

"You aren't going to high school?"

"Nope. School never learned me much. Ma needs my pay. Be a mechanic some day."

"We better be getting back. I have to be at work for seven."

"Yeah, shouldn't of kept ya out so late."

I pull on my dress. My underwear's just about dry.

We're almost at my house when Clinton says: "When's yer day off?"

"Monday."

"Come for supper. I'll pick ya up at six."

He kisses me.

"Okay," I mumble and jump out of the car, run in the house and close the door.

I lie in bed and think, stupid, stupid, stupid. Clinton's not my boyfriend and never will be. He doesn't even speak properly and not

even going to high school. The man I marry will use proper grammar. Clinton's supporting his ma and all those kids. Stupid, stupid, stupid. What came over me? I always make sure things don't go too far. If Clinton hadn't stopped? I could be Mom all over again. At 14, not 16. Thank God nothing happened. I'll never be so stupid again.

But I have to go to supper at his place. I'll make it clear Billy Sider's my boyfriend. Tell Clinton, Billy's the jealous type. School starts in two weeks. Tell him I'm too busy to date. What came over me? Never again.

***

Monday, all the time I'm pushing the diapers through the wringer, I think about not being here when Clinton shows up. That would be mean. Takes all morning to get the wash done—it'd really piled up. Not Mom's fault. She's sick again. Had a miscarriage a week ago. It's Gloria who should've done the wash. She's so lazy. Plays with the kittens when she should be helping. Debbie's a good little worker, but still has to stand on a stool to pin the clothes on the line. She's a cute kid, red hair and freckles. Looks a lot like me when I was little, except I don't have freckles.

I take a bath and put on my pale green sundress. The circle skirt and the cinch belt make my waist look really tiny. I fasten a black velvet clip to my ponytail.

Clinton's right on time. He's wearing new-looking blue jeans and a white shirt with the sleeves rolled up.

He doesn't talk on the way to his house. The house, a winterized cottage really, doesn't look any better than I remember. The paint's still peeling, but one thing's different: it has new wood steps instead of a crate. Really new—they're not even painted. I've never been inside their house.

When Clinton opens the front door, the kids, all six of them, are sitting in a row on an old sagging couch. The two bigger boys are holding the tiniest ones.

Clinton ushers me to the one chair, a beat up-looking rocker. "Sit here," he says. "Meet Patrick, Teddy, Jimmy, Susan, Brian, and Baby

Norma." He touches each one lightly on the head. The kids look solemn, except for one little boy who giggles.

I don't want to be here.

They've all been scrubbed and in clean clothes. The girl Susan, looks around three, is wearing a ruffled pink dress that's been washed so often it's faded almost white—probably from a rummage sale.

"Meet Ma," Clinton says.

Before she moves her hand up to her mouth, I see rotten teeth, blackened stubs. She smiles, mouth closed and cheeks sunk in. She reminds me of our old mother cat who's had so many kittens she's bones in a baggy skin, belly sags and fur has fallen out in patches.

His mother has two glasses on a tray and offers them to me and Clinton. "Lemonade?" she says with her odd smile. "Supper almost ready."

The row of kids watch us drink.

Clinton must know this makes me uncomfortable because he touches my hand and says: "They had some already." He's standing beside my chair.

Shortly, we're called to supper in the tiny kitchen. We sit at the table with the two bigger boys and the baby girl in a highchair. The other kids sit around a makeshift table—two orange crates pushed together with a raggedy towel over them. The kids sit or kneel on the floor. Except for the odd whisper, they're quiet.

The smaller boy at our table says with a proud grin: "Us havin' baloney steak."

Sure enough, supper is fried baloney, boiled potatoes and tinned peas—one tin as we each get a tiny spoonful. His mother serves me first, then Clinton. The children's eyes follow the baloney pan. She cuts the last few slices in half so there's enough to go around. She doesn't sit down—fries up more and offers us seconds.

"There's cake, too," the little brother whispers to me. He's the only kid who speaks. The others sneak looks at me and hide their faces when I smile back.

The cake is one layer and thinly iced. Mom's done that. When there's not enough icing sugar, add water and it goes further.

After supper the kids are shooed outside, and Clinton and I have

tea in the living room. I offered to help with the dishes, but his mother won't let me.

"Ya keep my boy, Clinton, company. He's a good boy."

"Wanna go for a drive?" Clinton asks.

"Okay."

He holds the car door open for me. I feel so awkward, and I've got to tell him Billy's my boyfriend. We drive a long way to that same beach. Clinton turns off the engine and reaches back for the blanket.

"Wait. Clinton, I've got to go home."

"What ya mean?"

"Billy Sider's my boyfriend. He won't like it. He gets really jealous. He might beat you up."

"I can handle im."

"Clinton, I like Billy. He's my boyfriend. Please take me home."

He stares at me. "You like me."

"Sure I do, but Billy's my boyfriend."

Clinton starts up the car, and the gears screech. We drive in silence all the way home. I want to reach out and touch him. I want to say something. Want to go back to that beach.

When he parks in front of my house, I leap out and race inside without saying goodbye.

I won't cry. Run upstairs into the bathroom and hook the door. I crouch down by the tub, my arms hugging my knees. Won't cry. Won't cry. "Us havin' baloney steak." I see that little kid's face, his excitement, and can't bear it. Somehow Clinton's face is his little brother's. Run away, run some place where no kid ever says: "Us havin' baloney steak."

DATE BILLY ALL through grade 10. He calls me a cock-tease, but says he loves me. I tell him, I don't want to get pregnant.

"Not to worry," and he pulls a rubber out of his wallet.

"They're not foolproof."

"I love you. Let's get married and have lots of babies," he says.

"I'm going to finish high school and get a job in an office."

"Whatya want to do that for?"

"I just do."

I hardly ever see Clinton. Once I spot his car on Main Street, and duck into the drug store so he won't see me. Another time I'm hauling groceries home from Newman's Store, and he offers me a ride. It's raining and I can't think fast enough of an excuse so I get in.

"How ya doin?" he says.

"Fine. Billy and I are going as Romeo and Juliet to the Halloween dance. My costume is emerald-green organza. I'm sewing on rows of sequins ..." I keep on describing my imaginary costume all the way to the Plum.

"See you around," I say as I get out of his car as fast as I can with my load of groceries.

"Okay," he says.

After, from the upstairs window, I watch him. He sits there for at least 10 minutes before he drives away. I won't cry, and I can't date Clinton. He'll be stuck here all his life.

***

Billy's a nuisance, but I handle him. Most of the time it's fun fooling around with him. If I'm even slightly tempted to go all the way, I just think of Mom. No way am I ending up pregnant. For Christmas Billy buys me a record player and an Elvis record. I work some weekends

at the Shady Glen when his mother's sick or just wants some time off. I'm afraid if I drop him, I might lose my job. That makes me so mad.

* * *

My second summer at the restaurant I solve the Billy problem. I'm encouraging him to date other girls. When a pretty girl comes into the restaurant, I say: "She's eying you, Billy."

He's got to catch on that I'm never going to marry him. I tell him I want to see the world. He tells me someday he'll own the Shady Glen, and when he gets married his dad will buy him a house. He says that me and him can take trips to Florida so I'll get to see the world.

Betty Moyer, my old enemy and Joanne's sidekick, has been trying to cozy up to me. She hangs around the restaurant and invites me to her birthday party.

"We're going to the drive-in to see *Seven Brides for Seven Brothers,*" she says.

Purely out of curiosity, not about the movie, but about Betty, I agree to come.

After the show we have cake and ice cream at her house. Her house is nothing special. They don't even have wall-to-wall and the kitchen sink has rust stains.

She's such a silly little twit, just dying for a boyfriend. "Where's Joanne?'" I ask her.

"Oh, she's attached herself to that snotty Grenville bunch."

I know exactly the girls she means. Their chief pastime is making fun of other people's clothes. Usually the ones they're talking about are from Orchard Park or the country.

The next day at the restaurant I ask Billy: "Don't you think Betty Moyer's cute?"

"Yeah, so what?"

"She really likes you."

"She does?"

I'd kinda like to see her married to Billy, working in the restaurant like his mother does. Or home with their six kids—he wants a big family. Betty deserves six kids. She was always a mean little thing teasing me and Gloria about our rummage sale clothes. And what a tattle-tale. In grade six I got the strap because of her.

Billy does think she's cute. He's six foot and dark haired. She's blonde and petite. I'm glad when they start dating. They look so nice together. She's welcome to my hand-me-downs.

＊＊＊

"Sorry to hear you broke up with Billy," Mom says.

I guess Gloria told her. Mom and me are doing the wash. It really piled up this week as I was on the breakfast shift. Today, I don't have to be to work till 11.

We've put two loads of sheets through the wringer when Mom says: "You never forget your first love."

"Oh, Mom, you're funny. Who was your first love?"

"Your papa, of course. He was so handsome. We went to the Crystal Ballroom every weekend all that summer. Duke Ellington, Tommy Dorsey. I was just your age. We were so in love."

"Mom, he knocked all your teeth out."

"Just the two front ones and they were so rotten they were ready to fall out."

"But you got false teeth."

"My teeth were so bad I had them all pulled. We had so many worries." She sighs. "I wasn't any better—broke his arm with a piece of cordwood. A few days before that, I threw a pot of hot soup at him."

"He deserved it. He hit Gloria."

"Sharon, he lost his temper. And no surprise—he went to get his slippers from behind the door and he put his hand right into a pile of Gloria's poop."

"That's no excuse."

"People lose their tempers and no wonder with all his troubles."

"What troubles?"

"He'd lost his job at the mine, for high-grading."

"That's stealing gold, right?"

"Yeah, high-grade ore. He was framed. Some ignorant bastards

worked in that mine. Maurice'd been in a fight. What was that jerk's name? Mike somebody. Maurice laid a real beating on him. I think Mike put the ore in Maurice's boot and then tipped off the foreman."

"How come the judge didn't believe Papa?"

She laughs. "They just fired the man if there were suspicions."

"That's not fair."

"What is? I was going to leave him anyway. We were going to be evicted. The punch in the mouth just settled it."

"Couldn't he have got another job?"

"Not in the mines. He was blacklisted. No mine would've hired him. He wanted to go join Yves on the farm."

"I remember the farm. We had so much fun there."

"Believe me Sharon, you wouldn't like it now. Nothing but miles of bush and corduroy roads. It was the family homestead and he'd been glad enough to leave it to Yves. When I met him in Buffalo, he swore he'd never go back North. Said he hated that farm. I was pregnant with you, and he'd lost his job, and there was good money to be made in the mines. He talked me into going to Cadillac. Anyway, I was head over heels in love with the guy. Mother and Jean just about had a fit. I was sixteen and, believe it or not, I thought going to Cadillac a romantic adventure. I changed my mind in a hurry once we got there. First place we lived didn't even have an indoor toilet. He promised me it was only temporary. We'd save some money and go back South. I agreed to Cadillac. Never agreed to that bush farm. I had to do something. Maurice was so bloody stubborn. We hadn't paid the rent in months, didn't even have enough money for the trip south. I said I'd get it from my mother. He walked out then. I knew he'd be in the beer parlour, bumming drinks till closing time. I packed up a few things, went to Belangers and phoned Mother. She wired the money."

"Gloria and me were already there, weren't we?"

"Yes, they offered to keep you girls while Maurice and I sorted things out."

***

In bed that night I twist and turn. All your life you remember something one way. What do you do when you find out it wasn't quite like that? Mom had already planned to leave him. Still, he was a bastard.

I wouldn't stay with a guy who punched me. I can't imagine Mom throwing the soup pot at anybody. If she ever yells at Jimmy, which is seldom, he goes out to the garage and rearranges his tools. I will be so glad when I can get the hell out of here. Give my pillow a good punch and try to get comfortable. As I'm falling asleep I see the log house and barn against a wall of spruce.

KEEP MY RECORD player in my room. Don't want Little Joey and Charlie wrecking the needle. My sisters are pretty good about not touching my stuff. I bought another Elvis record, but still prefer Hank Williams singing "Your Cheatin' Heart." My new favourite is Johnny Cash's "Cry Cry Cry." I can listen to that one for hours.

I go with boys from out of town, who are here for the summer at their parents' cottages—the up-along-the-lake cottages, fancier than any house in Grenville. I've been seeing quite a bit of Doug Brown. He's fun, but I'm careful. He's from London and will be starting college in the fall.

He took me to the Ravensbay Playhouse. I saw Gretchen Thorton there with her family. She smiled. I came over and she introduced me. Sometimes, I think she's just shy like Donna says. Martin Thorton's quite handsome. Too bad he's blind and walks funny.

***

The second week of July, Mike, the dishwasher, quits, right in the middle of a busy weekend. I tell Mr. Sider that Gloria would like a job. She's going to be 14 in October.

Gloria's really excited when I tell her. All she's been doing this summer is helping Mom or hanging around the pony track.

She works really hard and doesn't break too many dishes. She doesn't get to wear a uniform 'cause she's not waiting tables. She buys red pedal pushers and a sleeveless red gingham blouse. I realize my sister is pretty—still too skinny, but she's getting a nice figure. Awfully shy though. I tell her if she wants a boyfriend she'll have to smile more. If anybody speaks to her, she looks at the ground. You got to look guys in the eye, I tell her.

Doug takes me to some parties at his parents' or their neighbours' cottages. Everybody's older than me. I kinda liked one boy who's planning to be a doctor. He told me that with my hair and skin, I should go into modeling. I laughed. Like there's a real call for that around here. He's in his first year at the University of Toronto. Unfortunately, he has a girlfriend. When I flirted a bit, the girlfriend got mad. She's not much to look at.

Doug got mad, too, but I calmed him down with some heavy petting in the car afterwards. Give them a hand job and they're eternally grateful.

Mom tells me to keep an eye on Gloria. I assure her I am, but she's got nothing too worry about. Gloria's too shy to get into trouble.

September's almost here, and I'll be glad to go back to school. Just two more years and I can get a fulltime job.

The last couple of weeks at the restaurant are pretty hectic. The assistant cook doesn't show up for work one morning. Nobody knows where he's gone. He's been working at the restaurant for two summers. From Toronto originally. No great loss. Steve's a big dumb slob — really fat and homely. Still has pimples and he's at least twenty.

Too late in the season to hire somebody else. Mr. Sider's having to do all the cooking and yells at everybody. Gloria can't take anybody yelling at her and drops almost as many dishes as she washes. If it wasn't the end of summer, she'd get fired. If I tell her to be more careful, she bursts into tears.

* * *

The Thursday before school starts me and Gloria take the bus into London. Felt circle skirts are the latest thing. Mine is black with pale blue flowers. Gloria's is turquoise with a poodle appliqué. We both buy penny loafers. I get a pale blue nylon bra and panty set too, and a black cinch belt to show off my 23-inch waist. Emily starts kindergarten, and Debbie's in grade one. We buy them new clothes. Nobody's going to be teasing our little sisters.

I guess Gloria picked up a bug or the bus made her sick because she throws up all evening.

* * *

The first day of school I feel really good in my new clothes. My blouse is the exact same shade of blue as the flowers on my skirt. Gloria looks so pretty in her new skirt, and I did her hair in French braids, but she's quiet and pale-looking. She had the flu all weekend.

Emily keeps lifting up her dress to check she's wearing her Tuesday panties. "Don't do that at school," I tell her. I couldn't resist getting her and Debbie days of the week underwear. I remember mine from Grants when we lived in Buffalo.

I fasten a blue ribbon—to match her dress—in Debbie's curly red hair. She so reminds me of me when I was little.

Things are much better in our family. Only three of the kids aren't in school and only Baby Charlie still in diapers. Mom doesn't look as tired as usual. Me and Mom are the exact same height now. I bought her a yellow dress in London.

"You shouldn't have. Where'll I wear it?"

"To the Legion. Us redheads look good in yellow, remember?"

Mom smiled.

* * *

Some mornings Gloria's sick to her stomach and Mom lets her stay home. "Just nerves," I tell Mom. Gloria doesn't like her teacher. Who does? Mr. Blackwood, the principal, teaches grade eight. He's loud and a bully. I hated his guts, but still went.

"You should make her go," I tell Mom. "She's already a year behind."

CTOBER 2ND IS a date I'll never forget. When I come home from school, I've barely got the door opened before Mom starts yelling. "Why didn't you look after her?"

"Who? What are you talking about?"

"Gloria! Who else?" she shouts.

"Mom! What are you talking about?"

"She's pregnant."

"You gone crazy. She doesn't even have a boyfriend."

"I always thought you were looking out for her." Mom sinks down on a kitchen chair and buries her head in her hands.

"I do look out for her. She did walk home alone once in a while. Did some creep bother her? We didn't always get off at the same time. Mom, tell me what happened!"

"Never should've let her take that job. Too young." She's crying.

"Tell me what happened!"

"She says she loved him," Mom says, sobbing.

"Who?"

"She says he was the cook—Steve Bertram. He should be in jail."

"Fat Steve! She wouldn't like him."

"Why didn't you know what was going on?" She glares at me.

"But Mom, they never went out or anything."

"Well, she's pregnant. Not even fourteen. I thought you were the one we should be worrying about."

"You don't have to worry about me."

"Obviously. Too bad you didn't worry about your sister." She gives me a nasty look.

I leave the room. Shaking, I grab hold of the banister. How can it be true? She didn't even talk to him or anybody else for that matter. Fat Steve tried to flirt with me. To think I felt sorry for him. I could kill him!

I find Gloria curled up in bed, her arm around Pal. She must've lifted him up on the bed. He has arthritis and can't jump up. They both look at me with sad brown eyes. She looks like a kid, my little sister.

I remember us hiding under the iron pipe bed and running to Belangers, Gloria wearing only an undershirt. Her stroking the wool flowers on Grandma's rug and making the fringe all nice and straight. Me leading her away from the school in her wet pants. "Don't cry, I'll look after you." Her clinging to Pal—"When will Mommy be home?" Reading her stories. Knocking those snots to the gravel. They teased her because just once she had a rip in her underwear.

I sit on the side of her bed. "Is it true, Gloria?"

"Uhuh." She buries her face in the pillow.

"Steve Bertram?"

"Uhuh."

"He's a dumb slob."

She looks up at me. "He said he loved me. Nobody else ever will."

"You're only thirteen—there'll be lots of guys for you."

"No, I'm not like you. I'm not pretty."

"You're pretty."

"You don't have to say that."

"I'm not just saying it. You are pretty."

"You've always had boyfriends."

"That's because I'm a flirt. You're shy—that's all that's the matter with you."

"Not quite all, I'm going to have a baby."

"Yeah, and what are we going to do about that?"

"I can look after it." She manages a smile.

"You got to go to school so you can get a good job."

"I don't do good at school. Now I can quit."

"You do fine."

"I should be in grade nine."

"You didn't fail a grade. You started a year late."

"Doesn't matter now. Sharon, I want to go to sleep." She turns to the wall, her arm still around Pal.

***

I'm washing dishes, Debbie's drying, and Emily's putting away. Gloria didn't come down for supper.

"Girls, I'll help Sharon. Go outside and see what your brothers are up to." Mom shoos them out the door and picks up a tea towel. "What did she tell you?"

"What do you mean?"

"Well, obviously, it didn't happen in the restaurant kitchen." She scowls.

"We didn't talk about where."

"Maybe he raped her."

"I don't think so. She said he told her he loved her, and she didn't think anybody else ever would."

"Nonsense."

"That's what I said."

"Well, I want to know how it happened. You find out. She won't talk to me."

* * *

That night lying in bed, I can't get to sleep—almost midnight and a math test tomorrow. I sit up, pound and rearrange my pillow. Flop back down.

"Do you think he'll come back?" Gloria whispers.

"No. Do you want him to?"

"I don't think so. When I told him I'd missed my period, he got mad, called me names. Sharon, I'm a little bit scared of him now. I thought he was so nice. Didn't care people thought he was stupid—I'm dumb, too—but he was nice."

"Did you like doing it with him?"

"Um ... I ... That was nice too ... like never feeling lonely again."

"You never went on a date with him? I would've heard about it."

"He said we couldn't let people know because he's a lot older than me."

"So where did you go?"

"His place on my day off or when I got off work early."

I lie awake a long time—think about her saying: "That was nice

too, like never feeling lonely again." Gloria, who should be worrying, is fast asleep—I recognize her snuffling breath. My little sister doing it first, liking it. Would I like it? Sure I would. But I'm not doing it with anybody from around here. He'll have to be really rich. I like fooling around, but God, I hate men!

* * *

Mom and Jimmy both want to call the police.

"That bastard should be in jail. Not legal with a girl under fourteen." That's Mom.

Jimmy says: "That bugger gotta marry her, and look afta her and the kid."

"She's too young to get married."

"Havin a kid is time to get hitched," Jimmy says.

I finally talk Mom out of calling the police.

"You want her to have to go to court? That would finish her. Just let her quietly have the baby."

"Then what?"

"She could put it up for adoption."

"She won't, wants to keep it."

"Idiot!"

"I don't know," Mom says. "That's how normal people feel about babies."

"She hasn't even finished grade eight. She has to go back to school."

"I've told her that. One more kid around here won't matter. I'm pregnant, too."

I leave the house. Jump on my bike and pedal like mad. Haven't ridden much lately. High-school girls don't. I ride to the beach and push my bike through the field to Clinton's fort.

The vine tree is still here. And there's the sleeping bag. Doesn't look like he's been here in a while. I throw myself down on the musty bag and bawl like I haven't in years. Mom said it was my fault: "You got her the job. I thought you were looking after her."

It is my fault. Why didn't I pay more attention? Too busy thinking about myself. And Mom is having another baby. Hopeless, just bloody hopeless. What's the point in trying to help? I sit up and blow my nose. What's the point in crying? In less than two years I'll be finished school and be out of here. Never, never will I come back.

*　*　*

I date several hunks during grade 11. Send them all home with blue balls. It was one of the up-along-the-lake guys last summer who told me if the girl wouldn't give the guy a hand job he went home with blue balls. I was tempted to ask what shade—sky, royal, indigo, or maybe baby blue?

I get a reputation as a cock-tease. I don't give a damn. There's always another who thinks he'll get lucky.

Donna Evans is dating Rick Waddell the ex-football hero of Grenville High. He's a hunk, but she needn't think she's the cat's meow. His dad may own the Ford dealership, but Rick just sells used cars.

Meanwhile, back at the Plum, Gloria and Mom's bellies are swelling. Mom's healthy during this pregnancy, and Gloria's morning sickness has stopped. Jimmy moans about more mouths to feed. He should shut the fuck up. He hasn't worked for the past month. First, his back, then bronchitis. When he's not whining for a cup of tea, he's yapping on about the garden. His saintly mother grew and canned enough vegetables to see them through the winter. As I work weekends at the Shady Glen, I don't know when he expects me to work in the garden. Billy's mom has a bad hip and can't wait tables anymore. With Uncle Joey's army pension and my wages we're surviving.

Betty Moyer had to marry Billy. She struts into the Quick Stop like she's proud of herself. Boy, has she gained a lot of weight, swelling up like a giant squash. I should feel sorry for her. I don't. She was always a mean little thing.

One year and four months and I'm out of here.

April 15th Mom gives birth to James Edward Junior. That's Jimmy's full name. He's delighted.

"Three sons just like Bonanza," he says. Does he think he's Ben Cartwright?

We got a second-hand television last fall. Half the time it goes dizzle-y. Jimmy loves *Bonanza*. I like the *Ed Sullivan Show*.

We're all having supper. The new baby's wailing in his basket. Little Joey wants to feed him. "He's my new brother."

Mom fixes Little Joey in the rocker with the baby and a pillow on his lap. Charlie wants to help. "My brother, too."

Jimmy looks all serious, and says: "Three sons just like Pa had." Tears are running down his face, and now he's blubbering.

Mom hugs him, and I leave the room. I just hate it when the old fool cries.

I don't spend any more time around home than I have to. There's no privacy, can't even play my records in peace.

On May 27th Gloria has a baby girl, Tamara Louise, just five pounds six ounces. Mom tells me Gloria had a tough labour, there was a lot of tearing. "Fifteen stitches," she says.

But Gloria is ridiculously happy. I've seen her carry on over new kittens, but never like this. She walks around the house singing. She's always got Tamara with her even when the baby's asleep. She pushes her from room to room in that wreck of a buggy. At night Tamara sleeps in Gloria's bed even though Mom said she should be in the buggy. "What if you roll over on her?"

"I won't," she says with pathetic confidence.

How can she be so completely ignorant of what her life holds?

One year and one month and I'm out of here.

I get a job at the steak house that's just opened, up along the lake. And that's the crowd it caters to. The tips are better than ever. I go out with guys, but nobody important. Went out a few times with a millionaire's son. His dad owns some company in London. He took me to a nightclub. I can pass for 21. At least, nobody asks my age. I gave him a blow job after he bought me a 50-dollar dress at a fancy London store. Then I dropped him. Didn't want him thinking he'd get one every date.

In August, Donna tells me she's pregnant and is marrying Rick. Me and her sister Brenda are going to be the bridesmaids. Gretchen's the maid of honour. Donna always did prefer stuck-up Gretchen to me.

Brenda and me go to the Thortons' to plan the shower. First time

I've been in their house. They have a rug in the living room that reminds me of Grandma's that Aunt Jean stole. There are some fancy antiques, but you wouldn't think they had much money because the kitchen sink looks older than ours. Donna told me that Martin told her that, when his dad died, he left them 200,000 dollars. Now that's a lot of money. I didn't see Martin. I know he and Donna are friends. Kinda a strange friendship, but she's nice to everybody.

Mrs. Thorton's nice, but sure doesn't know how to dress. The day of shower planning she had on a rayon dress that must've been 20 years old. Once when I walked by their place, I saw her out raking leaves. She was wearing what looked like a pair of her son's outgrown trousers.

She had a book from the library on shower planning. Books were stacked everywhere in their house. I told her I'd been to a couple of showers and she asked me all about them. She really listened and wants to do everything I told her about. Even the dumb games, except she didn't think that one where you guess how many kids the bride will have was appropriate. Those were her actual words. She's pretty strait-laced. Maybe that's why Gretchen's so uptight. I am beginning to agree with Donna that Gretchen's not snobby, just shy. We played the guess-how-many babies game at Betty Moyer's shower.

Donna's situation is so different from Gloria's. It's no disgrace because the families have money and know each other. Rick couldn't have wriggled out of marrying her, even if he wanted to. His father and her father would've got together and made him. She's having a big wedding. What is it, Grenville's major social do of the year?

Money makes everything different. Grandma knew that. They were pleased when Aunt Jean was marrying Uncle John because his family was rich. They were right to be pleased even though he turned out to be a jerk. Aunt Jean is sittin pretty in a big house with a swimming pool. She and Barbara moved to Florida. They haven't visited us again, though Aunt Jean's always inviting Mom. As if Mom could go. She was the stupid one, naïve, marrying Papa who had nothing so when their marriage broke up we had nothing. Mom ridicules Grandma—making fun of her mending or her love of old sayings. Should've learned from her.

Gretchen's a fool. She went on about how cute Gloria's Tamara is. She said she saw her at the post office. "Gloria, let me hold her." Sounded like she thought Gloria lucky to have her.

"Doesn't it matter she quit school and has no husband?"

"That's not good, but she has such a sweet baby," Gretchen said. I'd swear I heard envy in her voice. She's not stuck-up, just an idiot.

ONCE SCHOOL STARTS me and Gretchen sometimes eat lunch together in the cafeteria. She's helping me with English. My marks aren't as good as they used to be. I miss too much school taking extra shifts at the restaurant. Now that the steak house is closed for the winter, I'm back working at the Shady Glen because Mrs. Sider is still laid up.

I'd like to win the business prize—be a help when I go job-hunting in Toronto. First I thought London, but that's too close. In Toronto nobody will have heard of Grenville.

In March, Donna has a baby boy. When I visit her, she moves like she has a sack of bricks in her gut. Less than a year ago she got a detention for doing handstands on the school's front steps.

She and Rick move into a brand new bungalow on Leaman Road, right across the street from the Thortons. Tamara still sleeps in Gloria's bed in our room with my bed and army cots for Debbie and Emily. At least when I'm gone, Debbie can have my bed. The room's so crowded we have to keep our clothes in cardboard boxes under the beds.

Three months and I'm out here. Toronto, here I come. I'll be walking to work in four-inch heels, a tight, tight skirt and a boxy jacket. I'll introduce myself, Sharon Desjardins, maybe just the hint of a French accent.

***

Today, June 15th, is my last exam, English. Going to Toronto, going to Toronto, runs like music through my head.

I won't have my graduation diploma until the end of the month. I've been to see Mr. Podger, and he gave me a letter and a transcript of my marks, all but the finals.

He said: "You've done very well, Sharon. You're the only one who came from Orchard Park Public graduating this year."

I know exactly what he meant. If you're me, just graduating from high school is an achievement. Graduating in grade 12 commercial wouldn't be doing great if you were Gretchen Thorton who's going to university. But I'll show them. Someday, I'll come back here in a fancy car. Let's see, yeah, a Cadillac. I'll drive down Main Street and be wearing a fur coat.

Joanne Newman who used to think herself so smart failed grade 11 physics and algebra. Had to repeat them this year, so she's not graduating. And dear roly-poly Betty is home washing diapers.

Mr. Podger wrote me a letter of recommendation. Mrs. Laurence did, too. They know my plan to go to Toronto. Mrs. Laurence gave me the address and phone number of a temporary employment agency. She said that's a good way to get started. She also told me about Willard Hall, this place where women travelling on their own can stay. She stayed there years ago. She said it costs just a few dollars a night. I've saved $169. Lately, Jimmy's been working pretty steady.

I figure I'll leave next week. Before I do, I've going to make my job-interview suit. With the exams on, I can go in the Home Ec room whenever I please. I've already got my pattern and fabric — a peacock-blue, linen-rayon mix.

When I hand in my paper, I'm sweaty, tired, and elated. I figure I got an A. Thinking of heading to the beach for a swim, I push open the heavy oak door, and who do I see? Clinton! Haven't seen him in ages. He climbs out of his funny car with the mismatched doors and waves me over. He's a good-looking guy even though there's always black grease under his fingernails, and he wears a faded t-shirt and old jeans.

"How about us go for a picnic by the lake?" he says.

"When?" I'm already thinking of excuses. "Tomorrow's Saturday, and I have to work."

"Right now. Just get your bathing suit and us'll be off."

I should say no, but I'm so sweaty and want a swim. "Okay."

We stop at my house. I change into my bathing suit, and put on shorts and a t-shirt over it. The kids aren't home from school yet or I'd bring them along.

I climb into his old car. One thing I have to say for him is, though that dump where he lives is a mess, there's no junk in his car. A wicker picnic basket, the kind a grandma would have, and a plaid motor rug are the only things on the back seat.

We drive a long way. "Where are we going?"

"New spot. You'll love it."

We go miles down a dirt road. We have to keep the windows closed to keep the dust out. Boy, it's hot. A swim will sure feel good.

We park and walk down a lane to the beach. I'm so hot I want to pull off my shorts and run in.

"Not here," he says. "Better place further along." He strides down the beach with his funny old picnic basket and blanket.

"Wait up."

After climbing over some rocks, and avoiding a swampy place with cattails, we come to sand hills. He shows me where just up above the beach, a big uprooted tree forms a sandy cave. We stash the basket and blanket. I pull off my shorts and t-shirt. I'm wearing my brand new, pale blue Janzen swimsuit. Clinton's in ancient swim trunks, the black wool kind from the 1940s. It would be unkind to laugh, so I run into the water.

Ah, that's the ticket.

We swim for a while and have a water fight just like old times. We end up kissing, but I can handle this, in spite of he's the only guy who gives me this crazy feeling. We're in the cave now. He's spread out the plaid blanket and we're necking like mad. Sharon, keep your wits about you, I think, don't say. He's tonguing my bare breasts and it's wonderful. I think what the hell, show him a good time, and I go down on him. He's pulling me back up and rearranging things, and god damn it, I stop thinking because he's spreading my legs, and he's in me, and I'm lost. This is everything, this pulsing—me, the cave, him. I don't care. I don't care about anything.

It's over. He's holding me, and I'm crying while blood trickles down my leg, and he says over and over: "I love you."

He takes my hand, leads me into the lake, and we wash ourselves off. Back in the cave, we pull on our clothes. I'm numb. Can't believe

this has happened. I can't eat, though he's made macaroni and cheese loaf sandwiches. Had I sometime told him that was my favourite?

I sit here like a dummy. Finally, he packs up the picnic.

"I want to show ya summin," he says.

He takes my hand, and we go back to his car.

We drive to Grenville in silence. He turns the wrong way, and pulls up in front of an old house on Vine Street.

"Me and Ma bought this place. Gonna fix er up nice. No more fuckin, excuse my French, landlords."

All I can think is, oh no, it's Jimmy's house all over again. Big old house with a long boxy wing on the back. Peeling blue paint, torn screens, one window is even boarded over.

"Know she needs a lot of work. I don't mind work."

Inside worn linoleum and rough floor boards. Stove pipes snake across the ceilings and through the upstairs to the chimney. A couple of abandoned iron pipe beds and an ancient gas cook stove. Wallpaper pulling away to expose laths and crumbling plaster.

Now he's showing me the big room attached to the kitchen. More worn off linoleum and Ten-Test walls just like the upstairs in Cadillac.

"Ma says this would've been the summer kitchen—twenty-two by twenty-eight feet. Gonna be my place."

There's a rusty sink with a pail underneath to catch the drips.

"See? Divide off the bedroom here." Clinton blushes.

Does he blush because he knows I can read his mind? Sorry, Clinton, won't be me in your bedroom. How many times do I have to tell you, I'm getting the hell out of this town?

"Gonna build a little bathroom and put in a toilet. Know it's not much, but marry me, Sharon. Us'll fix er up."

He's holding my hands. I yank them away. "You take me home."

"Ya gotta marry me now."

"I don't gotta do anything, you idiot. I'm not marrying you, dummy."

"Sharon, I love ya, have always loved ya. And ya love me."

"I don't. I don't." I run outside and jump in the car.

He follows.

"Take me home."

He gets in and starts up the car. Drives to my house. I'm about to jump out when he grabs my hand.

"A baby could be comin," he says.

I hate him. I really truly hate him. Bet he planned the whole thing. "I'll get rid of it."

"No, you wouldn't do that."

"Listen to me, Clinton McClary. I'm not marrying you now or ever. You think I'm gonna live with your ma and that bunch of shitty-assed kids."

"Us'll have our own apartment."

"I'm leaving Grenville and never coming back."

"Me too, if that's what ya want."

"You'll never leave Grenville. You're from here."

"So are you."

"Am not. I'm from Buffalo."

"Youse lived there two years."

"I'm from Cadillac, Quebec."

"Doesn't matter where ya from. Us'll get married."

"And live in a dump and have six kids, whose big treat will be baloney steak. You listen to me, Clinton McClary. If I'm pregnant, I'll get rid of it. I'll not have your kid and your baloney steak life."

"Whatcha talking about—baloney steak?"

"Big treat baloney steak. Your ma will even fry up more. Baloney steak. Baloney steak. Us gonna have baloney steak."

He looks at me funny. Dumb Clinton, but he must've caught on. His face goes all red and he mumbles: "Bitch."

I laugh. "I'll get rid of it, you hear me." And leap out of the car.

I head for the front door, think better of it. They'll all be home. I run around the back and go in the shed off the garage. I'm freezing cold and shaking so, my teeth chatter. I lie down on a pile of burlap sacks and pull one over me. Stupid, stupid bitch. I bite the burlap to keep from screaming. Dust and grit fill my mouth. I reach between my legs. There's blood on my fingers, but not much.

Dusk now. Still can't stop shivering. Stupid bitch, stupid bitch. Get rid of it. How? I don't know where to go. Here, girls just have babies. Babies, babies. Babies. Helen Dawes used a knitting needle. One of the country girls, fifteen, came to school in her mother's old housedress-

es. Bled to death. Stupid bitch. I won't do that. In Toronto I could find someone. Oh, yeah, just walk up to people on the street. "Where do you go for an abortion?" Throw me in jail or the loony bin. Stupid bitch.

You are a stupid bitch. Think straight. What are the odds? My period's due when? About ten days. Make a plan. Wait till they're all in bed.

I wait and wait. The outdoor kitchen light sends a weak beam into the shed. They turn it out last thing before they go to bed. I shiver and wait.

***

Must've fallen asleep. Pitch dark now. Ache all over. I stagger to my feet and go in the house. Fortunately, they never lock the back door. I long for a hot bath.

The water's lukewarm as usual. I think of the showers at the high school, all that hot water. If I broke into the school—but that is crazy. Still shivering, dry myself on a scratchy towel, and crawl into bed.

***

Just as the birds begin their predawn racket I'm up and packing. Got a suitcase in London two weeks ago.

"Are you leaving today?" Debbie says.

She's wearing my worn out t-shirt that barely reaches her scrawny thighs. Could be me—that mop of red curly hair. The rip under the arm is sewn up with big uneven stitches. No, not me—she's always quietly trying to fix things. Her age I was taking off on my bike and whining for new clothes. Can't look her in the eye. "Yeah, gonna get a job in Toronto."

"Can I come visit?"

"Sure, someday."

"Don't want you to go."

"I'll send you a present, okay?" She still looks about to cry. "And you can have my bed."

"Really?"

"Yes, really." I give her a hug.

"Come back and visit us."

"Sure." I pick up my suitcase and go downstairs.

Mom's feeding Jimmy Junior. That's the ridiculous name they've given him. "What's going on?" she says.

"Leavin now, Mom."

"You said next week."

"Plans change. If Clinton comes around, don't tell him where I've gone."

"Clinton? What's he got to do with it?"

"He's an ass. I'll write, Mom."

"Well, at least wait till people are up and say goodbye."

"Can't. Gotta catch the early bus. Bye, Mom." I kiss the top of her head, her fading red hair, and I'm out the door.

I stride up Plum Street with my suitcase in my hand. Think for a moment of the peacock blue suit I'll never wear. Maybe Mrs. Laurence will give the fabric to some pathetic Orchard Park kid in grade nine. I'm wearing my green and white striped sundress with white bolero jacket, and white pumps. My new shoulder bag matches them. I look pretty businesslike. I think I hear one of the kids calling. I walk faster. Don't look back. Selfish bitch, don't look back.

I have to walk to Leaman Road, and then to the top of the hill, Main Street. The sun's fully up now. I wish it were dark. Would've liked to leave in the middle of the night.

Half-hour early for the bus. I can tell it's going to be another warm day, but I'm shivering. This crazy feeling somebody's gonna come by and tell me I can't go. Who? Clinton? Not scared of him. He can go to hell. Don't want to see anybody. Please, bus, hurry up.

Why doesn't that stupid bird shut up? A robin chirping away, a piece of straw in its beak. Nest building. It'll keep right on chirping till some cat bites its head off. Idiot!

I'm sweating. I'll have deodorant stains on my dress. Am I bleeding? Doesn't matter. Wearing a pad. Should've put on perfume. I stink.

Chicken poop Sharon, chicken poop Sharon. I threw gravel in Betty's face and pushed her down. I had chicken dirt on my shoe. She saw it. Got the strap that time, third time caught fighting.

Forget it. All done now. I'll change before I go to the employment place. Spray on some Evening in Paris. Be in Toronto by noon. Better go to Willard Hall first, get settled in. Bus, hurry up, hurry up.

Wish I had a car. I'd gun the engine right out of here.

***

The bus driver sold me a ticket all the way to Toronto. That was good. Thought maybe I'd have to go in the London terminal to get one. The driver even told me: "The Toronto bus pulls into lane six." Found it —no problem. I'd never been further than London.

I put my suitcase on the seat beside me. Know you're supposed to put it on the overhead rack, but the bus isn't crowded. I don't want anybody to sit with me.

My stomach feels sick. The first sign. Then I remember I haven't eaten since lunch yesterday. Should've bought a chocolate bar in the bus terminal.

I must've fallen asleep because when I wake up we're passing factories—Maple Leaf Foods. They make macaroni and cheese loaf. I press my face against the window to keep from barfing.

We're passing a brewery, the sour-yeasty smell somehow familiar. There was a brewery in Buffalo. Christmas Eve. On the way to Aunt Jean's. I swallow back vomit and tears and dig my fingernails into my wrists. Pain stops stupid tears. Gloria in her red velvet dress held her new doll. "My baby," she called it. Gloria, looking at me with those trusting brown eyes, would reach for my hand on the way to school. I was mean to her, but she kept right on trusting. Too damn trusting. Now she holds her real live baby and is stupid enough to be happy.

Stop thinking about her. I'm here. Toronto. I'm here.

We're pulling into the terminal. A lot like the Buffalo terminal, but no legless man selling pencils.

With a trembling hand clutching my suitcase, I push through the doors into Toronto. Bay Street, the sidewalks are crowded with people. Men in suits carry briefcases. Women in smart outfits. Every woman in high heels. Glad I wore mine, though they pinch my toes. Tame pigeons waddle among the people. The sun shines, cars honk, a bus rumbles by. I'm here.

I spot a restaurant across the street—pictures of hamburgers, fish and chips and hot dogs painted above the door. Not too fancy—good. I haul my suitcase through the doorway. The place is long and narrow like Hank's. I find a booth. Stash my suitcase under the table. Before I can look around, the waitress is here. "A hamburger, fries, and a Coke, please."

Everything tastes so good. I smile. Order myself to stop worrying.

***

I take a cab to Willard Hall like Mrs. Laurence told me to. There's an elderly lady at the counter. Willard Hall smells old. Very clean though.

"I'm from out of town and would like a room, please. My teacher recommended I come here." I say exactly what Mrs. Laurence said I should.

"Yes, dear, this is a safe place for young girls like yourself." She hands me a form.

I fill it in and pay for a week.

"I'll be looking for an apartment once I get a job."

"You're going to live in Toronto, dear?"

"Just graduated from high school. I want to work in an office."

"Very good. Come along, dear. I'll show you to your room." She leads me down narrow halls, painted pale yellow. "This is our cafeteria, breakfast is six-thirty to eight-thirty, supper five-thirty to seven-thirty. We don't serve lunch, dear."

Down another long hall and she unlocks a door. The room is small, just space for the single bed, dresser, and chair.

"After you get settled in, dear, have a look at our bulletin board. Girls put up notices there of apartments to share."

"Thanks, I will."

I close the door after her, lock it, and sit down on the bed. Smooth the worn bedspread—my own room. I'm shaking. Go to the window. I'm on the second floor. There's a continuous stream of people walking along the sidewalk. A man in a grey suit and wearing a fedora shouts, waves, and a taxi pulls over. A truck—Flowers for Every Occasion— honks. A bus stops at the corner. I'm here. I'm here. I want to rush out on the street and cheer.

I don't. It's enough I'm here. I pull back the bedspread and crawl under.

WAKE UP STIFF and sore all over and look at my watch. Six o'clock. It can't be. I was supposed to go to the employment agency. Wasted my first day.

Still a little shaky, I get out of bed. Open my suitcase, get out my housecoat and cosmetic bag. Idiot, shouldn't have slept in my dress. I take the towel provided and find the bathroom. It too is very clean. I wash my hair, lovely hot water, scrub myself all over, no more blood. Good. Then remember, blood is what I want lots of. Don't think about it. I dry off and scurry back to my room.

Dummy, you're here. Don't hide in your room.

I can't decide what to wear. Settle on my plain blue skirt, and a white blouse, and sandals. My toes still ache from my pumps.

I scan the people in the cafeteria. Mainly older women, older than me anyway. Then I see two girls laughing together. One is sorta plump and dark haired, the other a skinny little blonde.

Ravenous again, I load up a tray. Beef stew comes with a roll, choice of Jell-O or pudding, and of milk, juice, coffee, or tea, no pop. I get chocolate pudding and milk.

Look around. Those girls are still giggling over something. Nothing ventured, nothing gained.

"Mind if I join you? I just got here today."

"Sure, sit down," the dark one says. "I'm Mary. She's Judy. We came yesterday. We're from Owen Sound."

"Sharon Desjardins. I'm from a little town you wouldn't know of. Before that I lived in Buffalo."

"Buffalo!" Judy says. "We went shopping there on our school trip to Niagara Falls. Great shopping, really cheap compared to home."

"Did you go to Grants? It's right on Main Street."

"That's where I got Levis jeans for $2.99. Couldn't believe it."

"Small world, eh?"

After supper we walk around the neighbourhood and agree to meet tomorrow at noon.

Lying in bed, I figure I haven't done too badly for day one. Judy has a job on the switchboard at Bell telephone, but she doesn't start till next week. Mary has an interview tomorrow at Eaton's. In September, she'll be going to the University of Toronto. Mary and Judy have been friends since kindergarten. Judy has been working fulltime at Bell in Owen Sound for the past year. I can't believe how nice they are. Just like that, they invited me to share an apartment. We're going looking tomorrow. They don't know me. I could be a murderer. Pretty trusting. Money's part of it. Mary said apartments would be cheaper with three.

But first thing tomorrow is the employment agency.

***

Toronto is magical. It was all so easy. I went to the temporary employment agency, filled out some forms. The girl said: "You're in luck. Montgomery Insurance needs somebody right away. Can you be there at eight tomorrow for an interview?"

"Sure." She handed me the address. I'm to see Mr. Rutledge.

In the afternoon Mary, Judy, and I go apartment hunting. We all want something downtown and cheap. We settle on the attic of a big old house for ninety a month. Three tiny bedrooms, a combined kitchen-living room, and a bathroom. We can move in Monday.

Giddy with our good luck, we go shopping. We could shop all day and never run out of stores. I buy a suit, $14.99, though I'm supposed to be watching my money. Rayon, looks like linen, and a lovely aqua blue. Boxy jacket and pencil skirt, just like the one I was going to make, and it fits me perfectly.

The next morning I'm up at five. After my shower I take a long time with my hair. For my birthday Mom gave me her silver clip. I try to fasten my curls up the way she used to when she went out on dates in Buffalo. My hair keeps falling down. Finally, I just fasten some back with the clip and let the rest hang down. Hope I look businesslike enough. I whiten my shoes and get dressed. The suit is beautiful.

By six o'clock I'm all ready, but too early for breakfast and too early to leave for the interview. I could use up some time if I walked. Montgomery Insurance is on College off Yonge. But don't want to arrive all sweaty. Better take a cab. I sit on the edge of my bed. Scared my suit'll be wrinkled, I go stand by the window, and wait. Toronto is already waking up. Cars go by. Across the street a garbage truck backs into a lane. There's a cab. Maybe I should go down and phone for mine. Too early. I wait. Look at my watch — 6:20. I wait and wait.

***

The cab drops me off at the front door. The office is on the fifth floor. I tell the receptionist I'm here to see Mr. Rutledge, and she says she'll buzz him.

I wait. My stomach growls. Should've eaten something. A man, I assume Mr. Rutledge, comes towards me. He's young and tall with wavy brown hair and is wearing a grey suit, white shirt, and a grey tie with tiny red squares.

"Ted Rutledge," he says.

I stand up. He shakes my hand. I think I'll faint, but I order myself to get a grip and hand him my papers.

He rifles through them. Smiles. "So you can type fifty-five words a minute?"

"Yes, sir."

"No *sir*, just Ted." And he grins.

I give him my best smile and know I've got the job.

He leads me into an office with four desks, women at three of them. The fourth is to be mine, he tells me.

"This is Beverly, our office manager."

I shake hands with her and figure I better watch it. She reminds me of the Bear, my grade three teacher.

"I'll leave you for now in her capable hands."

Unsmiling Beverly, plump, grey-haired, explains I'll be filling in for a secretary on vacation. She gives me a stack of letters in short-hand to type. "Have them on my desk by noon."

I type all morning, concentrating on not making a mistake. I do make mistakes and have to retype two of the letters. I hear people laughing and talking in the background. I don't even look up.

At 11:30 I place a stack of perfect copies on Beverly's desk. She looks through them. I have the feeling I'm about to be sent to the principal's office, when she looks up and grins. "Well, you are more than a pretty face. Okay, girls, let's take her to lunch. She's a keeper."

They take me to Fran's, this diner-type restaurant nearby. Beverly tells me that the last girl the agency sent couldn't read shorthand, and the one before that couldn't turn out a perfect copy if she typed all day.

Beverly's okay. As long as I work hard, we'll get on all right.

"I'm Cathy, and this is Pam, our office beauty until you arrived."

"Oh, stop it, Cathy, you're embarrassing the kid," Pam says.

Pam's pretty, blonde hair done back in a French roll. Older than me, but young, early twenties, I guess. Cathy has bouffant hair teased to perfection. She's nice enough looking and about the same age as Pam. Beverly has a hamburger and fries and I order the same.

Cathy and Pam have salads. Watching their waistlines, they say. "Sitting at a desk all day puts on the pounds," Pam tells me.

***

Mary and Judy went home for the weekend. I've stayed in bed this morning—Saturday, there's nothing I have to do. I'm stretched out in new cotton sheets on a rusty iron-pipe bed. Such beds must follow me around. Place came furnished, pretty shabby. Not what I planned. When Mary saw the beds, she said: "How quaint, I've only seen those before in cottages." They have a cottage on Lake Huron. Judy's family does, too.

I couldn't say: "Let's look for something better?" Cheap is good. I have sixty-seven dollars left. I've had a lot of expenses—two months rent, the bus ticket, my new suit, the nights at Willard Hall, too many restaurant meals, the sheets, and towels. This job is just for two weeks. I phoned the temp agency and they said they're pretty certain of having something lined up for me. Still, I'm earning less than back home. Thirty-eight a week sounds good, but at the restaurant I more than doubled my wages in tips. But it's plenty, unless ... My period's due today. I'm waiting, waiting, waiting.

What am I going to do if it doesn't come? That's the sixty-four-thousand dollar question. Mary and Judy can't help, little innocents. Nice, but don't know their way around. The girls at work are older. Pam, the youngest, told me she was twenty and Cathy twenty-two. Beverly, the office manager, is really old, at least forty. I can't imagine her in her tailored suits and sensible shoes, knowing. The receptionist wears tight skirts and spike heels. She might know, but what am I supposed to say: "Hey, Susie, you ever have an abortion?"

Oh God, what am I going to do? Relax. Just due today. Glad Mary and Judy are away. Wish I could go to sleep. Fat chance. Feel like pounding somebody—Clinton, dumb, idiot Clinton.

Have to get out of here. I crawl out of bed and pull on jeans, t-shirt, sneakers, and my old hooded windbreaker. Too warm for the jacket, but I don't want to be recognized. I don't know who I'm worried about—only know the people from work.

I walk for miles along Queen Street, all the way to the Sunnyside bus terminal, way out in the boonies. I cross Queen and go down to the lake. There's a beach, a merry-go-round, a couple other kiddie rides, a hot dog stand, and a playground. On the beach a man throws sticks for a black dog. Two dowdy mothers chat on the bench by the playground, and a few kids play on the swings.

I buy a hot dog and a coffee and choose a bench way off by itself. Pull my hood down over my face. I light a cigarette. Got to figure out what to do. God damn stupid Clinton.

Who am I gonna ask? Mr. Rutledge? The boss. Have I taken leave of my senses? He'd fire me. Maybe, maybe not.

Gave me a ride home that first day when I was headed for the bus stop. When he pulled up beside me, all I could think was oh no, my $14.99 suit that I thought was so great is all wrinkled. I look like a frump.

He leaned over and pushed open the door for me. I smiled and got in.

"How was your first day?"

"Good, Mr. Rutledge. Everybody's really nice." I gave him a big smile.

"Ted, call me Ted," he said returning my smile.

There was something in his smile. I recognized the look. Better be careful. Still, if I play my cards right? He knows his way around. Bet he could help me.

He dropped me off at the apartment with a fatherly pat on the arm. Was I imagining things before? I think not.

I finish my hot dog and another cigarette. It takes me two-and-a-half hours to walk back to the apartment. Almost crawl up the stairs —I'm that tired.

Flop down on my bed.

* * *

Must've fallen instantly asleep because I wake up with a start and look at the clock. Seven-thirty. I've slept three hours. What woke me up? Then I know and run to the bathroom. I've bled right through onto my jeans. I laugh and can't stop. Realize I didn't buy Kotex. This makes me laugh harder. I'm a dope. Why did I think I was doomed?

I get out clean underwear and stuff the crotch with wadded toilet paper. Pull on my pedal pushers, red, good thing they're not white. I head out to find some store still open.

The convenience store on the corner is open, and I buy the biggest box they have.

I come back to the apartment, fix myself up, and put my stained clothes in the bathtub to soak. I even bled on the sheet.

I stand at the window and thank God for my reprieve. No, God's more into punishment. Give thanks to Lady Luck. I've been given a second chance. Never, never will I be so damn stupid again.

I write Mom a quick letter, just telling her I'm here, and have a job. I include ten dollars for the kids.

* * *

On Monday Mr. Rutledge invites me for a coffee after work. Just as we're about to enter the restaurant he says: "What the hell, let's make it a drink." He takes my arm and leads me away.

He must know I'm seventeen, and the drinking age is twenty-

one. We go into a dimly lit place he seems familiar with. I've been in bars before with some of the up-along-the-lake crowd back home. My first time, I was fifteen and ordered a pink lady, a drink I knew from the *Thin Man* radio show. I'm more sophisticated now and order a rye and ginger.

I'm careful with alcohol. I remember Papa. I sip my rye and ginger and when Mr. Rutledge, Ted, is lighting his cigarette, I give the plastic rose centrepiece half.

After our drinks we go for dinner at a restaurant with white linen tablecloths. It's one of those places with three forks and two spoons. I know what's what, thanks to Mrs. Laurence's lessons on the proper way to set a table.

"Don't mention us coming here to the girls at the office." He grins. "They might think I'm playing favourites and that could jeopardize your job."

I flirt a bit during the meal and, when we park in front of my place, he kisses me goodnight. He has his tongue in my mouth, but I wriggle away, mumbling something about nosy landladies. We haven't seen our landlady since we rented the apartment, but he doesn't need to know that. Don't want him to think I'm a slut.

* * *

On Wednesday I'm busy typing away, when Ted comes up to my desk. "Can I see you in my office, please?" He looks serious.

I follow him into his office and he closes the door. He smiles. "Sharon, you're an excellent typist. You've got a full-time job here, if you want it."

"Really? That's great."

"Oh, if Beverly or the others say anything to you, just tell them I said you're replacing Jill permanently because she didn't get much work done. Was always talking to her friends on the phone. How about we go out for dinner after work to celebrate?"

"Thanks, I'd like that."

"Don't say anything to the girls about our date. I'm not supposed to date my employees, but I really like you, Sharon."

"I like you, too."

"So, we'll keep it hush-hush, eh?"

"Sure."

***

When us girls go out for lunch on Friday, Pam does complain about him firing Jill, who was on vacation when I was hired. "Did he say anything to you about her?"

"He said I was a good typist, and she phoned her friends when she was supposed to be working. That's all I know."

"Not your fault," says Beverly. "Jill did waste time, and she's getting married in the fall so she would've been quitting anyway."

HIRD WEEKEND IN July, Mary, Judy and I take the train to Owen Sound. I'll be staying at Judy's place. Mary's brother and his family are visiting so they're full up.

Judy's dad, driving a new-looking Buick, picks us up at the station. I love the smell of new cars.

When we get to the house, Judy's mother hugs her, shakes my hand, and offers us tea. She's wearing a navy and white dress, nylons, and pumps, also makeup, and her hair is teased to perfection. Maybe she was out somewhere and just got home.

The house is a big, two-storey brick—old, but very modern inside. The living room has light green wall-to-wall carpeting and beige fibreglass drapes. Fibreglass drapes are the latest thing. Mrs. Laurence told us about them. They don't have to be washed—just wiped clean with a damp cloth. The kitchen's all white, lots of cupboards, black counter tops, and a dark red vinyl tile floor. There's a dining room —the table has eight heavy wood chairs around it. We have our tea in the TV room, a big room off the kitchen.

The little sister, Janet, comes in, says hi, and then complains her mother didn't wash her red shorts, and she wants to wear them to the lake.

Hell, she's fifteen. Why isn't she looking after her own clothes?

The older sister isn't here. She's working as a camp counsellor in Muskoka for the summer. She goes to university in London, where Janet informs us she intends to go, too. After, when Judy's showing me to my room, she tells me she's the dummy in the family. She's not dumb—she has her grade twelve.

I have the older sister's room and her big double bed, all to myself. The white with gold trim bed, dresser, and night table, make me think of our beds in Buffalo. Gloria and Baby Tamara sleep on a stained mattress in a room with our little sisters. A room smaller than this. Here, pink ruffled sheers at the window, there, a cheap cotton print, faded almost white.

This house has five large bedrooms. Their mother uses one as a sewing room, and there's an attic playroom. Judy took me up there and showed me her old dollhouse—filled with miniature wooden furniture and tiny china dolls. Looked like the dollhouse in the Beatrix Potter book. I didn't know there really were such things. All their old dolls, stuffed toys, and board games were neatly arranged on shelves.

"Mom's saving everything for when we have kids." Strange for rich people to save old stuff, but I guess even their old stuff's too good to throw out.

Judy's nice. Not a snobby bone in her body, but hard to believe she's two years older than me.

* * *

Their cottage on Lake Huron is at a little place called Sauble Beach. The cottage is pretty fancy, imitation log painted dark brown with white trim, flower boxes filled with geraniums. Again, I get the older sister's room. This one has twin beds with mauve flowered spreads and drapes. No iron pipe beds that Mary thinks are quaint.

At the lake Judy's mother wears plaid Bermuda shorts and a sleeveless, spotless white blouse.

Janet goes off with her friends, and Mary joins me and Judy on the beach. She has her little nephew with her. She builds him a big sand castle. Judy and I go in swimming and flop on the beach to sun ourselves. A couple of not bad-looking guys who were in grade 13 with Mary come by. Within minutes they're down on the sand enlarging the castle, building moats and sending the little boy for pails of water. The one guy designs a drawbridge from a piece of cardboard and some string. He'll be doing engineering at Queen's University in the fall.

For the next hour-and-a-half they build sand castles and talk about school.

At suppertime Mary's whole family comes over. The dads barbeque steaks. There's potato salad, macaroni salad, rolls, fruit pies, and

ice cream. Too much food. Each steak is enough meat for a family. They throw the leftovers in the garbage. Wow, think of being that rich!

Getting dark by the time supper's over. We scour the beach for firewood. Mary's collie helps drag our finds back. Makes me think of Pal—now too old to drag sticks. He can't even climb up on Gloria's bed anymore.

The men make a bonfire on the beach and we roast marshmallows.

Mary's little nephew says: "Don't you just love camping?"

Hell, camping is no toilet and sleeping in the back of the station wagon. I'm going to sleep in a room that looks like something out of a magazine. "It's nice," I tell him. And it is. I stare at the starry sky and listen to the waves wash the shore.

Mary's brother has brought his guitar. They sing songs they all learned years ago at summer camp.

Everybody's friendly. These are nice people and I have never felt this lonely in my life.

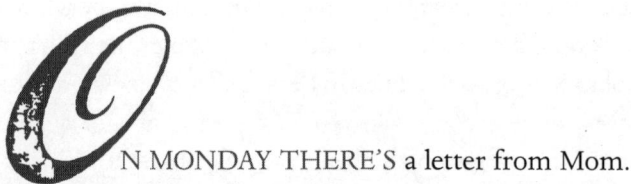ON MONDAY THERE'S a letter from Mom.

Dear Sharon,

I was so relieved to hear from you. It's wonderful you have a job and an apartment. What are the girls you're sharing with like?

Jimmy Junior is so cute. He took his first steps yesterday. The kids carry him around so much we figure he was just lazy and didn't feel any need to walk. Mind you, Tamara walked at ten months, and she was babied as much as Jimmy Junior. Each baby is different, I guess.

Clinton was here asking for you. I said I didn't know where you were, which of course was true. That Clinton's a good boy and has always been sweet on you.

Thanks for the ten dollars. I'll put it towards the kids' school clothes. Now that it's summer it doesn't matter what they wear.

Write again soon and tell me all about your job. Debbie and Emily are including their drawings.

Love,
Mom.

I grab a sheet of paper and write:

Dear Mom,

Don't ever mention Clinton to me again, and don't tell him where I am, or you'll never hear from me.

I don't feel bad about what I wrote and went right out and mailed—
until I'm lying in bed. Debbie and Emily's pictures are folded up in my
underwear drawer. Part of me wanted to put them up on the wall, but
I didn't want Mary and Judy asking questions. Emily's picture is of
Pixie and her latest kittens—four of them, two striped, one black and
one black and white. She's a good little artist. Debbie's is of herself
wearing bright blue shorts. *Me in my new shorts. They used to be Gloria's.*
Debbie, her red curls sticking out in all directions, is wearing a big
smile and kicking one leg in the air. I feel like crying. I don't though.
If I start, I'll never stop.

Mom is so stupid. "In the summertime, doesn't matter what they
wear." Mom, you just don't notice.

***

Me and Ted go out a couple of nights a week. He asked me up to his
apartment. I was a little nervous, but I can handle him. He's a hunk,
but before we get too involved, I want to make sure he's serious about
me. His apartment's great—a black leather couch and a glass and
chrome coffee table. I love how neat everything is, no junk lying
around. There's even a balcony. We had drinks out there. He's a good
kisser, but I'm not taking any chances. I flirt. We fool around, and
that's that. Billy Sider was a good kisser, too, but I'm sure glad I'm not
married to him and washing diapers.

***

In August, Pam gets engaged. On Monday she was showing off her
ring. A rather measly diamond. Today is Friday and we've gone to
Fran's for lunch. They're all talking about what they're going to do on
the weekend. Beverly and her sister's family are going to their parents'
cottage. Pam whispers something to Cathy and they both giggle.

"What's the big secret?" Beverly asks.

Pam laughs. "I went to my doctor and told him I was getting
married. He admired my ring. And"—she grins—"he fitted me with

a diaphragm. Of course, first he asked me when, and I told him in two weeks."

"Naughty girl," Cathy says, "Considering the big day's not till next June."

"Why wait so long?" I ask.

"Jake's going to teachers' college this September. He's going to be a high-school teacher. His course finishes in May. And I have to save for my dress and our honeymoon. My folks will pay for the wedding, of course."

"You're lucky to have your life planned out."

"You got a boyfriend?" Pam asks.

"Still waiting for Mr. Right."

"What are you, seventeen? No need to be in a hurry," Beverly says.

Maybe she should've hurried. She's 41 and still not married.

* * *

I'm learning a lot at work and not just office skills. I go to Eaton's and buy a gold ring with three tiny crystals. Fake gold, of course. I look up doctors in the phone book. Find one in the area we live, not too close, though.

"Hi, this is Sharon Desjardins. I'm getting married next month, and I'd like to make an appointment with Dr. Baker."

* * *

I act all giggly, show Dr. Baker my ring, and tell him it's less than a month to the big day. Then I pretend to be shy and whisper what I've come for.

At first, he suggests I come back in two weeks, but when I describe to him all there is to do, what with fittings for my wedding dress, centrepieces for the tables, favours for the guests, my flowers, two wedding showers, the trousseau tea my Mother's planning—he gives in. At work Pam talks endlessly about wedding preparations.

However, I'm playing it safe. Even though I have my brand new diaphragm, and it's all fun, I don't go all the way. Heavy petting, a

hand job, that's all he gets. After all, I might want him to marry me. I remember Mom's saying about the cow and the milk. I wonder if that too was one of Grandma's sayings. I have to know he really loves me before we do it. What will he think when he finds out I'm not a virgin?

***

On Friday, Beverly has all us girls over to her apartment for supper. I'm surprised by how ordinary her apartment is. After all, she's the office-manager. While she's warming up the casserole, we have white wine. I notice the drapes are a little faded. The apartment is roomy, but old—hardwood floors like Grandma's place had, and two bedrooms so her sister can visit.

She's a good cook. Supper is chicken in a cream sauce with mushrooms. Beverly talks about all the trouble she's having with her old car. "Why not buy a new one?"

She looks at me kinda funny and laughs. "Not on my salary."

"But you're the office manager."

"Listen, honey, an office manager makes less than any one of the insurance agents. They're men, of course."

𝒯HE LEAVES ARE off the trees and, even after buying clothes, I've got $140 in the bank. I'm not going to be another Beverly. I want to get married.

In September, I sent Mom fifty dollars for school clothes, and another twenty to Gloria for Tamara. I get a letter from Mom every couple of weeks and no more mention of Clinton. Good. I really can forget about him.

I don't buy many clothes because Ted often does. He bought me a really pretty blue dress and gold sandals with spike heels. Another time there was a one hundred percent wool suit—a dark purple. He has these surprises for me at his apartment. They're always gift wrapped in fancy paper. He makes me mad though. Going on about how much he loves me. Okay, Buster, if you love me so much, why aren't we engaged? No matter how hot and bothered he makes me, I'm waiting for a ring.

I handle him pretty well, but must admit, he's getting more and more persuasive. When he's holding me, and I'm rubbing him, I just want to rip off my clothes and let him do what he wants. I could—my diaphragm is carefully inserted before each date. Guys talk about girls who are easy. But he calls me a cock-tease. I tell him: "I want to be with someone who will love me forever and ever, and I don't want to get pregnant."

He says: "I love you a lot, but you're damn frustrating. Don't worry about getting pregnant." He opens his wallet and takes out a rubber.

I tell him my mom's saying about the cow and the milk.

Ted must think that pretty funny. He laughs and laughs. "Oh honey," he says when he stops laughing, "there may be some truth there, but there's another expression: 'You don't buy an overcoat without trying it on.'" He chuckles. "Listen honey, couples don't know if they're compatible, if they don't do it."

All evening free milk and overcoats battle it out in my head.

When I get home, Mary and Judy are already in bed. I make a cup of Nescafé and sit down in the living room. Light a cigarette. Mary and Judy'll complain. They fuss too much. I'm not at all sleepy. Not wildly in love with Ted—he's kind of flabby around the middle, not like Clinton. Oh, hell, why did I have to think of that idiot?

Do I want to end up like Beverly? Unless I get married that's all I can hope for. An ordinary apartment and an old car. Ted's calling me a cock-tease. He could easily find somebody else. Good-looking guy like him and he's rich. Though I'm not in love with him, we have fun fooling around. Look where crazy in love got Mom—pregnant at 16. What made me go all the way with Clinton? Just couldn't stop myself. All that felt great, but I'm sure as hell not going to marry somebody like Clinton and end up with six kids. Those wild crazy feelings aren't a good way to find a husband. Maybe better if you just like the guy.

***

Monday night we're in this new little Hungarian place on University, very posh. Hard to concentrate on the food. Ted leans across the table and offers me a taste of his chocolate pastry. His other hand, under the table, pushes its way up my nylon-stockinged leg. My purple suit suddenly feels way too warm.

I giggle and whisper: "You damn well better have that rubber with you."

***

We're lying on his big soft bed. His arm is flopped across my breasts. He snores lightly. Why do I feel empty? Like this guy could be anybody. It was fun while it was going on. He isn't just anybody. He's rich, good-looking, and my boss.

I slide out from under that arm and find my clothes. Damn, he tore a button off my blouse.

***

After that night things sorta settle into a routine. Dinner a couple of nights a week, then back to his place. I love getting dressed up, being ushered in across thick carpeting to a table set with white linen and shining silverware. I love Ted's arm around me and the smell of his aftershave. I love his apartment so new and clean, his black leather couch and his glass and chrome table. And we have a good time on that big soft bed. I'm really grateful he didn't seem to care I wasn't a virgin. I was going to make up some story, but he put his fingers against my lips and said: "Shh ... no problem at all."

In high school if you were going steady and doing it, everybody figured you'd end up getting married. After all, a guy wants to be the first with the girl he intends to marry. Otherwise he'd think she was a slut.

Most of the time me and Ted do have fun together, just some-times ... my mind wanders. We're in bed and I'm thinking about the emerald-green dress in Simpson's window. Once, I think of being in the sandy cave with Clinton. That makes me so mad. I hate that dummy, Clinton.

Even though I like Ted a lot, I'm not sure he's the one for me. The one big problem is his mother. She lives in Barrie and he has to visit her every weekend. She's not well and he's all she's got.

I'm sick of men who are so damn loyal to their mothers, like Clinton looking after his mother and all his brothers and sisters.

I asked Ted if his mother's poor and that's why he has to look after her. He said: "No, she's very well off, has a big house on Lake Simcoe. But she's lonely since my dad died and I'm her only child."

"Maybe I could go with you some weekend. I'd like to meet her."

"That would be nice, honey, but she's so reclusive, doesn't want anybody in the house but me. She got very odd after Dad's death. She's not well, has a heart condition. I figure I better do what I can for her. I don't expect her to last for more than another year."

At least Clinton's mother was friendly.

"Someday it'll be you and me in the big house on the lake," he said.

***

All very well that someday me and him might live in his mother's big house on the lake, but for now, I'm spending my weekends alone and I can't even brag about dating him. You're not supposed to date your boss. That's him showing favouritism.

MY SPIKED-HEELED SNOW boots make their sure-footed way along Bloor Street the day before Christmas. Snowing, big soft flakes — barely below freezing. My fur coat hangs lightly from my shoulders. My Christmas present to myself. Dyed rabbit, but looks like mink, and full length. Be three years paying it off. So what? Heads turn when Sharon Desjardins walks by. I have shed the Dutton name like a rummage sale coat.

I smile at my reflection in store windows. The rich brown fur shows off my long red hair, swept back with Mom's silver clip. Sterling silver, she said, when she gave it to me.

"A friend gave me that when we lived in Buffalo." She smiled. "I did have some fun."

"Yeah, Mom." Your big mistake was marrying Dumb Dutton. I didn't say that. Thought it though.

I turn down High Park Avenue. Snowing heavier now, turning High Park into bush. In the North they say bush. Grenville kids say woods. I left the North when I was six. I still think bush.

People like Clinton don't know it's a big world out there. He'll never leave Grenville.

Judy and Mary are in Owen Sound. Ted's spending Christmas with his mother. Mom wanted me to come home. Told her I didn't have enough time off. The office is closed till after New Year's.

I sent a big parcel. Tights for all the girls — so much nicer than those awful long brown stockings we used to wear. And come in colours — got a pair of red and a pair of blue for each of them. With tights no kid will be teasing them about their underwear. Got Joey and Charlie sets of cars made in England, and rubber animals for Jimmy Junior and Tamara. For the girls, these dolls, sorta like costume dolls, but the clothes come off. Really nice clothes like teenagers would wear. Orlon sweaters for Mom and Gloria, socks for Jimmy and

Uncle Joey. A five-pound box of chocolates for everybody. I put forty dollars in Mom's card and ten in Gloria's. I know from Mom's last letter Jimmy hasn't been working much.

I could still get a bus. The last bus to London leaves at six tonight. Mom could pick me up, if our ancient station wagon's still running.

I just can't. Christmas dinner will be two chickens, hens too old for laying, stringy and tough. Mom will put her red candles she never lights in the centre of the table and everybody will think it special.

I could buy a turkey and surprise them. Sure, just like Mr. Scrooge gave the poor Cratchit family a goose. The Sunday school put that on. Gloria was one of the Cratchit sisters. I refused to be in it. The whole performance made me so mad. I can't stand pathetic. The story I would've liked, would be for Bob Cratchit to steal Scrooge's money, and buy his family lots of presents. He would do it so cleverly, he wouldn't get caught, and Mr. Scrooge would end up in the poor house.

Last night Ted gave me a great gift — a rhinestone necklace, bracelet and earrings, all set in real silver. I was hoping for a ring, though I don't know if I want to marry him. Not with the mother problem. He did say he didn't expect her to live more than another year.

Our apartment is dumpy and I'm getting tired of Judy and Mary. They don't like it I'm not home every night to have supper with them. Mary had the nerve to say: "You came in awfully late last night."

None of her business. And Mary's dull friends! Lately, they play this game, something like charades, where you try and guess some famous character in literature. Hoity toity bunch. Judy's no better at it than I am. Since November, she's been going home every weekend. What's that all about? Maybe she's homesick.

I don't care I'm not head over heels in love with Ted. Liking is a better basis for marriage. Love made Mom marry a drunken bastard. Ted gave me fifty dollars too for a new dress to wear out to dinner at the Park Plaza first night he's back.

I used it for the down payment on my fur coat. I've got lots of dresses.

*O*N MARCH, ALL hell breaks out. I can't believe what an idiot I've been. Beverly spotted us in the Park Plaza dining room. Or her sister did. I never got that part straight. Ted said we were safe — none of the office crowd had the money to eat there.

Beverly, Pam, and Cathy took me out for lunch. I didn't suspect anything. We often go for lunch.

"So you're dating the boss," Beverly said.

"Huh?"

"Don't deny it, you were seen at the Park Plaza."

"I wanted to tell you guys, but couldn't. We were afraid you'd think he was playing favourites."

They all laughed.

"What's so funny?"

"I thought you were a smart girl," Beverly said. "You're good at your work."

"Don't you know he's married?" Cathy said.

"He is not."

"Where do you think he goes every weekend?" Pam asked.

"To Barrie to visit his mother."

"That's a good one." Pam giggled.

"He has a wife and two kids in Barrie. Ask him, if you don't believe us," Beverly said. Her tone was serious and she's not a mean person. "Nearly ten to one — we better get back to the office."

***

At his apartment that night I ask him, and he confesses, but says he loves me, not the wife, and is only still with her because of the children.

I want to spit in his face. I leave and walk home. I stomp through the slush. Don't give a damn I'm ruining the new silver pumps he bought me. So mad I'm not even cold. An hour later, I'm in front of our house and don't want to go in. I'm such an idiot. Never again.

Thank goodness Mary and Judy are in bed. I'm all shivery. Take a hot shower. The water sluices down my back like a man's hands. Damn him. I'm such a fool. Just playing with me. Dumb country hick. And I thought he wanted to marry me. How will I ever face anybody? I dry off, take two aspirin and crawl into bed. Can't get to sleep. First, I'm hot, then cold. Have three cigarettes in a row. Doesn't help.

The birds are beginning their predawn racket. I have a terrible headache. I take another shower, get dressed and am out of the apartment before Mary and Judy wake up. I go to this all-night diner. Drink coffee and smoke.

I'm the first one in the office. There are appraisals to type. I type and type. Lots of mistakes. Start over. Don't care. Just keep busy. Beverly leaves a butter tart on my desk. I don't look up.

"C'mon for a coffee," says Pam. "You'll feel better."

I shake my head and keep on typing.

At four o'clock I cover up my typewriter and leave. I walk all the way home. Don't go in. Go to the diner, order bacon and eggs. Force them down. Concentrate on not throwing up. Go home.

"Look what came for you." Mary greets me at the door. "I put them in water. Wish somebody would send me roses."

I tear them to pieces and stuff them in the garbage pail. My fingers bleed from the thorns. I don't care. "I've broken up with him."

"Oh, I'm sorry."

* * *

"How about a drink after work?" He's bending over my desk.

My steel letter opener would wipe that smile off his face. I continue typing. "We'll have coffee," I say.

When he catches up with me on the street as I leave work, I don't let him touch me. I stride away, and he follows.

"Don't be upset, honey. Let me explain."

I lead the way into a dumpy coffee shop. "Two coffees," I tell the waitress.

We sit down across from each other. One glance at his smirky face and I blurt out: "I have no intention of dating a married man, and you better leave me alone."

I walk out.

* * *

I expect to be fired, but nothing happens. Beverly, Cathy, and Pam are especially sympathetic after I tell them I've broken up with him.

I feel like a fool and can't bear to keep working here. I keep my head down and try to concentrate on my typing. I can't afford to quit. I need a job.

Ted keeps his distance. Thank God for that. Beverly brings me brownies. I want to throw them at her, even though I know she's trying to be nice. I'm such a pathetic loser.

As the weeks go by it should be better. It's not. I get angrier and angrier—want to punch him in the face.

Cathy and Pam invite me to the movies with them. I say I have a headache.

I just can't stand it any longer. I knock on his office door.

"Come in."

"I want to talk to you."

"Okay, how about over a drink tonight?"

"Right now."

He sorta lifts his eyebrows and frowns.

"I can't work here and you better give me a good letter of recommendation."

"Sharon, are you threatening me?" A rather nasty smile.

"Take it any way you like. I'm 17 and I've told you about my brute of a stepfather. You wouldn't want to meet him."

His smile disappears. He actually pales. I didn't realize he was such a coward.

"Look, honey, I'll gladly give you a letter of recommendation. There's no need to be unpleasant."

"Don't call me honey and thank you."

"I'll have it on your desk by the end of the day."

***

At four o'clock he places a letter on my desk.

"Thank you," I say.

The letter praises my typing, shorthand skills and all round competence. A separate note reads—*Here is your severance pay. I'm sorry you're quitting.*

Included are six twenty-dollar bills. Normally we're paid by cheque. I'm being paid off, but who cares?

I don't say anything to Beverly, Cathy, and Pam. Want to disappear.

***

I don't tell Mary and Judy I've quit. Judy's in Owen Sound and Mary spends all her time studying. She doesn't even notice if I'm around.

I spend the next day job hunting. I give Ted as a reference. He better come through. He's scared of my stepfather. This makes me smile and I haven't felt much like smiling. Imagining Jimmy Dutton threatening anybody makes me laugh out loud. He's afraid to chop off a chicken's head.

Lucky I told Ted the brutal stepfather story. He asked me why I didn't go home for a weekend or at Christmas. I combined Papa and Jimmy. Said Jimmy knocked out Mom's teeth. Said I was afraid of him.

I leave applications at several offices.

While I wait to hear, I'm plain miserable. Judy's still away. Did she quit her job? I don't bother to ask Mary, who's either at the library or shut in her room.

She said: "Too bad you broke up with your boyfriend, but I'm sure you'll find somebody else."

What's she mean by that? That I'm a slut?

Even though I don't see the office girls, I know they feel sorry for me—would rather they'd been nasty.

***

I'm going to have to go apartment hunting. Turns out Judy has moved back to Owen Sound. She's engaged to a boy she knew in high school. That explains all those weekends she went home. She's getting married in August. Wants me to come to her wedding.

Mary is going steady with Stephen, a medical student. He's one of the charade players. I didn't even know they were going out. I'm a complete fool. I thought Judy and Mary were such stick-in-the-muds, and now they are the ones with wedding bells ringing.

Neither of them will be working this summer. Judy needs the summer to prepare for her wedding. Mary's taking a reading course and plans to spend her summer at Sauble Beach. Stephen's parents have a cottage on Georgian Bay so they'll be able to see a lot of each other. Mary said when she's a teacher and Stephen's a doctor they plan to go to Africa and work with the poor. I don't know why this makes me mad.

Mary knows a couple of girls from the university who want to move into our apartment.

WO WEEKS LATER, my luck finally changes. I have a job at Brownlee, Crowley & Sutter: Barristers & Solicitors, a big legal firm. Six girls work in the office, plus the receptionist. More money—fifty-two dollars a week. I rent a bachelor apartment in a new building near College, not far from Yonge where the office is. A small building—just eight apartments. I'm on the second floor at the end and have a tiny balcony. I'm the very first person to live here. Even the white walls smell new. All one room except for the tiny bathroom—toilet, stall shower, and wash bowl. There's an alcove for my bed. A small fridge and stove—can't use the oven and elements at the same time. I love the newness. The rent is seventy-five dollars. Good thing I took Ted's money—almost broke. I bought a rollaway bed and a card table with two folding chairs. When I get paid next Friday, I'll buy some kind of couch. Have to be cheap, but it'll be new. Nothing second-hand is entering my apartment.

Reluctantly, I give Mary and Judy my new address and promise to stay in touch.

I won't though. They know too much about me. They saw me too many times get into Ted's car. They saw the gifts he gave me. I even hinted we were nearly engaged. They don't know much about my family except for my brutal stepfather story. They asked too many questions about why I never went home.

I want to start new.

Ted thought I was a slut and naïve. Me, who always figured I was calling the shots. I'm not a slut. I liked him, even thought we'd get married. To hell with him. I'm going to be different. People can change if they really want to.

I mind my own business and do my job. Don't flirt with the lawyers. Mr. Brownlee's fat and bald. I haven't seen Mr. Crowley. Mr. Sutter's young and good looking, but no doubt married. There are several young lawyers. I ignore them all.

In the lunchroom I listen to the other girls talk and don't say much. I think about the kind of person I want to be.

Sue and Tania talk about their boyfriends, where they went for dinner, and the gifts they got. They wear a lot of makeup and remind me of the old me.

At Eaton's there's a one-day makeup course. I sign up. Basically, what I learn is less is more—a little foundation, muted eye shadow, and paler lipstick.

I go to the library, as a little kid I loved reading, start with authors we studied in high school—Dickens, Thomas Hardy. I discover American authors like Faulkner and plays by Tennessee Williams, and read art books, go to the gallery.

I love my apartment. Spend summer weekends sitting on my tiny balcony, reading and smoking.

I'm eighteen. I remind myself that's not old—feels old. At the office, I get an invitation to Pam's wedding. She must've found out where I work through Ted. I gave him as a reference. I get an invitation to Judy's wedding. Judy is a year older than I am, Pam, three.

I line the wedding invitations up on the windowsill. The thick ivory paper is embossed with silver.

One morning I crawl out of bed with a headache and tear both invitations into tiny pieces, instant confetti.

I get regular letters from Mom. "You must get summer holidays, why not come home for a week?"

I reply: "I've changed jobs. No holidays." I send her ten dollars.

She writes back: "Come for a weekend then."

***

Labour Day weekend I go home. I get on the bus. It's crowded. An older woman sits beside me, and I listen to the story of her three daughters, of how well they're doing. All three of her girls are married, one even married a doctor. Her second grandchild will arrive in October.

I look out the window. The fields are brown. Did hear something on the radio about a drought. In Toronto I'm not much aware of the weather.

I've been away for over a year. The fields were green when I left.

As the bus pulls into the terminal I'm shocked when I see Mom. In a faded skirt and a blouse I made in Home Ec, she looks so old, even grey in her hair now. My mother had beautiful red curls and once wore a tight red blouse showing off her breasts. Now she doesn't appear to have any.

She grabs me in a great bear hug, then holds me at arm's length. "You look good, Sharon. So all grown up."

She's still driving Grandma's old station wagon. There's a fume-y smell and the engine knocks.

"You need a new car."

Mom smiles. "We're lucky how this one's lasted."

Then we're home and all the kids run out to meet me. And yeah, they're all cleaned up and in their best clothes. It's more than I can bear and burst into tears. I'm hugged, made much of, and served lemonade with ice cubes on the cleared off front porch. Debbie shows me the new-old refrigerator, the origin of the ice cubes. "It was all rusty, but Daddy painted it."

Gloria shows off Tamara in a pink nylon dress. "She's smart like you. She can count and she's only two. Count for Auntie Sharon."

"One, twos, five, eight."

"Pretty good," I say and notice Gloria is wearing a skirt I wore in grade nine.

Jimmy's on the couch and apologizes for not getting up. "Me back's like a knife."

Uncle Joey has changed the most. He's positively gaunt, and his hair is completely grey. "Hey, red spitfire," and he hugs me. He starts coughing. "Sorry," he splutters. He coughs up great gobs into a very dirty handkerchief. Not even an actual hanky, looks like a piece of an old sheet. I can't speak. If I do, I'll start crying.

"Poor Joey," Mom says later in the kitchen. "His cough's worse ever since his pneumonia this past winter. And he's so thin. Jimmy said he was a big strapping boy before he went off to be gassed in the war."

Supper is roast chicken, potatoes, and corn from the garden.

"Gloria has become quite the gardener. Debbie and Emily are helping, too," Mom tells me.

Later, when we're sitting on the porch, and the kids are doing the dishes, I ask Mom: "How on earth are you managing?"

Mom smiles. "I have news."

For an awful moment I think she's going to tell me she's pregnant yet again.

"I have a job," she says. "At Stedmans. Gloria watches the kids."

"What do they pay you?"

"Twenty-two a week. It buys the groceries."

***

Me and all the kids are playing a version of volleyball I invented years ago. There are no rules—just keep the ball in the air going back and forth over the clothesline. Even Jimmy Junior and Tamara are trying to play.

We're having a great time until Tamara trips over a toy truck hidden in the long grass. She's really crying, and when I pick her I see blood on her knee. "You kids keep the game going. I'll take her to her mom."

The kitchen's empty, and poor Tamara's wailing. "Gloria!"

"Down here," Gloria calls.

I carry Tamara down the cellar stairs.

Gloria stands up and takes her from me. "Oh my, what happened to you?" She kisses the scraped knee, and Tamara's sobs lessen.

I stare at the bucket on the floor, filled with blood-soaked rags, and I remember grade nine.

I was at school when it started. I folded paper towels into my panties and went to find Donna. She was at her locker talking to a couple of boys. I whispered in her ear, and she took a cosmetic bag from the shelf and stuffed it in her purse. "C'mon," she said.

"What's the big secret?" one of the guys asked.

"For us to know and you to find out," Donna teased. We went off arm in arm to the washroom.

"I always come prepared," she said, and lent me a belt and Kotex. "Now you're a woman," Donna said between giggles. "That's what Mom said my first time. She took me out for lunch just me and her."

"Not too likely at my house."

When we were walking home from school, she insisted on stopping at the Quick Stop.

"You're going to get your special lunch." She bought me a hamburger, fries, and a root beer.

When I got home, I told Mom I needed money for Kotex.

"My little girl's growing up." She smiled.

Maybe we were going to do something special.

We went into her room, and she got a box out of her wardrobe. It was filled with folded rags, and an elastic belt and safety pins. "I've got a bucket down cellar. You just put them to soak till washday."

"What the hell! I won't wear those. Do you want all the girls at school laughing at me? I need Kotex, Mom, Kotex!"

"Keep your voice down. The little kids don't need to know."

"At school we change for gym, Mom."

"So change in a toilet stall."

"I won't!" I yelled and ran upstairs.

I got in bed and stayed there. Didn't come down when she called me for supper. When Gloria and the kids came into our room, I yelled at them to get out. Sometime during the evening Mom came in with a big box of Kotex and a store-bought belt.

"If it's that important," she said.

I didn't say anything.

"Keep the box under your bed."

After she left the room, I went in the bathroom and cleaned myself up. We never discussed it, but she refilled the box under my bed. A few months later, I was working at Siders' restaurant and could buy my own. Gloria started in grade seven, and I showed her my supply. But nobody took her out for lunch. Why didn't I?

I stare at the bucket of bloody rags.

"I'll just take Tamara up and fix her knee," Gloria says. "What's the matter? Not your fault. Kids are always getting hurt."

"Guess so," I say, and we go upstairs.

***

Back in Toronto, I sit on my balcony, smoke, and brood. Poverty is a bucket of bloody rags.

I LIKE THIS JOB. The law office handles mainly real estate, and civil cases—one firm suing another, that sort of thing. Real estate's more interesting than insurance, and a lot of money changes hands. I enjoy doing deed searches. I've worked here six months before I'm sent to the registry office to search a deed. Only get to go then because one of the senior secretaries is ill.

Properties change hands frequently, usually for more money. A sudden jump often means a building went up on the lot. Now when I walk around the city, I think about long-ago Toronto.

I'm taking a night course: "Famous Women Writers." We read Jane Austen's *Northanger Abbey*. In grade 12 I read *Pride and Prejudice*. *Northanger Abbey*'s pretty good. Now we're reading *To the Lighthouse* by Virginia Woolf.

I don't date much. The girls in the office set me up with guys. They're just out for a good time. I'm sick of the game—the guy trying to get into my pants and me trying to keep him out.

* * *

At the Christmas party most people are pretty drunk. They talk and laugh too loud. The room is a smoky haze. I light another cigarette and pour my drink into a handy rubber plant. Stubbing out my cigarette, I head for the door.

Art Midwood blocks my way. He just started here a month ago. Tall, blonde, and good looking. I don't know him, but everybody seems to like him.

"Your glass is empty. Here's another."

"I was just leaving."

"Too early for a pretty girl like you." He hands me the drink. "Have you noticed how stupid people sound when they're drinking?"

"Yeah, I have."

"That fellow over there, one of the senior partners, tells the same dumb jokes every time he gets drunk."

"Is that Mr. Crowley?"

"You got it. He's a womanizer—can't stand that type. Just because he has money thinks he's entitled."

"You'll have to excuse me. The noise is giving me a headache. Nice to meet you, but I'm going home."

"Pretty nasty out there—the rain's turned to ice. How about we go to my place for a quiet cup of tea? Tea's good for a headache, and after, I'll give you a lift home."

Why do I go with him? He seems nice and I'm bored. It's Christmas, and let's face it, I haven't been having much fun lately.

He drives a brand new Chevy. Just finished school and has a new car, a graduation present from his folks, he tells me.

His apartment is as nice as Ted's. He lays my fur coat over a chair. I expect he'll put on the kettle, but he takes hold of my shoulders and kisses me.

"Christ, keep your hands to yourself!" I give him a good push.

"C'mon, honey, I know you want it." He shoves me up against the wall. His fingers gouge my shoulders, and his meaty tongue slurps my clenched teeth.

I dig my spike heel into his ankle.

"Like it rough, do ya?" He grips my arm with one hand and with the other yanks up my skirt.

I knee him in the crotch. With a surprised look, he lets go. I follow up with a full kick.

He's bent over and cursing.

I grab my coat and bag and make for the door.

I'm out in the hall.

He's at the door.

I run.

"Fuckin cunt," echoes in my ears.

Out on the street, I keep going until lack of breath and a stabbing pain in my side stop me. Have no idea where I am. My fur coat is soaking and getting heavier and heavier.

Idiot, idiot. I stand here in the icy rain, and bawl and laugh crazy. Shut up, get hold of yourself. No sign of that creep. He wouldn't dare attack me on the street. There's a steady stream of cars.

I walk to the nearest street sign—Woodbine, ah, the racetrack. I've been here with Ted. If I keep walking, I'll come to Queen. I walk for blocks and blocks and come not to Queen, but the lake. I'm going the wrong way. Oh, my feet hurt, and even my hair's coated with ice. What I'd give for a pair of sneakers right now!

Half an hour later, soaked with sweat, but with freezing ears and toes, I reach Queen and wait another half hour for the streetcar. My ice-coated fur weighs a ton. .

On the streetcar the ice melts off my coat and pools at my feet. My ears and toes burn. Nearly an hour ride to Yonge, then the subway to College, another streetcar to my stop.

It's one in the morning by the time I stumble into my apartment. I lock the door, pull off my shoes, throw my coat over a chair and crawl into bed.

Though I'm sweating, my teeth won't stop chattering,

All the guys I went out with in high school and nothing like this happened.

***

I wake up stiff and sore. Take a long hot shower. Back home, if I ran more than a few inches in the tub, the water ran cold.

I rescue my poor coat and hang it on the shower rod to dry. Dye from the lining has stained the carpet. Hope I can get it out.

In old jeans, sweat shirt, and wrapped in a blanket, I go out on the balcony for a smoke.

The morning sun melts the ice from the trees and makes last night a bad dream.

I bandage my blistered heels—my feet so swollen my sneakers barely fit. I grab my old windbreaker and leave the apartment. A kerchief hides my hair. I never dress like this. What if somebody from work sees me? Today, I don't care.

Keep looking over my shoulder. That creep has me spooked.

I go back to my apartment. Saturday morning—have the whole week off. Christmas isn't till Tuesday.

I shampoo the stain on the carpet. It cleans up perfectly. I vacuum the whole apartment. Scrub the bathroom. Wash my angora sweater. Lay it on a towel on the kitchen counter to dry. Wash out my lace-y underwear. Set up the drying rack in the kitchen. I clean the fridge, scour under the elements on the stove, and scrub the seldom-used oven. Ten to eleven. How will I endure a week of this?

Call somebody. The girls from the office are always ready to go for lunch, or shopping.

Who am I kidding? This morning they're sleeping off last night. Anyway, everybody either has relatives coming or they're going home for the holidays.

After another hour on the balcony, and three more cigarettes, I phone Mom. Gloria answers. "Sharon! Are you coming home for Christmas?"

"How are you?"

"Fine, Mom's not so good—bronchitis. We had to have the doctor. Are you able to come home?"

"What did the doctor say?"

"Oh, she should be okay."

"I've got some time off."

"I'll pick you up. I've got my license now. The kids'll be so excited. Sharon, we all miss you."

"Okay, there's a bus that gets in at five."

"I'll be there."

What have I done now? Wasn't Labour Day weekend bad enough? I already told them I didn't have time off and sent a big parcel. Still, if Mom's sick, I should go, but Christ, it's depressing.

***

As my bus pulls into the terminal, I look out the window. Oh my God, Gloria's wearing Mom's old coat with the ratty fur collar. Mom had that coat in Cadillac. On short little Gloria the coat hangs over her shoes. She's wearing a flowered kerchief, and could pass for forty.

Little Joey and Charlie are both trying to pull the wagon that holds Tamara, Jimmy Junior, and a ragged quilt. The wagon, we found long ago in Jimmy's garage, has rusty steel-rimmed wheels, one of which appears to have been replaced with a baby buggy wheel. Debbie, Emily, and Judy stand like little soldiers, though Debbie is holding Judy's hand. All three have crooked ponytails tied with red ribbons. Mismatched barrettes attempt to hold the hair the ponytails missed. They must've fixed each other's hair. Velvet and taffeta dresses show under stained coats. Emily's coat, I recognize — royal blue velvet from Grants. Grandma bought it for Gloria. It's missing a pocket.

"They all wanted to come meet your bus." Gloria hugs me. "With them out of the house Mom can rest."

The three little girls, all with big grins, hang back.

I just get a chance to say: "Hi everybody," before Little Joey and Charlie tip over the wagon and Tamara and Jimmy Junior roll onto the pavement. Tamara and Jimmy Junior are bawling. Gloria's yelling at the boys. The three girls stand with their smiles frozen in place.

I pick up Tamara and she rubs her runny nose against my fur. Jimmy Junior, already on his feet, is trying to pound his brothers.

The other passengers make a wide berth around us.

My homecoming.

We ride with the windows open so the fumes won't get us. I'm holding Jimmy Junior. Debbie's holding Tamara. We're up front with Gloria. The other four are in the back along with the wagon and assorted blankets. I'm surprised Gloria didn't add old Pal to the mix.

"How's Pal doing?"

"Oh Sharon, I should've written you. He died in November." Her voice falters. "The last while I had to feed him with an eye dropper — just milk and chicken broth."

"He was in pretty bad shape when I was home Labour Day weekend."

"Just kept getting weaker. Died one evening with his head on my lap. Gave sorta a big sigh, and a thump of his tail, and he was gone." She wipes at her eyes.

"Gloria, he was really old."

"Mom figured at least fifteen. I loved that dog."

"I know."

"Reubels' dog had pups. She brought us over one last week. Skippy is part collie, part hound. Awful cute."

Warm pee is dripping down my leg. "This kid just peed on me!"

"Oh my, I should've put a diaper on him. He's been so good lately. Tamara's been trained since September."

That doesn't change the fact my fur's going to have to go to the cleaners, I think, don't say.

***

I go right in to see Mom. On the way home Gloria told me that Mom doesn't only have bronchitis—she's pregnant and the doctor has ordered her to stay in bed. She's pale with great dark circles under her eyes. Her cheeks are sunk in and there's more grey than I remember in her hair.

"Hi, Sharon, come sit on the bed."

"Oh, Mom." I kiss her forehead.

"I know I look like hell. Just let me get my teeth in. I take them out while I'm resting. They make my jaw ache so."

She's got the teeth in now and looks only slightly better.

"How long have you been sick?"

"Been in bed the past week. Dr. Stewart said I better not take chances. I've had some bleeding. Oh, I'm so glad you're here to give Gloria a hand. How long can you stay?"

"A week."

"That's wonderful, dear. You look just beautiful, Sharon."

"Ah, Mom." I'm scared I'm going to cry. "Can I make you some tea?"

"That would be lovely, dear."

***

Jimmy's back bothers him and Uncle Joey has just been diagnosed with lung cancer. The house is dirtier than I remember. Gloria's puppy isn't housetrained, plus there's an old cat that pees everywhere. It has

runny eyes and has lost most of the fur on its face. I've seen road-kill that's better looking. The whole house stinks of cat pee.

"Gloria, why don't you get rid of that cat?" She gives me such a look, you'd think I'd suggested shooting Jimmy. Now that I think of it, that wouldn't be a bad idea. He's moaning away on the couch.

"That's Tiger, my first kitten. Don't you remember? The day we arrived here the old cat was on the porch. The kittens were just old enough to crawl off their blanket. Daddy said: 'Honey, you take anyone ya like.' I held Tiger and knew everything was going to be better. We finally had a home. You think I'd kill her?"

"Put her out of her misery."

"She's not miserable." Gloria picks up the dirty thing and cuddles it. "See, she can still purr."

Obviously, there's no point in saying anything.

It pours rain on Christmas Day. I bought new sleds at the hardware store downtown. Seven children stuck in the house, and the television isn't working. Instead of playing with their new toys, they're all down the floor, pretending to be dogs chasing the new puppy. Uncle Joey's laughing his head off.

Mom miscarries on Boxing Day. I help her into the back seat, and Jimmy climbs in beside her. Listening to Mom sob, I grit my teeth and drive to the hospital. Jimmy moans and wails: "Jesus, help us. Oh God, oh God!"

In the rearview mirror I see Mom wrap her arms around him.

* * *

Back at the Plum, me and Gloria bundle up all the kids and, with Debbie in charge, send them off to the hill with the new sleds. Thank goodness it snowed last night.

Me and Gloria tackle cleaning up Mom's bed. Fortunately, we put newspapers over the sheet when it all started. The mattress isn't stained. Well, no new stains. I'm about to gather up the whole mess, when Gloria puts her hand on my arm.

"Is the baby ... there?" she sobs.

"There isn't a baby," I snap. "She was barely three months pregnant."

"Well, a would-be baby?"

"It's just a disgusting mess." I gather up the sheet and newspapers and haul it all down to the cellar. Gloria follows me.

I rinse out the sheet in the laundry tub and then leave it to soak. I fold up the newspapers, take them back up to the kitchen. I'm about to stuff the whole mess in the kitchen woodstove when Gloria cries: "Stop, we've got to bury it." She tries to grab the papers.

"Don't be stupid." I stuff the whole mess in and slam the stove door.

Gloria, still sobbing, is searching the cupboard drawer for something.

"Bury it! There's a foot of snow, and the kids might come back any moment."

She lights a stubby candle, sits down at the kitchen table, and closes her eyes.

"What are you doing?"

She ignores me for a moment, before opening her eyes. "I was just saying a little prayer for the baby," she whimpers.

I leave the room.

***

Mom's home the next day. She can't sleep because of her cough, and I sit up with her.

"Your uncle Joey will be dead by spring. It would've been nice to have a new baby in the house. There's nothing like a new baby to make everybody feel better."

"Oh, Mom, think of all the crying, and the diapers — all that mess!"

"All that mess, you say. I love all that mess — a new baby in my arms, children playing with the kittens or running through the house, followed by the dog. In that neat frowning house where I grew up, I longed for all that mess, as you call it."

LEAVE IN THE MORNING. On the bus I grind my teeth and will us to go faster. At least in my Christmas parcel I gave all the kids new underwear and socks, tights for the girls. At least that.

Back in my tiny but clean apartment, I wrap up in a blanket, sit on my balcony, and smoke.

I take my fur coat to the cleaner's — a very expensive cleaning job, and he'll mend the spot the puppy chewed. "It'll hardly show," he says.

***

Snows a lot in January — so damn sick of wading through slush that invariably fills my boots. On the streetcar my wet feet ache and burn. I hate people in cars, whizzing by, spraying guck everywhere. By February my coat's been to the cleaners twice. I hibernate in my apartment — read a lot and smoke too much.

By March I'm going stir crazy and, when Gail from the office suggests a show Friday night, I agree. We see *The Apartment*. Gail thinks it's funny. I don't see anything funny about the higher-ups using their secretaries like prostitutes.

***

Me and Gail sometimes go shopping Saturday afternoons and occasionally to another show. She's from Toronto and introduces me to Brad, a guy she went to high school with. He and Gail's boyfriend Mike work at a Ford dealership on Queen.

We all go to the show together. Brad asks if I like tennis. I confess I've never played.

"We'll teach you," Gail says.

So here I am on a cool April morning, brand new racket in hand, wondering what I've got myself into. The tennis courts are in a park. Brad says you have to get here early or you'll have to wait for a court.

He stands behind me, holds my arms and shows me how to serve. He's funny looking—only a few inches taller than me and a bit chubby.

That first day we don't actually play a game just hit the ball back and forth while I get the hang of it.

That's how we start meeting every Saturday morning for tennis. I'm in for two surprises. One, I love tennis—the running, leaping. Haven't had this much fun since my bike-riding, tree-climbing days. Second surprise is Brad is the best player of all of us. Amazing how fast he moves on a tennis court. He doesn't look at all athletic.

Friday after work Gail and I buy new short-shorts for our tennis date tomorrow morning. She chooses blue so I get the pale pink ones. I buy a pink-and-white striped sleeveless blouse to go with them. The shorts come with a narrow white belt that shows off my 23-inch waist very nicely.

On Saturday I feel good leaping around the court. Brad's game's a little off which makes me giggle. He's a bit distracted by my new pink shorts.

The group waiting to use the courts is dressed all in white. The girls' outfits have these little skirts that look really dumb and don't show off their bums at all.

***

I got bored with my night course. Wasn't getting that much out of some of the stuff we read. *To the Lighthouse* was kinda dull. The teacher said Virginia Woolf drowned herself. She walked into a river with stones in her pockets—so she couldn't change her mind. I guess her writing didn't make her happy.

Brad and I go out occasionally on our own now. After the show or dinner we go back to his parents' place in Scarborough. Brad still lives at home. The house is a very clean three-bedroom brick bungalow with hardwood floors and a finished recreation room in the basement. Brad's their only child.

His parents are nice and so is Brad. On the couch in that recreation room we watch television and neck. We have a bit of fun, but he talks too much. I'm sick of hearing about the merits of Ford cars. I learn more than I ever wanted to know about V-8 engines. He's a nice guy, but I don't see him being a great success. And what if he lost his job?

Donna back home married Rick who works at a car lot. The difference is his dad owns Waddell Ford. Brad's father is a plumber.

***

May's a good month. I get a promotion and a raise. I'm Mr. Brownlee's private secretary. My job is interesting. I do all the research on deals he's handling — often commercial properties worth over $100,000.

Mr. Brownlee's nice, a real gentleman. His wife is nice, too. I've been to their house for dinner. Their kids, Ashley and Philip, go to the Toronto French School. Mr. Brownlee told me they'll be bilingual which is important if they ever want to work for the government. Philip, who's twelve, is considering law. Ashley, at ten, wants to be a doctor.

"Don't you mean a nurse," I say to her.

"No," she says, "Mummy said I can be a doctor."

"We're teaching the children to aim high. By the time Ashley's in university, there'll be lots of women in medicine," her mother says.

"That's wonderful," is all I can think to say.

***

June is not so good. Mom phones.

"Uncle Joey died last night. The funeral's on Saturday. Will you come, please?"

"I'll take the early bus. Gets there at eleven."

Poor Uncle Joey. At least no more mean kids teasing him. What a life.

***

This time Mom meets my bus. I hug her. She's skinnier than ever. Her Evening in Paris perfume makes me want to cry.

All she talks about is Jimmy. "He's taking it hard. His little brother. He beats himself up over letting the boys join the army. Showed me a picture of the three of them before the war. Joey and Raymond were both over six feet, big muscular boys, and looked so young. Hard to believe it's them. Jimmy keeps saying if anybody had to go, it should've been him. I tell him that's nonsense. He was the one supporting the family. But it doesn't do any good."

"How have you been, Mom?"

"Oh fine, working at the store. Poor Uncle Joey. When I first came here, I resented him. Wanted it to be just our little family."

"We were pretty hard up."

"I was a selfish, immature girl. One thing Jimmy has taught me is there's always room for one more at the table."

A debatable point, I think, don't say.

When we come in the door, Little Joey and Charlie are wrestling on the living room rug.

"Get upstairs and get dressed." Mom yanks them to their feet and gives them a push.

In the kitchen, Gloria's slapping together peanut butter sandwiches. Debbie's all dressed up in a plaid taffeta dress two sizes too big for her. She's doing Tamara's hair. Emily and Judy's hair is already up in crooked ponytails and mismatched barrettes.

Jimmy Junior runs naked through the kitchen and Gloria tells Debbie to get him dressed.

Mom gathers him up just as Jimmy Senior, wearing only trousers, storms into the room.

"Poor Joey," he wails. "Never had a chance. Oh boy, oh boy, my poor little brother. What'll I do? Oh dear God, what'll I do?" Snot and tears dribble down his face.

What a clown! Get a grip, Jimmy.

Mom hands me the squirming kid, who I hold at arm's length. At least I'm not wearing my fur.

She wipes her husband's face with a tea towel and leads him off to their bedroom.

I tuck Jimmy Junior under my arm and carry him upstairs. Let him down in the babies' room. There's a basket of clean laundry on the floor, but I can't find a diaper. "Where are the diapers?"

"Me big boy, wear pants."

"Do you now? So where are they?"

He points at the basket.

Finally, I locate a pair of little boys' underwear and help him into them. Laid out on the bed are navy pants and a white t-shirt. I dress him, find socks, but no shoes.

I lead him downstairs and ask Gloria where his shoes are.

"In the pile by the back door—he knows which ones."

Jimmy Junior with a proud grin holds up a mud-encrusted sneaker.

* * *

I'm surprised at the number of people at Uncle Joey's funeral. A lot of veterans. At the cemetery a bugler plays *The Last Post*. He's white haired, maybe was in the First World War. His red coat decorated with medals stands out from the grey crowd. The people aren't really grey—just dowdily dressed. The music is sad, like Uncle Joey's life. Uncle Raymond wasn't going to live like that. Who can blame him?

We go back to the house and drink beer, eat baloney and mock chicken sandwiches with the crusts cut off, and the desserts the neighbours have brought. Jimmy's wearing that same worn-out suit he wore for Holly's wedding in Buffalo. The jacket still won't button over his belly. Mom's wearing the yellow dress I bought her in London when I was still in high school. Looks new. She must've kept it for good. Too big on her now and why doesn't she wear a bra? She sits with her arm around Jimmy while me and my sisters serve the food. The kids, though well scrubbed, are all wearing rummage sale clothes.

After everybody leaves, Jimmy, at Mom's insistence, takes a nap. Gloria and her boyfriend pack up all the kids and take them to the park. Brian Hoffman, a big fat slob, reminds me of that jerk who got her pregnant. She told me he moved here from Nova Scotia with his parents and two younger brothers. "He's looking for a job," she said.

Me and Mom sit down with a cup of tea. I should shut up, but what the hell I sent her thirty dollars last month. "Mom, why don't you buy the kids some decent clothes?"

"I do the best I can. Both Jimmy Junior and Tamara had strep throat. Antibiotics are expensive."

All evening Gloria and her boyfriend sit on the couch and paw each other.

I go to bed early, but wake up in the night. One of the kids is crying —must be Jimmy Junior or Tamara. Not my problem. I try to go back to sleep. Can't. I'm in my old bed—Debbie insisted. I look for her on the feather tick on the floor. She's gone. Whoever was crying has stopped.

I go downstairs to investigate, and find her in the kitchen. She's holding Jimmy Junior on her lap. He's sucking on a baby bottle. Too old for that. Debbie's rocking him in Mom's chair. "Mom finally got Daddy to go to bed," she says.

My old t-shirt she wears as a nightie doesn't cover her skinny legs. Her curly red hair is lighter than mine, and her eyes are grey, but oh boy, she reminds me of me.

"How do you do in school?"

"Good. Miss Shupe says I'm real smart."

"What do you plan to do when you're finished?"

"Be a secretary like you."

I'd like to tell her she could be a doctor. It would be a lie.

ULY 24TH, 1960

Dear Sharon,

Happy news. Brian and I are married. We got married in Rev. Miller's office. Maybe I should've asked you to come, but I know you don't like coming home too often, and it wasn't like a formal wedding, just Mom and Daddy and us. I wore a pink eyelet sundress Mom helped me make. We made Tammy a pink dress too. I never was good at sewing like you, plus Daddy's mother's old treadle is the pits.

Big weddings are nice, but expensive, and we got better ways to spend our money. Afterwards, the five of us went to that new southern fried chicken place.

We're staying on here. Brian's working at the lumberyard, and we could get a little apartment, but Mom and Daddy need our help. Anyway, Tammy would find leaving the other kids awfully hard, and I wouldn't want to leave my garden behind.

We have Charlie and Little Joey's room. They've moved into Uncle Joey's room off the kitchen. Jimmy Junior, we call him J.J. now—he and Tammy are sharing the babies' room.

Hope you're having a good time in the big city. Come visit us when you can.

Love,
Gloria

P.S.
Skippy finally got housetrained. He's a good dog, but there'll never be another Pal.

She's never going to get away and I can't bear it. I was supposed to look after her. When she was scared, I used to tell her stories. In my story the children get on the train, escape the big bad wolf, and get their heart's desire. I should've told her more about big bad wolves, how they drag you down, chew up your life. Run, little sister, run. Vite, vite. Too late now.

I send her twenty dollars, stick it in a nice card, but don't go home.

***

First day in October I buy a brand-new red Volkswagen Beetle. I got another raise, making sixty a week now. I'll be five years paying for my car, but who cares.

Once the weather gets too cold for tennis, I make excuses not to go out with Brad. Gail and Mike broke up. That makes it easier for me not to see Brad.

Saturdays I clean my apartment and do my hand-wash. Bought a small television and I read a lot. I've discovered historical fiction. I go from Napoleon's court to the carryings-on of Henry the Eighth. I've had enough of Tennessee Williams and Virginia Woolf. There's plenty misery in the world without reading about it. Historical novels don't dwell on the misery, more about sumptuous meals, exotic places, and lots of sex.

By Sunday, I'm usually bored with my own company. My little red car is freedom. I drive and drive. One time I take Highway 2 and drive all the way to Kingston, stopping in little towns along the way. Have delicious chocolate cream pie at a greasy spoon restaurant. I people-watch and then drive on. In Kingston there's a ferry that goes to an island. I love the island. Park my car and sit on a rocky beach. A few snowflakes fall, but I don't care. I get my emergency blanket out of the car and wrap up in that. I watch the waves roll in over flat rocks and the last few leaves drop from grey limbs. Stay so long, I almost miss the ferry back.

Kingston was too far to go — midnight before I get home. I have to drag myself to work the next morning.

* * *

I don't attend the Christmas party. There'll be no repeats of last year. I sit on my balcony in my fur coat, drink tea, and smoke. A mild night. A bit of wet snow fell earlier, but it's gone. Most likely be a green Christmas. I don't care one way or another. A mild night, but the lights glitter cold. All those cars with places to go even at one a.m.

I'm not going home. Can't take another family Christmas.

* * *

In January Mrs. Brownlee calls me up. "Hi Sharon, this is Marion."

It takes me a moment to realize it's her. "Oh, hi." In my head she's Mrs. Brownlee.

"We'd like to have you over for dinner on Friday. Of course, maybe you already have plans."

"No plans."

"We're having a little dinner party—Judith and Stan Dawson, and Jack will be there. You know Jack Sutter?"

"I know he's one of the lawyers."

"It's nice to have an even number at a dinner party. Oh, my." She laughs. "I'm not doing this very well at all. Jack would like to meet you."

"He would?"

"Is that all right?"

"Is he married?"

"No, of course not. Sharon, you're no doubt wondering why he doesn't just ask you out. He's a very nice man, but he is shy around women. I think he got his heart broken in university and hasn't asked a girl out since ... most likely you're already going with someone."

"Not at the moment."

"Will you give him a chance then?"

"I guess."

"Here, I've embarrassed you."

"No, but how can he be shy? Mr. Brownlee's called him a killer in the courtroom."

"Oh Sharon, men are strange beings. Can you make your own way over here? Or Bill could pick you up."

"I can get there on my own."

"You remember we're at 55 Beech Avenue. You'll take a cab, dear?"

"Sure."

"See you Friday, Sharon."

"Yes, thanks." I hang up. How peculiar. At least now I know Jack Sutter's not married. He's around thirty, good looking. Maybe, just maybe, my luck has changed.

I won't waste money on a cab. I'll take the streetcar.

***

By Friday I wish I'd said no. It's just too peculiar. I went to dinner at Brownlee's before, and that was fine. The Brownlees are easy to talk to, but who are the Dawsons? Jack is sorta my date? I wouldn't mind going out with him, now that I know he's not married. Alone with him I could handle things. But a formal dinner at my boss's place? I can't mess up. I'll wear my little black dress and won't flirt. In Home Ec Mrs. Laurence said you couldn't go wrong with a little black dress.

***

I've just settled myself on the Queen car when a stinky fat man in grubby clothes sits next to me. I pull my fur coat tighter around me. I should've stood. Can't imagine being able to eat anything—my stomach hurts. I'm wearing Mom's silver hair clip. Have lots of others, but hers makes me feel safe. She used to be so pretty. I mustn't screw up.

Oh no, there's a traffic jam, and we're just sitting here. I hear a siren—must've been an accident. The stinky fat man crowds me. Wish I could stand up.

Finally, we're moving. By the time I get off at Beech, I'm really late. I hope the fat man's stink didn't rub off on me. I touch Mom's silver clip for luck and ring the bell.

Mr. Brownlee takes my coat.

"Sorry I'm late."

"Doesn't matter, dear." Mrs. Brownlee gives me a hug. She's awfully nice.

The men stand up when I enter and Mrs. Brownlee introduces me. Both Mr. Dawson, a grey-haired guy, and Jack shake my hand. Jack has blue eyes, cold until he smiles and says: "So nice to see you outside of the office."

I smile back, just a little smile. "Nice to be here."

Mrs. Brownlee takes my hand, "Oh, your fingers are like ice. Sit by the fire, dear."

She seats me by the fireplace, right next to Jack. Mrs. Dawson is on his other side.

"May I get you a glass of white wine?" Mr. Brownlee asks.

"Yes, please."

Mrs. Dawson asks: "Where are you from, Sharon?"

"A small town in Quebec. You wouldn't have heard of it." None of her business.

"What brought you to Toronto?"

"I like the city."

Mr. Brownlee hands me my wine.

"Toronto's growing rapidly — lots of job opportunities," Jack says.

I turn to him and smile, not a flirty one. "I like how Toronto's growing. Deed searches are interesting because you can see all the times a property's changed hands."

"Yes, history written in real estate."

"Jack, haven't seen you since Stratford," Mrs. Dawson says, touching his arm.

She's got a tan in the middle of winter. Her blonde hair looks lacquered, not a strand out of place. Why doesn't the nosy bitch butt out and let me talk to him?

"Yes, it was at *Othello*, wasn't it?" Jack says.

"That's right. What did you think of the production?"

"They've done better. Sharon, do you enjoy Shakespeare?"

"I haven't been to Stratford."

"I don't suppose you've had the opportunity," the old bitch says.

"I like reading plays," I tell Jack.

"I do, too. I often think you get more out of a Shakespearean play reading it than seeing it produced."

Thank goodness Mrs. Brownlee announces dinner, and I'm spared any more discussion of Shakespeare. People are leaving their glasses on the coffee table so I do, too. Mine's still full.

We all file into the dining room—white linen cloth, and sparkling gold and white china. Oh God, don't make me sit anywhere near that bitch. And where are the children?

For once, God must be listening. Mr. Brownlee's on one side of me and Jack on the other.

There are fresh wine glasses on the table and Mr. Brownlee fills them. Mrs. Dawson who, damn it, is on the other side of Jack, is discussing some ski trip. Sounds like they all went together. She talks right through the clam chowder, Caesar salad, and home-baked bread. I say a silent thank you to Mrs. Laurence who taught me which fork is which, and don't cut your bread in half, tear it, and whatever you do, don't pick up a whole slice and chomp it down like we do at the Plum.

"So, you like Toronto?" Jack says.

"Yes, there's more to do here than in a small town."

"What kind of things do you like to do?"

"Oh, um ... go to the art gallery."

"What kind of art do you like?"

"Rembrandt is my favourite."

"Ah, the Old Masters."

"Jack, on your next trip to Ottawa, drop in at the National Gallery. The MacDougal family donated their collection—some fine canvasses." Mrs. Dawson just won't stop talking. She has one of those super-cultured voices I can't stand. She talks all through the chicken done in some spicy sauce.

Thank God, Mrs. Brownlee brings in the dessert and ends the art discussion. "That looks too lovely to eat," I say eying the cherry cheesecake.

***

Finally, finally, dinner is over. The Dawsons have to leave early. They are going skiing in the morning. This gives me an excuse to leave, too. Jack offers to drive me home.

"I live on Brunswick, off College, it's a long way."

"Not a problem. I'm going that way. My place is just off Bloor."

As I climb into his Lincoln, I breathe normally for the first time tonight. This I can handle. Before the light goes off I give him, yet another polite little smile.

He returns my smile and starts up the car. He turns on the radio, some station playing dull classical music.

The car warms up almost instantly, and as I sink into the soft leather seat, I know I could get used to this quite easily.

"This music, okay?"

"Fine."

"Some of the music the young people like today is so loud."

"I guess."

"I forget you are a young person. Perhaps you like rock and roll."

"This is nicer." He's only about thirty, but sounds older.

We don't talk much the rest of the way. He gets out and opens the car door for me. We walk up to my building together, but he doesn't even hold my hand or kiss me goodnight. "Thanks for the ride home," I say.

"My pleasure," he says.

***

He doesn't phone the next day, and I figure he doesn't much like me. Maybe I should've flirted just a bit, but I didn't want him to think I was a slut. That was my mistake with Ted. I flirted even in the job interview.

Sunday night I'm wrapped in my fur on the balcony having a smoke. Only nine-thirty, but I'm bored with my own company and thinking about going to bed. The phone rings.

"Oh, hi, Jack." Play it cool, Sharon, play it cool.

"I enjoyed meeting you," he says. "You mentioned you liked the gallery. The Picasso exhibit opened this past week. Have you seen it?"

"Not yet."

"Perhaps we could go this Saturday and out for dinner afterwards."

"Sure, that'd be great. And thanks for the ride home."

"I enjoyed driving you home. Would three o'clock be all right on Saturday?"

"That's fine."

"Goodnight then and see you Saturday."

"Yeah, see you then." As I hang up the phone I'm grinning. Maybe my luck has changed. He asked me out for dinner. He's good looking and must have lots of money, drives a Lincoln. Maybe, just maybe, I've met my millionaire. Whatever will I wear? Can't be the same black dress.

Both Monday and Tuesday I go shopping after work, but nothing suits me. But on Wednesday, when I think I've gone through every rack in Simpsons, I find the dress—jade-green, soft wool. A scoop neck combined with an empire waist, shows off my breasts nicely. The gored skirt flows softly around my hips. A good girl dress, not at all slutty.

***

As I climb into his Lincoln in my jade dress and fur coat, I feel quite sophisticated. He's wearing a charcoal-grey suit, white shirt, and a grey tie with fine blue stripes. The tie looks like silk. We go to the gallery. He's more talkative than he was at dinner. We look at the paintings and he tells me all about them. All about cubism, far more than I ever wanted to know.

I don't say much, too afraid I'll say something stupid. I'm relieved when I spot the exit sign.

"It's only five. We have time to see a few of the Old Masters, if you would like."

"Sounds good," I say even though my toes are on fire. I shouldn't have worn these spike heels.

One church-y painting after another and all I can think about is my feet. As he appears to know the history of each painting, I better act interested.

Finally, we're on our way to dinner.

Jack pulls out my chair for me, and I sit down. The restaurant's lovely with white linen cloths and candles.

"Will you have a glass of wine?"

"Okay."

"White or red."

"White, please." I ease my feet out of my shoes and rub my toes together. They hurt like after skating. Wish we were whizzing around a pond.

"They have a nice chardonnay."

"Sounds good."

"Sharon, was it rural Quebec where you grew up?"

He thinks I'm a hick. "I grew up in Buffalo."

"Oh, I thought you said Quebec."

"I was born in Quebec, but we moved to Buffalo."

"I don't know that city well."

"Oh, it's wonderful—beautiful restaurants, lots of theatres and stores."

"So you moved here from Buffalo."

"No, my family moved to Ontario, to a little place you wouldn't have heard of, didn't even have a decent newspaper."

"Oh?"

"The Buffalo paper had coloured funnies." Why'd I say that? Boy, I sound dumb. "Where are you from?"

"Ottawa."

"Did you like it there?"

"Unless you're in the government, it's very provincial, rather staid. Toronto is much more vibrant. I went to law school here and never left."

I know what staid means, but how can Ottawa be provincial? It's the capital. "I love Toronto."

"I like it, too. What will you have? The braised sole looks good."

"Sounds lovely." Actually sounds like shoe leather. What in the hell is a braised sole?

***

I sit on my balcony and smoke. Jack held my hand as we walked back to the car, but he didn't kiss me goodnight. Does he like me or not? He's nice, not a bit like Ted. That smoothie would've had his hand on my ass guiding me through the door.

***

I don't hear from him for six days. Figure I messed up—should've flirted. Tonight, I'm curled up on my couch with a book of George Bernard Shaw's plays. At least in them everything doesn't end tragically. Not like Tennessee Williams. At dinner Jack mentioned a theatre here that's going to be doing *Arms and the Man*. I figure I better read it, just in case he asks me to go. I sounded pretty stupid at the gallery. I said I liked Rembrandt, because that was the only name I could think of. A pot of tea is beside me and I'm on my second cup—turning into an old grandma. Wish I could've tried out for the plays in high school, but the practices were after school, and I was either heading off for a shift at the Shady Glen or Mom needed me home.

The phone rings. It's him.

"Sorry I haven't called. Been snowed under with work."

"That's okay. I've been busy, too."

"Would you go to dinner with me on Friday?"

"I'd like that."

"I'll pick you up at seven then."

"That would be lovely. I'll look forward to it."

"See you then."

He's sure not one to gab. I don't seem to be able to talk to him like other guys. Want too much for him to like me.

***

He takes me to a dining room in the Royal York hotel. A carpet something like Grandma's—Axminster, I now know that's what they're called. This one is beautifully soft and I think how a little Gloria would love to curl up on it.

The tables have linen cloths and shining silverware. We sip our wine. Jack's blue eyes look distant until he smiles. I smile back and feel like he kissed me, but what the hell—when's that going to happen? I love this room and think I could easily love Jack.

"How do you spend your evenings?" he asks me.

"I like to read."

"What kind of books?"

"Lately plays. I like reading plays—George Bernard Shaw's one of my favourites."

"We must go that production of *Arms and the Man*. Would you like that?"

"Sure."

"I'll phone about tickets."

"Do you visit your folks much, Jack?" It's high time we talked about him.

"Not very often our schedules mesh. Dad's a government lawyer and my mother works in the Department of Finance. How about you? Are you close to your family?"

"No."

"Why is that?"

"It's a mess, that's why."

"Oh?" He's waiting expectantly.

I've got to make this good. "Let me tell you about my mother. She came from a nice family, her father a high school principal, her sister went to university and married a bank manager. They were all members of the Buffalo Country Club. My mother was the rebel. She married too young, had me and my sister. The marriage didn't last. She went home and lived with her mother. Those were good years when we lived in Buffalo. But after our grandmother died, my mother had a hard time." I take a deep breath. "I know she married again just to have a roof over our heads. Jimmy Dutton has health problems and ... not much education. They had several kids. I couldn't wait to get out of there. I'm not that close to any of them."

***

Later, lying alone in bed, I feel guilty. Debbie so looks up to me. What have I ever done for her? Never brought any of them here for a holiday. I'm so fuckin selfish.

If I invited Debbie, I'd have to invite Emily and Judy, and what about Little Joey and Charlie? Could take them to the CNE this summer. They've never been to a big fair like that. If they all stayed here, my landlord would evict me, and what if Jack saw me with a bunch of shabbily dressed kids? He'd know me for the piece of Orchard Park riff-raff that I am.

$\mathscr{A}$ WEEKEND IN MARCH I decide to go home. I don't know why. Jack's away this weekend on business in Ottawa. We have reached the point where he lets me know when he'll be away. He takes me out for dinner almost every weekend. And we did go and see *Arms and the Man*. I enjoyed it, but the next weekend he took me to a concert. I was hoping for Johnny Cash or somebody like that, but I knew it wouldn't be. The Toronto Symphony—boring.

Something I've learned is that rich people don't like country music. We were in a coffee shop, and "Your Cheatin' Heart" was on the radio. "Those hayseeds don't even use proper grammar, and that awful twang," Jack said. I didn't say anything. What could I say? When he asked me if I enjoyed the concert, I said I did, but that I didn't know much about music. "You were deprived of a musical education," he said. I never should've told him anything about my family.

He keeps asking me out, but I don't even know if he likes me. A week ago he kissed me goodnight—a closed-lip kiss. I opened my mouth and poked his with my tongue. He stopped kissing altogether. Then he hugged me and planted little kisses all over my hair. That was sweet, but he's the most confusing man I've ever met. Does he like me or not? I know one thing: I end up frustrated after every date. I lie in bed and touch myself and wish it was him.

***

I want to go home, but I sure as hell don't want to have to see that slob Gloria married. Maybe he'll be at work. More likely he's lost his job and is stretched out on the couch, watching TV, unless Jimmy's already there. Maybe they've bought a second couch for the new man in the family.

I don't tell them I'm coming. Don't want them making a big fuss.

***

I leave just as it's getting light. Most of the snow's gone, the fields just beginning to green. My little red car is a snug humming cocoon.

When I pull into our driveway, Mom's getting out of a rusty, green station wagon. I honk my horn, jump out, run over and hug her. "Hi, Mom."

"Sharon, how wonderful!" She kisses me, and I get a whiff of Evening in Paris. Jack bought me Chanel No 5.

"Mom, you like my car?"

"I do. How could you afford that?"

"On payments—almost like rent. You have a different car, Mom. Grandma's finally quit?"

"It did, and Jimmy got this one from Waddells. He's been building an addition on Moyer's house. Be steady work for the next few months. He hasn't been sick as much either. Oh, Sharon, if I'd known you were coming, I would've killed a couple of chickens."

"No need, Mom, I brought a ham. You got a new coat?"

"Got it at Stedmans. Some of their stuff's not bad. You look just lovely, Sharon."

"How are you finding having Gloria and her husband living here?"

"Brian's a really nice guy, so good with Tammy, and Gloria is so happy. Everything's working out just fine. Sharon, the kids'll be so glad to see you."

Gloria greets me at the door. She's huge, must be six months pregnant. Great, following in Mom's footsteps. Brian's here too and looks as if he's gained another twenty pounds.

Gloria tells me she's just four months pregnant. "I've gained a lot of weight this time. Food tastes so good."

This is my little sister who always ate like a bird.

"Come see the new couch Brian and me bought. He's full-time now at the lumberyard."

Skippy jumps on me with muddy paws and Little Joey drags him away. The kids, all watching cartoons, aren't even dressed. They jump off the couches and up off the floor and crowd around. I hug Debbie

and hand her the shopping bag. "You can hand out the gifts — they're all labeled."

With lots of oohs and aahs, the kids tear open their presents. The new couch is cheap ugly brown tweed, one corner already chewed by the ill-behaved Skippy.

All evening Gloria and Brian sit on their couch. They can't keep their hands off each other. Oh, little sister, you could've done much better. I'd like to get in my car and go back to Toronto.

Sunday afternoon I drop in on my friend Donna from high school. She's home alone with her two kids. Rick's out — she doesn't say where. Donna is very pregnant and obviously miserable. She bursts into tears and we talk. Rick, the ex-football hero, doesn't like rubbers, and she forgets to put in her diaphragm. Donna used to be a bright, pretty girl, the most popular girl at Grenville High. She just turned twenty-one and looks like a middle-aged housewife.

On the drive back, I remember my narrow escape at seventeen. Life in Toronto is good.

N APRIL JACK invites me to a party at the Gladstone Club. I ask him what I should wear. He says: "Something quite formal. Would you be offended if I bought you a dress?"

"I don't know if that's proper."

"Just practical, dear. Evening gowns are expensive, and secretaries aren't paid as much as they should be."

He takes me to this store where there aren't even price tags on the dresses. He buys me a long black sheath, body hugging to the knees then flaring out—real silk.

* * *

We're at a table with three other couples. I look nice in my new dress, but I'm scared I'll drop my fork or say something stupid. Jack knows everybody. They chat about trips they've had and their cottages. All older than me. Then the talk turns to tennis and I say how much I like it.

After, there's dancing. Jack's a wonderful dancer. But the music is slow and, for a moment, I wish to be back jiving at Grenville High. I couldn't jive in this dress anyway. The skirt's too tight. I look around and smile—me and Jack are the best-looking couple here. The band plays, the lights are soft, and his arms around me feel good, like something out of a fairy tale.

* * *

The next Saturday Jack invites me to play tennis at the Gladstone Club.

I don't exactly know what to wear, but I figure my pink shorts and striped blouse, and sneakers, will be okay.

I greet him at the door, and he's wearing a white shirt and tan

trousers. Won't he be too warm playing tennis? He's carrying a small duffle bag.

He looks at me kind of funny.

"Is something the matter?"

"They're a little fussy about apparel," he says.

"You don't like my shorts?" I twirl around.

"I like them fine. We'll surprise them."

"Okay, let's go," I say.

"Better put on a dress and bring a bag. There are change rooms at the club."

I should've known that. Even Grenville High had change rooms. I obediently go to my closet and don't know what the hell to pick. My mauve dotted shirt-waist, that should be sedate enough for them. I go in the bathroom and change. Stuff my shorts and blouse into my beach bag.

At the club everyone anywhere near the tennis courts is in those silly white outfits. A couple of the women give me disapproving looks. Just jealous, I bet.

Jack's dressed like the rest of them and is much better at tennis than I am. I know he's sending me easy shots. I'm sweating and out of breath by the game's end, but he looks as cool as when we started.

But tennis is fun. And after I've showered I meet him for lunch in the dining room that looks over the golf course. Linen tablecloths at lunchtime—back in high school I never even dreamed of this.

The next Saturday, when he picks me up for our tennis date, he hands me a small duffle bag like his—a sports bag, he calls it. I open it and there is one of those cutsie tennis dresses and a pair of white shoes.

"There's a rule that everyone must wear tennis whites," he says.

"Why?"

"Less distracting maybe." And he smiles.

"Okay." I set down my beach bag. "Let's go." I'm already wearing a dress, a turquoise cotton I bought after work on Thursday.

In the club's change room I put on the tennis outfit. The dress with its silly skirt looks dumb, but if that's what they wear who am I to complain?

Jack is waiting for me by the courts. "You look lovely," he says.

"The dress and shoes fit perfectly—Jack, you're amazing."

"Important to wear proper shoes or you could injure your feet."

I'm not much better this week than last, but I love the speed, the leaping around. Jack plays so effortlessly. I know he's still sending me easy shots.

He doesn't even sweat. Meanwhile, I'm dripping.

I shower and change into my dress. We said we'd meet in the club bar. When I walk in Jack's talking to some men. The one guy is plump with a big beer belly, the other is going bald. Jack's so handsome, his wavy dark hair, flashing blue eyes and not an ounce of fat on him.

When he introduces me to the two fellow lawyers he was talking with, I realize how completely different he is from Ted who never wanted me to meet his friends.

***

I love playing tennis and every time we go I get better at it. Today our game ended in a tie. Playing tennis is the only time I see him relaxed. It's also the only time I feel we're actually talking to each other which is strange, because there's not much talking during tennis. But as he serves and I return we're having fun. Tennis is a kind of dance. I know he's playing down to me, being kind, but I don't care. We're having fun, not like those dreary concerts and trips to the art gallery.

He may be playing down to me on the tennis court, but he must respect me because he invites me to meet his parents. That'll be scary, but it's great that he wants me to meet them. Me and Jack will be together for a whole weekend. Something has to happen.

I pack carefully, starting with my diaphragm. Not taking any chances. That's the part about Jack that puzzles me. He holds my hand, kisses me—at least now he opens his mouth. He touches my breasts, but never tries to take off my clothes. Things just don't proceed. This suited me fine at first, but now I don't know. Every date I end up hot and bothered.

But we're going away for the weekend. All will be fine.

* * *

I'm sweating, even my palms are wet as we turn onto the curving flag-stone drive. The house is a sprawling ranch bungalow, red brick. They won't like me, I just know it.

Jack rings the doorbell. Why doesn't he just walk in?

Mrs. Sutter opens the door. She's tall, silver-haired, and wearing a white blouse and grey tweed skirt. Reminds me of the Bear in grade three.

"Hello there, Jack." They hug, barely touching—bizarre.

"Mother, I'd like you to meet my friend, Sharon Desjardins."

"Hello, Sharon." She has this really polite smile, a bit like pictures of Queen Elizabeth. She shakes my hand.

I mumble: "Hi."

"Do come in," she says with just a hint of an English accent. "Jack, you'll find your father out on the patio, engrossed in the *New York Times* as usual on a Saturday afternoon."

We make our way across shining hardwood floors and fancy car-pets, and through glass doors to a massive flagstone patio.

A tall white-haired man stands to greet us, looks old enough to be Jack's grandfather. He has Jack's profile and piecing blue eyes. "Good to see you, son." He shakes Jack's hand. "And this must be Sharon." He smiles at me.

"Do sit down. I'll make us a cup of tea," Jack's mother says. "You can bring in your bags later."

"What do you think of Diefenbaker's plans for the Arctic?" Mr. Sutter says.

"He'd do better to pay attention to economic development right here in Southern Ontario," Jack says.

They talk politics and I stop listening. The spacious lawn is a perfect even green, not a dandelion in sight. There's a swimming pool. The water very blue. I'd like to dive in. Sweat trickles between my breasts. Oh, I hope they can't smell me. Good thing my dress is a print—stains won't show. In Eaton's window the purple and green flowered sheath looked just right for spring. Maybe I shouldn't have worn it—it's awfully bright. Both Jack and his dad are wearing dull tweed jackets. Aren't they hot? Why didn't Jack tell me there was a pool? I didn't even bring my bathing suit. It's early May, but plenty warm enough.

Here comes his mother with the tea tray, and she's wearing a grey cardigan. Do they have something against colour?

I sit and sweat as tongue-tied as a ten-year-old. The men talk tennis. Sounds like his dad plays, too.

"So where did you go to school, Sharon?" his mother asks.

"Oh, um, we moved quite a bit. I graduated from Grenville High."

"And then?"

"I got a job. I'm Mr. Brownlee's secretary."

"Oh."

Teatime is endless. Finally the talk turns to where we might go for dinner.

"Sharon, would you like a rest before dinner?" Mrs. Sutter asks.

"I am a little tired."

Jack brings in our bags and rejoins his dad on the patio. His mother shows me to my room. When are me and Jack going to have a chance to be alone?

I strip off my too-bright sweaty dress and take a shower in my room's own bathroom stocked with Yardley lavender soap and big fluffy towels. Dry myself with the softest towels I've ever felt. I use two. There's a whole pile of them on the bathroom shelves. A far cry from the scratchy towels at the Plum.

I wrap up in a towel and stretch out on the double bed. Jack's mother said she'd call me half-an-hour before it was time to leave. She doesn't like me. A secretary's not good enough for her son.

* * *

We go to dinner at a snazzy French restaurant and I wear my little black dress. His mother wears a plain black dress, too, looks like silk, and a single strand of pearls. I've got on my silver and turquoise pendant, earrings and bracelet. Maybe I should get some pearls. They all talk politics. I just listen.

The subject turns from politics to art. All I can say when his dad asks me what I think of the Picasso exhibit Jack and I went to is that I liked it. They must think I'm a hick. Dinner is endless.

When we get back to the house Jack's mother says she's going to turn in early and I say I will too. "It's been a busy day." And I smile at Jack. That smile I've been practicing since I turned twelve, a smile no man could misinterpret. He says he'll be off to bed soon too, just going to have a brandy with his dad.

Me and his mother say goodnight and I go down the hall to my room. Jack's is right across from mine, and his parents' room is through a double door at the end of the hall. I shouldn't have long to wait.

I take another shower and carefully insert my diaphragm. I put on the pale blue negligee I bought at Holt Renfrew. It cost half a week's wages. Worth it. I twirl before the mirror. Leave on the bedside lamp and all atremble climb into bed.

I wait for the knock on the door.

Wait and wait and wait. I get out of bed and look out the window. A full moon mocks me.

Why did he bring me here if he doesn't want to go to bed with me? Since I've been thirteen, every guy I meet has been trying to get in my pants. Finally, I'm with the man of my dreams and here I am, alone, staring at the moon. What's going on?

***

On our way back to Toronto, Jack asks: "What did you think of my parents?"

"Nice. Very polite."

He looks at me kind of funny. Did I say the wrong thing?

"They liked you."

"I liked them, too. It must've been nice growing up with a swimming pool in your backyard."

"I wasn't home that much. Went to boarding school when I was eight and camp in the summers. Being with the government, my parents travelled a lot."

"That couldn't have been too great for you."

"I enjoyed my school. Always lots to do. I know a lovely little restaurant where we might stop for lunch. Would you like that?"

"Sure."

"Nothing fancy, but they make good sandwiches."

We don't talk much, and the miles roll by.

The restaurant is pretty with red gingham cloths and daisy centrepieces. We've just ordered when Jack reaches across the table and takes my hand.

"I know my parents are awfully formal. My dad's a bit of a stuffed shirt ..."

"It's okay. They were fine."

"I like you a lot, Sharon."

"I like you, too."

* * *

When we get back to my apartment, I invite him in for coffee. I'm just putting the coffee pot on when he puts his arms around me and kisses me.

"I love you, Sharon."

"I love you, too."

The kiss goes on for a while till I figure if things are to proceed, it's up to me. I sneak a hand down and rub his trousers. He's hard.

He removes my hand and leads me to the couch.

I sit down, and can't believe it, he kneels at my feet.

He takes a tiny box out of his jacket pocket and yes, it's a ring.

"Will you marry me, Sharon?"

Without stopping to think I say: "Yes."

He slides the ring on my finger and now we're kissing. I reach again for his cock.

He stops my hand and says: "Let's wait till we're married."

My confusion must show because he says: "I want everything to be perfect. Can we get married right away? Or do you want a big wedding?"

"Right away's good."

"You would want to invite your mother, of course. And maybe your sister?"

That's what he thinks. Damn it, what'll I say? "They couldn't come. My mother isn't well, and my sister is looking after all the kids."

"My parents, as you know, are off to Europe and won't be back for two months. Maybe as neither set of parents is available, we could just go to City Hall and then have a party at the Gladstone Club afterwards for our friends."

"Okay, that's a good idea." Big weddings are nice, but go with proper families.

He kisses me a bit and, just when I'm getting all hot and bothered, he stops.

We have our coffee and he leaves, giving me a quick goodbye kiss.

I pour myself another coffee, fetch my smokes, and go out on the balcony. Light a cigarette and sit down. The diamond's a good size surrounded with tiny engraved flowers in the gold. Pretty. I don't know what I feel. With all my dreams coming true I'm supposed to feel a little different from this.

"You don't buy an overcoat without trying it on." He loves me so much he doesn't care what I'm like?

I know he's not a fairy. Mrs. Brownlee said he was shy. A truly awful thought crosses my mind. Is it possible he's a virgin? Some girl at university broke his heart. Maybe she wouldn't go out with him. Maybe he's never been to bed with any girl. Could a guy be that shy? Not in Orchard Park, that's for sure. And, a much worse thought — what if he thinks I'm a virgin?

***

Wedding plans proceed and I don't tell anybody back home. Me and Jack go shopping to that same place where he bought me the evening gown. He buys me a cream silk suit to be married in. Then we go to Simpsons and he buys me a lot of clothes for our honeymoon that he just told me about when he picked me up today. We're flying to Bermuda for a week. I can't decide between two bathing suits. I model

them for him and he buys both. The Saturday after we're back there'll
be the party at the Gladstone Club. We go to Birks and pick up our wedding rings. His is plain gold, mine is gold with three small diamonds
—matches my engagement ring. We go for dinner at the Royal York.
He suggested the Park Plaza, but I don't go there. I'm scared I might
see Ted.

The Brownlees are going to stand up for us. Bill and Marion—I
find it difficult to call them by their first names. The night before we're
going to be married we have dinner at their place. Mr. Brownlee says
he'll be sorry to lose me as a secretary.

"The best secretary I've ever had. You're marrying not only a
beautiful woman, but a smart one, too," he tells Jack.

This is the first I've heard that I won't be working after I'm married. I don't know how I feel about this. I like my job and was looking
forward to me and Jack going off to the office together each morning.
I would like to discuss this on the way back to my apartment, but
there is something more important I've got to tell him. I ask him in
for coffee.

"It's late and the big day's tomorrow," he says.

"There's something I need to talk to you about."

"Not having cold feet, I hope?" He looks solemn.

"Nothing like that."

He comes in, and I make the coffee. We sit on the couch. I'm scared.

He takes both my hands in his. "Darling, what did you want to
tell me?"

"I'm not a virgin," I blurt it out and see him wince.

"That's all right," he says, very formal like.

"When I was in high school, I dated one of the football players.
We had just gone out a couple of times, when he invited me to a corn
roast out at the lake with some of the other fellas on the team and
their girlfriends. The boys were drinking, and my date suggested a
walk on the beach. I was glad to get away from the party. I don't like
that sort of thing, and as you know, I don't drink much. We went for
our walk—it was an isolated spot. He kissed me and ... started to paw
me, and I told him to stop, and he wouldn't." I burst into tears.

Jack's holding me. "It's all right, darling. That's all in the past. We have each other now."

He's hugging me, my face buried against his chest, against the fine wool of his suit. He massages my back. "It'll be fine, dear," he says, and offers me his neatly-folded clean white hankie.

I stop crying. Blow my nose and lift my face to be kissed. He kisses me gently, tenderly. I really do feel like crying—I'm such a lying shit.

THE WEDDING CEREMONY is brief, doesn't feel like a real wedding. No wedding dress, no music, no guests, just the Brownlees. Mom's friend, Holly, carried a bouquet of red roses, and her satin dress had a train, and a long veil. I have a pale orchid pinned to my suit. The men wore tuxedos, and the organ played. The church hushed when the Holly walked up the aisle. Donna's gown, princess style, was white silk. Us bridesmaids wore fuchsia taffeta. Mom should be here. Haven't even told her. We do the rings and he kisses me, a little peck on my lips. Mrs. Brownlee hugs me, and there are tears in her eyes. I feel like crying, too. What have I done?

We stop at this snazzy restaurant, have champagne, and the Brownlees drive us to the airport.

I'm thrilled to be flying. The stewardess tells me to pull down the blind—the movie's starting. I keep it up and stare out the window. We're flying above white fluffy clouds. Me and Gloria, it must have been after I read her *Jack and the Beanstalk*, pretended we were sledding high above the clouds. Cloud Mountain, we called it. I look out the window and can almost see us there.

The pink stucco hotel is like a palace. Our room has dark wood furniture, white carpeting, and a giant bed with a white silky covering.

After dinner we go back up to our room.

"Maybe you would like to shower first?" he says.

I take my cosmetic bag and my negligee from Holt Renfrew into the bathroom. I take a quick shower—he's certainly into cleanliness. Carefully I insert my diaphragm and put on the nightgown.

When I open the door I see he's changed into pyjamas and robe. He excuses himself and hurries into the bathroom.

I sigh and get into bed.

I hear the shower running.

When he comes out, he's again wearing his bathrobe. He switches off the light and climbs into bed. Too dark to see much, only the outline of his naked body. That was quick. He reaches for me and I turn to him. Figure better let him lead the way.

He's on top of me with the sheet pulled up over both of us. He locks his lips on mine, pushes up my nightgown and caresses my breasts. He guides my hand to his stiffened cock. He's already wearing a rubber. I ease him in. It's all over much too quickly.

He kisses and thanks me, lies down beside me, keeps his arm around me and falls asleep. I lie awake for a long time.

Morning when I wake up and he's straddling me with the sheet pulled up over both of us. He kisses me lightly and whispers: "Is this okay, darling?"

"Sure, okay." And reach for his cock—already hard and wearing a rubber.

This time he goes a little slower, but I'm still just getting hot when he comes.

He thanks me profusely, kisses me, and lies down beside me.

"I didn't hurt you, did I?" he asks. "Darling, with your past, you must find all this a bit frightening."

"Not at all, Jack. You're nothing like he was." And I'm telling the truth about all the men in my past.

"How about a swim before breakfast?" he says.

"Sure, be ready in a jiffy"—and scurry into the bathroom. Take a long hot shower. He's okay, just inexperienced. But he's thirty-two? Strange.

I come out wrapped in a towel. He's wearing his robe.

He takes me in his arms, holds me. "You're so beautiful, Sharon."

"Not bad looking yourself." And give him my best smile.

He doesn't unwrap my towel.

***

We swim, eat beautiful meals, go for walks along white sand beaches, and make love frequently. It's all very nice and, when he slows down, it's good for me too, once in a while. Very occasionally, my body tingles with pleasure.

On one of our walks we find a secluded spot among big trees. Early morning and nobody else is around. We lie down on the sand. Clinton and our sandy cave. His grease-stained fingers. The soft hair on his chest. My nipples stiffen. Jack kisses me and I reach for him.

He removes my hand. 'Not here, quick, let's get back to our room."

In our room while we're doing it, I remember being fourteen — he wrapped the blanket around me, held my hand, and told me all his plans. Poor, dumb Clinton. Oh, why am I crying?

Jack's finished. I climb out of bed and take a long shower.

I'M GLAD TO be back in Toronto. Jack goes to work, but not me. It feels weird, but I'll get used to it. All day to do what I please. His apartment has a black leather couch and chair, and a really pretty teak table and chairs. My furniture wouldn't have looked right. I just had the rollaway that I used for a couch too, and my card table and chairs. Jack sent it all to the Salvation Army. I should've at least sent the towels and bedding to Mom. I haven't told Mom yet—going to write her a letter soon.

Jack says on Saturday we'll start looking at houses. The party at the Gladstone Club is tonight. My new sheath dress is sea-green silk with a low back and spaghetti straps. I'm wearing the real emerald earrings Jack gave me for my birthday.

***

Jack pulls out my chair and I sit down. We're side by side at the head of the table in a private dining room. Twelve couples, I didn't invite anybody.

The guests are lawyers, doctors and such, and their wives. My husband is the best-looking man here. Mrs. Brownlee is the only woman I know. I like her.

Presents have been arriving at the apartment ever since we got back—sterling silver serving dishes from his parents and sterling silver candle sticks from the Dawsons. I now know the difference between sterling and silver-plated. We get sets of Waterford crystal—glasses for white wine, cocktails, sherry, and claret. I didn't know there were different glasses for different drinks. That stuff's expensive. Betty Moyer bragged about the four Waterford crystal wine glasses her mother bought her. The English china shop in Grenville carried Waterford crystal, but ours come from Birks or Eaton's College Street.

***

The party was a little dull. The men talked business, and the women, clothes or their kids. All Jack's friends are a lot older than me. Most of them are older than him. But everything's fine. Jack goes to work, and I clean the apartment, plan what I'll make for his dinner, go shopping, and cook supper. I have lots of time to lounge around and watch television—his set never goes dizzly. I smoke and read on his balcony. His balcony is about four times the size mine was. We're on the sixth floor and I can see City Hall and the lake from here.

Evenings we sit together on the couch. He keeps his arm around me and tells me about his day, and asks about mine. I talk about the book I'm reading or the fun I had trying a new recipe. His arm around me makes me feel safe.

***

I've been out shopping and got a lovely pale yellow linen sheath. I plunk my shopping bags on the floor and unlock our mailbox. There's a letter from Mom. Jack'll be home soon. I tuck my letter in with the dress. Better get the chicken in the oven—making Chicken Parmesan for his dinner.

After supper we take our coffee into the living room and Jack puts on a record.

"I got a new dress today."

"Let's see it."

I'm just pulling out the dress when my letter falls on the floor.

He picks it up. "Letter from home?"

"Yeah."

"Well, aren't you going to open it?"

"Of course." I sit back down and tear open the envelope. Check that he's not reading over my shoulder. He's drinking his coffee.

Dear Sharon,

Happy Birthday, darling. I can't believe my daughter is twenty.

We haven't heard from you for awhile. I hope everything is going okay. Are you still dating that lawyer?

Everything's fine here. Only the third week of June and eighty degrees. I'm on the porch with a cup of tea. Not often I have the house to myself. Gloria just took all the kids to the beach, even J.J. and Tamara. The little ones rode in the wagon. The water's going to be cold, but they all wore their bathing suits. Debbie has outgrown hers and the only one she could find was that old blue tank suit that belonged either to you or Gloria. It was way too baggy on tiny Debbie, and she kicked up a fuss. I tore a piece off your worn-out purple sundress and fashioned a sash, and a tie for her ponytail. She strutted off proud as a peacock. She often reminds me of you.

This is such a good place for kids, at the beach from May till October. As a kid I never got to go swimming. The only places to swim in Buffalo were public pools. Jean and I weren't allowed to go. Mother was too afraid we'd catch something. Polio was her big fear. So much better here.

Pixie's latest kittens are rolling around on the floor. The little tiger one's awfully cute. He's wrestling with my foot. Thinks he's a jungle animal.

So lovely to have it warm. Such a cold winter, and one child or another was always sick. But Gloria has been healthy during this pregnancy and has so much energy. Her baby's due in August and here she is off to the beach. It'll be lovely to have a new baby in the house.

Lilacs scent the air—those late Persian ones. The wild lilacs are finished. I do love this place.

Write soon.

Love,
Mom

You're such a god damn Pollyanna, Mom. You send Debbie to the beach in rags and fool her into thinking she looks good. Bet some kid —the equivalent of Joanne Newman—sets Debbie straight and she won't say a word about it to you. Mom, how can you be so blind?

"Everything okay?" Jack asks.

"Yeah, fine." I can see he's waiting for more. "Mom goes on about the lilacs and my sister who's pregnant."

"Nothing about our marriage?"

"I haven't told her yet."

"Why not?"

"We've been so busy. I'm going to phone her tomorrow."

"Do that and we should drive down some weekend."

"Their place is an awful mess."

"Doesn't matter. It's you I married, but only proper that I meet your family."

"I suppose."

***

A week later, when I bring the tea tray into the living room, Beethoven or somebody like that is playing softly on the stereo. Jack looks very solemn. Is something wrong?

"How do you feel about babies?" he says.

I set the tray down very carefully on the glass and chrome coffee table and pour him a cup. The tea set was a wedding present from the Brownlees. Wedgwood—very expensive. Blue and white—pretty. At the Plum we were lucky if two cups matched. Jack's looking at me and waiting for an answer. "There are a lot of them around," I tell him.

"Yes, the world is over-populated and, if something isn't done about it, in another hundred years, we could all die of starvation. Even zero population growth isn't enough. There are already too many people."

"Everybody should practice birth control."

"Darling, would you mind if we didn't have children?"

"Fine with me."

"I wouldn't want to share you with a child. I've seen my friends' wives go from attentive partners to all their focus on their babies."

"More tea?"

"Not yet. Haven't started this one, silly girl."

I'm glad he doesn't want babies. Back home that's all they think about. I don't want a baby. The babies wear Mom out, and she sure as hell shouldn't have had so many, but what I've always resented is just how much attention she pays Jimmy. "How's your back, dear?" And she brings the whimpering idiot more ice wrapped in a tea towel. She went over to Reubels and borrowed ice cubes. "How about a cup of tea to get your mind off it? Sharon, Emily's awake, could you fix her a bottle?" I don't want a baby. Too much of my life was spent looking after Mom's, but I don't owe Jack one hundred percent of my attention. If I wanted a baby, I'd make room for one.

"Have I upset you? I guess most women want a baby, but it would so disrupt our lives."

"I don't want a baby. I miss not going to work. I liked my job."

"Maybe you might consider going back to school. Take some interest courses at the university. You know what you said about not having had a chance to go to college."

"I might like that. My friend Gretchen went to university."

"This weekend might be a good time to meet your family. Why don't you phone your mother and see if it's convenient? You said she was pleased we were married."

Damn it, I don't want to take Jack there. Mom was really excited when I told her. "Oh Sharon, I can't wait to meet him." Oh hell, I can sure wait.

"Phone your mother right now, darling. It's only proper that I meet them. There's nothing for you to worry about. I know your family is poor."

$\mathcal{S}$O HERE WE are on Highway 3 heading towards Lake Erie. At least we're not staying at the Plum. Jack agreed it would be too crowded. We've got a room at the Pleasant View motel—the new motel just outside of town.

I don't want Jack to meet my family. I can't stand how hard they'll try to make things nice.

***

I'm amazed to see the house has been painted—pale blue. Still has its two tarpaper sheds, but looks a hell of a lot better. Maybe this won't be as bad as I thought.

Then I spot all the kids in their best clothes, sitting in a row on the cleared-off porch.

***

"You and Jack sit at the head of the table," Mom says. She's given us the matching pink-flowered plates.

Gloria, with just a month to go, waddles to the table. Pudgy Brian fixes a pillow for her to sit on. "Hafta look after my little broody hen." He has a guffaw that makes me remember poor Uncle Joey. At least Joey had the war as an excuse.

"Brian painted the house," Mom says. "Doesn't it look nice?"

"Yeah, it does." What I'm wondering is how pudgy Brian managed to get up on a ladder.

The old card table has been set up at the end of the big table—the three-legged card table, though now it has four—the fourth being a piece of a two-by-four. New-looking red gingham oilcloth covers both tables.

From the dressed-up kids to the luncheon meat sandwiches and Campbell's chicken noodle soup—all so fucking pathetic. What? Mom thought her chicken soup wasn't good enough?

Debbie has arranged wild flowers for a centrepiece. The Queen Anne's lace makes Jack sneeze. I didn't know about his hay fever. The flowers are removed and lunch continues. Only for a moment though, as now a black-and-white cat drops a large dead mouse at Jack's feet.

He leaps up from the table. Even Jimmy's not afraid of mice.

I grab his arm. "Jack, it's just a mouse."

"They carry vermin."

"I got it," Little Joey says, proudly holding the mouse up by its tail.

"Take it outside," Mom says.

Jack sits back down, but doesn't finish his lunch.

"How about a cup of tea?" Mom says.

"Thank you," he says in a voice I imagine he uses in the courtroom.

Debbie carries in a cake, "Congratulations Sharon and Jack" written on it in garish blue icing.

"We found a cake decorating set at the church sale," Mom says. "The girls have had such fun with it."

Over tea and cake we are presented with several gifts. A Corningware casserole dish from Mom and Jimmy. "It's the big one," she says. "Figure you'll be doing quite a bit of entertaining."

A cut glass wine decanter from Gloria and Brian. "We knows youse drink wine," Brian says.

Handmade cards from all the kids, and Debbie gives me a china figurine of a Victorian lady. "I got it at Stedmans," she says.

"She's been babysitting for your friend Betty," Mom says.

"Betty Moyer?"

"Betty Sider now, of course. They have a little girl and twin boys."

Bully for them. Why doesn't Betty look after her own shitty-assed kids? I hug Debbie. "I'll keep it right on the centre of my dresser."

A muddy-pawed cat takes this moment to leap on Jack's lap and lunch ends with him heading to the bathroom to clean off his light grey trousers.

He returns when we're all still at the table. He smiles at Mom.

"Thanks for the gifts, everyone. I'd like to take the family out for dinner tonight. Just a little thank you for raising such a wonderful girl. I have never met a girl like Sharon."

"You don't have to do that. I was going to roast a couple of hens," Mom says.

I can tell she's embarrassed. Bet she knows he doesn't want to eat another meal in this dump.

"I would like to." He turns to Jimmy. "What's a good restaurant to go to?"

"Southern fried place is pretty spiffy. Us took Gloria and Brian there."

"Do you have their number? I'll phone and make a reservation."

"I don't think we need one," Mom says.

"With a big group, I've found it's usually a good idea."

"You're right," Mom says. "We won't have to wait in line. I'll do the phoning."

"Thanks." He turns to me. "Darling, weren't you going to take me on a tour of the area this afternoon? I'd like to see the schools you went to and that beach where you played."

"Okay."

"Let's take the children along. We can get them a treat."

I can't believe he wants to take them anywhere.

"Come along, children," he says. "Everybody into the car."

"Maybe J.J. and Tammy better stay here," Gloria says.

J.J. starts shrieking.

"Let them all come. We'll manage," Jack says with a smile.

"Okay," Mom says. "Everybody upstairs to the bathroom. Pee and wash your hands."

I feel Jack wince.

We all pile into the car. Debbie with J.J. on her lap sits up front between Jack and me. The other five squeeze into the back.

"Did you notice my dress?" Debbie whispers. She's wearing a yellow dress with white eyelet collar and pockets.

"Yellow goes nice with your hair."

"It's your dress. Mom had it put away."

"I remember. That's the dress I wore to Mom's friend's wedding. I was nine, but tall for my age."

"I'm the shortest in my class, but Mom says I'll get a growth spurt soon."

I take a ten-dollar bill out of my purse and stuff it in her pocket. "Buy yourself a new dress."

"I like wearing stuff that was yours or Gloria's."

We're driving down Main Street. A Lincoln Continental is more expensive than a Cadillac. I should feel triumphant.

"Is there a store that sells children's books? When the Brownlee children were small, and we were going out for dinner, I'd bring some activity or story books in case they got bored."

"Just Stedmans."

He parks in front, and we all parade in. We choose books. He picks *All About Stars* and *All About Trees*. Look at him trying to improve them.

"Too bad I didn't think of this in Toronto where there's a better selection," he says.

"Yeah, Grenville's not much."

"Lovely trees arching over Main Street, typical small town Ontario. Attractive in its way, but you and I, darling, would miss the bustle of Toronto."

"Very true."

Even Little Joey and Charlie, who are usually getting into trouble, are strangely quiet.

Jack also buys five big packs of coloured pencils, Laurentian, not the cheap ones that break all the time, pads of drawing paper, and jumbo crayons for J.J. and Tammy.

"I saw a restaurant next door to Stedmans. Let's take the children for ice cream."

And we all parade into the Quick Stop.

Mrs. Taylor pushes two tables together to make room for us. "Hi, Sharon, we haven't seen you for a long time."

"Hi." I can't think of anything else to add.

"I see a wedding ring. You must be married."

"Yep. This is my husband, Jack Sutter."

"Nice to meet you," says Jack. "And you are?"

"Eva Taylor."

"Nice little place you have here."

"Bill, that's my husband, and I have had the restaurant for twenty-six years now. He does the cooking."

"The kids would like ice cream," I say, cutting her off. Next, she'll be telling some story about me, or even worse, congratulating me on how well I've done.

"There's chocolate, vanilla, strawberry, butterscotch ripple, and orange." She rattles them off.

"Do all of you like chocolate?" Jack asks.

Solemn nods around the table.

"Nine large chocolate it'll be," he says.

"That makes it simple," Mrs. Taylor says, smiling at Jack who returns her smile.

I know for a fact that Emily and Little Joey prefer strawberry, and Judy's favourite is vanilla.

The large cones make the expected mess. J.J. drops his on the floor, and Mrs. Taylor replaces it with a small one. I go to the bathroom, get wet paper towels and Debbie and me clean the kids up. I gobble down my cone. Jack's barely touched his.

Finally, we're leaving. The table's a big mess and I notice him leaving a two dollar tip. I'm tempted to pocket it.

"Let's take the children home now," he says. "That'll give us time to check into the motel for a rest before dinner."

"Okay."

Back at the Plum we unload the kids with all their parcels. Debbie, holding J.J. by the hand, solemnly thanks Jack.

I want to run away.

"We'll be back at five-forty-five to pick all of you up for dinner," he says.

***

"They're a surprisingly well-behaved group," he says unlocking the door to our motel room.

What did he expect that they'd pee their pants or bite him?

"Think I'll take a nap." I kick my shoes off and lie down on the bed.

"Good idea." And he heads into the bathroom.

Wish I could go to sleep. I listen to the shower run. Bet he's trying to wash off all traces of The Plum. He showers for twenty minutes. I time him.

He comes out fully dressed. He's changed into tan trousers and another white shirt. He lies down beside me.

"Guess you found my family a big shock," I say.

"A tough life. We could send them a cheque each month."

"I've sent them what I could."

"Good. Now you can send more."

We lie here side by side, and neither of us speaks for a few minutes.

He clears his throat. "You deserve a lot of credit, darling, that you rose above your circumstances. You're a very bright girl."

"Thanks."

"Amazing, really. You don't look a bit like any of them. Who was your father?"

"I told you. An unemployed miner."

"Maybe, or maybe they married her off to him when she got into trouble, and the guilty party at their country club wouldn't marry her."

"That's silly."

"Or maybe you were adopted."

"That's even more ridiculous. Debbie looks just like me."

"Debbie?"

"The redhead."

"That carrot-haired urchin looks nothing like you. You're beautiful."

I god damn fuckin hate him.

SIGN UP FOR a history course, *The Evolution of the British Empire and Commonwealth*. The first few lectures I take lots of notes about the struggles in England between the king and parliament after the American Revolution. It's interesting to learn about the past, like those deed searches taught me about Toronto.

After a while, there are just too many facts to keep straight, and I find myself dozing off during lectures.

I really did like my job.

I'm late handing in my first essay. It conflicted with my first dinner party. We had three couples over for dinner.

***

Every Sunday afternoon we look at houses. The area we've pretty well settled on is in York Mills, either Bridle Path Road or Shires Way.

As we walk up to an immense place with dark beams crisscrossing white stucco, Jack holds my arm.

"This is called Tudor style. Do you like it?"

"Sure, but can we afford a house this big?"

"Honey, we can afford any house you like."

He smiles down at me in my pale blue linen suit with a pencil-slim skirt and matching pumps. Best of all is the pure silk bra and panties. A girl moves differently in silk underwear.

This house has light grey carpeting. I'm actually going to live in one of these big houses with acres of wall-to-wall. The staircases curve into the living rooms. There are crystal chandeliers in the dining rooms. Master bedrooms are as big as the whole upstairs at the Plum. Walk-in closets are the size of bedrooms. And best of all, everything is brand new.

"We have time for a couple more today," Jack says.

We decide on a two-storey red brick that has an open fieldstone front porch with white pillars. It reminds me of Tara from *Gone with the Wind*. I loved that movie. Our house has a beautiful oak staircase rising right out of the front hall and wall-to-wall everywhere, except in the kitchen and bathrooms, of which there are three. The shag carpeting is so thick it feels like you're walking on a mattress.

We go to Eaton's College Street and pick out our furniture. We only have an hour and Jack spends two thousand dollars. I'm giddy from the richness of it all. He picks cream brocade French Provincial couches for the living room. They match the cream carpeting. The family room furniture is less formal, a rich burgundy plush that goes nicely with the pale grey wall-to-wall. I let him choose. It all looks great to me.

Jack says he doesn't expect me to clean this big house. We're having a cleaning lady two days a week.

When Jack's at work, I vacuum the whole house. My Electrolux vacuum cleaner is the most expensive model. I have a special rug comb for the shag carpet. I love keeping everything perfect. It all smells new. "My house," I say as I run my hand along the polished oak banister. "My house," and I stretch out on the cream shag carpet. I never run out of hot water. Sometimes I use the dishwasher, but here I like doing dishes, swishing my hands through the hot sudsy water in the double stainless-steel sink. No need to conserve soap. I polish the Italian black marble L-shaped counter and scrub and wax the black and white tiled floor. The cleaning lady is supposed to do all this—well, not lie down on the carpet—but I love cleaning my house twice the size of Aunt Jean's or Donna's family home.

We have dinner parties. Jack is amazed I can put on dinner for twelve.

"Shouldn't we have it catered?"

I laugh. "Nonsense, I like cooking." What I love is going shopping and not even looking at the prices. I buy more than what I need and try out the recipes a few days before we're having company. Sometimes a dish doesn't come out that well. I throw the food in the garbage and experiment till it comes out perfect.

Before each dinner party, I stand in my sock feet on the dining-room table and wash and polish each teardrop of my crystal chandelier. I never dreamed I'd own anything so beautiful. Our dining-room suite, just like his mother's, is solid walnut and seats twelve.

We have a bar in the living room, built into a unit that looks like a fancy cupboard. There are glass shelves for the four kinds of Waterford crystal glasses and two decanters. I put the glass one from Gloria and Brian away in the kitchen.

I've never much liked drinking because of Papa, because of Clinton's pa, because of Jimmy, Mom, and Uncle Joey sitting on the front porch, drinking beer right out of the bottles. Uncle Joey all giggly singing that stupid "It's a long, long way to Tipperary." He'd be prancing around barefoot, big feet and overgrown yellow toenails like something out of a cartoon. Mom and Jimmy would be laughing, and more times than not, she'd be sitting on his lap. I was always scared one of my friends would come by and see them.

With Jack in our cream-carpeted living room, I sip red wine from a crystal goblet and listen to Beethoven or Bach on the record player. My records, Hank Williams, Willie Nelson, Johnny Cash, are on the back shelf in my closet.

W E'RE GOING TO the Stratford Festival with the Brownlees to see Shakespeare's *Macbeth*. Mr. Brownlee's driving because they have a station wagon. Jack said our Lincoln was too small to hold everybody. It held all the kids when we took them for ice cream.

The Brownlee children are treated like little adults. Mr. and Mrs. Brownlee are in the front seat, Jack and me in the second row, and Philip and Ashley in the back. The station wagon's leather seats makes me think of Grandma's the first time we rode in it, before Jimmy stunk it up with his junk.

"Is this your first time to see a play?" I ask the kids.

"No, we go every year," Philip says.

"Well, you should enjoy *Macbeth*, all the battles and everything."

"Yes, it should be a better production than when I saw it before," Philip says.

"You've already seen it?" Even these kids are more cultured than me.

"The Earle Grey Players put it on at our school."

"I haven't seen it," Ashley says. "But we both read it with Mummy, and I want to see the witches."

"Me too," I tell her. "They're my favourite part." When I took *Macbeth* in grade twelve, I had a hard time keeping the story straight. Never did get that speech—something about the petty pace of time —memorized properly. I was working too many shifts at the Shady Glen and both Mom and Gloria had bronchitis that winter. I made a joke about getting mixed up, said: "I wish the 'petty pace of time' would speed up, and the bell ring." The boys laughed, but Miss Stevenson gave me a detention. That was grade twelve. I wanted to do well and did win the business prize.

***

The play is great. I expected to be bored. In high school, the class read-ings put me to sleep. The fight scenes are really something—actors run up the aisles waving their swords. Little Joey and Charlie would love it.

***

We have the Brownlees over for dinner to thank them for taking us to Stratford. I do a ham, parsley-cream potatoes, and baked yams. Everybody compliments me on my cooking. We have homemade apple pie for dessert.

***

Almost every weekend we attend a dinner party or host one. Our dinner parties go off fine until one fateful Saturday. My dinner is perfect and the four couples, including Stan and Judith Dawson, im-portant clients of Jack's, are having a quiet after-dinner glass of wine in our cream-carpeted living room. I've never liked Judith from the first time I met her at Brownlees. The way she looks at me makes me feel like if I've got chicken dirt on my shoe.

Stan Dawson knocks over his glass and I watch the red stain wreck our beautiful carpet. I jump up and yell: "What have you done, asshole!"

Complete silence follows my outburst.

Then Jack has his arm around me. "Excuse her." He gives a high-pitched laugh. "Must be that time of the month."

I wrench myself away, run upstairs, and crouch down in the corner by the closet. Everything's ruined. My beautiful carpet. I'm shivering.

Jack stays downstairs with our guests. I'm really scared.

Then he's here, leaning over me. "Whatever is the matter, Sharon?"

"The carpet's ruined."

"Nonsense, it'll clean up, though the Dawsons must wonder what's the matter with you."

Suddenly I know how stupid I've been. "I'm sorry."

"Are you ill, Sharon?"

I get to my feet. "I have a migraine. That must be why I acted so dumb." Migraine sounds better than headache. Aunt Jean had migraines.

"Better get in bed. I'll get you some aspirin."

I'm undressed and in bed before he gets back. I dutifully swallow the pills and curl up into a ball away from him.

"I'll just serve the coffee, and then they'll go. Good night, dear." He turns off the light.

"Night," I whisper.

It's a long time before he returns and comes to bed. He presses against me. Why does he wear those dumb striped-flannel pyjamas? I pretend to be asleep.

I get up at five. Jack's still sleeping. He never wakes up until his alarm goes at six.

The kitchen's cleaned up. The leftover food put away. The dishwasher filled. I put the coffee on to perk and wash what dishes are piled in the sink.

I go in the living room. There's a slight pink stain.

I go back in the kitchen and pour myself a coffee.

***

"Feeling better, dear?" Jack has showered and is fully dressed. I'm still in my housecoat.

"Yes, fine. I'll make some toast."

We sit stiffly across from each other. Neither of us speaks until he says: "I've never heard you talk like that."

"Sorry." What the hell, has he never heard the word asshole before? Hardly the way to address his client, though. "I really am sorry."

"You must've been overtired. You'll write Judith a note and we'll hire caterers next time."

When breakfast is over, he disappears into his study. I look in the phone book for carpet cleaners and call the first name on the list. Of course, they don't answer. Not open on Sunday.

***

Jack never mentions my little outburst. The carpet is cleaned, though if I look really hard, I can see a slight pinkness. Maybe not. It's not perfect anymore. I told Jack I wrote Judith a note, but I didn't. I can't stand that bitch.

HE PROF'S TALKING about the British in India. I can't keep straight what he's saying long enough to write anything down. The plaid-skirted girl beside me is scribbling away. Penny loafers—looks like she belongs in high school. Damn it, I want out of here.

Last night Gloria phoned to tell me she has a baby boy. She was so bubbly and excited. After, I said to Jack: "Babies are all she's interested in."

"How did she do in school?"

"Not that great."

"That's what I thought. Do you really believe you and Gloria had the same father? You obviously have a much higher IQ than any of them."

"Gloria was sick a lot."

"I suppose you were never that close."

"When we were little me and Gloria did everything together."

"Gloria and I. Nominative case. Gloria and I played."

"Okay, sure." I felt my face go red. I know perfectly well *I* is for the subject, but I've always said me and Gloria. Do I make other mistakes I've not noticed?

The class is half over and I still I haven't taken any notes.

We're having some important clients of Jack's over for dinner on Friday, and what shall I feed them? Beef stroganoff or stuffed chicken breasts? I'll try out the stroganoff recipe tonight on Jack. He again suggested caterers. Doesn't he think my cooking's good enough?

By the end of the lecture I'm bored with the recipes and the British in India.

When I get off the subway and find my little red car, I'm in a hurry to get home.

Why on earth do I drive right past our house and keep going

north? I've been driving for over an hour, almost to Barrie before I turn back.

I get home just before Jack and crawl into bed. It's the only thing I can think to do. There's no time to thaw the beef, and I didn't stop at the supermarket for vegetables.

I hear him on the stairs.

"What's the matter, darling?" he asks.

Wish I knew. "I have a terrible headache." I don't, but can hardly tell him I'm going crazy.

"Can I get you some aspirin?"

"Thanks."

"Maybe I should call the doctor?"

"No, don't. It'll go away, if I sleep for a while. Do you think you can find something for your supper?"

"Of course, don't worry about me. I'll be right back with the pills."

When he returns, he pulls the drapes shut and offers me pills and a glass of water. "How about a cup of tea?"

"No, thanks. I just want to sleep."

I close my eyes and hope the aspirin will do the trick. I can't get comfortable. What the hell's the matter with me?

Buffalo, Grandma's rug, soft wool—swirls of blue, red, purple flowers.

The monkey bars, hand over hand. Numb fingers. Hot cocoa. Grandma: "You're half-frozen." Warm hug. Grandma smells like lavender.

Soda fountain at Grants, grape phosphates. We stick out our purple tongues and giggle.

Gloria's furry pink toilet seat Grandma made.

Stuck-up Barbara with her perfect parents, perfect house, and shelf of perfect dolls. Barbara, a year older, would be grown up now. They never visited us again—moved to Florida. What did they do with Grandma's rug? Every room in that house had wall-to-wall.

Gloria wails all through Grandma's funeral. Mustn't cry. Wimps and babies cry.

Delivering the *Buffalo Courier News*, fingers and toes numb, relief in seeing this porch has two steps instead of six. Itchy wool snow

pants weighing me down. At last, can climb in the back with coughing, sniffling Gloria nestled in the quilt with her dolls.

Some nights we're home alone. Where's Mom? Out on a date or out with Holly Holmes, of the movie star name, a waitress at Grants discount department store. Gloria bawling and me not letting on I'm scared too. Reading to her. I learn to swim at Crystal Beach, hold my breath, go under, kick hard, reach out my arms, move like a fish, surface, gulp in air. I did it. Much later, the floating raft at Grenville Beach. Push them all off, Clinton last. I'm lord of the raft. Clinton buys me a Coke. Me and Clinton in the sandy cave.

After, waiting for the bus, terrified I'll never get out of Grenville. But I did. I did. Whatever is the matter with me? Oh God, let me go to sleep and never wake up.

GREY SKY, GREY pavement, and leafless trees—November. My course is Monday and Wednesday. That leaves Tuesday, Thursday, and Friday.

Sometimes I go for walks and admire all the beautiful houses. Even though the houses are all different, there's a certain sameness. Easy to get lost. There's never anybody on the street and not even anywhere to go for coffee.

Thank God for my car. I go downtown, sometimes to the art gallery. Most often shop. I can buy whatever I want. Once I got six pair of pure silk underwear in all different colours—the fuchsia pair is my favourite. Sometimes, I just walk—explore Toronto. I went past my old apartment building. What a plain, ugly little building! Funny, I used to think it was grand. Who would have imagined I would end up in a big house in York Mills?

Jack's awfully busy. Often has to bring work home with him, but always at ten o'clock, he stops, makes tea, and we sit down together. He puts on one of his records—something classical. He identifies the instruments for me. When we first moved in, he picked up one of my Hank Williams records and said: "I've never pictured you as a Hank Williams fan."

"At home those were the only records I had."

"You were deprived of a musical education."

"Guess so."

Very occasionally, I play my records during the day. "Your Cheatin' Heart" and Johnny Cash's "Cry Cry Cry" are my favourites. I know they're low-class hillbilly music. I should be listening to Jack's records, educating myself. Maybe, when I finish the British Empire course, I'll take a music appreciation course.

Some evenings Jack tells me about the case he's working on, but often he goes in his study and doesn't come out till it's time for tea. An odd thing has happened. He used to always sit with his arm around me. I liked that. Now he seldom touches me, except in bed. When he hasn't brought work home, we both sit and read. He's reading Churchill's history of the Second World War. I should be studying for my course, but more often I'm reading a historical novel or an Agatha Christie.

We do have fun at the Gladstone Club. Nearly every Saturday morning we play tennis. Marion Brownlee, I remember to call her Marion now, invited me to join the Women's League. So now I play Thursday mornings, too.

***

The Women's League is planning a Christmas party for underprivileged children. They hold it every year at the Club—first Saturday in December. Seemed a little early. Marion said any closer to Christmas, the members would be too busy going to parties. There are a lot of parties planned leading up to The Gladstone Ball, just a week before Christmas. Thank goodness Jack didn't suggest we hold a big party. We've had a couple more small dinner parties. Jack wanted caterers. I said: "Something wrong with my cooking?" He didn't mention caterers again. I'll not let him boss me around. He hasn't suggested having the Dawsons over again. Good! I wonder if they're having a party.

The Club spends a lot of money on the party for poor kids. A hundred are invited and there's a gift for every one of them. Not cheap stuff either—garage sets, Meccano, expensive games like Scrabble, beautiful dolls, art supplies, and sets of books.

For entertainment the women hired a clown troupe, and some members' children are leading the carol singing, others are demonstrating Highland dancing, or playing the piano or violin.

A lot of the food is being catered, but we're making the desserts ourselves. Most of the women do fancy Christmas baking. I've been collecting recipes and trying them out.

Two days before the party I have my baking all done. I made lemon-coconut squares and some other fancy squares with dates. I look at my desserts and wonder if the kids will actually like them. There's peel in the lemon squares — Little Joey and Emily hate peel, and come to think of it most little kids don't like dates. I go to the store and buy three bags of those chocolate mallow cookies that Mom buys as a special treat at Christmas. Chocolate-coated marshmallow, a dab of red jam and a yummy cookie. I don't allow myself to sample.

Everything looks lovely as the kids file in, the gifts under the giant tree are wrapped in shiny expensive paper and satin ribbon, no plain tissue or yarn ties like we used at home.

The big tables along the side have white linen cloths and live poinsettias. The children file into their seats for the show.

I know what the Club's doing is nice, but I feel rotten for these kids in their cheap or hand-me-down clothes, the girls in rummage sale velvet or frilly nylon dresses.

I cheer up, laughing with them at the silly antics of the clowns — the big one on a tiny tricycle, and the little one on a giant scooter.

The choral group leads the singing — "Away in a Manger," "We Three Kings," and "Silent Night." The guests are supposed to join in, but some are looking at the tree and others are poking each other and giggling. The carolers are good, but I can't help but notice their new Christmas dresses and expensive three-piece suits. Ashley and Philip play a piano duet — must've had years of lessons. The Highland dancers in their red plaid kilts and green velvet jackets put on quite a show. By the time three more girls have played the piano, I'm ready for food.

Santa first. The kids go up shyly to get their gifts. As they start tearing them open there's much oohing and ahhing. One little girl sits holding hers unopened. She's stroking the shiny paper — makes me think of Gloria and how she used to stroke the ratty fur collar on Mom's coat.

Finally, the food. A lot doesn't get eaten. I'm not surprised — creamed salmon tarts, mini quiche stuffed with broccoli, no kid would like that. Even the desserts are left half-eaten. But every one of my chocolate mallows is snatched up.

When us ladies are in the kitchen organizing the clean-up staff, Judith Dawson says to Jan Pritchard: "Did you see them gobbling up those cheap cookies? I suppose it's what they get at home — welfare

food. I wonder who brought them. I thought it was supposed to be home baking."

"Deprived children can't appreciate quality," Jan says. "A lot weren't paying attention during the concert."

"I sometimes wonder why we bother," Judith says. "We might as well hand them each a five-dollar bill and be done with it."

"At least it's a learning experience for our children in helping others," Jan says.

*A*FEW DAYS AFTER the children's party, me and Jack —I mean Jack and I—are sitting reading. I can't keep straight all the battles. Ladysmith, that's a funny name. Wish I'd never started this course. Soon be bedtime. The phone rings. He answers—makes sense, usually for him.

"It's your mother," he says. "Sounds upset."

Mom never phones. We write monthly letters back and forth.

I take the receiver from Jack. "Hi, Mom."

"Oh, Sharon," Mom wails. "Jimmy's dead."

"Mom, what happened?"

"A heart attack. He died in the night, in his sleep. Never had heart trouble." She's sobbing.

"Oh, Mom, I'll come first thing in the morning."

"Thanks, Sharon. The kids are in an awful state. Too young to lose their daddy. Brian's made all the arrangements. The visiting ... is to-morrow ... night. I can't ..." She's crying again.

"I'll be home by noon at the latest."

I say goodbye, hang up, and tell Jack.

"I'm in court tomorrow, but Friday I could drive you up."

"She was crying and said the kids are really upset. I don't mind driving. You can come for the funeral."

"Of course, but if you drive, we'll have both cars there. Wait a day and we can go together."

"She needs me right now. I'll go pack a few things."

He follows me upstairs and into our bedroom. Watches as I pull my honeymoon suitcase down from the closet shelf, and stuff clothes into it. My black dress I wore to Uncle Joey's funeral. Maybe my dark purple suit. Everybody doesn't wear black to funerals nowadays. Throw in my jeans—we'll have to get the place cleaned up for the reception.

"You're taking a lot of clothes."

"Hard to know what I'll need."

"I would think just a dress for the funeral. If you let me drive you, we wouldn't have to two cars to contend with."

Why's he going on about the cars? "I can drive from Toronto to Grenville."

"But dear, you're upset. And what if it snows? I don't like you driving on bad roads."

"I can manage. Going to bed now so I can get an early start." I head to the bathroom.

When I return, he's still standing there.

I quickly pull on my nightgown and get under the covers. "Night, Jack."

"Would you like an aspirin?"

"No thanks."

I curl up in a tight ball, my face to the wall, and close my eyes.

I hear him moving around the room. A few minutes later, the light goes off, and he's in bed beside me.

He tries to put his arms around me. I shrug him off. "Not tonight, Jack."

He awkwardly pats my shoulder. I wish he'd stop. There's something about the feel of his flannelette pyjamas that bugs me. "Jack, I want to go to sleep."

He lies stiffly beside me.

Finally, gets up and leaves the room.

Thank goodness.

I'm not at all sleepy. Jimmy is dead. Poor Jimmy, but Mom is finally free. She's only thirty-eight. Still time to meet somebody nice. Maybe, but not likely with all those kids. Jimmy was old, over fifty. No more moaning about his back. No more pleading for cups of tea.

I twist and turn, but can't get to sleep. When Jack comes back, I pretend to be sleeping. He gets into bed, but doesn't try to touch me.

I must've fallen asleep, because when I next look at the clock it's ten to six. I head for the shower.

When I come back in our room, Jack, in his bathrobe, is sitting on the side of the bed. "Do reconsider, dear. I'll drive you up tonight and then come back for the funeral."

"Jack, what's the big deal? You come for the funeral, I imagine it'll be Saturday, and right after we'll come home."

"I'll miss you."

"I'll miss you, too. Now let me get dressed."

He goes downstairs and, when I come down with my suitcase, he's making bacon and eggs. The table's all set with the blue linen place mats.

"You shouldn't have bothered."

"You need a good breakfast before you set out. The forecast says snow flurries. That little car of yours doesn't handle well in snow."

"I'll be fine." Why doesn't he shut up about my driving?

* * *

I drive out of Toronto, through the subdivisions with all their new pretty houses. Even the streets have grand names—Saxon Gate, Bridle Path Way—no Plum Streets, that's for sure. I'm glad Jack's not with me. He fusses.

A grey sky, just ten days till Christmas, and no snow. I'm driving into a grungy landscape. The barn roofs sag and the old houses have stains under every window, like they've been crying. What a time for Jimmy to die. Raymond died at Christmas. We had a lot of snow that year. I got my skates. Poor, pathetic Jimmy. Mom had to marry him because of me and Gloria. Without us she could've had any man she wanted. But now she's free. That's a laugh—six kids.

Still, Jack's willing to help. Get her an automatic washer and dryer for a start. And she does have a job—not stuck home babysitting. Gloria doesn't seem to mind. Anyway, she's home with her own two. Mom doesn't earn much. She could take a few night-school courses and get a job in an office. Could dye her hair. Too young to be going grey.

I pull into the driveway behind a car I don't recognize. Somebody forgot to turn off the Christmas lights on the porch. Jimmy only allowed the lights on for a couple of hours in the evening—afraid for his electric bill. They put all the Christmas decorations away when Raymond died.

I open the door. Mom's having tea with Mrs. Ruebel and some woman I don't know. I hear Gloria in the kitchen with the kids.

Mom sets down her teacup in a hurry, rushes over, hugs me. "Oh, Sharon, I'm so glad you're here."

* * *

In the evening we are no sooner through the door of the funeral home than an officious, smiling man leads us into the visiting room. He murmurs something to Mom that I don't catch. I hold Charlie by the hand. At least they didn't bring J.J. and Tamara. Mrs. Reubel's babysitting. Charlie shouldn't be here. He's just the age Gloria was at Grandma's funeral.

We all traipse up to see Jimmy. Mom fusses with his shirt. Even for his funeral he's not wearing a tie. She bends down and kisses him. I hate funerals. When I die I want to be cremated and my ashes scattered. Anywhere away from this grotesque business.

I lead Charlie over to look at the flowers. There are a surprising lot of them.

"Your flowers are lovely," Gloria says.

"Huh?"

"Right here." She points to a big arrangement of cream and yellow roses.

Sure enough, the card says from Mr. and Mrs. Jack Sutter. Leave it to Jack to do the proper thing.

"We better sit down," Gloria says. "People will be arriving soon."

She's carrying her new baby. Why didn't she leave him at home? Brian takes her arm and leads the way to the chairs lined up by the door. The back of his suit jacket is all wrinkled. Where did he get it? The Salvation Army?

We sit in a solemn row. Most of the kids are wearing grubby sneakers. Tomorrow I'm taking them shopping. New clothes and new shoes for everyone. Debbie and Emily flank Mom. Debbie holds Mom's hand.

So many people come. Who would've thought Jimmy had so many friends?

A man I don't know gives Mom an envelope. "The money I owes him. He never bugged me. Knew us was having some trouble. Jimmy was a good guy."

"I know," Mom whispers.

* * *

All the kids are in bed and Gloria and Brian are in their room. I find Mom on the couch with her head in her hands. She's still wearing that awful dress she bought at Stedmans this morning—aqua with black triangles. Poor Mom. "You okay?" I ask. "Can I make you a cup of tea?"

"Thanks, might help me sleep."

I make the tea and put some cookies on a plate. The neighbours have brought over so much food.

"Oh, I just don't know how I'll manage without him."

She must feel desperate. I put my arm around her. "Don't worry, Jack and I will help out."

She pulls away with a really cross look. "I didn't mean money. I miss him so. How many evenings we sat together on this couch. I thought I'd grow old with him. We only had twelve years. Should've had longer."

She's crying. I look at her in amazement.

"Don't look at me like that. I love him. Is that so hard to understand?"

I can't think of anything to say.

"You think I married him to have a roof over our heads. Sure, that was part of it, but I loved him and always will. Little miss-who-knows-so-much-about-men is surprised, is she?"

In shock more like it.

"No, you don't have to say anything. You think a guy has to be tall, dark and handsome. You're wrong. Looks have very little to do with it. I've never understood why you resented Jimmy so."

"We had a good life before he came along."

"A good life? I was leaving you kids alone in city parks. We were homeless, sleeping in the car."

"We had the tourist cabin."

"Oh, Sharon, that was the worst time in my life — Phil Whitmore."

"Was he so bad?"

"You have no idea."

"Why did you go out with him?"

"You are clueless. That's how I got my job, and the loan to rent the cabin. Had to pay a month in advance on that dump."

"I loved our cabin."

"And if that woman who owned the camp had found out you girls were alone, she would've called the Children's Aid."

"Maybe they would've given you the money for a sitter."

"No, Sharon. They would've put you girls in foster care. And if, within a year, I couldn't provide a proper home, you and Gloria would've been put up for adoption. Most likely separated. Once you're adopted, the records are sealed. I never would've been able to find you."

"Oh, Mom, I didn't know you worried about stuff like that."

"It was pretty bad."

"But Mom, that summer was the happiest of my life. Remember the time Teddy's family was over and we had sparklers and everybody, even the adults, ran around in the field, and Teddy's mom lost her shoe?"

"Teddy's mom?"

"You know, Norma. Her husband worked with you on the painting crew."

"Oh yeah, I know who you mean. Fancy you remembering all that."

* * *

I stare at the cracked plaster and the string dangling from the single light bulb. Dawn and still not asleep. Mom loved Jimmy. Mom loved Jimmy. I carefully stretch out my cramping leg. Don't want to wake Judy who's curled up next to me. She's sweaty, and her straggly hair's stuck to her cheek. When I came to bed, she was awake and crying with Debbie trying to shush her. Debbie's asleep now on the feather tick.

Judy said: "Don't let them put Daddy in the ground. He can't breathe."

"He doesn't need to breathe. He's dead, and it's not really him they'll bury, just his body. His soul's in heaven with God."

"I want my daddy!" she wailed.

I let her get in bed with me. Oh, the dumb things we say to kids. Oh, Jimmy, they all love you. I'm such a cold-hearted bitch.

* * *

Jack arrives on Saturday just as me and Gloria are making lunch for the kids. The funeral's in a couple of hours. He gives me a peck on the lips. "Let's go for a quick coffee," he says.

"Can't. We're just getting lunch." In his black suit and black cashmere overcoat he looks like a judge or an undertaker.

"It would help you relax, dear."

Mom comes in from the living room where she's supposed to be resting. "Girls, have you seen my butterfly brooch? I wanted to wear it. Jimmy gave me that last Christmas."

"Mrs. Dutton, let me express my deepest sympathy," Jack says.

Mom mumbles something and I take her arm. "I'll help you look."

When I come back in the kitchen his overcoat is hanging over the back of a chair, and he's sitting at the table with a peanut butter sandwich and a cup of tea. I bet he's never eaten a peanut butter sandwich in his life.

"Do you take milk in your tea?" Gloria asks.

"Yes, please."

She sits the milk bottle on the table. Has she never heard of a cream pitcher?

"These cookies our neighbour made are pretty good." She offers him the tin. She used to be so shy.

* * *

"I am the resurrection and the life, saith the Lord: he that believeth in me, though he were dead, yet shall he live: and whosoever liveth and believeth in me shall never die," the minister says.

A Christmas snow so softly falls covering the raw grave, the dead

grass, Jimmy's wife and kids. A white Christmas after all. Bloody pathetic. Let's all sing "Jingle Bells".

Jack's arm around me feels good. Just let me get through this and back to Toronto and I'll be fine.

When we're walking away from the grave, Jack says: "If we don't spend too long at the house, we could get back to Toronto in time for the Club Christmas ball."

All I wanted was to get back to Toronto, yet I say: "I better stay and help Mom." I'd completely forgotten that the dance was tonight.

"She has Gloria and the neighbours to help her."

"I should stay."

"But you were so looking forward to the dance and wearing your new dress."

"It wouldn't feel right going to a dance right after his funeral."

Jack looks at me kinda funny. "If that's what you want, dear."

"We've got both cars. Jack, you go on ahead. I'll drive back tomorrow."

***

I do stay, but he's right, I'm not needed. The neighbours keep bringing food, and Debbie and Emily wait on Mom hand and foot.

Worst of all, they tell stories. Even the neighbours — Mrs. Reubel talks on and on about how Jimmy wouldn't take any money for fixing their roof. "'Nah, wouldn't be right,' he told us, 'Youse been so good to my wife.'" Gloria tells again about Jimmy giving her the kitten and how she knew right then he would be her good daddy. Debbie tells some long story about Jimmy building her and Emily a dolls' table and chairs out of scraps of wood. Little Joey remembers breaking the garage window and being scared he was really going to get it. "Daddy didn't even get mad. Me and him just nailed some plywood over to keep the rain out."

I have nothing to say, and when it's time to leave the next morning, I'm glad.

E GO TO the Brownlees' party on Christmas Eve. Just four families. One other couple besides the Brownlees has kids, two girls younger than Ashley. When we arrived Ashley and Philip took our coats to an upstairs bedroom. Philip's wearing a pale grey suit and white shirt, Ashley, a blue velvet dress. The visiting girls, around the age of Emily and Judy, are both in dark green velvet dresses with white collars. The three girls serve the appetizers—salmon in puff pastry and other fancy things that these children actually eat. The men talk about business and city politics. The women talk about how hard it is to get a good cleaning lady. The two older women both agree it was much easier before the war.

"My mother," Eleanor Pearson says, "during the Depression, had a live-in nanny for ten dollars a month."

I wouldn't want to be that nanny.

After dinner the children go upstairs to play Monopoly, and we take our drinks into the living room by the gorgeous Christmas tree—ten feet tall and decorated with silver angels and bells and only blue lights.

Some people have had quite a few drinks, but it doesn't seem to affect them. Nobody acts drunk. If Uncle Joey had more than one beer, he'd start singing "It's a long, long way to Tipperary" and something about "my old kit bag." His singing was worse than his hyena laugh. Sometimes Mom and Jimmy would get up and dance even though Jimmy didn't know how. Around the porch or in the front yard—really stupid. The kids would dance, too. Did nobody know how dumb they looked?

I have one drink. Alcohol makes me sleepy. I used to be afraid it would make me violent like Papa.

I'm glad when it's time to go home.

When we get home, Jack hands me a big box wrapped in silver

paper. Inside is the most beautiful coat I've ever seen. I stroke the unbelievably soft fur, the real thing. How could I have ever thought dyed rabbit looked like mink?

"Thanks, Jack. It's beautiful."

"Try it on," he says.

I slip it on and twirl around.

He takes me in his arms. "My beautiful Sharon. You deserve the real thing, not some shoddy fake."

He really likes the solid gold cufflinks and tie pin I got at Birks.

After midnight by the time we're in bed. We wish each other Merry Christmas and we make love. After, Jack falls asleep immediately. I can't get to sleep. Is Mom sleeping? Is she lying awake wishing Jimmy were beside her? I always knew he loved her, but didn't think she could love him. He was so bloody ignorant. But she said: "He made me so happy."

How is that possible?

The night after the funeral, when the kids were all in bed, and Gloria and Brian, too, Mom and I sat up late talking. That's when she said how happy he'd made her feel. Her eyes filled with tears. "We both had so little family left. My parents dead and Jean and me not even speaking for years. Jimmy and I both wanted a big family. He talked a lot about his childhood. You know, Sharon, what we call the garage was his dad's blacksmith shop. They were a close loving family. Unlike mine. Sad how, one after another, all his family died. I wanted to make it up to him."

"But Mom, we were so poor."

"You kids had a good childhood." She sounded indignant. "Living by the lake, in swimming from May till October. And think of all the pets you had, all the cats, and getting to see kittens born. All the fun you had with the kittens, better than dolls any day. Jean and I weren't allowed pets. Oh, I know you kids wore shabby clothes, but what difference did that make? Everybody's in the same boat around here."

"It matters to kids what they wear. Remember how you told me you hated to wear darned stockings?"

"Sharon, that was different. None of the other children had to wear mended stockings."

"Everybody wasn't the same at Orchard Park. Joanne and Betty were well dressed and lorded it over the rest of us."

"But surely what matters is how most are dressed. And you were better off than a lot of them. Jimmy always made sure all of you got new shoes every September. And our house is pretty nice. A lot of people are living in falling-down cottages."

"We were still poor."

"That didn't matter. Jimmy's mother had to take in laundry after his dad died, and he quit school to get a job. But they still had good times—all the kids, even Annie, going out to the beach for a swim."

I said nothing. What could I say? You romanticize everything, Mom. Why didn't you see the mess we lived in?

The clock says a quarter to five. The kids would just be getting up, and rushing downstairs to their stockings lined up on the couch. All excited over an orange, some candy, a colouring book and crayons and, if it was a good year, new underwear and socks.

Be better this year though. I send them a hundred every month, and for Christmas, a big parcel, and a cheque for two hundred. Mom's never had money like that. I should talk to her about having a furnace put in. That space heater barely heats the living room. The only cozy place is by the wood stove in the kitchen. Imagine, 1961 and still heating with wood.

Stop worrying about them. I have a real mink coat. How could I have thought dyed rabbit looked like mink? That shoddy fake, he called it. I'm fuckin pathetic.

* * *

I don't finish my British Empire course. Too boring. Also I'm scared to write the exam. I know I would fail. I don't tell Jack that, just say it's boring.

I'm relieved he doesn't make a big fuss. Says maybe I'd prefer an English course. I agree, but don't get around to signing up. I shop. Sometimes buy things for the kids and send parcels home. I don't go there. Too depressing.

Saturdays, if Jack hasn't brought too much work home from the office, we play tennis.

I play every Thursday in the Women's League. Marion Brownlee can't play now. She broke her arm skiing. They're all better than me, and only Marion was friendly. Well, that's not exactly true. Sometimes, we go for drinks afterwards in the Club bar. They talk about their kids and which private school is better, Bishop Strachan or Branksome Hall. The Toronto French School is good. Two women fret whether their sons will get into Upper Canada College. The women with babies discuss ways to make their babies smarter—listening to good music, flash cards, lots of visual stimulation. Once the conversation is whether dancing lessons are better than piano for little girls. Dancing trains the whole body to listen, to feel the music. Dancing lessons make little girls more confident.

I don't add anything to these conversations. What do I know, except it's no wonder their kids'll grow up to be doctors and lawyers.

Rich people don't have to worry whether there's enough milk and eggs to go around, but there are all these other things. I'm glad I'm not going to have kids.

***

More and more, I simply stay home, or go shopping, or for drives. I get bored shopping. More and more, I just stay home. I really liked my job.

***

I sign up for the committee working on the Spring Gala—a dance to raise money for under-privileged children. I don't understand their interest in poor kids. I cringe when I think of my chocolate mallows.

Raising money's a good idea, but the meetings are boring— making silk flower arrangements, menu planning, and door prizes, bottles of good wine (yes, I'm learning there's good and bad, mainly a matter of price, I think) or would the women like cosmetics? But each woman likes to choose her own. The women mostly discuss clothes or the concerts and plays they've been to. It's not that I haven't been to concerts, but the only comment I could make is they're boring. I went to Stratford last summer. Better than concerts, but I like a good movie. We don't go to movies much.

What I'd like to go to is a Hank Williams concert. Listen to him sing "Down on the Bayou" or "Your Cheatin' Heart." Or Willie Nelson or Johnny Cash. I just can't appreciate classical music—puts me to sleep. I don't listen to my records much now. "Cry, Cry, Cry" just makes me want to. I should be happy.

*O*N AN EARLY spring day, I hear the mail drop through the slot. I go see if there's a letter from Mom or Gloria. There isn't. But there's a square white envelope addressed to me and Jack.

We get lots of invitations, but something's different about this one. Worded wrong—Sharon and Jack Sutter instead of Mr. and Mrs. Jack Sutter. Handwriting sorta messy, certainly wouldn't rate an A for penmanship.

I open it:

Elizabeth and Frank Hadley
and
Mary Stinson
Invite you to the wedding of their children
Clinton John McClary
and
Marlene Gail Stinson
The ceremony will be held at St. Mary's Roman Catholic Church
Grenville, Ontario
At eleven a.m., April 23rd, 1962
Reception to be held at five p.m.
At the Royal Ontario Legion
19 Queen Street, Grenville

Written by hand in the bottom corner: *Be great if you come. Your friend, Clinton.*

Who in the hell is Frank Hadley? His mother must've remarried. Shacked up more like it. She wouldn't have got divorced from that drunken bully, Jim McClary. The Catholic church doesn't allow divorce. Anyway, they wouldn't have the money.

I'm laughing and can't stop. It's just dawned on me that Mom and Jimmy weren't really married. She's still married to Papa. My, I'm dense.

So Clinton's getting married. How in the hell did he get my address? And marrying little Marlene Stinson who came to school all winter barelegged in cotton dresses, and rubber boots with no socks.

Reception at the Legion. I can picture that—white crepe paper streamers, and wedding bells made from Kleenex roses. White paper tablecloths on folding plywood tables. I can even guess the menu—a cold buffet, ham or turkey, maybe both if they're going all out, potato salad, Jell-O salad and coleslaw.

Well that's one wedding I won't be attending. Why did he invite me, and why would Mom or Gloria give him my address?

***

A week after I get the invitation, I show it to Jack.

"I'm meeting an out-of- town client for tennis that day," he says.

"On a Saturday?"

"He's a friend of my dad's. Just going to be in Toronto for the weekend."

"I could go on my own," I tell him. When did I decide to go to the wedding?

"Why do you want to go at all?" He looks at me kinda strangely.

"I dunno, just do."

"Is he an old boyfriend?"

"No, we were friends in public school. Lost track of him after that. I went to school with Marlene, too."

"I can be home by one. It's only a two-hour drive. We could be there in time for the reception. If you really want to go, it's all right with me."

***

A few days later we've just started supper when he asks: "Have you bought them a gift?"

"Not yet."

"Only two weeks away. You have to have time to mail it."

"Mail it?"

"You send the gift to the bride's house."

"In Grenville you bring them to the reception."

"How odd."

"I don't see anything odd about it."

"Well, there's a correct way to do things."

"Your way?"

He shrugs. "Sharon, don't be like that. I just meant there are rules of etiquette."

"I'll look after the gift."

We don't talk for the rest of the meal.

*   *   *

I wander around Eaton's, but can't decide what to get them. Diapers and baby bottles are most likely what they need. That's unkind, but no doubt true. Little Marlene Stinson was a couple of grades behind me. She was one of the perpetual carriers of lice and every time she got them her dad ran the clippers over her head. Poor kid. Joanne and Betty called her Cootie Cut. I don't remember her in high school. Did she even make it that far? Clinton didn't.

Why did they invite me? Clinton sent the invitation—his little note on the bottom. Was it to prove he'd recovered from my nastiness? I was mean to him. Had to be, if I was going to get out. Poor, dumb Clinton will spend his life in Orchard Park. I'm glad he's getting married. Things can't be too bad. At least they're having a wedding. I can imagine her lace-curtain dress. Will it have sequins or rhinestones? People like her, when they get dressed up, always overdo it. I hope her parents stop drinking long enough to attend the ceremony. Poor Marlene, poor Clinton.

If Jack thinks my family are hillbillies, wait till he meets Clinton and Marlene.

I should stay home.

I'm too curious.

I could go alone. Jack wouldn't like that. I wouldn't like it either. Grenville would think he'd walked out on me. No doubt think I got my just desserts.

I want Jack by my side. Just setting myself up to be embarrassed. Maybe Donna will be there. Not likely. The Waddells and the Evans don't hang out with the likes of the Stinsons and McClarys. I wonder who this Frank Hadley is. No doubt more Orchard Park trash. Who else would marry a woman in her forties who looks about sixty and has seven children? Her breasts and belly hung like sacks, and she talked with her hand over her mouth to hide the blackened stumps.

I buy them a breakfast set of Wedgwood. They won't know the difference between Wedgwood and dishes from Stedmans. Oh well, I can afford to be generous.

When we set out for Grenville, Jack's in a bad mood. "We could've gone out for a nice dinner," he says. "And we're missing the symphony tonight."

"We don't go to Grenville very often."

"I never thought you wanted to."

"I don't. We don't have to stay long."

"Quite a drive to just put in an appearance."

"I suppose I should stop in at Mom's."

"Yes, of course. Will your mother be at the wedding?"

"I doubt it."

"Sharon, does your mother know we're coming?"

"Nope."

"You should've arranged something. What if she's out?"

"Not likely."

"If I didn't have so much work to do, we could've reserved a motel. I'm in court Monday."

"Don't worry, we won't stay long."

We arrive just as the reception line is starting.

I never pictured Clinton in a tux. Marlene's in the cheap lace gown I expected. I smile—both rhinestones and sequins. Her wispy blonde curls make me remember her buzz cut.

That must be Frank Hadley beside Clinton's mother. Old guy, at least he's got a suit. She's all dolled up in a chartreuse dress and when she smiles I see her new teeth. And the kids are in new clothes. Somebody's scraped together the money. Marlene's father's not here. Maybe home drunk. No, now I remember, his name wasn't on the invitation. Must've kicked the bucket or took off. Her mother, as big as Marlene is tiny, is decked out in a red flowered, full-skirted outfit.

"Sharon, I'm so glad you could make it." Clinton takes my hand. "You remember Marlene?"

"Sure. Hi, Marlene. Congratulations to you both." Something's odd—he doesn't speak like my Clinton. Jack introduces himself. I was supposed to do that. Just can't get my words out.

I'm relieved when we can sit down. The meal is exactly what I expected—they've gone all out—both the ham and the turkey.

The speeches start. Mrs. Stinson gets up. I'm surprised she's sober. She talks about Clinton and how good he's been to her family. No surprise there—he was always too damn nice for his own good.

Then the best man gets up, the guy in the army, no, air force uniform—he was in the reception line. I didn't catch his name.

He's talking about Clinton and the air force. When was Clinton in the air force?

Finally, dinner and speeches are over. They're pushing the tables against the walls for the dancing.

Clinton and Marlene are dancing. She's looking up at him, such delight in her eyes. He grins, wraps his arms tightly around her. They stumble, must've forgotten they're supposed to be dancing, come to halt, laugh, and hug each other.

They're so obviously in love.

"Can we leave now?" Jack says. "If we're going to call in at your mother's."

I ignore him. What about Clinton and the air force? How could he join the air force?

Clinton stands beside our table. "Hi, Sharon, long time no see. I'm glad you came."

"You were in the air force?"

"Yep, two years. Did my high school there, and trained as an airplane mechanic. I'm in Toronto now. Not far from you. I work at Malton airport."

"That's great." He uses proper grammar. Who would've thought it possible?

"Maybe you and your husband could come for dinner sometime."

"That would be nice," Jack says.

"Marlene loves to see people from home. So do I. We've bought a new bungalow. Move in right after our honeymoon. We're going to Niagara Falls."

"How did you come to join the air force?"

"Thanks to Frank. He married Ma. He's a good dad to the kids. Freed me to do what I wanted."

"That's great," I mumble.

"Guess better be getting back." He hands me a slip of paper. "Here's our phone number. Hope you're enjoying the party. Thanks for coming, Sharon. And nice to meet you, Jack."

"Yes," Jack says. "I'm sorry we'll have to leave early. It's a long drive back to Toronto."

"Do give us a call. Shirley Brown's in Toronto. You used to hang out with her, remember? We should all get together."

"Yeah, we should." I can barely speak.

"Bye for now, Sharon."

"Bye."

He's walking away, back to Marlene. I want to get out of here.

"Can we leave now?" Jack asks. "We want to have time to visit your mother."

"Let's go straight home. I'm so tired."

STRIDE FROM THE living room to the kitchen. Pour myself a coffee, but don't drink it. I go out on the deck. Light a cigarette. The daffodils we planted last fall are in full bloom. Even they annoy me.

This terrible discontent, this anger. I always thought I knew what was going on, knew the score. Poor, dumb Clinton would always be a loser.

From the beginning I saw things clearly, none of this through a glass darkly. My glass was filled to the brim with crystal clear water.

Mom introduced me and Gloria to Jimmy, and one look at his funny clothes, old jalopy, bad grammar, and I saw what she was getting herself into. I knew if he owned a house, it would be a dump, and he would never earn enough to support us. The man was forty and look at him.

Once the babies started coming Mom was just digging the pit deeper and was never going to get out.

Clinton's family was worse than ours, brutal father, slovenly mother. And poor Clinton—didn't even get to high school. And his atrocious grammar. He would always have a baloney steak life.

He would never get out of Grenville. He was Orchard Park personified. I saw his good qualities—hard-working, honest, loyal. So was Mom. But those qualities don't buy groceries. I couldn't bear to watch anymore. Kids in holey underwear. Little girls all dressed up in faded pink dresses, somebody else's discards. And the blessed baloney steak. That little boy's face so proud of the big treat.

Not that I'm suddenly in love with Clinton, but he was always my friend, and I didn't treat him like a friend. That awful time after Raymond's suicide, Clinton didn't tease us. He threatened the kids who did. He gave me a cat's eye marble. I saved it for a long time.

Not that suddenly I wish I'd married Clinton McClary and had his baby. I don't.

I recognize he's the guy who could make me tingle all over. Figured I was better off without that. Getting carried away is how Mom got pregnant at sixteen and married to an unemployed miner.

So there was Ted and there's Jack. Ted took me for the sucker I was. I should've known he was married with him not available on weekends and holidays. Jack's different. He's a gentleman and we have beautiful things. And yes, he wanted to marry me.

Does he love me? Even in bed we're controlled, polite.

Getting carried away with Clinton could've ruined my life.

Do I love Jack? I don't know him. What terrified him as a kid? I have no idea.

I knew Clinton. Brought him a sleeping bag so he wouldn't freeze in his fort. I saw his battered face. He spent his pay helping his mom feed all those kids. Unselfish Clinton made me feel ashamed. Selfish me planned to escape first chance I got.

I wanted to go away where I was unknown, could make myself new. I've done that. When I finally let Jack meet my family, he couldn't believe I came from there. Thought someone at the country club got Mom pregnant, that her parents made her marry Maurice just to avoid scandal. Debbie's so much like me as a kid, but he called her that carrot-haired urchin.

Jack doesn't know me.

Most nights I wake up shivering and scared. Occasionally, I had nightmares in the past—not often, not like Gloria. She'd wake up screaming and the next morning she'd be telling us her dream in great detail. The few times I had a bad one, I never could remember what I'd been dreaming.

I felt safe with Jack.

Don't now.

He said: "Don't you think that smoked salmon was a little off? Better try a different deli." I expected praise for my dinner party. Didn't expect passion, knew that the smoked salmon, as imperfect as it was, had more passion than Jack ever has.

What else will Jack notice? Never should've taken him to that wedding. Did I give off some vibe that I was once part of that life?

Did I expose some yearning for my old life? Surely not. I don't long for Clinton or anything or anyone else that's part of Grenville.

That I was wrong has changed everything. I knew Clinton wasn't at all stupid when it came to things outside of school. Could build a shelter out of spruce bows and vines, could fix a bike or a car.

But a baloney steak life wasn't for me.

I was wrong about Clinton. He could change his life just as much as I've changed mine. Could join the air force, finish high school, become an airplane mechanic, learn proper grammar. Most of all, leave Grenville. They're buying a house in Malton, for Christ's sake.

They know each other. Little Marlene Stinson who went to school barelegged all winter, in rubber boots with no socks, doesn't have to hide anything from Clinton.

I have no friends. I told lies for so long, saying what I thought those around me wanted to hear.

I need to start over. That little girl who looked after Gloria, helped kill chickens, she was ready to take on the world and fight for her place in it. I have fought, but dishonestly.

Go back to that kid running with her cousins on that bush farm somewhere outside Cadillac.

This time grow up honest.

***

I can't get to sleep. Jack snores softly beside me. He always falls asleep immediately after lovemaking. I treated Clinton very badly. I was such a mean little thing. He knew all about me and still loved me. With him didn't have to pretend to be somebody I'm not.

A lie that I don't want Grenville. I want my family back. Want to know my little sisters and brothers. Want to wake up to a rooster crowing. Want to make a big batch of pancakes and watch the kids eat them. Want the cats meowing at my feet while I do the dishes. I want to throw a pancake for Pal to catch in his mouth and carry off.

Gloria told me he died with his head on her lap. I wasn't there. She buried him under the lilacs.

This bed is so damn cold, as cold as Jack. Cold as me. Clinton's grease-stained hands roughened from garage work, stroked my bum. Maybe I do want him, just a little.

Too late. I missed my chance.

Jack's been different since Clinton's wedding. I notice him watching me. When he saw me with Clinton, did he realize I belonged with the people there more than I ever would belong at the symphony or the Gladstone Club?

Never should've married him. Don't love him. Never did. Don't even have the excuse I didn't know what love was. I knew, but thought I was better off without it.

Jack is a decent man—don't want to hurt him. My leaving will. I'll never be able to explain why. Thought he was everything I wanted. My dream man. Intelligent, sophisticated, and rich. I wear nice clothes. Go in the grocery store and put everything I want in my cart. I don't even look at prices. Never in my life will I have to put something back.

I go to concerts and sit among rich people. The music begins and the audience is riveted to the stage. I'm falling asleep. I wouldn't fall asleep at an Elvis concert. Or if Hank Williams was up there singing "Your Cheatin' Heart." "That hillbilly music," Jack says. Of rock and roll he says: "They're not singing, they're shouting." Classical music is good, but isn't my music.

Why has everything gone wrong? I did get away from Grenville, got a job, my own apartment. With a coffee and a cigarette, in my fur coat I sat on that little balcony, and watched the beautiful city. I was free. Why didn't I know that?

With Jack I've done nothing but pretend. He deserves better. Ahh, does that allow me to think that by leaving him I'd be doing him a favour? Maybe in the long run, but not now.

He'll feel I've betrayed him, which I have. In his own controlled way he has loved me. What's worse is I know too much about him. How shy he is in bed. Confident at the Gladstone Club, how I imagine he is in the courtroom, but an uptight easily embarrassed lover.

Will I have permanently soured him on women? A virgin at thirty-two.

But I can't live with him any longer. I want my real life back. Want to go back to that bike-riding, tree climbing little kid who went exploring with Clinton. We told each other everything.

I want to walk down the street, just being me, not trying to be somebody else. I don't want to be ashamed of my family.

Never should've been. We weren't the lowest of the low. Marlene Stinson in her ragged clothes, stood all recess with her back against the wall. She looked half-starved. The first time I handed her half a peanut-butter sandwich, she cringed. I wrapped it up and stuffed it in her coat pocket. After that, if I offered her something, she'd take it. Never invited her to play though. Being friends with Shirley and Norma made Joanne and Betty sneer. Even Shirley and Norma kept away from Marlene, the perpetual carrier of lice.

Don't want to study history or music appreciation. I want a job. Liked working in an office. I also liked working in a restaurant. Need to make my own way, whatever that is.

***

Morning and I don't think I slept at all. I pull the covers up to my ears and curl into a tight ball. Jack's not in bed. I hear the shower running.

When he comes into the room, I say: "Got a terrible headache."

"Better stay in bed. Can I get you an aspirin?"

"Thanks."

I pretend sleep, but watch him dress and leave the room.

He returns with two aspirin and a glass of water. "Thanks." I dutifully swallow. "Have a good day," I say.

"You have a good rest. Let's go out for dinner tonight. I'll make a reservation."

"Okay."

I listen to him moving around in the kitchen. Finally I hear the front door close. Listen to the click as he locks it.

Get out of bed and from behind the curtain see him open the

garage door. Watch him back out the Lincoln. Such a gorgeous car. I'm crying as he drives away.

I take a long hot shower. Do have a headache. A couple of cups of black coffee and a cigarette and I'll feel better.

I reheat the coffee Jack made and go out on the deck. The brightly blooming daffodils mock me. I would like to trample them into the mud.

I go back upstairs and pack. Not the formal gowns—don't imagine I'll need those. I take my jewellery. Might need to sell it some day. I stroke my mink. I could sell it too, if I had to. My old fur coat is at the very back of the closet. I leave them both. Take my tennis racket and all my shoes. I take Debbie's figurine from my dresser. I have almost three thousand dollars in the bank. Should return that money. I won't. Be too afraid to leave with nothing. A braver woman would go with just the clothes on her back. That woman wouldn't have once been a kid who had to sleep in a car or make ketchup and macaroni for supper.

I snap shut my suitcase and push it to the back of my closet.

Jack doesn't deserve this. I'm not so cowardly that I won't tell him face to face. None of it is his fault.

Y FIRST STOP is the supermarket. Take a long time to decide what to buy. Settle on a roast, prime rib. I'll make scalloped potatoes—Jack doesn't care for gravy. Asparagus tips all the way from California. Fresh strawberries, also from California, for the strawberry mousse. At the LCBO, I buy his favourite French wine.

I set the dining room table with the white damask cloth, our best china, and the Waterford crystal.

When Jack comes in from the office, I meet him at the door in that green dress he likes and receive his customary peck on my lips.

"Dinner's all ready."

"Oh, I thought we were going out. I made a reservation."

"I was feeling better and did a roast."

"I'll shower and be right down," he says.

Jack showers twice a day—a third time, if it's a night he intends to make love. He smells of Old Spice and Lifebuoy soap.

Lately, I've been showering before bed. I didn't used to worry about smells. While supper cooked, I showered, got dressed, and put Mom's silver clip in my hair for luck.

I go to the table, pour our wine, and sit down.

***

"But why, Sharon?"

"I never should've married you. I'm sorry. I want a different life."

What a ridiculous thing to say.

"It's that wedding we went to—that man."

"No."

"He was your old boyfriend."

"No, but he made me think."

"And you decided you prefer that hillbilly mechanic to me?"

"No."

"He's married. Do you intend to break them up?"

"Of course not. I don't want Clinton."

"Well, what do you want?"

"I don't know."

"Listen, Sharon, I know you're unhappy. Your life has changed dramatically in the past year. You've faced a lot of challenges. Meeting new people, having people over for dinner. It's time we made some changes here. We'll hire a housekeeper like I wanted to."

"I don't need a housekeeper."

"And I'll make an appointment for you to see someone about your nerves. You try too hard, darling. A rest is what you need."

"Jack, this isn't working."

"Don't worry, dear. The doctor will give you something to help you relax, and in a few weeks you'll be fine. That roast smells delicious. We better eat before it gets cold. You've made a lovely dinner, my darling."

***

Tonight Jack is urgent in his lovemaking. Takes him a long time to come. I haven't got it in me to help him. He said I try too hard. I'm too tired to try at all.

Afterwards, he holds me. "Sharon, I love you very much." For a moment, I think he's going to cry. Can't bear it if he does. He swallows several times, turns away, and lies there stiff as a corpse. He's not asleep, but doesn't move a muscle.

I should put my arms around him, comfort him. I can't. The cold-hearted bitch that I am lies awake and listens to nothing. Wish it would rain. Rain pounding a roof can put me to sleep. I never hear the rain here, the house too well insulated.

Must've fallen asleep because I jerk awake from a nightmare. What was I dreaming? Have no idea, but I'm left shivering. The house is always at seventy-two degrees, but I'm cold anyway. Jack's curled up away from me. I listen to him breathe. Why didn't he get mad? He's never yelled at me. I wait for morning.

The sun glints from between the shut drapes. Jack's not in bed. I don't hear the shower. I'm scared. Nonsense. Jack wouldn't hurt me. Or himself? He can't even cry. Isn't that the kind who does it? Takes a gun and blows his head off. Like Uncle Raymond.

I've trashed my life. Jack's been so good to me. I thought I could just walk away. Do what? Could I even get a job? So tired all the time. Do I even remember how to type? That awful dream. What was so awful? I can't remember. Something terrible is going to happen. Poor Jack, he can't even cry. How can I be so mean?

I take my jeans and blue plaid shirt from my closet, grab some panties, and carry it all to the bathroom. Want to get dressed in private. I turn the shower on hot and let it wash over me. The heat's making me dizzy. The room's all steamy and I step out and grab the towel rack for support.

"Jack!" I scream.

What I think I see is a body lying on the floor. Uncle Raymond in his blue plaid shirt.

As the vomit comes into my throat, I drop down by the toilet bowl. Throw up until I'm gagging on dry heaves. Cling to the toilet. Do something. I'm too scared.

Holding on to the toilet for support I stagger to my feet and make myself look. No one's there, just the pile of clothes I left on the floor. Must be going crazy. Like I saw my dream I never can remember—Uncle Raymond in his blue plaid shirt. Why now? An omen? Jack! Something's happened to him. My fault. All my fault.

I rub myself dry, pull on my clothes, and run downstairs.

"Good morning, darling," he says.

The table in the breakfast nook is already set. He brings me a coffee. Pours orange juice for us both. He's frying bacon and eggs. "A hearty breakfast will help build up your strength."

"I feel a little dizzy."

"I've made an appointment for you for eleven with Dr. Harris. He's at 449 Bloor. Why don't you take a cab? I'd drive you, if I wasn't in court this morning."

"How'd you get an appointment that fast? No office would be open yet."

"I phoned him at home. Please, darling, promise me you'll talk to him. He'll help you see things clearly."

"I'm not sick."

"You're overtired. Your mother's troubles may have affected you more than you realize. Promise me, you'll go to the appointment."

"Okay."

***

Jack left for the office an hour ago. I'm still at the table with my coffee and my third cigarette. Maybe I should see a doctor. I'm not sleeping well, always thinking about Grenville, and all the stupid stuff I've done. I called one of Jack's clients an asshole just because he spilt his wine.

Being overtired could give me nightmares. Wasn't a nightmare. I was fully awake. Just nerves. Why else would I hallucinate? That's what it must've been. When Mom had pneumonia she had hallucinations, thought Mrs. Reubel was her mother. That was scary. Maybe Jimmy dying made me remember his brother. But Jimmy died months ago.

Just feeling a bit down. Guilty, maybe. Jimmy didn't mistreat any of us. Didn't treat me and Gloria differently because we weren't his. Clinton said: "At least he don't hit nobody." I could've done a lot worse than Jimmy for a stepfather. And Uncle Joey. I didn't feel much when he died. He brought me and Gloria treats after Raymond's funeral. He didn't have to do that. That long day we were shut in our room. Did I even thank Joey? Most likely not. What a little shit I was.

His crazy laugh. Kids teased him. Once, some boys threw stones at him. I didn't even try to make them stop. Uncle Joey laughed his crazy wild laugh, waved his arms, and started towards them like he thought it was a game. They ran away. Uncle Joey turned to me and winked. I ran away, too. It wouldn't have killed me to walk home with him.

***

The doctor's an older man, maybe fifty, in a grey, well-pressed suit. When he shakes my hand, I'm reminded of Mr. Brownlee, a real gentle-

man. I liked working for him, never talked down to me. He's like that with his wife and kids, too. Dr. Harris sits me down in a comfortable chair. Doesn't make me lie down on some couch. I don't even see a couch. I know he's a psychiatrist—I saw his name on the directory in the lobby.

"I'm Dr. Harris. Your husband tells me you're feeling depressed."

"I've been having nightmares."

"That's a symptom of anxiety."

"I do always feel a little anxious."

"Has getting married changed your lifestyle?"

"Yes, I used to work in an office and live in a tiny apartment."

"And now?"

"My whole apartment would fit in our living room with space left over."

"Do you like your new house?"

"Of course. Who wouldn't?"

"You know, Sharon—may I call you Sharon?—young women, in the first year of marriage, often get feeling down. Marriage is such a big step, so many adjustments to make. Most find it a little scary—feel down or on edge. You wouldn't believe how many young women like yourself come to me with similar problems."

"Really? Other girls feel like me?"

"Oh, yes, feeling on edge, down, often feeling the whole marriage was a mistake. Now, I'm going to write out a prescription for you to try. These little pills work wonders. Try them for a month, then come back and see me. I think you'll be amazed at how differently you'll feel. Will you do that?"

"Okay."

"I've had many a young woman come back and thank me, and say they can't believe how close they came to ruining their lives. There's a drugstore on the main floor where you can get the prescription filled."

"Thanks." I guess he knows what he's talking about.

"You're welcome, dear. I'll see you in a month. I do believe you'll be feeling a lot better."

I get the prescription filled and drive home. I didn't take a taxi.

Not so out of it I couldn't drive my car. *Take two with a glass of water.* I've never felt this tired in my life. I sink down on my bed and close my eyes.

I'm in the whirlpool at Niagara Falls. Try to scream as I'm being sucked into the dark. I jerk awake. Sit up. I've got to get out of here. So dizzy. I'm going crazy. Lie down. Just relax. Be quiet. Breathe in, breathe out. I pull the blanket right up to my nose. Go to sleep—I'm safe here.

***

My eyelids feel heavy, but I force them open. Look at the clock. Four-twenty—slept all afternoon. I must get up. My suit's all wrinkled. Slept in my clothes.

A shower will wake me up. I strip down and open my closet to get my housecoat. See the suitcase I packed yesterday. Must've been crazy. Where did I think I was going to go?

I'm a little shaky going into the shower. What if it happens again? Just a nightmare. But I was fully awake. I woke up really scared and couldn't remember my dream. That business after my shower was just remembering. But it felt so real. Dreams feel real when you're dreaming them. Stop thinking.

I do feel better after my shower. Pull on a shirt and my old jeans. Maybe I'll go for a walk.

Already five, no time for a walk. I better think about supper.

In the kitchen I find a note tucked into a dozen red roses. Jack must've come home while I was sleeping.

> *My darling, don't bother about dinner. We'll go to the Royal York. I'll be home at five-thirty.*
> *Love, Jack.*

> *P.S. Wear your blue-green silk. It matches your eyes.*

Five-thirty! At least I already showered.

By the time I hear Jack's key in the lock, I'm wearing the blue-

green silk, and my hair's done up with Mom's silver clip. I meet him at the door.

He takes me in his arms. "Feeling better, darling?"

"I am."

* * *

I order roast beef, but can't finish it. Jack's more talkative than usual. He tells me he's arranged a housekeeper to start tomorrow.

"She's just temporary," he says. "If you don't like her, Sharon, we'll hire someone else."

"I should be able to do the housework."

"It's a big house and a lot of work. You should be doing fun things."

"I don't know."

"Why not take an English course? You love to read."

"I might like that."

"Or just take it easy. You've been overdoing it."

"I am tired."

"Let's go home. We'll get to bed early."

* * *

I take another pill, like I'm supposed to. We lie side by side. Jack reaches out, pulls me to him. I fall asleep with my head on his chest. Very peaceful.

I drag myself awake. Thank God, it's morning. What was I dreaming? I was on some dark street. Desperate to get somewhere. There were all these chickens flapping around. Chicken dirt and blood. Oh, I can't remember. All mixed up. Crazy. The Raymond dream again?

I do remember. Me and Gloria opened the chicken-house door. He was there on the floor. Blood everywhere. A strange smell. And I saw it, an ear, all bloody and off by itself in the straw. I had forgotten all about that. When Gloria would go on and on about seeing the body, I'd get mad and smack her. I knew I'd seen the body, but I couldn't remember anything about it. An ear, a Dumb Dutton ear, lying in the straw.

I take a shower, wrap up in my housecoat. Go downstairs. A plump middle-aged woman is at the sink, like it was her kitchen. The water's running.

Jack's in the breakfast nook with his newspaper.

I stand in the doorway.

He comes to me, takes my hand. "This is Julie Benson."

"Hi, Mrs. Sutter," she says over her shoulder.

"Hi." She calls me Mrs. She's old enough to be my mother.

Jack seats me in the breakfast nook and she brings me coffee. I look out the window. Lots of daffodils, so what?

I'M IN MY usual spot—the cream velvet wing chair by the window. Been back to see Dr. Harris. Told him: "I'm so tired all the time." Jack took me out for dinner on our anniversary, and I fell asleep in the car on the way home. I have fallen asleep while we're making love. Dr. Harris said that was just my body adjusting to the pills.

I pull the afghan right up over my shoulders. Always cold. I watch the street. Nothing much happens, occasionally a car goes by. I told Dr. Harris about seeing Uncle Raymond. He said: "That's not unusual when a person's under stress." He called it a flashback—a repressed child-hood memory surfacing. And was I still having nightmares? When I said I wasn't, he said: "That's proof the pills are helping you relax."

True—no more hallucinations or flashbacks or whatever it was. The trouble is I'm so tired. Good thing Jack hired Mrs. Benson as I don't care what the house looks like. I'm supposed to call her Julie, but she's older than Mom.

The mail plops through the slot.

"A letter for you, dear." Mrs. Benson hands me an envelope. I turn it over. From Mom.

May 28th, 1962

Dear Sharon,

We haven't heard from you in a long time. I know you're busy, but do stay in touch.

We got your cheque, but there wasn't a letter. I hope you're not sick.

We're all fine here. Gloria's little William is the cutest thing. Just nine months and already walking. Not just walking, he runs. Such a bright little fella—wants to see everything at once.

It's my day off so I'm babysitting. The kids are at school and Gloria's downtown.

A beautiful day. The lilacs are in full bloom, such gorgeous mauves and purples. The scent alone is enough to make one glad to be alive. I wish Jimmy were here to share this day. Yesterday I took lilacs to his grave.

I picked some blossoms for the baby, and he's delighting in pulling them apart, and sniffing. Won't matter if he eats a few. I remember how you kids sucked the blossoms for their sweetness.

We've had lots of rain, and everything is so green. The wild phlox has turned our rather unkempt lawn into a giant flower garden. Baby William's rolling in the phlox now. He can't wreck them. They'll spring up again with the next rain.

I miss Jimmy, but I can still delight in a spring day. If the world wasn't so beautiful, we wouldn't mourn the dead. We would think they were better off.

Write soon and tell me all the exciting things you're up to in the big city.

Love,
Mom.

I look out the front window. The twin lilacs we put in last fall are blooming. The sun shines, the lilacs are purple, the grass spring green. I feel nothing.

I go outside and sniff the lilacs. I do remember as kids we pulled off the flowers and sucked the ends of each tiny blossom. I know they taste sweet, but who the hell cares?

I'm so tired I wish I was dead. Then I wouldn't have to walk back in the house, eat supper, listen to music, go to bed.

***

Days turn into weeks with me hardly noticing. One evening after supper when I'm dozing in the wing chair I used to think was beautiful, the phone rings.

"I'll get it," says Jack.

Then he's back, telling me my mother's on the phone.

"Okay, I'm getting up." I'm still half asleep, but make it to the phone. "Hi, Mom." I yawn.

"Hi Sharon. Happy birthday. I was going to call on the day, but figured you'd be out."

"Jack gave me diamond earrings and ... we went out for dinner."

"Nice dinner, I bet."

"Yeah." I yawn again.

"You sound tired, dear?"

"I am. Think it's these pills I'm on."

"For what?"

"Just to help me relax."

"Well, stop taking them."

"I can't."

"Why not?"

" Mom, I'm too tired to talk. I'll call you back tomorrow."

I don't call her back, not the next day, or the one after. I really am too weary to talk. I make myself go for a walk. Everything looks so blah. I come home and take a nap on the couch.

The doorbell rings. Damn, it's Mrs. Benson's day off. I'll have to get up.

I drag myself off the couch and go to the door. What? It's Mom, and she's wearing that awful aqua with black triangles number she got for Jimmy's funeral. At least she's left off the aqua cloche that looked like an upside down bucket. "Mom, what are you doing here?"

"You didn't sound right." She grabs me and hugs me. She smells of Evening in Paris.

"Oh, Mom" — and I burst into tears.

I lead her into the living room and over to the couch.

"Sharon, whatever is the matter? Does Jack mistreat you? Does he hit you?"

"No, nothing like that."

"Sharon, what's going on?" We sit down on the couch and she holds both my hands in hers.

I tell her everything, how down I was feeling, how I even considered leaving Jack, and how the doctor gave me pills, and now I don't feel much of anything.

"Get your pills."

"They're all the way upstairs. Why don't I make us some tea?"

"Good idea, but first I want to see those pills." She takes my arm and leads me upstairs. I get the pills from the medicine cabinet and hand them to her.

She studies the label. "Valium, no wonder you feel tired. Your Aunt Jean was on Valium. That's how she got addicted. Now, it's booze."

"Mom, I'm not addicted."

"No, and you're not going to be."

I don't believe it. She flushes my pills down the toilet.

"Mom, what are you doing?"

"You're coming home for a few days, until you feel better." She takes my arm and leads me into my bedroom. "Now, where's your suitcase?"

"In the closet. What about Jack?"

"No problem. You'll leave him a note. Not against the law to visit your family. He can come on the weekend."

She pulls open my closet door, reaches around and finds my suitcase.

"It's already packed." I giggle.

"What?"

"After Clinton's wedding, I was going to leave. I made dinner, told Jack ..."

"Clinton? Clinton McClary? You went to his wedding? Sharon, what's this about?"

"Not what you think. I just wasn't happy so I went to the doctor."

"Jack's suggestion?"

"Yes, but Mom, I wasn't well. I was having nightmares."

"Well, pills aren't the answer. You come home for a few days and get yourself sorted out."

Just like that she takes my arm, picks up my suitcase, and we go downstairs. She hands me the pad by the phone and a pen. So shaky, I can't even write neatly: *Dear Jack, Mom came. I'm going home for a few days. Love, Sharon.*

She tells me to lock the door, and we get in the old green station wagon Jimmy bought when Grandma's finally gave out.

Mom curses when she makes a wrong turn and has to circle back. "These subdivisions all look alike," she says.

"Beautiful houses, eh, Mom?"

"I've always preferred the country."

Once we're on the highway, she speeds up.

What will Jack think? I'm too tired to care. Like she said, not against the law to go home for a few days. I'll just close my eyes and rest for a little while.

The next thing I know is we're stopping in front of the Plum.

The kids all rush out to meet us. They're all squealing and touching me.

"Sharon, you're home," Debbie says, hugging me.

"What'd you brings us?" J.J.'s got hold of my leg.

Mom shoos them away, leads me in, and tells Gloria: "What she needs is a strong cup of coffee."

Gloria in a soiled housedress is at the sink. From the swell of her belly I bet she's pregnant yet again. "Hi, Sharon." She pours me a coffee. Touches my hand. "What's the matter? Are you sick?"

"Just tired." I drink my coffee. "What I need is a nap."

"No, I don't think so. Let's go for a walk," Mom says.

"I'm tired."

"You slept all the way from Toronto."

"I'm still tired."

We walk down Plum to Cherry, past the school, down Leaman, to the park, and onto the beach.

Finally, we sit down on the big rocks.

"So, you went to Clinton's wedding?"

"Yep."

"Why didn't you stop in?"

"Had to get back."

"Clinton married Marlene Stinson. I saw the write-up in the paper."

"They looked so happy."

"I didn't know you'd stayed in touch with Clinton."

"I hadn't, but he invited me to his wedding. I never thought he'd leave Grenville."

"The paper said he's working in Toronto."

"An airplane mechanic at Malton. Hard to believe, eh, Mom?"

"He was a nice boy and was sweet on you. I've always wondered—did you two have a fight just before you left home?"

"Sorta. He wasn't my boyfriend, Mom. I'm really tired. Can't we go back now?"

"Sure. But you'll need lots of walks to get those pills out of your system."

***

Supper is hamburgers and fresh lettuce, green onions, and radishes from Gloria's garden.

"It was such an early spring, the garden got a head start," Gloria tells me.

I want to eat, but chewing is such an effort. I give up and just sit there with my elbows on the table and my chin in my hands. Elbows on the table, were you born in a stable? Jack's mother said that when he was a little boy. I had my elbows on the table. One of the few times he mentioned his mother and himself as a kid. Here, nobody notices elbows—too busy eating before the grub runs out.

The phone rings, and Mom gets it. I know it's him, hear her telling him off about the pills. "You want her to get addicted? So what? That's not the answer. Whether she was thinking straight or not, drugging her wasn't right. No, don't come down now. Sharon'll call you. Of course, you can talk to her. Well, if she wants to, that is."

I shake my head.

"She doesn't want to talk right now. She'll call in a few days. Don't worry, Jack, she's safe with us. Bye."

***

I'm going to sleep in Mom's room. She offered me the bed, as if I'd sleep in her and Jimmy's bed. I opt for the cot she wheels in.

Finally, I can go to sleep. I pull the covers over my head. I must've fallen asleep immediately, because I wake up with the moon shining in the window. I'm shivering I'm so scared. Can't get back to sleep. What's Jack doing?

I had the dream again. Know I did. There was a lot of blood. The chickens were pecking at it. No, the chickens were pecking at an ear. The gun there, too — glistens with blood. I shouldn't have left Jack. Supposed to look after him. Poor Jack, all the lies I told him. Why dream about Uncle Raymond? A sign Jack's in danger? I'm such a shit.

I'm crying and can't stop.

"It's okay. Everything'll be all right," Mom says. "Get in the big bed."

I curl up in her bed, clutching a pillow to my chest. I can't stop shaking. She puts her arms around me.

"Remember your eighth birthday party when we had sparklers? We all ran around in the field. You were such a joyous little girl. Afterwards, you said: 'The stars fell out of the sky and danced with us.' Only you would come out with something like that."

"Mom, I'm scared."

"It's withdrawal from the Valium. Go to sleep now."

***

Morning, when I wake up again — something's different. I'm alone in Mom's bed. Not that. I didn't hear the rooster. In Toronto I woke up to traffic noises, well, when I lived in the apartment. I liked that. In Jack's house, there wasn't any noise from the street. Jack's house? Isn't it mine, too? What have I done? So fuckin stupid. Back at the Plum. Crow, rooster. At least give me that.

Stop feeling sorry for yourself. Get up and take a shower.

I wrap up in Mom's housecoat and go upstairs. Somebody's in the bathroom. How do they manage with one bathroom for eleven people? And only a tub. I need a shower. Feel all gritty.

I hide behind the girls' bedroom door and wait. I need to pee, too. The bathroom door opens, and Little Joey comes out. Not so little now. What is he — nine? Or ten? I don't know — can't think straight. Scurry into the bathroom and hook the door.

I use the toilet and start a bath. The water dribbles from the tap. Somebody's running water in the kitchen. I pick up the bottle of cheap shampoo, climb in the tub crouch down, and stick my head under the tap. The water's lukewarm.

I want my own bathroom, hot water gushing down my back. I soap my hair and now can't get the soap out. The tap dribbles, and I'm crying. I'm smelly and there's not enough water to clean myself. Try to stop crying, but can't. Cry and cry and pull at my hair.

Somebody rattles the door.

I freeze until they go away.

"Sharon, open the door." Mom's cross voice.

I crouch down in the tub and listen to her footsteps retreating. She's back, has the door open. She's holding a nail file.

"Get out of the tub. Come down and have coffee."

"I ... can't get ... the soap out ... useless loser."

She's filling a plastic bucket. "Lean over. I'll rinse it for you." She pours the water over my head and kneads my scalp. Her fingers feel good and I stop crying.

She wraps my head up in somebody's already used towel and wraps me in another one.

We go downstairs and she sits me down on the side of her bed and brushes out my hair. A long, long time ago I brushed her long red hair.

"That feels nice," I say and Mom keeps on brushing. "I didn't hear the rooster crow."

"What?"

"The rooster, why didn't he crow?"

"We got rid of the chickens last fall."

"But why?"

"Eggs have got so cheap and chicken feed's gone up in price. Not worth the bother."

To be a kid and jump out of bed when the rooster crows. Throw a few things in Uncle Joey's army packsack, hop on my bike, and ride off to the beach.

Mom lays out my clothes and I get dressed.

"Come and have some coffee," she says.

I follow her into the kitchen and think about going back to bed.

HE NEXT FEW days are a blur. I fall asleep, but can't stay asleep. My head hurts. Mom's always making me go on walks. She takes time off work. Tells me she's assistant manager now, can afford to take some time off. When I get crying jags, she makes me go for walks with her. At first, I'm scared we'll meet people. What a good laugh they'll have. I don't want to talk to anybody.

Mom says, don't worry—she'll handle it. And she does. Whenever anyone speaks to us, she nods hello, and we go on.

One day I'm out in the yard, and I see Mrs. Reubel coming over. I run back in the house, into Mom's room and under the covers. Feel like an idiot, but I'm not talking to anybody.

I have nightmares. Me and Gloria with Mom at Niagara Falls. "Keep away from the edge." "Don't worry I can swim." I swim round and round in the whirlpool—fun and easy to breathe underwater. I look down, want to see the fish. Uncle Raymond—the water turns to blood. I wake up screaming.

Mom holds me. "What were you dreaming?"

"I saw Uncle Raymond and the water all bloody." I'm shivering and she massages my back.

"Strange you're dreaming about him now. When he died, you handled it so well. We worried about Gloria. She told me she couldn't forget because kids at school kept talking about it. I guess the kids bothered her because she was an easy target. You were never teased."

"Oh, Mom, you have no idea about that school. Whether it was the uncles, or lice, or our shabby clothes—there was lots to tease about."

"But you got on so well."

"Knocked a few kids to the gravel and got on just fine."

"Because of your troubles with Jack, things are bothering you now. Nothing did as a child. When you were only seven, you could stay home alone and look after Gloria, get her supper. You helped me kill chickens — your sister, of course, ran off screaming. You could take on the world and wrestle it to the ground. How I admired my tough little girl."

Oh, Mom, that's how much you knew me.

***

On one of our walks Mom starts talking about her life with Papa. "It wasn't all his fault. Oh, the fights we had. Once I broke the milk pitcher over his head. He was cut so bad he had to go to the hospital and get stitches. I had a bad temper."

"Really? I don't remember that."

"The fights were usually after you and Gloria were in bed."

"You and Jimmy didn't fight."

"No, I'd smartened up a bit. Anyway, you couldn't fight with him. He'd never get mad. If I started yelling, he'd offer me a cup of tea. If I got too bad, he'd go out and putter around in the garage. Maurice and I just wound each other up. We were too much alike. Opposites make a better marriage. Boy, I miss Jimmy."

"Do you ever think about Papa? Wonder what became of him?"

"I did for a while. Not anymore. During the tough times in Buffalo I used to fantasize he'd show up. Tell me he'd got his job back on the railway and had stopped drinking. Wanted us to be a family again. In my saner moments I knew it would never happen."

"Just as well. No woman should stay with a man who hits her and the kids."

"Sharon, he never hit you, and there was only that once with Gloria. And that wouldn't have happened if he hadn't lost his job and taken to drinking in the daytime."

***

I sleep a lot. Seems all I do is sleep and go for walks. I don't allow myself to think about Jack. He calls every day, demands to talk to me. He's not like Papa — wouldn't hurt anybody. I should phone him, but

what on earth would I say? Maybe he's glad I'm gone. I didn't even make dinner. We'd stopped having parties. Good riddance to bad rubbish—is that what he's thinking? What am I going to do? Can't just stay here. I've trashed my life. Here I am a grown woman sleeping in her mother's bed. If I could just go to sleep and never wake up.

***

Sunday morning I lie in bed—Mom's bed. I can hear Gloria urging the kids to get dressed for church. She and Brian take all the kids to church, and Gloria still sings in the choir.

Stretch my arms over my head. I feel a little better today. Actually hungry. I'll get a coffee, a hunk of bread and go out and sit on the swing. At least I feel like getting out of bed.

Got to make a plan. Have to talk to Jack. When he calls, Mom talks to him. I heard her say I was feeling better and would soon be ready to talk. Not today—a coffee and the swing is all I can manage.

***

We're sitting on the rocks by the lake when she says: "Jimmy was a great storyteller."

"I don't remember him telling us stories."

"You never stayed around to listen. You were a very independent little girl. From when I first met him, he would talk about growing up in Grenville, all the fun they had. Which is amazing when you think about it—his father dead and his sister handicapped. He talked about them going sledding on pieces of cardboard. Or going for hikes, all of them, even Annie in her wheelchair."

"Her chair's in the garage. Gloria and me played with it once. He told us to leave it alone and to thank God we didn't need one. I'd never seen a wheelchair like it, tall backed, made of wicker."

"From when he was thirteen, he worked in the gravel pit. He even liked that. He drove the team. He was good with horses. You know, Sharon, after dealing with your papa, and then Phil Whitmore and others like him, I was ready for a man like Jimmy—someone so gentle and loving. And another thing, not having much money never bothered him. In my family being poor was a disgrace. Jimmy and his brothers and sister had more fun as children than I ever did. He was a man who had known real tragedy. His father dying. I think the family was well enough off until that happened."

She talks on and on.

"Jimmy always said if only his brothers hadn't joined the army. They wanted to stop Hitler and they wanted the adventure. Sad, Jimmy would say, that boys look on war as an adventure. Then during the war Annie, his beloved little sister, died."

"Of cerebral palsy?"

"Cerebral palsy's not a disease. She died of pneumonia."

"What did his mother die of?"

"Cancer. To think by the time his brothers came home, both their sister and mother were gone. At least she didn't have to see what happened to the boys."

✳ ✳ ✳

A walk is Mom's answer to everything. I can barely keep up with her the way she strides along in her cotton skirt and ratty t-shirt. I'm short and sluggish beside her. And though there's grey in her hair, she's wonderfully tough.

Once we walk all the way to Blackstone Point. When we get back, I'm so tired, I fall asleep for several hours. Of course, then I'm wide awake at two a.m.

Mom must've heard me get up or smelled my cigarette. When she comes into the kitchen, I'm sitting with my head in my hands.

"How about a cup of tea?"

"Okay, thanks."

She turns on the gas, boils the water, and dips a teabag into two mugs. Hangs the bag over an upside down mug to dry for next time. I think of Jack's mother warming the Wedgwood pot and how shocked Jack was to see me dip a teabag in a cup.

She hands me my tea and sits down. "So you went to the wedding and then you were going to leave Jack?"

"I know it's crazy. I'm really grateful to him."

"For what?"

"Marrying me, of course."

"He was lucky to get you."

"You just say that because you're my mother."

"Sharon, you're a beautiful, intelligent girl. You could have any man you wanted." She sighs.

"Oh, Mom."

"Is there someone else?"

"No, it's not that. Ever since I got married I've been so damn lonely, even when we were sitting together listening to music."

"What about in bed?"

"Then, too."

"Best you two take a break. It's not as if there's a baby to worry about."

"He's been so good to me, and I'm such a lying shit."

"Don't talk about yourself like that. And stop worrying about him. Think about yourself for a change."

"That's selfish."

"It's your life. You have a right to make your own decisions."

"I don't know what I want."

"Do you know what you don't want?"

"My life with Jack."

"Then leave him."

"What'll I do for money?"

"Get a job."

"I wouldn't be able to help you as much."

"I've been wanting to talk to you about that. We're doing much better here. I'm the assistant manager, and Brian's earning good money. And there was a small insurance policy. I put that money in the bank for the kids' education. Jimmy would be proud of us. Even the kids are working—Debbie and Emily babysitting, and Joey has a paper route. We don't need help. I didn't want to hurt your feelings, but the money coming from Jack feels like charity."

"Oh, Mom, I had no idea you felt that way."

"Sharon, you don't have to worry about us. Look after yourself."

"I don't know what I want."

"Go and find out."

***

I'm so ashamed. All the neighbours must be laughing. Mom says: "Quit worrying about what people think. You ran and hid when Mrs. Reubel came over. Believe me, she's not thinking about you. Her husband has stomach cancer, and Billy and Lynne have separated, and they have three children—the baby not even a year old. People have their own problems to worry about."

***

Wednesday afternoon I'm sitting at the kitchen table with *Pride and Prejudice,* my copy from high school. I read a page, and my mind wanders. Got to talk to Jack.

"You comin on the picnic?" Gloria, her swelling breasts bursting the buttons on a ragged old shirt, is stirring something at the work table. She's barefoot and in shorts. Her legs are skinny. Just her belly's fat.

"I'm so tired," I tell her.

"We're celebrating Tammy and J.J.'s birthdays together. We're having the party at the beach. The town's put new picnic tables up back of the sand."

"You don't need me to go."

"Actually, we do. Mom won't leave you home alone."

"Nonsense, I'm fine."

"Sharon, what's wrong with you?" She sits down beside me, puts her hand over mine.

"Just getting over those pills."

"You've been off them for weeks. And why'd you take them in the first place?"

"I was depressed. Are you happy, Gloria?"

"Yes—I'm so lucky to have Brian and Baby William and Tammy. And now another one coming. Sometimes I just can't believe it. My

cup runneth over." She smiles and I realize how pretty she is with her big brown eyes and long dark hair. "Weren't you happy with Jack?"

"No, I guess I wasn't."

"He reminded me of Mr. Blackwood." She giggles.

"The principal? How come?"

"I dunno — stern, didn't like animals. I couldn't imagine him changing a diaper."

"Neither could I." And I laugh.

"That's the first time I've heard you laugh since you came home."

"Guess so."

She puts her arm around me. "Come on, the picnic. We'll have a big water fight with all the kids. Brian loves water fights. Forget your troubles, Sharon."

"I just don't want to talk to outsiders."

"No need to. We'll all be there."

"Okay."

"Great. Guess what? We're getting Tammy and J.J. brand new trikes. Mom gets a twenty percent discount."

***

On a Sunday afternoon there's a knock on the door. I run upstairs to the girls' room. Don't want to see anybody. I look out the window. Oh, what'll I do? Jack's Lincoln is in front of our house.

I open the door a crack and listen. Can't make out what he or Mom is saying. At least nobody's yelling.

Debbie's coming up the stairs. "Mom says you should come down and say hello."

"I can't. I'm not dressed."

"You're dressed."

"In jeans and an old t-shirt!"

"I bet Jack'll buy you new clothes, if ya want. He's nice." What does this kid make of all this? Must think I'm crazy.

I pull myself together and go down followed by barefoot Debbie.

"Hello, Jack." He's in his charcoal-grey suit, and I'm in old jeans and didn't wash my hair this morning.

"Sharon, how are you feeling?" Jack steps forward and I move back. He mustn't touch me. "Much better, but I can't talk right now. I'll phone you."

"When are you coming home?" He isn't demanding. His tone is quiet, sad.

"Soon, I'll call." I turn and walk back upstairs. Want to run, but don't. He must think I'm a nutcase. I can't go back, can't live with him. I've told too many lies. Don't love him. I crawl into Debbie's bed and bawl. What on earth am I going to do?

I sit up as I hear his car pull away. He didn't try very hard to get me back.

THIS WEEK I really do feel a lot better. I can't stay here much longer. The kids, the dogs, Gloria has two now, and at least six cats in the house, are just too much. And with Gloria expecting again.

"What? You're going to follow in Mom's footsteps and have eight?"

"No, me and Brian plan to have four."

It's time I left.

Where to? That's the sixty-four thousand dollar question. I have almost three thousand in the bank. When we got married, Jack paid off my car loan. My car's in Toronto. I have to go back. A better person would return the three thousand. Jack's money—he gave me a cheque every month for clothes and such. A lot more than I needed. I'm not that better person. Not going to end up sleeping in my car and living on bread and peanut butter.

I tell Mom I'm leaving and no, she doesn't need to come with me to face Jack. I'll take the bus, get my car and things, and look for a job. "No, Mom, you don't need to worry Jack might be violent. He's far too cultured for that."

"You can't be sure," she says. "Let me go with you. Help you find an apartment."

"Mom, you've helped me a lot, but I'm better now."

"That's my tough little girl," she says with a smile and hugs me. "You're sure you'll be okay?"

"I can handle him."

***

Not going to be sneaky about it. I phoned and told him I would get the bus back. He wanted to come pick me up. "No, thank you," I said in my iciest voice. "I'll see you when you get home from work Tuesday."

***

Mom drives me to London and I take the bus from there. We hug goodbye and I thank her again. "I'm so glad we've had this time together. I love you, Mom." She smells of Evening in Paris. The little blue bottle has its place of honour on her dresser. Jimmy bought her a fresh bottle on her birthday and one at Christmas.

"I love you, too," says Mom. "You sure now about finding an apartment and all?"

"I'm fine. It was just the Valium—it messed up my head."

As the bus pulls out, I really do feel okay. When I talked to him on the phone, I told him I was coming back to pick up my car, and the rest of my clothes, that I'd be getting my own apartment. That it was best this way—a trial separation. He didn't say much. He'd see me when I got there and help me arrange everything. He's a decent man. Never did deserve him. I have my suitcase beside me. Don't want anybody to sit with me.

We're passing Maple Leaf Foods—almost there. I'll go to Willard Hall for a few nights, until I find something. Oh, God, right back to the beginning. I've got to look for a job. Even with a job what future will I have? Someday be an office manager like Beverly who can't even afford a new car. Can I even get a job? Interviews, I can't do it. Don't want to talk to anybody. I can't face Jack. He was always too good for me. I'm such a shit. A liar and a shit.

Jack greets me at the door. He's thinner, but more handsome than ever. He takes me in his arms. Why on earth do I let him?

"Oh, Sharon, thank God you're back." His voice cracks.

Oh, please don't cry.

Over a lovely dinner at the Royal York, he tells me he only sent me to a doctor because I was so unhappy and not sleeping well.

"I'm fine now."

"I'm so glad. I'm taking some time off. I'll finish up a couple of cases. Then we're off to Europe. You've never seen Paris, my darling."

"Jack, I don't know ... I ..." Paris, Europe. A cheap perfume is as close to Paris as Mom will ever get.

"It's what we both need," he says.

* * *

I was supposed to tell him I was leaving. Instead, I'm in bed with him. He's so urgent in his lovemaking. I do my best, and after, he thanks me and falls asleep.

I lie awake a long time. Why am I here? I feel like shit.

* * *

A week later, we're in Paris. The hotel dining room has luxurious, gilt-framed mirrors and paintings on the walls. In perfect French, Jack orders *pain du chocolat* and strong coffee for our breakfast. The waitress smiles and I see us in the mirror, a handsome blue-eyed man with a red-haired mannequin beside him. Once, I lived in Cadillac and spoke French.

We go to the Louvre.

I see the Mona Lisa. She's much smaller than I expected.

Jack leads me to the Monet exhibit. "At first, he wasn't well received, but now his paintings are worth millions. This is an early one."

I don't say anything. I know the paintings are beautiful, but there are so many people here and not enough air. I could curl up on the floor and sleep. I'm that tired.

"It's a lot to take in," he says. "We mustn't overdo it."

On the way back to the hotel he buys me a very expensive shimmering blue dress.

We walk by the Seine. It's hot, Paris in July. We cross over on the old bridges. We go to Notre Dame Cathedral—very grand—and I remember the church in Rouyn-Noranda where, long ago, I went with Papa. We have lunch in sidewalk cafés and watch the people go by. French people dress very well. I wear my shimmering blue dress and we eat in a candle-lit restaurant overlooking the Seine.

"Do try the wine, dear. France is the birthplace of fine wines."

I watch the girl in the shimmering blue dress sip. She tastes nothing.

Paris, the most beautiful city in the world. I admire the bridges, all different, some have carvings, some arches, many have stone benches for resting.

I stand at the centre of this bridge and look down at grey water and the barges slowly passing. I run my hands over the ancient stone and wonder. How many people jumped from here? I can almost see the long-ago girls in corsets, full skirts. As they leap, their laced-trimmed white petticoats and ruffled bloomers change them into pretty water-flowers floating down the river. Not a bad way to go. But is the bridge high enough? Their heavy skirts would weigh them down. I'm wearing a yellow sundress and white spike-heeled sling-backs. This bridge isn't high enough. Anyway, I'd most likely start swimming. Maybe those other girls didn't know how.

***

The city of lovers, who walk arm-in-arm on this hot humid night. She's barefoot, her sandals hanging from her purse strap. He whispers something in her ear. She laughs, and right there on the street, twirls. Her long cotton skirt lifts, displays her supple legs and bare feet. He makes a playful grab for her, and she pokes him in the belly. He hugs her and her feet lift right off the ground. She laughs and wraps her legs around his waist. They disappear into a dark passageway.

Jack holds my arm. He tells me how impressed he is with the cleanliness of Paris subways.

***

Today we're on a different bridge—there are so many. I lean over the stone railing and study the murky water. Men jumped too. Their clothes weren't as heavy and more of them would've known how to swim. Can you will yourself to drown? My head hurts.

"I don't feel well."

"We'll go back to the hotel. You can have a nap." Jack leads the way.

***

I'm lying on a white duvet in a darkened room when I remember Virginia Woolf put stones in her pockets.

* * *

My headaches get worse and I'm afraid to walk on bridges. We cut our vacation short. Jack makes all the arrangements.

"We need to get you home and to the doctor."

* * *

With Jack beside me the plane ride is endless. He complains about the wailing baby and the little boy across the aisle, making engine noises for his matchbox car. "Babies and small children shouldn't be allowed on planes," he says.

Yell louder kids, drown him out.

* * *

The day after we get home Jack has to check in at the office.

"You just rest, dear. Your appointment with Dr. Harris is tomorrow. He'll try something different. There are lots of ways to get rid of chronic headaches. Have a good sleep. I'll only be gone a couple of hours." He gives me a quick peck on the lips and leaves.

Poor Jack, I'm out of bed the moment I hear his car start up. My head hurts. I'm scared I'll throw up. I take a 222 and start packing.

Our suitcases from Paris aren't unpacked, but I take things out. The shimmering blue dress stays behind. My old things go in.

I take a shower. My head feels slightly better. I put on jeans, an old shirt and running shoes. I take most of Jack's emergency money, over a hundred bucks, out of his handkerchief drawer and leave him a cheque in its place. I write a note. *I need to be on my own.* Just sign my name. Not even love. I'm not coming back.

I get in my little red car and drive east to the new highway, the 401. I drive, don't think. Concentrate on passing that slow truck spewing diesel fumes. A heavy sky, grey scudding clouds. I want speed. My little Volkswagen can't make it past sixty. It's going as fast as it can and so am I. Where? I don't know. Just drive. I'm tremble-y all over. Know what heart in your mouth means. My heart is blocking my throat. Could bite down and chomp it in two. Silly Sharon, drive, your life depends on it. Breathe in, breathe out. Concentrate on your breathing. Drive.

The traffic thins out. What day is this? I don't know. Jack went to the office. My appointment with Dr. Harris is Thursday. We got home yesterday. Today must be Wednesday. Wednesday's child is full of woe. Drive, just drive.

I pull in at a service centre. With aching head and cotton batten legs I go in the restaurant and order a coffee. I swallow another 222 with a gulp. My throat burns. Hope I don't throw up. I light a cigarette. Can't smoke. Feel too sick.

When did I eat last? I sip my coffee. Ask the waitress for toast.

I chew very slowly, have trouble swallowing. That damn heart in my mouth. I actually giggle. I finish my coffee and drink a little water.

Pay the bill. Drive on.

The grey strip of highway goes on and on. Less nauseated now, and though should be tired, I feel more awake.

The sign says Napanee when I realize I'm low on gas. I turn off the highway and find a gas station.

"Fill 'er up, please."

While the tank fills, the young man cleans my windshield. A slouching kid in grease-stained jeans and once white t-shirt. Could be from Orchard Park. What will he make of himself? A year ago I would've thought he'd be pumping gas all his life.

"Want me to check your oil, miss?"

"No thanks." I hand him a five-dollar bill.

"I'll get your change."

"Keep the change. Would you know where I could get a road map?"

"We have some in the office. I'll get you one."

Looking for a restaurant, I drive on into the town. I pull in at a little place, Aunt Sarah's. Don't feel quite so shaky.

I sit on a red vinyl chair, mended with electrical tape. The grey Arborite table is scratched, but clean.

"What can I get you?" A plump older woman in a yellow apron hands me a menu. She smells of Johnson's baby powder.

"I dunno."

"The pecan pie's good. Made it myself. Or maybe you want a sandwich or a burger?"

"Pecan pie sounds fine, and a coffee, please."

I spread out my map. Find the 401. I'm near Kingston. I was there before, when I went to the island. It snowed and I was really late getting home. Home, where is home now? Don't think. Thinking is dangerous.

"Here's your pie, hon. Hope you like it. Just give a shout if you want more coffee."

"I like your yellow apron."

"Thanks. I made it, too." She smiles and I smile back.

The pie's delicious, heaped with whipped cream. I am hungry. I drink my coffee and study the map. I could go to Montreal. Another big city. I'm not ready. Where do I want to go? Uncle Yves' farm. No, not there. Back though, to that tough little kid who left Cadillac ready for the next adventure. North to somewhere I've never been before. Those miles and miles of rocks and bush. Highway 41 goes north.

I pay my bill. "The pie was great," I say. Drive back to the highway and turn north. I pass farms and the odd cluster of houses and a general store with gas pumps.

Now there are fewer farms and miles since the last village, just rocks and bush. Far from Toronto. Good.

I drive and drive. The clouds are darker now. Travel on through a grey landscape. I like the grey road, the grey rocks. Even the trees are greyish green. Spruce or are they pine? Tasselled sumac, the occasional silver birch.

The rain comes. My wipers swish-swash, swish-swash. I'm behind an old station wagon pulling a camper. Children are sticking their arms out the windows, waving them in the rain. When I try to pass, I wave to the kids. A truck's coming and I pull back in.

The road curves and up and down hills and another big curve. Finally, I can pass and I'm alone on this road going north.

A truck loaded with logs hurtles by, and my little red Bug trembles. On and on. More logging trucks. I lose another station on the radio and turn it off. The campers have found their spots for the night. The rain has slowed to a drizzle. I roll down my window, let the rain in. Love the feel on my skin.

At dusk three deer stand at the side of the highway. I slow to get a better look. Everything—the wet trees, the rocks, the deer—shines with a silver grey light. The deer flash their white tails and disappear into the bush.

Later, the rain is heavy again, and I can barely keep my eyes open. I jerk awake as the tires hit the shoulder. Slam on the brakes, stop, and stumble out. I'm less than a foot from a deep embankment. I laugh and laugh. Just when I know I want to live, almost kill myself. I've been so stupid. Damn you, Jack, what did you want? A pretty girl to prove you were a man. You didn't even notice I was a wooden doll. Was that what you wanted?

No more pretending. Us Duttons are as good as anybody. I thought money was safety. Mom knew better. I turned my back on the one I might've loved. Clinton, I was scared to love you.

Don't go there. Thinking is dangerous. Almost as dangerous as driving.

I drive on. Drive and drive. Rest-Rite Motel. That's what I need. Rest.

This motel could do with a coat of paint. I open the warped aluminum door marked Office.

The owner, in an easy chair losing stuffing, has thinning grey hair and sticking out-ears like Jimmy's.

"I need a room."

"Long drive, miss?"

"Longest in my life."

"Some days are like that." He smiles. "Our rooms are clean and quiet." He hands me the key to number eight, and I give him the ten dollars.

A battered Philco is playing "Your Cheatin' Heart." "I like your music."

"Yep. Hank Williams sure can sing," he says. "Sleep well."

"Thanks, I will."

My room is shabby, but clean. I don't cringe at the sight of the iron pipe bed. An honest bed without pretentions. So unlike Jack's king-sized mahogany one. I turn on the lamp, china base with pink roses. Grandma had one like that by her bed. The dim yellow light warms the room. The mattress is old and soft, sinks in the middle, the blanket thin. I wear my sweater to bed, roll into the centre and curl up in the blanket. The rain drums on the roof, patters against the windows—bang, patter, bang, a strange lullaby. I feel myself dozing off. Plenty of time to find a new town, somewhere I can get a job. For now nothing hurts, my nest is snug, and sleep is good.

I wake up with the sun shining on my face. I smile and stretch. Take a shower—let the water sluice over me and wash away my mistakes.

Rub my hair dry and fasten it up in a ponytail. Pull on jeans and a clean t-shirt, pack up my things and head outside. The clean, cold air stops me. I can smell the trees growing.

I get in my car and locate my map. Only a short distance to Mattawa. I'm starving. I drove over three hundred miles yesterday. I laugh. When I need a new world, I go find it. Not entirely new since Cadillac is about a hundred miles from here. But far enough to find that honest little girl ready for the next adventure. I like the kid I was much more than the woman I became.

I drive into town. Spot the Northland Café. Several cars and two trucks in the parking lot. The coffee must be good.

It is. I've finished my bacon and eggs and am on my second cup when I notice the harried-looking woman behind the counter. She's doing all the cooking and serving. She's wearing jeans and has a red bandana tied around her head to keep the sweat from dripping in her eyes. Run off her feet, but a ready smile for everyone, even for the jerk in the suit who wants the music turned down.

"Not everyone can put up with Willie Nelson caterwauling at seven in the morning," he says.

I hear Jack say: "That whining, hillbilly music. Should be against the law." I set my cup down so hard, I fear I've cracked it.

The woman behind the counter laughs. "Willie wakes me up," she says, and sings along: "Yesterday is dead and gone, and tomorrow's out of sight."

I get up and go to the counter. "I'm Sharon Desjardins. I'm looking for a job and you look like you could use some help."

Acknowledgements

I would like to thank Guernica Editions' publishers, Michael Mirolla and Connie McParland, and my editor, Lindsay Brown. It was my great pleasure to work with Lindsay during the editing process.

I am indebted to Sylvia Andrychuk for her editing skills and technical support.

I would also like to thank the Ban Righ Writers' Group, especially Maureen Garvie, Bill Hutchinson, and Darryl Berger for their long-time support and encouragement.

A chapter from this novel was published with some modification as a short story in *Room's* fall issue 2010.

Excerpts in *Cadillac Road* from: *The Three Smart Squirrels And Squee* by Margaret Friskey, Philadelphia: David McKay Company, 1942 and *The Adventures Of A Brownie* by Dinah Maria Mulock, New York: McLoughlin Brothers, 1908.

About the Author

Kristin Andrychuk was raised in an area of stark contrasts between the conservative village of Ridgeway, Ontario, the vibrant summer resort town of Crystal Beach, and just a few miles away from the bustling American city of Buffalo, New York. All three places majorly influenced the stories she tells in her poetry, short stories, and novels. She has been widely published in literary magazines and anthologies. *Cadillac Road* is her third novel. Her two previous novels are *The Swing Tree* (Oberon 1996) and *Riding the Comet* (Oberon 2003). She has three times been the recipient of scholarships to attend the Banff Centre's writers' studios. She resides in Kingston, Ontario with her husband Don.

Printed in December 2016
by Gauvin Press,
Gatineau, Québec